Maisie Dobbs

Maisie Dobbs

A Novel

JACQUELINE WINSPEAR

SOHO

Copyright © 2003 by Jacqueline Winspear

Published by
Soho Press, Inc.
853 Broadway
New York, NY 10003

Library of Congress Cataloging-in-Publication Data
is available in the office of the publisher.

ISBN 1-56947-330-7

10 9 8 7 6 5 4 3 2 1

$\mathcal{T}$his book is dedicated to the memory of
my paternal grandfather and my maternal grandmother

JOHN "JACK" WINSPEAR sustained serious leg wounds during the
Battle of the Somme in July 1916. Following convalescence, he
returned to his work as a costermonger in southeast London.

CLARA FRANCES CLARK, née Atterbury, was a munitions worker at the
Woolwich Arsenal during the First World War. She was partially blinded
in an explosion that killed several girls working in the same section
alongside her. Clara later married and became the mother of ten children.

Now, he will spend a few sick years in institutes,
And do what things the rules consider wise,
And take whatever pity they may dole.
Tonight he noticed how the women's eyes
Passed from him to the strong men that were whole.
How cold and late it is! Why don't they come
And put him to bed? Why don't they come?

Final verse "Disabled," by Wilfred Owen. It was drafted at Craiglockhart, a hospital for shell-shocked officers, in October 1917. Owen was killed on November 4, 1918, just one week before the armistice.

SPRING 1929

CHAPTER ONE

*E*ven if she hadn't been the last person to walk through the turnstile at Warren Street tube station, Jack Barker would have noticed the tall, slender woman in the navy blue, thigh-length jacket with a matching pleated skirt short enough to reveal a well-turned ankle. She had what his old mother would have called "bearing." A way of walking, with her shoulders back and head held high, as she pulled on her black gloves while managing to hold on to a somewhat battered black document case.

"Old money," muttered Jack to himself. "Stuck-up piece of nonsense."

Jack expected the woman to pass him by, so he stamped his feet in a vain attempt to banish the sharp needles of cold creeping up through his hobnailed boots. He fanned a half dozen copies of the *Daily Express* over one arm, anticipating a taxi-cab screeching to a halt and a hand reaching out with the requisite coins.

"Oh, stop—may I have an *Express* please, love?" appealed a voice as smooth as spooned treacle.

The newspaper vendor looked up slowly, straight into eyes the color of midnight in summer, an intense shade that seemed to him to be darker than blue. She held out her money.

"O' course, Miss, 'ere you are. Bit nippy this morning, innit?"

She smiled, and as she took the paper from him before turning to walk away, she replied, "Not half. It's brass monkey weather; better get yourself a nice cuppa before too long."

Jack couldn't have told you why he watched the woman walk all the way down Warren Street toward Fitzroy Square. But he did know one thing: She might have bearing, but from the familiar way she spoke to him, she certainly wasn't from old money.

At the end of Warren Street, Maisie Dobbs stopped in front of the black front door of a somewhat rundown Georgian terraced house, tucked the *Daily Express* under her left arm, carefully opened her document case, and took out an envelope containing a letter from her landlord and two keys. The letter instructed her to give the outside door a good shove after turning the key in the lock, to light the gas lamp at the base of the stairs carefully, to mind the top step of the first flight of stairs—which needed to be looked at—and to remember to lock her own door before leaving in the evening. The letter also told her that Billy Beale, the caretaker, would put up her nameplate on the outside door if she liked or, it suggested, perhaps she would prefer to remain anonymous.

Maisie grinned. I need the business, she said to herself. I'm not here to remain anonymous.

Maisie suspected that Mr. Sharp, the landlord, was unlikely to live up to his name, and that he would pose questions with obvious answers each time they met. However, his directions were apt: The door did indeed need a shove, but the gas lamp, once lit, hardly dented the musky darkness of the stairwell. Clearly there were some things that needed to be changed, but all in good time. For the moment Maisie had work to do, even if she had no actual cases to work on.

Minding the top step, Maisie turned right on the landing and headed straight for the brown painted door on the left, the one with a frosted glass window and a To Let sign hanging from the doorknob. She removed the sign, put the key into the lock, opened the door, and took a deep breath before stepping into her new office. It was a single room with a gas fire, a gas lamp on each wall, and one sash window with a view of the building across the street and the rooftops beyond. There was an oak desk with a matching chair of dubious stability, and an old filing cabinet to the right of the window.

Lady Rowan Compton, her patron and former employer, had been correct; Warren Street wasn't a particularly salubrious area. But if she played her cards right, Maisie could afford the rent and have some money left over from the sum she had allowed herself to take from her savings. She didn't want a fancy office, but she didn't want an out-and-out dump either. No, she wanted something in the middle, something for everyone, something central, but then again not in the thick of things. Maisie felt a certain comfort in this small corner of Bloomsbury. They said that you could sit down to tea with just about anyone around Fitzroy Square, and dine with a countess and a carpenter at the same table, with both of them at ease in the company. Yes, Warren Street would be good for now. The tricky thing was going to be the nameplate. She still hadn't solved the problem of the nameplate.

As Lady Rowan had asked, "So, my dear, what will you call yourself? I mean, we all know what you do, but what will be your trade name? You can hardly state the obvious. 'Finds missing people, dead or alive, even when it's themselves they are looking for' really doesn't cut the mustard. We have to think of something succinct, something that draws upon your unique talents."

"I was thinking of 'Discreet Investigations,' Lady Rowan. What do you think?"

"But that doesn't tell anyone about how you use your mind, my dear—what you actually do."

"It's not really my mind I'm using, it's other people's. I just ask the questions."

"Poppycock! What about 'Discreet Cerebral Investigations'?"

Maisie smiled at Lady Rowan, raising an eyebrow in mock dismay at the older woman's suggestion. She was at ease, seated in front of the fireplace in her former employer's library, a fireplace she had once cleaned with the raw, housework-roughened hands of a maid in service.

"No, I'm not a brain surgeon. I'm going to think about it for a bit, Lady Rowan. I want to get it right."

The gray-haired aristocrat leaned over and patted Maisie on the knee. "I'm sure that whatever you choose, you will do very well, my dear. Very well indeed."

So it was that when Billy Beale, the caretaker, knocked on the door one week after Maisie moved into the Warren Street office, asking if there was a nameplate to put up at the front door, Maisie handed him a brass plate bearing the words "M. Dobbs. Trade and Personal Investigations."

"Where do you want it, Miss? Left of the door or right of the door?"

He turned his head very slightly to one side as he addressed her. Billy was about thirty years old, just under six feet tall, muscular and strong, with hair the color of sun-burnished wheat. He seemed agile, but worked hard to disguise a limp that Maisie had noticed immediately.

"Where are the other names situated?"

"On the left, Miss, but I wouldn't put it there if I were you."

"Oh, and why not, Mr. Beale?"

"Billy. You can call me Billy. Well, people don't really look to the left, do they? Not when they're using the doorknob, which is on the right. That's where the eyes immediately go when they walk up them steps, first to that lion's 'ead door knocker, then to the knob, which is on the right. Best 'ave the plate on the right. That's if you want their business."

"Well, Mr. Beale, let's have the plate on the right. Thank you."

"Billy, Miss. You can call me Billy."

Billy Beale went to fit the brass nameplate. Maisie sighed deeply and rubbed her neck at the place where worry always sat when it was making itself at home.

"Miss . . . ."

Billy poked his head around the door, tentatively knocking at the glass as he removed his flat cap.

"What is it, Mr. Beale?"

"Billy, Miss. Miss, can I have a quick word?"

"Yes, come in. What is it?"

"Miss, I wonder if I might ask a question? Personal, like." Billy continued without waiting for an answer. "Was you a nurse? At a casualty clearing station? Outside of Bailleul?"

Maisie felt a strong stab of emotion, and instinctively put her right hand to her chest, but her demeanor and words were calm.

"Yes. Yes, I was."

"I knew it!" said Billy, slapping his cap across his knee. "I just knew it the minute I saw those eyes. That's all I remember, after they brought me in. Them eyes of yours, Miss. Doctor said to concentrate on looking at something while 'e worked on me leg. So I looked at your eyes, Miss. You and 'im saved my leg. Full of shrapnel, but you did it, didn't you? What was 'is name?"

For a moment, Maisie's throat was paralyzed. Then she swallowed hard. "Simon Lynch. Captain Simon Lynch. That must be who you mean."

"I never forgot you, Miss. Never. Saved my life, you did."

Maisie nodded, endeavoring to keep her memories relegated to the place she had assigned them in her heart, to be taken out only when she allowed.

"Well, Miss. Anything you ever want doing, you just 'oller. I'm your man. Stroke of luck, meeting up with you again, innit? Wait till I tell the missus. You want anything done, you call me. Anything."

"Thank you. Thank you very much. I'll holler if I need anything. Oh, and Mr. . . . . Billy, thank you for taking care of the sign."

Billy Beale blushed and nodded, covered his burnished hair with his cap, and left the office.

Lucky, thought Maisie. Except for the war, I've had a lucky life so far. She sat down on the dubious oak chair, slipped off her shoes and rubbed at her feet. Feet that still felt the cold and wet and filth and blood of France. Feet that hadn't felt warm in twelve years, since 1917.

She remembered Simon, in another life, it seemed now, sitting under a tree on the South Downs in Sussex. They had been on leave at the same time, not a miracle of course, but difficult to arrange, unless you had connections where connections counted. It was a warm day, but not one that took them entirely away from the fighting, for they could still hear the deep echo of battlefield cannonade from the other side of the English Channel, a menacing sound not diminished by the intervening expanse of land and sea. Maisie had complained then that the damp of France would never leave her, and Simon, smiling, had pulled off her walking shoes to rub warmth into her feet.

"Goodness, woman, how can anyone be that cold and not be dead?"

They both laughed, and then fell silent. Death, in such times, was not a laughing matter.

CHAPTER TWO

*T*he small office had changed in the thirty days since Maisie had taken up occupancy. The desk had been moved and was now positioned at an angle to the broad sash window, so that from her chair Maisie could look up and out over the rooftops as she worked. A very sophisticated black telephone sat on top of the desk, at the insistence of Lady Rowan, who maintained that "No one, simply no one, can expect to do business without a telephone. It is essential, positively essential." As far as Maisie was concerned, what was essential was that the trilling of its authoritative ring be heard a bit more often. Billy Beale had also taken to suggesting improvements lately.

"Can't have folk up 'ere for business without offering 'em a cuppa the ol' char, can you, Miss? Let me open up that cupboard, put in a burner, and away you go. Bob's yer uncle, all the facilities for tea. What d'you think, Miss? I can nip down the road to my mate's carpentry shop for the extra wood, and run the gas along 'ere for you. No trouble."

"Lovely, Billy. That would be lovely."

Maisie sighed. It seemed that everyone else knew what would be best for her. Of course their hearts were in the right place, but what she needed most now was some clients.

"Shall I advance you the money for supplies, Billy?"

"No money needed," said Billy, winking and tapping the side of his nose with his forefinger. "Nod's as good as a wink to a blind 'orse, if you know what I mean, Miss."

Maisie raised an eyebrow and allowed herself a grin. "I know exactly what that saying means, Billy: What I don't see, I shouldn't worry about."

"You got it, Miss. Leave it to me. Two shakes of a lamb's tail, and you'll be ready to receive your visitors in style."

Billy replaced his cap, put a forefinger to the peak to gesture his departure, and closed the door behind him. Leaning back in her chair, Maisie rubbed at tired eyes and looked over the late afternoon rooftops. She watched as the sun drifted away to warm the shores of another continent, leaving behind a rose tint to bathe London at the end of a long day.

Looking again at her handwritten notes, Maisie continued rereading a draft of the report she was in the midst of preparing. The case in question was minor, but Maisie had learned the value of detailed note taking from Maurice Blanche. During her apprenticeship with him, he had been insistent that nothing was to be left to memory, no stone to remain unturned, and no small observation uncataloged. Everything, absolutely *everything,* right down to the color of the shoes the subject wore on the day in question, must be noted. The weather must be described, the direction of the wind, the flowers in bloom, the food eaten. Everything must be described and preserved. "You must write it down, absolutely and in its entirety, write it down," instructed her mentor. In fact, Maisie thought that if she had a shilling for every time she heard the words, "absolutely, and in its entirety," she would never have to work again.

Maisie rubbed her neck once more, closed the folder on her desk, and stretched her arms above her head. The doorbell's deep clattering ring broke the silence. At first Maisie thought that someone had pulled the bell handle in error. There had been few rings since Billy installed the new device, which sounded in Maisie's office. Despite the fact that Maisie had worked with Maurice Blanche and had taken over his practice when he retired at the age of seventy-six, establishing her name independent of Maurice was proving to be a challenge indeed. The bell rang again.

Maisie pressed her skirt with her hands, patted her head to tame any stray tendrils of hair, and hurried downstairs to the door.

"Good. . . ." The man hesitated, then consulted a watch that he drew from his waistcoat pocket, as if to ascertain the accurate greeting for the time of day. "Good evening. My name is Davenham, Christopher Davenham. I'm here to see Mr. Dobbs. I have no appointment, but was assured that he would see me."

He was tall, about six feet two inches by Maisie's estimate. Fine tweed suit, hat taken off to greet her at just the right moment, but repositioned quickly. Good leather shoes, probably buffed to a shine by his manservant. *The Times* was rolled up under one arm, but with a sheet or two of writing paper coiled inside and just visible. His own notes, thought Maisie. His jet black hair was swept back and oiled, and his moustache neatly trimmed. Christopher Davenham was about forty-two or forty-three. Only seconds had passed since his introduction, but Maisie had him down. This one had not been a soldier. In a protected profession, she suspected.

"Come this way, Mr. Davenham. There are no appointments set for this evening, so you are in luck."

Maisie led the way up to her office, and invited Christopher Davenham to sit in the new guest chair opposite her own, the chair that had been delivered just last week by Lady Rowan's chauffeur. Another gift to help her business along.

Davenham looked around for a moment, expecting someone else to step out to meet him, but instead the young woman introduced herself.

"Maisie Dobbs. At your service, Mr. Davenham." She waved her hand toward the chair again. "Do please take a seat, Mr. Davenham. Now then, first tell me how you came to have my name."

Christopher Davenham hid his surprise well, taking a linen

handkerchief from his inside pocket and coughing lightly into it. The handkerchief was so freshly laundered and ironed that the folds were still knife sharp. Davenham refolded the handkerchief along the exact lines pressed by the iron, and replaced it in his pocket.

"Miss, er, Dobbs. Well, um, well . . . you have been highly recommended by my solicitor."

"Who is?"

Maisie leaned her head to one side to accentuate the question, and to move the conversation onto more fertile ground.

"Oh, um, Blackstone and Robinson. Joseph Robinson."

Maisie nodded. Lady Rowan again. Joseph Robinson had been her personal legal adviser for forty-odd years. And he didn't suffer fools gladly unless they were paying him—and paying him well.

"Been the family solicitor for years. I'll be frank with you, Miss Dobbs. I'm surprised to see you. Thought you were a chap. But Robinson knows his stuff, so let's continue."

"Yes, let's, Mr. Davenham. Perhaps you would tell me why you are here."

"My wife."

Maisie's stomach churned. Oh, Lord, after all her training, her education, her successes with Maurice Blanche, had it come to this? A love triangle? But she sat up to listen carefully, remembering Blanche's advice: "The extraordinary hides behind the camouflage of the ordinary. Assume nothing, Maisie."

"And what about your wife, Mr. Davenham?"

"I believe . . . I believe her affections are engaged elsewhere. I have suspected it for some time and now, Miss Dobbs, I must know if what I suspect is true."

Maisie leaned back in her chair and regarded Christopher Davenham squarely. "Mr. Davenham, first of all, I must tell you that I will have to ask you some questions. They may not be questions that are easy or comfortable for you to answer. I will have questions about your responses, and even questions about your questions. That is my job. I am unique in what I do. I am also unique in what I charge for my service."

"Money is not a problem, Miss Dobbs."

"Good. The questions may be, though."

"Do continue."

"Mr. Davenham, please tell me what personal evidence you have to suspect that your wife is betraying your marriage in any way?"

"Tuesdays and Thursdays, every week, without fail, she leaves the house immediately after I have departed for my office, and returns just in time to welcome me home."

"Mr. Davenham, time away from the house is no reason for you to suspect that you are being deceived."

"The lies are, though."

"Go on." Maisie wrote in her notebook without taking her eyes off Davenham, a skill that unnerved him.

"She has told me that she has been shopping, visiting friends or her mother—and upon investigation I find that if such visits have occurred, they have taken only an hour or so. Clearly they are a smokescreen."

"There are other possibilities, Mr. Davenham. Could your wife, perhaps, be visiting her physician? Is she undertaking a course of study? What other reasons for her absences have you explored in your investigations, Mr. Davenham? Such absences may have a completely innocent explanation."

"Miss Dobbs. Surely that is for you to find out? Follow her, and you will see that I am right."

"Mr. Davenham. To follow a person is an invasion of the right of that individual to privacy. If I take on this case—and I do have a choice in the matter—I am taking on more than the question of who did what and when. I am taking on a responsibility for both you and your wife in a way that you may not have considered. Tell me, what will you do with the information I provide?"

"Well, I . . . I'll use it. It will be a matter for my solicitor."

Maisie placed her hands together in front of her face, just touching her nose, as if in prayer. "Let me ask you another question. What value do you place on your marriage?"

"What sort of question is that?"

"A question to be answered, if I am to take on this investigation."

"A high value. Vows are meant to be honored."

"And what value do you place on understanding, compassion, forgiveness?"

Davenham was silent. He crossed his legs, smoothed the tweed trousers, and leaned down to rub away a nonexistent scuff on his polished leather shoes, before responding. "Damn and blast!"

"Mr. Davenham—"

"Miss Dobbs, I am not without compassion, but I have my pride. My wife will not divulge the nature of her business on those days when she is absent. I have come here in order to learn the truth."

"Oh yes. The truth. Mr. Davenham, I will ascertain the truth for you, but I must have an agreement from you—that when you have my report, and you know the truth, then we will discuss the future together."

"What do you mean?"

"The information I gather will be presented in a context. It is in light of that context that we must continue our discussion, in order for you and your wife to build a future."

"I'm sure I don't know what you mean."

Maisie stood up, walked to the window, then turned to face her potential client. The bluff of the stiff upper lip, thought Maisie, who keenly felt the man's discomfort, and was immediately attuned to his emotions. Intuition spoke to her. *He talks about pride when it's his heart that's aching.*

"My job is rather more complex than you might have imagined, Mr. Davenham. I am responsible for the safety of all parties. And this is so even when I am dealing with society's more criminal elements."

Davenham did not respond immediately. Maisie, too, was silent, allowing him time to gather his resolve. After some minutes the stillness of the room was broken.

"I trust Robinson, so I will go ahead," said Davenham.

Maisie moved back to the desk, and looked down at her notes, then to the rooftops where pigeons were busy returning to newly built nests, before she brought her attention back to the man in the leather chair before her.

"Yes, Mr. Davenham. I will, too." Maisie allowed her acceptance of the case to be underlined by another moment of silence.

"Now then, let's start with your address, shall we?"

CHAPTER THREE

aisie rose early on Tuesday, April 9. She dressed carefully in the blue skirt and jacket, pulled a navy blue wool overcoat across her shoulders, placed a cloche on her head, and left her rented room in a large three-story Victorian terraced house in Lambeth, just south of the Thames. It was cold again. Blimey, would spring ever spring up? she wondered, pulling gloves onto already chilled fingers.

As usual Maisie began her morning with a brisk walk, which allowed her time to consider the day ahead and enjoy what her father always called "the best of the morning." She entered Palace Road from Royal Street, and turned right to walk toward Westminster Bridge. She loved to watch the Thames first thing in the morning. Those Londoners who lived just south of the river always said they were "going over the water" when they crossed the Thames, never referring to the river by name unless they were speaking to a stranger. It had been the lifeblood of the city since the Middle Ages, and no people felt the legacy more keenly than those who lived with it and by it. Her maternal grandfather had been a lighterman on the water, and like all of his kind, knew her tides, her every twist and turn.

Londoners knew she was a moody creature. Human beings possessed no dominion over the Thames, but care, attention, and respect would see any vessel safely along her meandering way. Maisie's grandfather had all but disowned her mother when she had taken up with Maisie's father, for he was of the land, not that Frankie Dobbs would have called the streets of London "the land." Frankie was a costermonger, a man who sold vegetables from a horse-drawn cart that he drove from Lambeth to Covent Garden market every weekday morning. To Frankie Dobbs the water was a means to an end, bringing fruit and vegetables to market, for him to buy in the early hours of the morning, then sell on his rounds and be home by teatime, if he was lucky.

Maisie stopped at the center of the bridge, waved at the crew of a pilot boat, and went on her way. She was off to see Celia Davenham, but Celia Davenham would not see her.

Once across the bridge, Maisie descended into the depths of Westminster underground railway station and took the District Line to Charing Cross station. The station had changed names back and forth so many times, she wondered what it would be called next. First it was Embankment, then Charing Cross Embankment, and now just Charing Cross, depending upon which line you were traveling. At Charing Cross she changed trains, and took the Northern Line to Goodge Street station, where she left the underground, coming back up into the sharp morning air at Tottenham Court Road. She crossed the road, then set off along Chenies Street toward Russell Square. Once across the square, she entered Guilford Street, where she stopped to look at the mess the powers that be had made of Coram's Fields. The old foundling hospital, built by Sir Thomas Coram almost two hundred years before, had been demolished in 1926, and now it was just an empty space with nothing to speak of happening to it. "Shame," whispered Maisie, as she walked another few yards and entered Mecklenburg Square.

Named in honor of Charlotte of Mecklenburg-Strelitz, who became queen consort upon her marriage to George III of England, the gracious Georgian houses of the square were set around a garden protected by a wrought-iron fence secured with a locked gate. Doubtless a key to the lock was on a designated hook downstairs at the Davenham residence, in the butler's safekeeping. In common with many London squares, only residents had access to the garden.

Maisie jotted a few more lines in her notebook, taking care to reflect that she had been to the square once before, accompanying Maurice Blanche during a visit to his colleague, Richard Tawney, the political writer who spoke of social equality in a way that both excited and embarrassed Maisie. At the time it seemed just as well that he and Maurice were deep in lively conversation, so that Maisie's lack of ease could go unnoticed.

While waiting at the corner and surveying the square, Maisie wondered if Davenham had inherited his property. He seemed quite out of place in Mecklenburg Square, where social reformers lived alongside university professors, poets, and scholars from overseas. She considered his possible discomfort, not only in his marriage but in his home environment. As Maisie set her gaze on one house in particular, a man emerged from a neighboring house and walked in her direction. She quickly feigned interest in a window box filled with crocus buds peeking through moist soil. Their purple shoots seemed to test the air to see if it was conducive to a full-fledged flowering. The man passed. Maisie still had her head inclined toward the flowers when she heard another door close with a thud, and looked up.

A woman had emerged from the residence she had been observing, and was now depositing a set of keys in her handbag. She adjusted her hat and made her way down the steps and onto the pavement. Christopher Davenham had provided Maisie with an excellent description of his wife, Celia, a petite, fair-complected woman with fine features, no taller than five feet two. Celia Davenham had silky blond hair that tended to unsettle a hat that already required more than one hatpin to render it secure, and hands that seemed constantly to fiddle with bag, gloves, hat, and hair as she walked to the main road.

Even from a distance of several paces, Maisie noted the quality of the woman's deep burgundy gabardine suit, and the soft leather gloves and felt hat chosen to complement the expensive ensemble precisely. Her shoes had clearly been chosen with care as well, for they were of fine burgundy leather with half straps at each side that met in the center and were secured with a grosgrain ribbon tied in a small bow. Maisie was intrigued by the bow, for it suggested a certain girlishness, as if the woman could not quite accommodate the maturity her age suggested.

Celia Davenham made her way toward Heathcote Street and turned into Grays Inn Road, where she hailed a taxi-cab outside the Royal Free Hospital. Fortunately Maisie managed to secure a taxi-cab at once, so that she could travel immediately behind Mrs. Davenham. As she sat in the rear seat of the heavy black motorcar, she hoped that the journey would be a short one. For Maisie travel by any means other than her own two feet was nothing but an indulgence. The journey by underground to Warren Street was a treat she allowed herself in the morning only if she considered that she had worked hard enough to warrant the additional expenditure.

At Charing Cross railway station, Celia Davenham climbed out of the cab, paid the driver, and proceeded to the ticket counter. Maisie followed closely. She stood behind Mrs. Davenham at the ticket counter, and pretended to fumble in her bag for her purse, listening keenly as the childlike woman with the soft blond hair stated her destination.

"Nether Green, please. First-class return, thank you."

What on earth could this woman want at Nether Green, a small town on the outskirts of London, where it met with the county of Kent? Apple orchards giving way to terraced houses, an old station, a few good homes. Now if she had asked for Chislehurst, with its new-money grandeur, Maisie thought she might have understood. But Nether Green? Maisie requested a second-class ticket for the same destination, then proceeded to the correct platform to await the train. She stopped only to buy a newspaper, which she carried under her arm.

The train pulled in with a loud hiss, pumping clouds of smoky steam as the engine reached the buffers and the screeching brakes were applied. The olive green livery of the Southern Railways, painted on each carriage, was tarnished by coal dust and wear. Celia Davenham immediately walked toward the first-class compartments, whereupon a guard hurriedly stepped forward to open the sturdy, iron-framed door, and to extend a steadying hand as she stepped up into the carriage. Maisie passed on the way to the second-class carriages, and just before the door closed, noticed that the collar and cuffs of Mrs. Davenham's burgundy suit were edged with the same ribbon used to form a bow on her shoes. She quickly reestimated the cost of the clothes the woman was wearing that day.

Having ensured that the object of her investigation was aboard the train, Maisie claimed a seat in a second-class carriage, pulled down the window to observe the platform, and waited for the whistle to blow and the train to chug out of one of London's busiest stations. Eventually the guard walked down the platform, instructing Maisie as he passed that it would be better for "yer 'ead, Miss," if she sat down. He checked that the train was clear of all platform onlookers, blew his whistle, and waved the green flag, signaling the engine driver to move out of the station.

As the train chugged and puffed its way through south London and out into the city's border with Kent, Maisie pondered the changes she had seen in the city in her lifetime. London was creeping outward. Where there had been fields, houses now stood. Rows of shops were doing brisk business, and a new commuter class was working to improve itself. By the time the train reached Grove Park, Maisie had brought her notes up to date again, ensuring that each small detail of her journey, from the time she left her rented flat in south London that morning until the present moment, was recorded—along with every penny she had spent along the way.

The next stop was Nether Green. Maisie stood, inspected her reflection in a mirror strategically placed between two dim lights on the carriage bulkhead, adjusted her hat, and took her seat again to wait for the train to slow down, for the hissing of brakes. As the carriages rolled into the station, Maisie stood once more, pulled down the window, and poked her head out to keep an eye on the first-class compartments. When the train came to a halt Maisie put her arm out of the window so she could open the heavy carriage door from the outside and, keeping the first-class compartments in view, she jumped smartly from the train and walked at a brisk pace toward the ticket collector. Celia Davenham was ahead by only a few yards, obscured slightly by other passengers, including a very slow old lady who would not be rushed.

"Now just you wait, young man," said the old woman to the ticket collector. "It's a sorry state of affairs if you can't give your elders and betters a minute or two to find the ticket."

The ticket collector stepped back a pace, as if anticipating a blow to the head from the doughty woman's black umbrella. Maisie waited impatiently, for Celia Davenham had passed through the barrier and was leaving the station. Finally she reached the ticket collector, handed over her ticket, and walked as quickly as she could to the station gate. Glancing both ways, Maisie saw that Celia had paused by a flower stall. Luck indeed. She walked toward the stall, rearranging the newspaper under her arm and consulting her watch, even though she knew the time to the second. She approached it just as Celia Davenham was walking away.

Maisie looked over the bunches of fragrant blooms while addressing the stallholder. "Lovely flowers, the ones you wrapped for that lady."

"Yes, Ma'am, very nice indeed. Always has the irises."

"Always?"

"Yes, twice a week. Never fails."

"Oh well, she must like them," said Maisie, picking up a small bunch of Jersey daffodils. "I think I'll have something a bit different, though."

"Color of mourning, those irises," observed the man. "These daffs are a lot more cheerful by half!"

Maisie looked at her watch and made sure that Celia Davenham was still in sight. She walked slowly, but was not distracted by goods displayed in shopwindows. Keeping her eyes focused on the ground, she seemed to be avoiding any contact with people passing by.

"Well, I think so, too. I'll take the daffs, thank you very much."

"We sell a lot of irises, what with the cemetery up the road. That and chrysanths, always popular."

Maisie took the bunch of daffodils and handed over the exact change in pennies.

"Thank you. Very nice indeed."

She set forth at a steady pace, and was soon just a few steps behind Celia Davenham. They had passed the shops now, and although there were still passersby, the number of pedestrians heading in the same direction was thinning out. Celia Davenham turned right, then left onto the main road. She waited for some motorcars and a horse-drawn cart to pass, looking ahead to the green-painted iron gates of Nether Green Cemetery. Maisie followed, careful to maintain her distance yet still keep the other woman in view.

Celia Davenham walked with purpose, her head lowered but her step firm. Maisie watched her, mentally noting every detail of the other woman's demeanor. Her shoulders were held too square, hunched upward as if on a coat hanger. Maisie copied the woman's posture as she walked, and immediately felt her stomach clutch and a shiver go though her. Then sadness descended, like a dark veil across her eyes. Maisie knew that Celia Davenham was weeping as she walked, and that in her sadness she was searching for strength. With a sense of relief, as she walked along Maisie shook off the other woman's way of holding herself.

She followed Celia Davenham through the open gates, and along a path for about fifty yards. Then, without changing her pace, the object of Maisie's investigation turned in from the path and walked across the grass, pausing by a relatively fresh grave. The large marble angel towering above a neighboring grave caught Maisie's eye, and she made a mental note of this landmark. She knew she'd have to be careful. One grave can seem much like the next one when you are in a cemetery.

The cold seemed to close in around Maisie as she walked past Celia Davenham. A train chugged along the tracks nearby, its sooty vapor lingering for a moment over the headstones before being carried away by a chill breeze.

Maisie stopped by a grave that had clearly received no attention for years. She bowed her head and, carefully, looked sideways between the marble memorials, toward Celia Davenham. The woman was on her knees now, replacing dead flowers with the fresh irises, and talking. Talking to the dead.

Maisie, in turn, looked at the headstone she had unwittingly chosen as her cover. It bore the words: "Donald Holden. Born 1900. Died 1919. Beloved only son of Ernest and Hilda Holden. 'Memory Is A Golden Chain That Binds Us 'Til We Meet Again.'" Maisie looked at the weeds underfoot. They may have met already, she thought, while keeping a keen but inconspicuous watch on Celia Davenham, who remained at the immaculate neighboring grave, her head bowed, still speaking quietly. Maisie began to clear the weeds on Donald Holden's grave.

"Might as well look after you while I'm here," she said quietly, placing daffodils in the vase, which was mercifully full of rainwater. She couldn't afford to trudge all the way across the cemetery to the water tap: Celia might depart while she was gone.

As Maisie stepped to the side of the path to deposit a pile of weeds, she saw Celia Davenham move toward the headstone where she had held her vigil. She kissed the cold, gray marble, brushed away a tear, then turned quickly and walked away. Maisie was in no hurry to follow. Instead she nodded at Donald Holden's headstone, then walked over to the grave that the Davenham woman had just left. It said "Vincent." Just "Vincent." No other name, no date of birth. Then the words, "Taken from all who love you dearly."

The day had warmed by the time Maisie reached the station for the return journey to London. Celia Davenham, already on the platform, glanced at her watch repeatedly. Maisie went into the ladies' toilets, walked across chilly floor tiles that radiated more moisture into the damp air, and ran icy water into the porcelain sink to rinse the dirt from her hands. She looked up into the mirror and regarded the face that looked directly back at her. Yes, the dark blue eyes still held a sparkle, but the small lines around her lips and across her brow betrayed her, told something about her past.

She knew that she would follow Celia Davenham this afternoon until the woman returned to her home in Mecklenburg Square, and believed that nothing else of note would occur that day. Maisie knew that she had found the lover, the man who had caused Christopher Davenham to pay a princely sum for her services. The problem was that the man Christopher Davenham thought was cuckolding him was dead.

CHAPTER FOUR

aisie sat in the early morning half-light of her office considering her subject. Only one small lamp illuminated the room, but it was angled downward toward Maisie's notes and a clutch of small index cards. Maurice maintained that the mind was at its sharpest before dawn.

In the early days of her pupilage with Maurice, he had told Maisie of his teachers, the wise men who spoke of the veil that was lifted in the early hours, of the all-seeing eye that was open before the day was awake. The hours before dawn were the sacred time, before the intellect rose from slumber. At this time one's inner voice could be heard. Maisie had strained to hear that inner voice for days, since the single word "Vincent" had piqued her curiosity, since the apparent ordinariness of Celia Davenham's grief had given rise to more questions than answers.

Slipping off her shoes and pulling her wool cardigan around her shoulders, Maisie took a cushion from her chair and placed it on the floor. Lifting her skirt above her knees to allow freedom of move-ment, she sat on the cushion, crossed her legs and placed her hands together on her lap. Maurice had taught her that silencing the mind was a greater task than stilling the body, but it was in those still waters that truth could be mirrored. Now, in the darkness, Maisie sought the guidance of intuition and formed the questions that, in time, would give her answers.

Why only one name? Why no dates etched into the headstone? What was keeping the relationship between Celia and Vincent alive? Was it simply grief, perpetuated by disbelief that a dear one has parted? Or another emotion? Maisie saw the grave in her mind's eye, allowed her eyes to regard all aspects of the place where Vincent was laid to rest. But if he was at rest, why did she feel compelled to seek a path that was not as yet marked?

What is this question I cannot voice? Maisie asked herself. Donald Holden died just a year after the war. His grave bore signs of age. Vincent's seemed fresher, as if the ground had been disturbed only in recent months.

Maisie sat for a while longer, allowing the stillness to calm her natural busyness, until the brighter, grainy light of the waking hours signaled her to move. She stood, stretching her arms high while standing on tiptoe. Today she would follow Celia Davenham to the cemetery again.

Celia was a creature of habit. This day she left the house promptly at nine o'clock in the morning, immaculately dressed in a suit of shamrock green wool, the broad collar of a cream silk blouse flat against her jacket, and pinned with a jade brooch, clearly part of a set that included her jade earrings. Matching shoes and bag with a carefully coordinated hat and umbrella completed the ensemble. This time the shoes were plain in design, but each shoe bore a fashionable clip in the shape of a leaf pressed onto the front. Maisie wore her navy skirt and jacket. Her serious business clothes. The journey to Nether Green was uneventful. Once again Celia Davenham traveled in first class, while Maisie sat in the prickly discomfort of a second-class carriage. Celia bought her customary bouquet of irises, while Maisie decided upon something different for Donald—and for her purse—this morning.

"I'll have a nice bunch of daisies, please," said Maisie to the flower seller.

"Right you are, Miss. Always look cheerful, daisies, don't they, Miss? Last a while too. Newspaper all right, or do you need them wrapped special?"

"Yes, they are cheerful, aren't they? Newspaper will be fine, thank you," she said, holding out the correct change for a bunch of daisies.

Then Maisie quickly walked on, trailing Celia Davenham toward the cemetery. She entered through the green gates, and by the time she walked past Vincent's grave toward Donald Holden's resting place, Celia was standing in front of the marble headstone, tracing Vincent's name with the shamrock-green-gloved fingers of her right hand. Maisie walked past, her head lowered, and stopped in front of Donald's grave. After a respectful silent prayer, she busied herself, emptying water from the vase and pulling a few weeds. Picking up the now-dead daffodils from her previous visit, she walked over to the tap, threw the dead flowers onto the compost pile, and filled the vase with fresh water. Maisie returned to Donald's grave, replaced the vase, and arranged the daisies. As she worked, she looked sideways at Celia, who had removed her gloves and was arranging her bouquet of irises at the base of Vincent's headstone. Having placed them to her satisfaction, she continued to kneel by the stone, staring at the name.

Maisie observed Celia Davenham, and once again moved her body to mirror the woman's position. Her head seemed to sink lower on her long neck, her shoulders rounded, her hands tightened with pain. Such melancholy. Such an unending yearning. Maisie instinctively knew that Celia was dying inside, that each yesterday was being lived anew and that there could be no place for her husband until Vincent was allowed to rest in peace.

Suddenly the woman shuddered and looked straight at Maisie. She did not smile; it was as if she were looking beyond Maisie to another place. Regaining her own natural posture, Maisie nodded acknowledgment, a small movement that brought Celia Davenham back to the present. She nodded in return, brushed at her skirt, stood up, replaced her gloves, and quickly left Vincent's grave.

Maisie was in no hurry. She knew that Celia Davenham would go home now. Home to play the loving wife, the role she would assume as soon as she walked through the door. It was a role that her husband had seen through easily, although his conclusions had been erroneous. Maisie also knew that the second's glance and the deliberate acknowledgment she had initiated between herself and Celia ensured that the other woman would recognize her when they met again.

Maisie lingered for a while at Donald's grave. There was something healing in this ritual of making a comfortable place for the dead. Her thoughts took her back to France, to the dead and dying, to the devastating wounds that were so often beyond her skill, beyond everyone's. But it was the wounds of the mind that touched her, those who still fought their battles again and again each day, though the country was at peace. If only she could make the living as comfortable, thought Maisie, as she tidied a few more stubborn weeds in the shadow of Don's headstone.

"Making a nice job of that one."

Maisie swung around, to see one of the cemetery workers standing behind her, an older man with red, bony hands firmly grasping the handles of a wooden wheelbarrow. His ruddy complexion told of years working outdoors, but his kind eyes spoke of compassion, of respect.

"Why yes. It's sad to see them so uncared for, isn't it?" replied Maisie.

"I'll say, after what those boys gave for us. Poor bastards. Oh, Miss, I am sorry, I forgot—"

"Don't worry. It's as well to voice one's feelings," replied Maisie.

"That's the truth. Too much not said by 'alf."

The man pointed to Donald's grave.

"Haven't seen this one being tended for a few years. His old Mum and Dad used to come over. Only son. Killed them, too, it did, I reckon."

"Did you know them? I would have thought it would be difficult to know all the relatives, with so many graves," said Maisie.

"I'm 'ere every day 'cept Sundays, that is. Been 'ere since just after the war. I get to know people. 'Course, you don't 'ave long talks, no time for that, and folk don't always want to talk, but, there again, there's those that want to 'ave a bit of conversation."

"Yes, yes, I'm sure."

"Not seen you before, not 'ere." The man looked at Maisie.

"No, that's true. I'm a cousin. Just moved to the city," said Maisie, looking at the man directly.

"Nice to see it being taken care of." The man firmed his grip on the wheelbarrow handles, as if to move on.

"Wait a minute. I wonder, could you tell me, are all the graves here, in this part, war graves?" asked Maisie.

"Yes and no. Most of these are our boys, but some lived a long time after their injuries. Your Don, well, you'd know this, but 'e 'ad septicemia. Horrible way to go, 'specially as 'e was brought home. Lot of folk like to bury 'em 'ere because of the railway."

The man set the wheelbarrow down, and pointed to the railway lines running alongside the cemetery.

"You can see the trains from 'ere. Not that these boys can see the trains, but the relatives like it. They're on a journey, you see, it's a— you know, what do they call it, you know—when it means something to them."

"Metaphor?"

"Yeah, well, like I said, it's a journey, innit? And the relatives, if they've come by train, which most of them do, can see the graves as the train pulls out of the station. They can say another good-bye that way."

"So, what about that one there? Strange, isn't it? Just one word, the Christian name?" asked Maisie.

"I'll say. The whole bleedin' thing was strange. Two years ago 'e came, this one. Small family burial. 'e was a captain. Injured at Passchendaele. Terrible show was that one, terrible. Wonder 'e came 'ome at all. 'e'd lived away from the family, apparently, after bein' 'ome for a bit. Wanted to be known only by 'is Christian name. Said it wasn't important anymore, seein' as they were all nobodies who could just be written off like leftovers. Shame to 'is family, accordin' to a couple of 'is mates that came up 'ere for a while after. Now only that woman comes. Think she was 'is mate's sister, known 'er for years, 'e 'ad. Keeps the grave nice, you'd think 'e only went down yesterday."

"Hmm. Very sad indeed. What was his surname, do you know?"

By now the man was well into the telling of stories, and seemed glad of the opportunity, and importance, that a question brought him.

"Weathershaw. Vincent Weathershaw. Came from Chislehurst. Good family, by the looks of them. Mind you, 'e passed away where 'e was living. A farm, I think it was. Yes, 'e lived on a farm, not that far from 'ere—though more in the country, like. Far as I know, quite a few of 'em lived there."

Maisie felt a chill as the stillness of the cemetery seeped through her clothing and touched her skin. Yet the shiver was familiar to Maisie, who had felt that sensation even in warm weather when there was no cooling breeze. She had come to recognize this spark of energy passing across her skin as a warning.

"Quite a few of them?"

"Well, you know." The man rubbed his stubbled jawbone with the flat of his thick, earth-stained hand. "Them who got it in the face. Remember, we're not far from Sidcup 'ere—you know. Queen Mary's, the 'ospital where they did all that special work on faces, trying to 'elp the poor sods. Amazin' when you think of it, what they tried to do there—and what they did do. Miracle workers, they were. Mind you, I wouldn't mind bettin' a few of them boys still weren't fancy-looking enough for their sweethearts, and ended up at that farm."

The old gardener picked up the handles of the wheelbarrow. Maisie saw that he was ready to move on, away from recollections of war.

"Well, I had better be getting on, Mr. . . . ."

"Smith. Tom Smith."

"Yes, I have to catch the two o'clock, Tom. And thank you."

Tom Smith watched as Maisie picked her way past the graves to the path, and as he turned to leave he called to her. "I 'spect I won't see you 'ere again . . . but you know, Miss, the funny thing about this 'ere Vincent is that 'e wasn't the only one."

"The only one what?"

"The only one buried with just a Christian name."

Maisie held her head to one side, encouraging Tom to continue.

"There was a few of them, and you know what?

"What?" said Maisie.

"All lost touch with their families. Tragic it was, just tragic. Seeing their parents. You should never 'ave to go through that, never. Bad enough seeing 'em go off to war, let alone losing them when they come back."

"Yes, that is tragic."

Maisie looked at Tom, then asked the question that had been with her since the man had first spoken to her. "Tom . . . where is your boy resting?"

Tom Smith looked at Maisie, and tears rimmed his eyes. The lines etched in his face grew deeper, and his shoulders dropped. "Down there." He pointed to the row of headstones nearest the railway line. "Loved trains as a boy. Loved 'em. Came back from France not quite right up 'ere." He tapped the side of his head. "Would scream in the middle of the night, but it was all you could do to get a sound out of the boy in the daytime. One mornin' the missus goes up to take 'im up a cup of tea and there 'e was. Done 'imself in. She was never the same. Never. Broke 'er spirit, it did. Passed away three years ago come December."

Maisie nodded, held out her hand, and laid it upon his arm. They stood in silence.

"Well, this will never do," said Tom Smith. "Must be getting along. Got to look after them, 'aven't I? Good day to you, Miss."

Maisie Dobbs bade the man good-bye but didn't leave the cemetery immediately. Later, while waiting on the platform for the train back to London, she took a small notebook from her handbag and recorded the events of the day. Each detail was noted, including the color of Celia Davenham's shamrock-green gloves.

She had found two more graves whose headstones bore Christian names only, not very far from the final resting place of Vincent Weathershaw. Three young "old soldiers" who had withdrawn from their families. Maisie sat back on the bench and started to compose her questions, the questions to herself that would come as a result of her observations. She would not struggle to answer the questions but would let them do their work.

"Truth walks toward us on the paths of our questions." Maurice's voice once again echoed in her mind. "As soon as you think you have the answer, you have closed the path and may miss vital new information. Wait awhile in the stillness, and do not rush to conclusions, no matter how uncomfortable the unknowing."

And as she allowed her curiosity full rein, Maisie knew what her next move should be.

CHAPTER FIVE

*T*he Celia Davenham file comprised several pages by now, and included details beyond excursions to Nether Green Cemetery. Celia's birthdate (September 16, 1897), parentage (Algernon and Anne Whipton), place of birth (Sevenoaks, Kent), school (St. Mary's), and miscellaneous other details were recorded. Her husband was ten years older, not such a division in years at thirty-two, but it would have been something of a chasm at the age of nineteen or twenty, especially when the past offered more in the way of excitement than the day-to-day round of life in a maturing marriage.

Maisie knew where Celia shopped for clothes, where she took afternoon tea, even of her interest in needlework. Maisie also observed her comfort in solitude, and wondered how such a solitary soul could build a bridge to another. Did the Davenham marriage endure behind a veil of courtesy? The mundane communication that one would accord an acquaintance met on the street, but the formality of which could stifle the bond of affection between man and wife? It was evident that only one person could answer certain questions, and that was Celia Davenham herself. Maisie carefully replaced the pages in the file, placed it in her desk drawer, pushed back her chair, and made ready to leave her office.

A sharp knock at the door was followed by Billy Beale's freckled face and shock of wheaten hair, topped by a flat cap, poked around the dark wood doorjamb.

"Good afternoon to you, Miss Dobbs. 'Ow's business? Don't seem to 'ave seen much of you lately, though I 'eard that you'd 'elped old Mrs. Scott get something out of that thieving son of 'ers. Thought I'd pop me 'ead in to see if you need anything done in the way of 'andi-work in the office 'ere."

"Billy, yes, Mrs. Scott is a client. But you know better than to expect a comment from me, don't you?"

"Miss Dobbs, you're spot-on right there. But you can't stop folk talking about your business, 'specially when you've 'elped them. People round 'ere don't miss a trick, and we've got memories like elephants into the bargain!"

"Have you now, Billy? In that case, perhaps you can tell me if you know someone I think you might have heard of."

"Fire away!"

"Confidential, Billy."

"Nod's as good as a wink . . ." Billy tapped the side of his nose to emphasize the integrity of any information he might receive—he could keep a secret.

"Vincent Weathershaw. Captain. Know him?" asked Maisie.

"Weathershaw. Weathershaw. Now that name rings a bell. Let me think."

Billy took off his cap and scratched at his golden hair.

"You know, 'ere's what it is—I've 'eard about 'im. Never actually took an order from the man, but 'eard about 'im. By reputation, like."

"What sort of reputation?" quizzed Maisie.

"If I remember rightly, a bit devil-may-care. Mind you, you saw it a lot. Some of them got so as they couldn't care less about their own lives. Like they were in it so long that the shelling didn't scare them anymore. Poor sods. Some of them, the officers, that is, came out of their fancy schools and straight into the trenches."

"Was he reckless?"

"If it's the fella I'm thinking of, not reckless with 'is men. No, 'e was reckless with 'imself. Got so as 'e would just climb out of the bunker, no 'elmet, to go up and look around for the Kaiser's boys. Reckon they were more surprised than us when they copped sight of 'im walking around without a care in the world."

"Ever hear about him again, Billy?"

"Miss Dobbs, it's not like I talk about it much. Best left behind. But you know that, don't you? You saw enough, must've done."

"Yes, I saw enough for this lifetime, Billy."

Maisie buttoned her coat, secured her hat in place, and pulled on her gloves.

"But tell you what, Miss. I'll ask around down the Prince of Wales, some of the lads might know something. This Weathershaw, he a client, like?"

"No, Billy. No, he's not. He's dead. Two years ago. See what you can find out, Billy."

"Right you are, Miss," replied Billy. Maisie ushered Billy out of the office and locked the door behind her as she left with him.

"It's confidential, Billy. Just bring it into the conversation," instructed Maisie.

"Yes, Miss. Don't worry. Like I said when you moved in. Anything you want, you just ask Billy Beale."

Maisie decided that a brisk walk to Piccadilly Circus would be just what she needed to clear her head for the next part of her task: information gathering, as Maurice would say.

Fortunately there had been several new clients since she had moved into the office in Warren Street. Christopher Davenham's appearance had represented the beginning of a respectable stream of visitors. There were a couple of referrals from Lady Rowan's solicitors, along with three of Maurice's former clients who finally overcame any reticence they might have had about completely confiding in his former assistant, who happened to be a woman.

The work ranged from simple analysis of correspondence to reveal anomalies in funds paid to a company to a report on a "missing" daughter. As Maisie expected, there had not yet been the requests for assistance from government or from the legal or judicial services that Maurice had enjoyed, but she knew that such business would come in due course. She was qualified to consult on matters far beyond those that had come to her. Maurice had seen to that.

Maisie was now busy, and more to the point, had the money to research matters that presented themselves for investigation without initiation by an actual client. Unless you could call Vincent Weathershaw a client.

The restaurant at Fortnum & Mason's was busy, but as she walked in and feigned interest in the menu, Maisie quickly scanned the room and immediately saw Celia Davenham sitting by a window. She was looking out at the rooftops as if in a dream, with her hands clasped around a cup of tea.

"May I have a seat by the window?" requested Maisie of the tall waiter with slicked-back, brilliantined hair who greeted her.

Taking the table next to Celia, Maisie deliberately sat facing the woman, although she did not look at her as she removed her gloves, placed them on top of her bag, and set the bag on the chair next to her. Maisie opened the menu and read down the list of dishes until she felt the woman's eyes upon her, then she looked up, meeting Celia's gaze. Maisie smiled. Her "planetary" smile, as Simon had once said. She quickly banished all thought of Simon; her concentration had to be on the job in hand.

"Hello," said Maisie in greeting. "Such a lovely day today, isn't it?"

"Yes. Yes it is," responded Celia. She smiled at Maisie. "Forgive me . . . but, have we met?"

"You know, I must say, you look very familiar, but I . . . I can't think where." Maisie smiled again.

"Nether Green. I've seen you at Nether Green." Color flushed Celia Davenham's cheeks as she recognized Maisie.

"Why, yes, yes. Look, would you like to join me?" Maisie moved her bag and gloves from the seat next to her, an invitation to Celia Davenham.

A waiter quickly came to assist Celia, and placed her teacup, saucer, and place mat on Maisie's table. The perfectly dressed woman sat down opposite Maisie, who held out her hand.

"Blanche. Maisie Blanche. How do you do."

"Celia Davenham. I'm very well, thank you."

For a while the two women talked of small matters. The price of flowers at the stall, the late arrival of trains this past winter. Before Celia could ask, Maisie offered the story of her visits to the cemetery.

"Donald was a cousin. Not close, but family all the same. I thought that now I'm here in town, it would be easy to go out to Nether Green. One doesn't like to forget, does one?"

"No. Absolutely. No. Not that I could," replied Celia.

"Did you lose your brother?" asked Maisie.

"Yes, one of them. In the Dardanelles. The other was wounded. Seriously wounded."

"I'm sorry. You were lucky to have your brother come home from the Dardanelles," said Maisie, knowing that often brother fought alongside brother, which led to many a mother grieving the loss of not one child but two or three.

"Oh, no. No. My brother's body was never found. He was listed missing. I visit the grave of my other brother's friend. Vincent." Celia fussed with her handkerchief.

"I see. Is your brother, your other brother, recovered?"

"Um. Yes, yes, in a way."

Maisie held her head to one side in question but added, "Oh, this is such a difficult subject—"

"No, I mean, yes. Yes. But . . . well, he has scars. Vincent had scars too."

"Oh. I see."

"Yes. George, my brother who survived, is like Vincent. His face—"

Celia slowly moved her finely manicured hands and touched her cheek with delicate fingers. She flinched and tears filled her eyes. At that moment Maisie saw her chance for connection. A connection that was deeper than she would admit. She reached out and touched

Celia lightly on the arm until the other woman's eyes met hers. Maisie nodded her understanding.

"I was a nurse," said Maisie, her voice lowered, not to avoid being heard but to draw Celia toward her. "In France. When I returned from France I nursed again in a secure mental hospital. I understand the wounds, Mrs. Davenham. Those of the body—and of the soul."

Celia Davenham took Maisie's hand. And at that moment Maisie knew she was in the woman's confidence, that she was trusted. Maisie had anticipated that it would take no longer than the twenty minutes that the women had sat together at the same table. Such was Celia's hunger for connection to someone who understood. And the depth of Maisie Dobbs's understanding of her situation was greater than Celia Davenham could possibly imagine.

Celia Davenham sat for a moment before speaking again. Wave upon wave of grief seemed to break across her heart with such force that she made a fist with one hand, and gripped Maisie's offered hand of understanding with the other. A waiter coming toward the table to inquire if more tea was required stopped suddenly and moved away, as if repelled by the force of her emotion.

Maisie closed her eyes, concentrating her calming energy on the woman who sat opposite her. The moment passed, and Maisie opened her eyes to observe Celia relax her shoulders, arms, and the tight grasp on her hand. But she did not let go.

"I'm sorry."

"Don't be, Mrs. Davenham. Don't be. Take some tea."

Keeping Maisie's hand in hers, the woman took the cup in her other hand and, shaking, lifted it to her lips to sip the still-hot tea. The two women sat in silence for several more minutes until Maisie spoke again.

"Tell me about Vincent, Mrs. Davenham."

Celia Davenham placed the fine bone china cup in its saucer, took a deep breath, and began to tell her story.

"I fell in love with Vincent—oh, dear me—it must have been when I was about twelve. I was just a girl. He came to the house with my brother George. It was my brother Malcolm who died. George was the oldest. Vincent was one of those people who could make anyone laugh—even my parents, who were very stiff indeed. It was as if the sun shone upon Vincent and everyone felt compelled to look at him, just to warm themselves."

"Yes, I have known such people. I expect he was quite the charmer," said Maisie.

"Oh yes, quite the charmer. But he didn't realize it. He just went through his life bringing out the best in people. So, he was definitely officer caliber. His men would have followed him to death's door."

"And no doubt beyond."

"Yes. And beyond. Apparently when he wrote to the parents or wives of men who had fallen, he always mentioned some small detail about them—a joke they had told, an act of courage, a special effort made. He didn't just say, 'I'm sorry to tell you this, but . . . .' He cared."

Celia took up her cup again, keeping one hand on Maisie's. Maisie, for her part, made no move to withdraw, realizing the strength her touch gave the other woman. She moved only to pour more tea and to bring her own cup to her lips.

Occasionally she would look out of the window, and as dusk drew in saw the reflection of Celia Davenham in the windowpane as she told her story. In this way Maisie observed her as an onlooker might, rather than as a confidante. As Celia spoke, releasing the weight of hoarded memory, she seemed to gain strength. She sat straighter. Celia was an attractive woman, and in the reflected scene, Maisie saw the faces of other people in the tearoom occasionally looking toward them, drawn to a conversation they could not overhear but could not help observe.

Maisie knew well, more than the onlookers, that they were drawn by the power of revelation. They were witnesses to the unfolding of Celia Davenham's story, to the unburdening of her soul, though they might not be aware of it. And she knew that once outside, wrapping a scarf around a neck to shield it from the biting wind, or holding on to a hat, a woman might say to her companion, "Did you see that woman, by the window, the well-dressed one?" and her companion would nod and they would speak for a while of what might have been said by the woman near the window to the woman who allowed her hand to be held so tightly. And the picture of Celia Davenham squaring her shoulders to tell her story would come back to them on occasion, especially when they were sad and looking for the answer to a question of the heart.

Celia Davenham paused, as if to summon the fortitude to continue. Maisie waited, then asked, "Tell me what happened to Vincent."

"It was at Passchendaele."

"Ah yes. I know. . . ."

"Yes, I think we all know now. So many—"

"—and Vincent?"

"Yes, although some might believe him to be lucky. He came home."

Celia stopped again, closed her eyes, then continued. "I try, sometimes, to remember his face before. When it was complete. But I can't. I feel awful, that I can only remember the scars. I try at night to close my eyes and see him, but I can't. I can see George, of course; his injuries weren't so bad. But I can't think of *exactly* how he was before the war either."

"Yes, it must be very hard."

"There was something about Vincent, his enthusiasm for life, that turned into something else, as if it had another side. His company came under intense enemy fire. Vincent was hit in the face by shrapnel. It is a miracle he lived. George lost an ear and has scars on the side of his face, which you would think were unbearable but seem light compared to Vincent's."

Maisie looked at the woman, whose grip had relaxed as she told Vincent's story. Celia was exhausted. Maurice had counseled her, in the early days of her apprenticeship, when she was the silent observer as he listened to a story, gently prodding with a question, a comment, a sigh, or a smile, "The story takes up space as a knot in a piece of wood. If the knot is removed, a hole remains. We must ask ourselves, how will this hole that we have opened be filled? The hole, Maisie, is our responsibility."

"Mrs. Davenham, you must be tired. Shall we meet again another day?" she asked.

"Yes, Miss Blanche, do let's meet."

"Perhaps we might walk in Hyde Park, or St. James's; the lake is so lovely at this time of year."

The women made arrangements to meet the following week, for tea at the Ritz, then a stroll through Green Park to St. James's. But before they parted, Maisie suggested, "Mrs. Davenham, you probably have to rush home soon, but I wonder. Liberty has some lovely new fabrics, just arrived from India. Would you come with me to look at them?"

"Why, I'd love to."

*L*ater, when Celia Davenham reflected upon her day, she was surprised. For though she still felt sadness, the memory she reflected upon most was that of huge bolts of fabric being moved around at her behest by willing assistants who could sense in her the interest that led to a purchase. With an enthusiastic flourish, yards of vibrant purples, yellows, pinks, and reds of Indian silk were pulled out, to be rubbed between finger and thumb, and held against her face in front of the mirror. And she thought of the person she knew as Maisie Blanche, who suddenly but quietly had to take her leave, allowing her to indulge her love of texture and color for far longer than she had intended. Thus a day that had seen so many tears ended in the midst of a rainbow.

CHAPTER SIX

*M*aisie made her way back to her office. It was dark
by now, and although she was gasping for a cup
of tea much stronger than the light Darjeeling
served at Fortnum & Mason's, she needed to work. She reflected upon
the Davenham story, knowing only too well that there was a lot more
to elicit. But by leaving much of the story untold, Maisie allowed the
door to remain open. Instead of being exhausted by her own revela-
tions and memories, Celia Davenham was being helped to shed her
burden gradually, and Maisie was her guide.

Jack Barker greeted Maisie outside Warren Street station, doffed his
cap and bid her good evening.

"Miss Dobbs, and a good evenin' to you. My, you are a sight for
sore eyes at the end of the day."

"Mr. Barker, thank you, although I am sure I'll be better when I
get a cup of tea inside me."

"You should get that Billy to make you a cuppa. Does too much
jawing of a working day, that one. Do you know, I 'ave to tell him
sometimes that I'm busy and can't keep puttin' the world to rights
with 'im."

Maisie grinned, knowing by now that Jack Barker could talk the hind leg off a donkey, and that the same complaint about Jack was likely to come from Billy Beale.

"Well, Billy's a good 'un, isn't he, Mr. Barker?"

"'E is that. Amazing how fast 'e can move with that leg. You should see 'im sometimes, running 'ere and there, 'dot and carry one' with that leg. Poor sod. But at least we got 'im back 'ere, didn't we?"

Maisie agreed. "Indeed, Mr. Barker, at least he came home. I'd best be on my way, so I'll bid you good evening. Any reason to buy the latest edition before I rush off?"

"All bloomin' bad if you ask me. Threadneedle Street and the City in a rare two-an'-eight. They're talking about a slump."

"I'll leave it then, Mr. Barker. Goodnight."

Maisie turned into Warren Street, walking behind two women students from the Slade School of Art, who were making their way back to lodgings nearby. Each carried an artist's portfolio under one arm, and giggled as the other recounted her part of a story about another woman. They stopped to speak to a group of young men who were just about to enter the Prince of Wales pub, then decided to join them. They pushed past a woman dressed in black, who had been standing outside the pub smoking a cigarette. She shouted at them to look out, but her warning was met with more giggles from the students. She was soon joined by a man, who Maisie suspected already had a wife at home, for he betrayed himself by quickly looking up and down the street before taking the woman by the arm and hurrying her inside the pub.

"It takes all sorts," said Maisie in a low voice as she passed, and continued on down Warren Street to her office.

Maisie opened the door that led to the dark stairwell, and as she went to turn on the dim light to see her way up the stairs, the light over the upper stairwell went on and Billy Beale called out.

"'S only me, Miss. See your way up?"

"Billy, you should be knocking off work by now, surely."

"Yeah, but I've got some more news for you. 'Bout that fella you was askin' about. Weathershaw. Thought I'd 'ang about in case I don't see you tomorrow."

"That's kind, Billy. Let's put the kettle on."

Maisie led the way into her office, turned on the light, and went to put the kettle on the small stove.

"And that telephone has been ringing its 'ead off today. What you need is someone to help you out, Miss, to write down messages, like."

"My telephone was ringing?"

"Well, that's what it's there for, innit?"

"Yes, of course. But it doesn't ring very often. I tend to receive messages via the postman or personal messenger. I wonder who it was?"

"Someone with an 'ead of steam, the way it was ringing. I was working on the boiler, making a fair bit of noise meself, and every now and again, there it went again. I came up a couple of times, t'see if I could answer it for you, but it stopped its nagging just as I got outside the door—I c'n use me master key in an emergency, like. I tell ya, I nearly got me kit and put in a line so that I could answer it downstairs meself."

"Pardon?"

"Remember, Miss, I was a sapper. Let me tell you, if I could run a line in the pourin' rain and on me 'ands and knees in the mud—and get the brass talkin' to each other while the 'un's trying to knock me block off as I was about it—I can bloomin' well do a thing or two with your line."

"Is that so, Billy? I'll have to remember that. In the meantime, whoever wants to speak to me will find a way. Now then, what do you have to tell me?"

"Well, I was askin' round some of me old mates, about that Vincent Weathershaw bloke. Turns out one of the fellas knew someone, who knew someone else, you know, who told them that 'e wasn't quite all there after one of the big shows."

Billy Beale tapped the side of his forehead, and Maisie inclined her head for him to continue.

"Lost a lot of men, 'e did. Apparently never forgave 'imself. Took it all upon 'is shoulders, as if 'e was the one that killed them. But what I also 'eard was that some funny stuff went on between 'im and the big brass. Now, this is all very shaky, but . . . ."

"Go on, Billy," Maisie urged.

"Well, Miss, you know, if truth be told, we were all plain scared 'alf the bloomin' time."

"Yes, I know, Billy."

"O' course you do, Miss. You know, don't you? Blimey, when I think of what you nurses must've seen . . . anyway, if the truth be told, we was all scared. You didn't know when you were going to get it. But some of 'em. . . ."

Billy stopped, turned away from Maisie, and took the red kerchief from his neck and wiped his eyes.

"Gawd—sorry, Miss. Don't know what came over me."

"Billy. It can wait. Whatever you have to tell me. It can wait. Let me pour that tea."

Maisie went to the stove, poured boiling water from the kettle onto the tea leaves in the brown earthenware teapot, and allowed it to steep. She took two large tin mugs from the shelf above the stove, stirred the tea in the pot, then poured tea for them both, with plenty of sugar and a splash of milk. Since her time in France, Maisie had preferred an army-issue tin mug for her private teatimes, for the warmth that radiated from the mug to her hands and to the rest of her body.

"There you are, Billy. Now then . . ."

"Well, as you know, Miss, there were a lot of lads 'o enlisted that were too young. Boys tryin' to be men, and blimey, the rest of us weren't much more than boys ourselves. And you'd see 'em, white as sheets when that whistle blew to go over the top. Mind you, we was all as white as sheets. I was barely eighteen meself."

Billy sipped his tea and wiped his mouth with the back of his hand.

"We'd 'ave to get 'em under the arms, shove 'em over, and 'ope that the push would get 'em through. And sometimes one of 'em didn't make it over."

Billy's eyes misted over again, and he wiped them with the red kerchief.

"And when that 'appened, when a boy was paralyzed with fear, like, 'e could be reported for cowardice. If 'e'd been seen afterwards, not 'avin' gone over with the rest of his mates, the brass didn't ask too many questions, did they? No, the poor sod's on a charge and that's it! So we 'ad to look out for each other, didn't we?"

Drawing the red cloth across his brow, the young man continued his story for Maisie.

"Court-martialed, they were. And you know what 'appened to a lot of 'em, don't you? Shot. Even if some of 'em weren't quite so innocent, villains getting up to no good when they should've been on the line, it ain't the way to go, is it? Not shot by their own. Bloody marvelous, ain't it? You pray your 'ead off that the Kaiser's boys don't get you, then it's your own that do!"

Maisie allowed silence to envelop them and held the steaming mug to her lips. This was no new story. Only the storyteller was new to her. Happy-go-lucky Billy Beale.

"Well, this Vincent Weathershaw, as far as the brass were concerned, was a soft one with 'is men. Said it was enough with the trenches and shells killing 'em without their own 'avin' it in for 'em. Apparently they wanted to 'arden this Weathershaw up a bit. I don't know the 'ole story, nowhere near, but from what I've been told, 'e was commanded to do a few things 'e didn't want to. Refused. There was talk of strippin' 'im of 'is commission. The word is that no one quite knows what 'appened, but apparently, it was after these rumors went about, that 'e sort of lost 'is 'ead and started to do all that daft business, walkin' around without the 'elmet on in front of the other lot. Then, o' course, they got 'im—at Wipers—Passchendaele. Not far from where I copped it, really, but it seemed like 'undreds of miles at the time."

Maisie smiled, but it was a sad, reflective smile as she remembered how men made easy work of pronouncing "Ypres," referring to it as "Wipers."

"Mind you, they didn't get me coming out of a trench and over the top. No, it was all that business at Messines, not knowing whether the other lot were in the trench next door, or below us, and not knowin' whether the buggers—pardon me language, Miss—but not knowin' where they'd laid mines. Us sappers 'ad our work cut out for us there."

Billy lowered his head, swirled dregs of tea to soak up sugar at the bottom of his mug, and closed his eyes as memories pushed through into the present.

Maisie and Billy Beale sat in silence. Maisie, as she so often did nowadays, remembered Maurice and his teaching:

"Never follow a story with a question, Maisie, not immediately. And remember to acknowledge the storyteller, for in some way even the messenger is affected by the story he brings."

She waited a few more minutes, watching Billy sip his tea, lost in his memories as he looked out over the rooftops.

"Billy, thank you for finding this out for me. You must have worked hard to track the details down."

Billy lifted the mug of tea to his lips.

"Like I said, Miss—you need anything doing, Billy Beale's your man."

Maisie allowed more time to pass, and even wrote some notes in her file, in front of Billy, to underline the importance of his report.

"Well, Billy," said Maisie, closing the file and placing it back on the desk, "I hope you don't mind me changing the subject, but there is one thing. No rush, in your own time."

"You name it, Miss."

"Billy, I really need to have this room painted or wallpapered. It's as drab as yesterday's black pudding and needs a bit of cheering up. I noticed that on the ground floor you did such a nice job with Miss Finch's room—the door was open as I came through one day and I looked in—it was so bright and cheerful. What do you think?"

"I'll jump right to it, Miss. I'll put my mind to the colors on the way 'ome, and tomorrow I'll go by me mate's place—painter and decorator, 'e is—and see what 'e's got in the way of paints."

"That'll be lovely, Billy. And, Billy—thank you very much."

And so another storyteller fell asleep that night thinking not of the telling of the story but of the possibilities inherent in color and texture. But for Maisie, there was a different end to the day. She made notes in her file, simply named "Vincent," and started to sketch a diagram, with names and places linked.

Maisie Dobbs was even more convinced that her instinct had not betrayed her, that Vincent's death was simply one thread in an intricate web that led to no good. She knew that it would not be long before she discovered what connected the bright thread that was Vincent to the other boys who were buried with only one name at Nether Green Cemetery. And it was her intention that the next meeting with Celia Davenham would reveal how Vincent had spent the time since the war, and his exact location at his death.

More important, Maisie wanted an explanation as to why he was simply "Vincent."

CHAPTER SEVEN

$\mathcal{M}$aisie sat back in the wooden office chair and brought her knees up to her chest so that her heels rested on the edge of the seat. She had slipped off her shoes an hour or so ago, to put on the thick bed socks that she kept in her desk drawer. Maisie leafed through her report to Christopher Davenham and wondered how she might best advise him. It was at times like this that she missed the counsel of Maurice Blanche. The relationship between teacher and pupil was an easy one. She had opened her mind to learning his craft, and he had passed on to her the knowledge gleaned in a lifetime of work in what he referred to as "the forensic science of the whole person." Although he could still be consulted, Maisie knew that now that he had retired, it was his intention for her to make her way in the world alone.

She could hear his voice now: "Remember basics, Maisie, dear. Whenever you are stuck, go back to our earliest conversations. And remember connections, that there are always connections."

Now Maisie had to decide how far she should go in her report to Christopher Davenham. The man simply wanted to know where his wife was going and if another man was involved. Any information over and above what he had requested would not be necessary. Maisie thought for one more moment, put her feet back on the floor, placed the file on the table in front of her, and stood up.

"No, that's enough." She said to the empty room.

"*Do* sit down, Mr. Davenham." Maisie's chilled feet were now smartly clad in leather shoes.

"You have a report for me, Miss Dobbs?"

"Yes, of course. But first, Mr. Davenham, I must ask you some questions."

"Haven't you already asked enough? I would have thought my purpose for coming here was clear. I seek information, Miss Dobbs, and if you are half as good as your reputation, you will have that information."

"Yes, I do. But I would like us to discuss openly how you might use this information once you have it."

"I'm not sure I understand, Miss Dobbs."

Maisie opened the file, took out a blank sheet of paper that had previously covered her extensive notes, closed the file, and placed the paper on top. It was a technique learned from Maurice, which had proved to be most useful: The blank sheet of paper represented the future, an empty page that could be filled as the observer chose. Pages of notes brought out during conversation were a distraction, so a written report was given only at the end of meeting. "Mr. Davenham, if there were no other man, no reason for you to suspect that your wife's affections lay elsewhere, what would you do?"

"Well, nothing. If there's no reason for my suspicions, then she's in the clear. There would be no problem to do anything about."

"I see. Mr. Davenham, this is a delicate situation. Before I proceed, I must ask for you to make a commitment to me—"

"Whatever do you mean?"

"A commitment to your marriage, actually. A commitment, perhaps, to your wife's well-being and to your future."

Christopher Davenham stirred uneasily in his chair and folded his arms.

"Mr. Davenham," said Maisie, looking out of the window, "it's a very fine day now, don't you think? Let's walk around Fitzroy Square. We will be at liberty to speak freely and also enjoy something of the day."

Without waiting for an answer, Maisie rose from her chair, took her coat from the stand, and passed it to Christopher Davenham who, being a gentleman, stifled his annoyance, took the coat, and held it out for Maisie. Placing her hat upon her head and securing it with a pearl hatpin, Maisie smiled up at him. "A walk will be lovely."

She strolled with Davenham along Warren Street, then turned left at Conway Street into Fitzroy Square. The sun had broken through the morning's gray clouds, and there was a promise of warmer weather to come. The walk was by no means an idle suggestion. Maisie had learned from Maurice Blanche the importance of keeping the client open to whatever was being reported or suggested. "Sitting in a chair gives too much opportunity to retreat into the self," Blanche had said. "Keep the person moving, in the way that an artist keeps the oil moving when he is painting. Don't give them a chance to dry up; don't allow the client to shut you out."

"Mr. Davenham, I have decided to give you my report and my recommendations. I say 'recommendations' because I believe you are a man of compassion."

Davenham maintained an even pace. Good, thought Maisie. She matched his stride, keenly observing the position of his arms, the way he held his head forward and tilted back slightly, as if sniffing the air for a predator. He's terrified, thought Maisie, feeling fear rise up as she began to imitate his manner of walking and carriage. She closed her eyes for just a few seconds to be clear about the feelings now seeping through her body, and thought: He's afraid to give, for fear of losing.

She had to be quick to banish the fear.

"Mr. Davenham, you are not being deceived. Your wife is faithful."
The tall man breathed an audible sigh of relief.

"But she does need your help."

"In what way, Miss Dobbs?" The tension that ebbed with her revelation had no chance to reclaim him before Maisie spoke again.

"Like many young women, your wife lost someone she loved. In the war. The man was her first love, a puppy love. Had he lived, no doubt such an affection would have died with the onset of maturity. However—"

"Who?"

"A friend of her brother. His name was Vincent. It's in my report. Mr. Davenham, may we slow down just a little, you see, my feet . . . ."

"Of course, yes, I'm sorry."

Christopher Davenham settled into a more relaxed gait, to match Maisie, who had reduced her stride to allow him to consider her words.

"Mr. Davenham, have you ever spoken with your wife about the war, about her brother, about her losses?"

"No, never. I mean, I know the facts. But one just has to get on with it. After all, you can't just give in, can you?"

"And what about you, Mr. Davenham?"

"I didn't serve. I have a printing company, Miss Dobbs. I was required by the government to keep the people informed."

"Did you want to serve?'

"Does that matter?"

"Perhaps it does, to your wife. Perhaps it matters to your wife to be able to discuss her past with you, for you to know—"

"Your report will give me the facts, Miss Dobbs."

"Mr. Davenham, you may know the facts, but it isn't a catalog of facts that is causing your wife's melancholy. It is the storage of memories and of feelings. Do you understand?"

The man was silent, as was Maisie. She knew she was out of bounds. But this was not new for her. She had spent much of her life out of bounds, living and speaking where, according to some, she had no business.

"Allow the past to have a voice," Maisie continued. "Then it will be stilled. It's only then that your marriage will have a future, Mr. Davenham. And Mr. Davenham . . ."

"Yes."

"Just in case you were considering such a move, your wife does not need medication, and she does not need a doctor. Your wife needs *you*. When she has you, Vincent will be allowed to rest in peace."

The man took a few more steps in silence, then nodded.

"Shall we go back to the office?" Maisie asked, her head to one side.

Davenham nodded again. Maisie allowed him his thoughts, allowed him the room that he needed in which to take her words to heart. If she persisted, he might become defensive. And this was a door that needed to remain open. For there was something about the experience with Celia Davenham that nagged at Maisie. She didn't yet know what it was, but she was confident that it would speak to her. Maurice Blanche maintained that amid the tales, the smokescreens, and the deceptive mirrors of life's unsolved mysteries, truth resides, waiting for someone to enter its sanctum, then leave, without quite closing the door behind them. That is when truth may make its escape. And Maisie had ensured that the door was left open when she last saw Celia.

It was Maisie's intention that Thursday's meeting would reveal what she needed to know about Vincent's passing, about the mystery of the single name on his headstone, and what had occupied his time between the end of the war and his death. She wanted her next meeting with Celia to reveal Vincent's whereabouts just prior to, and at the time of, his death.

Maisie felt that she understood much about the relationship between Celia and Vincent. Their love had been more of a youthful infatuation—Celia had admitted as much herself—and in going forward with marriage to Christopher Davenham, she had tried to bury her feelings for Vincent at a time when emotions were running high throughout the country. But the ordinary rituals of marriage to the seemingly bland Christopher Davenham could not erase the memory of Vincent, the hero of her imagination, the handsome, fearless knight she might have married. Maisie believed that, to Vincent, Celia had remained simply the younger sister of a dear friend. Yet it was among the friends of one's brothers that so many young women found suitable partners.

Maisie met Celia Davenham at the Ritz for afternoon tea on Thursday, as arranged. As she made her way from the main doors of the Piccadilly entrance to join Celia, Maisie caught her breath when she saw the heavy marble columns at either side of the Winter Garden ahead. She walked toward the steps leading up into the venue for tea, and felt soothed by the warm shafts of light that entered through the windows at either end of the room. For a minute she allowed herself not to consider the expense of the expedition. The opulent grandeur of the Winter Garden, designed to resemble a French pavilion, with decorated cornices and a skylight that allowed soft natural light to bathe the room, almost took Maisie's breath away. With perfect white damask tablecloths, shining silver cutlery, and voluminous swags of fabric hung around the windows, the Winter Garden might not have encouraged intimate conversation between the two women, but the surrounding mirrored panels, and calming presence of water in the golden mermaid sculpture, brought a certan serenity to the room. Instead, with the delicate sound of Royal Doulton china clinking in the background, as cups were replaced on saucers, talk between the two women was light, skimming over the surface of confidence like a fly buzzing over a tranquil millpond.

Maisie touched each side of her lips with her table napkin, and placed it at the side of her plate. "I think it's time for that walk, Mrs. Davenham. Such a lovely day, one feels as if summer is almost here." She reached for her handbag and gloves.

"Oh yes, indeed. Let's walk . . . and please, do call me 'Celia.' I feel as if we know each other so very well now." Celia Cavendish inclined her head in invitation.

"Thank you, Celia. It does seem as if the time for such formality has passed, so I expect you, in turn, to use my Christian name."

With the bill settled, waiters hurried to pull back chairs for the women, their deep bows signaling the exit of a well-satisfied customer, and that the table must be cleared and prepared for the next duo of well-heeled ladies. Maisie and Celia left the Ritz and entered Green Park.

"It's so lovely here—the daffodils are pretty, but they're late this year, aren't they?"

"Indeed they are."

"Maisie, the fabrics at Liberty were simply gorgeous, almost overwhelming, as always. I have to confess, I bought three yards of the most exquisite sheer lilac silk."

"Good for you. How very clever of you to be able to sew."

"I learned from one of our maids who was an absolute whiz with the needle. Mummy insisted upon such drab colors and styles—it was the only way for me to avoid looking like a dowdy schoolmistress. Of course, during the war it wasn't as easy to get fabric, but remember there *was* the passion for all things Indian, wasn't there?"

Maisie nodded, remembering the demand for goods from the Indian subcontinent after the Gurkha regiments joined British forces in France. She remembered Khan, laughing as he told her about the invitations he was suddenly receiving from the very best houses, simply to have the presence of one who seemed, in the eyes of hostesses of the day who were not always clear about the geography of the Indian subcontinent, to be an ambassador for the legion of small, hearty, fearless Nepalese men fighting alongside the regular British soldiers.

There was a comfortable silence as Maisie and Celia made their way along Queen's Walk toward St. James's Park. Strolling alongside St. James's Park lake, they commented that it would have been a good idea to save some pieces of bread to feed the swans, and laughed together at an anxious nanny running in pursuit of a pair of mischievous children toddling on chubby legs toward a pair of mallards. Yet as she brought her step into line with that of her companion, and held her shoulders, arms, and hands as if she were her shadow, Maisie felt once again the melancholy that gripped Celia. But Maisie also knew that Celia would soon confide in her as she had when they last met, for her feelings for Vincent had been dammed inside her, and having been once unleashed, demanded to be heard.

"It was 1917 when Vincent came back to England. He was admitted immediately to hospital, for his wounds were so, so . . . ."

Celia put her hand to her face again, searching for a word to describe Vincent's wounds that would reflect her newfound bravery in telling the tale.

"Utterly devastating, Maisie. I could hardly recognize him when I visited. I had to beg my brother to take me with him—George had arrived home some time before Vincent, as his injuries were not as severe. Vincent wore a linen mask and only removed it when I assured him that I would not flinch."

"Go on," encouraged Maisie.

"But I couldn't contain myself. I burst into tears and rushed from the room. My brother was furious. Yet Vincent wasn't angry with me. But he was angry at everything else."

"Many men were angry when they returned, Celia. Vincent had a right to his anger."

Celia stopped in her walk, shielded her eyes from the sun, which was now late-afternoon low in the sky, then looked again at Maisie.

"That was when he said that he wanted to be just 'Vincent.' He said that as far as Britain was concerned, he was just a piece of meat anyway, he might as well buck the whole system. He said he'd lost his face, so he could be whomever he wanted to be. Except he wasn't quite as polite as that."

"Indeed. Do you know what happened in France? To Vincent?"

"I know, mainly from my brother, that something happened—more than being wounded. I believe there was some . . . discord. With his commanding officers."

"What happened when Vincent was discharged from hospital?"

"Convalescence. By the sea, in Whitstable. The army took over one of the large hotels. Vincent wanted to write about his experiences in France. He was very upset. But each time we sent him a quantity of paper, it was taken away from him. The doctors said that writing distressed him. My brother was furious. He gave Vincent a typewriter, which was confiscated and returned. Vincent maintained he was being silenced, but said he was determined to speak before the war was long gone and no one wanted to know anymore."

"The poor man."

"Then I met Christopher. A very solid man. Of course, he hadn't gone to France. I have to admit I never really found out why. I believe his business protected him from conscription. I seemed to go forward into marriage with a numbness in my mind. But I'd lost one brother, and of course Vincent was deeply, deeply injured. Christopher was a port in the storm. And he is, of course, so very good to me."

"What happened to your friend Vincent after the war, Celia? It seemed that he died some time later."

"Yes, he died only a few years ago. He returned to his parents' home, but as he was terribly disfigured, he became a recluse. Oh, people tried to get him out of the house socially, but he would sit in the drawing room, looking out the window, or reading, or writing in his diary. He worked from home after a while—for a small publishing house, somewhere not far from here, I think."

Celia rubbed her forehead as if pressure would squeeze memories into the present moment.

"He read manuscripts, wrote reports. He had obtained the connection through his uncle's business contacts. Very occasionally he would have someone drive him to the office, to discuss something. He'd had a mask made, of sorts, out of that very fine tin. It was painted in a glaze that matched the color of his skin. And he wore a scarf which he bundled around his neck and lower jaw—well, where his lower jaw used to be. Oh, poor, poor Vincent!"

Celia began to cry. Maisie stopped walking and simply stood next to her, but made no move to console by placing a hand on Celia's shoulder or a comforting arm around her.

"Allow grief room to air itself," Maurice had taught her. "Be judicious in using the body to comfort another, for you may extinguish the freedom that the person feels to be able to share a sadness."

She had learned, with Maurice Blanche as a teacher, respect for the telling of a person's history.

Maisie allowed some time to pass, then took Celia's elbow and gently led her to a park bench, set among a golden display of daffodils nodding sunny heads in the late-afternoon breeze.

"Thank you. Thank you for listening."

"I understand, Celia," replied Maisie.

As Maisie imagined Vincent's brutal disfigurement, she shuddered, recollecting the time she had spent in France, and the images that would remain with her forever, of men who had fought so bravely. She thought, too, of those men who had cheated death, only to struggle with the legacy of their injuries. And, in that moment, she remembered Simon, the gifted doctor who was himself a soldier in the struggle to tear lives free from the bloody clutches of war.

Maisie was brought back from the depths of her own memories by Celia, who was ready to continue her story.

"It was a bit of luck, really, that one of the patients he had been in hospital with remembered him. I wish I could recall his name. He had returned to France for a time after the war and saw that men with facial disfigurement were looked after in a different way. They were brought together for holidays, taken to the country to camps where they could live together for a while without having to worry about people drawing away—after all, they all had wounds. And, I suppose, more importantly, the public didn't have to look at them. Terrible, isn't it? Anyway, this man came back to England and wanted to get the same sort of thing going here."

Celia Davenham looked around her and briefly closed her eyes in the warmth of the waning spring sunshine.

"He bought a farm that was on the market, then got in touch with the men he had met while recovering from his own wounds. According to Vincent, he—heavens, what was his name? Anyway, this man had been deeply affected by the war in a way that made him want to do something for those with disfiguring wounds. Vincent was a strong supporter of the idea. It gave him an energy I certainly hadn't seen since before the war. In fact, the man was rather taken with Vincent's stubborn refusal to be known by anything but his first name. So Vincent went to live at The Retreat."

"Was that what it was called? The Retreat?"

"Yes. I think it was Vincent's idea. The name. There was a connection to 'Beating The Retreat,' I think, in that they were withdrawing from society, which for many of them had become the enemy. Vincent said that it commemorated each man who died in France, and every man brought home to live with injuries. He said that it was for all those who suffered and should have had a place to go back to, when there never was one."

"Did he remain there, at The Retreat?"

"Yes, he did. He became very reclusive. My brother would visit occasionally. Of course, by then I was married to Christopher, so I did not visit. I wanted to, though. In fact, I have considered making the journey, since Vincent died. Just to see where—"

"He died at The Retreat?"

"Yes. I'm not really sure what happened. My brother was told by Vincent's people that he slipped and fell by the stream. Breathing was difficult for him anyway, due to his injuries, but perhaps he hit his head. His parents have passed on now. I think they didn't really ask questions. Everyone agreed that it was a terrible accident, but it might have been a release for him."

"Did The Retreat close?"

"Oh no. It's still very much open. The farmhouse has been converted so that the residents each have a room, and specialist craftsmen were employed to work on the outbuildings, so that they could also be used for accommodation. I understand that new residents are welcomed. They are all men who have suffered injury of some kind during the war, and need a place to go."

"How does this man who set up The Retreat pay for everyone?"

"Oh, *they* pay. Resources are pooled. Christopher thought it was all very odd in that respect. But, you understand, Christopher would think that. He's very careful with money. Vincent gave Adam—that's it, Adam Jenkins, his name is Adam Jenkins—Vincent gave Adam Jenkins control of his finances when he decided to become a resident rather than a short-term visitor. The residents work on the farm as well, so it's still a going concern."

"Well, well, well. Vincent must have had tremendous respect for this man, Adam Jenkins."

The two women had started walking back towards the north entrance of St. James's Park. Celia looked at her watch.

"Oh my goodness! I must hurry. Christopher is taking me to the theater this evening. It's quite amazing, you know. He's always been such a stick-in-the-mud, but now he's planning all sorts of outings. I love the theater. I thought I would never go again when I married Christopher, but he's suddenly become quite agreeable to an evening out."

"How lovely! I must dash too, Celia. But before you go, could you tell me where The Retreat is? I have a friend who may be interested to know about it."

"It's in Kent. Near Sevenoaks, that area. In fact, it's not too far from Nether Green. Good-bye, Maisie—and here's my card. Do call me again for tea. It was so lovely. I feel so very light after spending time with you, you know. Perhaps it's being out here in the fresh air of the park today."

"Yes, perhaps it is. Have a lovely time at the theater, Celia."

The two women parted, but before making her way to the St. James's Park underground station, Maisie walked back into the park to reconsider their conversation. She would probably not see Celia again.

Vincent had died while living in a community of ex-soldiers, all of whom, initially, were facially disfigured in some way, although it seemed that the doors were now open to those who had other injuries. There was nothing untoward about the motives of Adam Jenkins, who seemed to want to help these men. It must cost a pretty penny to arrange care for the residents, but then again, resources were pooled, and they were self-sufficient and working on the farm. A farm called, ambiguously, The Retreat. Maisie considered the meanings of "retreat," and wondered if the soldiers were, in fact, relinquishing their position, seeking a place of shelter from the enemy. For such men perhaps life itself was now the enemy.

Maisie picked up the heavy black telephone and began to dial BEL 4746, the Belgravia home of Lord Julian Compton and his wife, Lady Rowan. There was a short delay, then Maisie heard the telephone ring three times before being answered by Carter, the Compton's long-serving butler. She checked her watch immediately the call was answered.

"Compton residence."

"Hello, Mr. Carter. How are you?"

"Maisie, what a pleasure. We are all well here, thank you, but not looking forward to Cook's retirement, though it's long overdue."

"And what about you, Mr. Carter?"

"Now then, Maisie, as long as I can manage these stairs, I will be at the house. Her ladyship has been very anxious to speak with you, Maisie."

"Yes, I know. That's why I've telephoned."

"Oh, well. . . . I should know better than to ask how you know, Maisie."

"Mr. Carter, that really doesn't take a lot, does it? Lady Rowan is a terrier in disguise."

Carter laughed and connected the call to Lady Rowan, who was in the library reading the late-edition newspapers.

"Maisie, dear girl. Where have you been? I thought you'd gone off somewhere."

"No, Lady Rowan. I've been busy."

"Excellent news. But you really must not be a stranger to us. Are you sure that you wouldn't like to move into the upstairs apartments? I know I keep asking, but this is such a big house now. It never used to seem this big. Perhaps I'm getting smaller. They say that about age."

"No, Lady Rowan. Not you. Shall I come to see you this week?"

"Yes. Definitely. Come tomorrow. And I insist that you have dinner with me, and that you stay. I simply cannot have you traveling on your own after dark, and I know that you will refuse any offer to drive you home."

"Yes, Lady Rowan. I'll stay—but just for one night. Is everything all right?"

There was a silence on the line.

"Lady Rowan, is everything all right?"

"I want to talk to you about James. I thought you might have some advice for a poor misunderstood mother."

"Lady Rowan—"

"Yes, I'm laying it on a bit thick. But I'm worried about him. He's talking about going off to live on a farm in Kent. Sounds very strange to me. In fact, it sounds more than strange. Maisie, I confess, I'm frightened for James. He has been in the depths of melancholy since the war, it seems, and now this!"

"Of course. I'll do anything I can to help," replied Maisie.

"Thank you so much, my dear. What time will you be here?"

"Will six o'clock be all right?"

"Perfect. I'll tell Carter. Mrs. Crawford will be delighted to see you."

"Until then, Lady Rowan."

"Take care, Maisie. And remember, I want to know everything about what you are doing."

"I will leave no story untold, Lady Rowan."

The two women laughed, bade each other good-bye, and replaced their respective telephone receivers. Without a second's delay Maisie checked her watch. She reached into the top drawer of her desk and took out a small ledger with "Telephone" marked on the cover. Inside she made a note that the call to Lady Rowan Compton had taken four minutes. Maisie replaced the ledger and closed the drawer before walking to the window.

Of course she would offer Lady Rowan any assistance in her power, for she was indebted to her for so much. And Maisie knew, too, how difficult the aftermath of the war had been for James—but not, perhaps, as hard as it had been for the likes of Vincent. Yet Maisie was sympathetic to his melancholy, which was as much due to a loss still mourned as to his injuries. Maisie wondered whether Lord Julian had concerns regarding the ability of his only son to take on the family's business interests, and she was aware that Lady Rowan had often been the peacekeeper between the two. Tall, blond, blue-eyed James had always been the apple of his mother's eye. Years ago, when his son was no longer a child, Lord Julian had been heard to say on many an occasion, "You're spoiling that boy, Rowan." And now the once mischievously energetic James seemed hollow and drawn. Lady Rowan had been secretly relieved when James, a flying ace, was injured—not in the air but during an explosion on the ground. She knew his wounds would heal, and that she would have him safe at home at a time when so many of her contemporaries were receiving word that their sons had been lost to war.

Maisie turned from the window, and walked toward the door. Taking her coat and hat from the stand, she looked around the room, extinguished the light, and left her office. As she locked the door behind her, she reflected upon how strange it was that a man who had significant financial resources, time, and a beautiful house in the country would seek the peace and quiet that might dispel his dark mood by going to live on a stranger's farm. Making her way downstairs in the half-light shed by the flickering gas lamp, Maisie felt a chill move through her body. And she knew that the sensation was not caused by the cold or the damp, but by a threat—a threat to the family of the woman she held most dear, the woman who had helped her achieve accomplishments that might otherwise have remained an unrealized dream.

SPRING 1910–SPRING 1917

CHAPTER EIGHT

orn in 1863, and growing up in the middle years of Queen Victoria's reign, Lady Rowan had delighted her father, the fourth Earl of Westavon, but had been the source of much frustration for her mother, Lady Westavon, who was known to comment that her daughter was "a lady in name only!" It was clear that, far from being content with pursuits more becoming her position and upbringing, she was happiest with her horses and with her brother, Edwin, when he came home from school in the holidays. From an early age she had questioned her father, disagreed with her mother, and by the time she was on the cusp of womanhood, caused her parents to wonder if a suitable match would ever be found.

Maurice Blanche was ten years Lady Rowan's senior, a school friend of her brother. At first Rowan was fascinated by Maurice during those weekends when Edwin brought Maurice home from Marlborough School.

"His people are in France, so I thought he might like to get out for a bit of a break," said Edwin, introducing the short, stocky boy who seemed to have little to say.

But when Maurice spoke, the young Rowan hung on his every word. His accent, a hybrid that came as a result of his French father and Scottish mother, intrigued her. As she grew older, Lady Rowan realized that Maurice moved with ease among people of any background, often changing his accent slightly to echo the nuances and rhythm of the other person's speech. The listener only vaguely appreciated the distinction, but nevertheless leaned in closer, smiled more easily, and probably shared a confidence to which no other person had been privy. Gradually his influence on the life of Lady Rowan challenged and inspired her, and in turn, his trust in her honest opinion was unfailing.

In the course of his life's work, Maurice Blanche could count among his friends and colleagues: philosophers, scientists, doctors, psychologists, and members of the judiciary. It was a self-designed career that had rendered him invaluable to an extraordinary range of people, whether government ministers, those investigating crime, or simply people who needed information.

In 1898, the year in which Lady Rowan celebrated the tenth anniversary of her marriage to Lord Julian Compton, it was clear to Maurice that Rowan needed to be engaged in more than simply London's social calendar. Her only son, James, had just been sent away to a preparatory school, an inevitable event Lady Rowan had dreaded. During a heated political discussion Maurice dared the very vocal and opinionated Lady Rowan to follow her own challenging words with actions.

"It's not enough to say that you want equality, Ro. What do you intend to do about it?

Lady Rowan swallowed hard. Soon after, she became a fully fledged and active suffragette.

Eleven years later Lady Rowan Compton shocked Belgravia by marching on Westminster, demanding the vote and equality for women, rich and poor. Lord Julian was long suffering, but the truth of the matter was that he adored Rowan and would walk on hot coals rather than cross her. Questioned about his wife's involvement,

Lord Julian would simply reply, "Oh, you know Ro, once she's got the bit between her teeth . . . ." and people would nod sympathetically and leave the subject alone, which was exactly what Lord Julian wanted them to do. However, it was Maurice Blanche who challenged Rowan once again on the depth of her commitment.

"So you march on Westminster, and you have these meetings with your sister suffragettes, but what are you actually doing?"

"Maurice, what do you mean, what am I *doing?* This house is full of women meeting together three times a week—and we're forging ahead, make no mistake!"

Lady Rowan had barely taken a sip from her glass of sherry when Maurice issued an instruction. "We're off. Got something to show you. Go and change. Plain walking skirt and a jacket will do. And good sturdy shoes, Rowan."

Blanche stood up and walked toward the window, a move that suggested she should be quick.

"Maurice, you had better have good reason—"

"Hurry up, Rowan, or I shall leave without you."

Lady Rowan went immediately to her room, and when Nora, her personal maid, came to ask if she was needed, she was turned away.

"No. That's quite all right, Nora. I can help myself, you know."

Lady Rowan dressed quickly, with only a cursory glance in the mirror. She cut a handsome figure, and she knew it. Not that she was quintessentially pretty, but with her height and aquiline profile, she was striking. She was an athletic woman, a keen and competitive tennis player, an accomplished equestrienne, and a notoriously reckless skier on the slopes of Wengen until she was well into her forties. Her once rich chestnut hair had dulled slightly and was peppered with gray, but mercifully her weight had changed little since the day of her marriage. On the day Maurice Blanche demanded she accompany him, Lady Rowan Compton was forty-seven.

Rowan was excited. Maurice was prodding her at a time when life had lost some of the edge it had had in her youth. Yes, she was involved in the suffragette movement, she had her horses at the country estate, and of course there was the London social calendar, engagements and reciprocal entertainment making up an important part of her life in town during the season. James had just finished his schooling. She had looked forward to his company at home when his school years were over, but she rarely had it, for no sooner had he returned from the city than he seemed to vanish again. James was a man now, if still a very young one.

As she dressed, Lady Rowan tingled with anticipation, Maurice might provide her with a diversion to fill a gap that seemed to be widening with the passing years. She returned to the drawing room, and they left the house quickly. The two old friends walked along the tree-lined street, conversation unnecessary, although Lady Rowan was aching to know where they were going.

"I'm not saying that you are not busy, Rowan," Maurice broke their silence. "Not at all. And the cause is a worthy one. For women to have a place of account in this society, they must have a political voice. And having had one queen on the throne in the modern age does not constitute such a voice. But Rowan, with you the voice always comes from a safe place, does it not?"

"You should have been on the march, Maurice. That wasn't safe at all."

"I'm sure. But we both know that I'm not talking about marches. I'm talking about the safe place that we remain in, within the world we were born to. Swimming forever in the confines of our own pond. Socially, intellectually—"

"Maurice—"

"Rowan, we will speak again of equality later, for it is equality that you claim to want. Now then, we must wait here for an omnibus."

"A *what?* Now, I told you, Maurice—we should have called for the motor."

"No, Rowan. We are stepping out of your pond today. I have the fare for us both."

It was dark when they returned to Belgravia in silence. Rowan was deep in thought. She had seen much that troubled her. But nothing troubled her more than her own emotions.

"You'll come in . . ."

"No, Rowan. You are tired from swimming in another pond today. A pond that, though discussed in your meetings and debates, you could not truly imagine. Poverty is something we think we understand from description. It is only when it is close to hand that we have a grasp of what it means to be unequal."

"But what can I do?"

"No need to wear a hair shirt, Rowan. But perhaps opportunities will present themselves. One only has to ask, 'How might I serve?' Goodnight, my dear."

Maurice bowed slightly, then left Rowan in the entrance hall of her grand home.

He had taken her to the East End of London. First to the noisy markets, which thrilled her, although she could not look directly at some of the street urchins. Then into the depths of London's poorest areas. And it seemed that always someone knew him.

"Evenin', Doc, awright then?"

"Well, very well. And how is the youngest?"

"Comin' on a treat, Doc. Thanks to you."

Rowan didn't ask about his relationship to the people who greeted him so readily. Maurice was certainly a doctor, but after attending King's College Medical School in London, he had studied at the University of Edinburgh's Department of Legal Medicine. Rowan was under the impression that he no longer practiced. At least not upon people who were still alive.

"To answer the question that is written all over your face, Rowan—once or twice a week, I attend women and children at a small clinic. There is precious little set aside for the poor, there is a constant need for help, for . . . everything. And, of course, bringing children safely into the world and providing care when they are sick is a refreshing change for me."

Rowan rung the bell in the drawing room. She had dismissed Carter, the butler, as soon as she arrived home, but now she craved inner warmth.

How may I serve? What can I do? What would be sensible? What would Julian say? Well, that was something she would not have to think about. If Maurice was her challenger, Julian was her rock.

"Yes, Your Ladyship?"

"Carter, I'd like some hot soup, please—something simple, nothing too clever, you understand. And a sherry please, Carter."

"Very good, Ma'am. Cook prepared a tasty vegetable soup this afternoon, as soon as the delivery arrived."

"Perfect. Perfect, Carter."

Carter poured sherry into a crystal glass and held it out on a silver salver.

"Oh—and Carter. Before I forget. I would like to speak to you about the dinner next week and our guests. Lord Julian's business associates. Tomorrow morning after breakfast, tell Cook to come to my study as well. Ten o'clock."

"Very good, Your Ladyship. Will that be all?"

Later, as Lady Rowan finished the hot soup that had been brought on a tray to the drawing room, she leaned back in her chair and contemplated what she had seen that day, and about the conversation with Maurice. It is so easy, she thought. All I have to do is snap my fingers and someone runs. Equality. Maurice is right, I can do more.

While Lady Rowan readied herself for bed in her grand house in Belgravia on that night in the spring of 1910, a thirteen-year-old girl cried herself to sleep in the small back room of a soot-blackened terraced house in southeast London. Her jet black hair, released from a neat braid and purple ribbon, cascaded over the pillow, and the deep blue eyes that so easily reflected joy were rimmed with dark circles and red with tears. She cried for her loss and cried, too, for her father, whose dreadful, deep breathless sobs echoed from kitchen below.

Maisie had held her tears back for days, believing that if her father did not see or hear her crying, he would not worry about her, and his burden would be lighter. And each day, his heart breaking, he rose in the early hours of the morning, harnessed his horse to the cart, and made his way to Covent Garden Market.

At first, after her mother died, Maisie would pinch herself three times on the right arm before sleeping, assured that this one action would make her rise at three o'clock in the morning, in time to make his tea and spread a thick slice of bread with beef dripping for him eat in front of the coal stove before he set off for the market.

"You don't 'ave to do that, love. I can watch out for meself, Maisie. You go on back to bed. And mind you lock that door after I leave."

"I'm all right, Dad. You'll see. We'll be all right."

But Frankie Dobbs was at a loss. A widower with a thirteen-year-old daughter. She needed more, and Lord knows that the girl and her mother had been close, thought Frankie. No, he had to find something better for the girl than for her to be little woman of the house.

Oh, there was so much that they had wanted for Maisie, the child that had come to them in later life, and who was, they said, the answer to many prayers. She was a bright one, they knew that almost from the beginning. In fact, people would remark on it, that even as a newborn it seemed that Maisie could focus on a person and follow them with her eyes. "That girl can look right through you," people would say, when she was still a babe in arms.

The Dobbses had been putting money away for Maisie's education, so that she could stay on at school, perhaps even go on to be a teacher. They were so proud of their girl. But the money was gone, long gone to pay for doctors, medicine, and a holiday at the seaside, just in case the fresh salty air worked a miracle. But nothing had worked. Frankie was alone with his girl now, and he was afraid. Afraid that he couldn't do well by her, that he had nothing left to give her. No, it was settled. He had to find a place for Maisie.

It seemed to Frankie that even Persephone, his old mare, had lost pride in her step. Frankie always made sure his horse and cart were well turned out; it made a difference to business. He might be a costermonger, but there was no excuse for looking shabby. With trousers pressed under the mattress each night, a clean white collarless shirt, fresh brightly colored neckerchief, his best woolen waistcoat, and a cloth cap set jauntily on the side of his head, Frankie himself was always well turned out. "Just because I use me 'ands to make a livin' doesn't mean to say I can't do with a bit of spit and polish," Frankie had been heard to say.

And as he climbed up onto the driver's seat of his cart, Frankie was more than proud of his shining horse and the gleaming leather and brass traces. Persephone, a Welsh cob, trotted proudly down the street, lifting her hooves high as if she knew how good she looked. But since the death of Maisie's mother, Frankie's inner malaise was felt keenly by Persephone, who now trotted in a desultory manner, as if the family's grief had added several hundredweight to her load.

In the kitchen of the house in Belgravia, Carter and Lady Rowan's cook, Mrs. Crawford, were deep in conversation about the morning's meeting to discuss the week's dinner plans.

"What time will Mr. Dobbs be here, Cook? You'll need to have a complete list of fresh vegetables for Lady Rowan, and your menu planned for the week."

Cook rolled her eyes. Just what she loved, being told how to do her job.

"Mr. Carter, menu suggestions are in hand. I asked Mr. Dobbs to stop by again today to give me a list of what is best at market this week. He is going out of the way to be at our service, poor man."

"Yes indeed, Cook. Mr. Dobbs certainly has his hands full. I quite agree."

Outside the rear entrance of the house, a horse and cart came to a halt. They could hear Frankie Dobbs talking to Persephone, putting on her nosebag of oats, telling her he wouldn't be long, then setting off down the stairs that led to the back door of the kitchen.

"That'll be him now." Cook wiped her hands on a cloth, and went to answer the door.

"Mr. Dobbs," she said, standing aside so that Frankie Dobbs could enter the large warm room. As he removed his cloth cap, Mrs. Crawford cast a glance at Carter, frowned, and shook her head. Frankie Dobbs looked pale and drawn.

"Good morning, Mr. Dobbs. How are you?"

"Very well, all things considered, Mr. Carter. And you?" It was a thin response, and both cook and Carter glanced at each other again. This was not the jovial, robust Frankie Dobbs they were used to doing business with. "I've brought a list of the best vegetables and fruit this week. If I take the order today, I can deliver tomorrow morning. The broccoli and sprouts are looking very nice indeed, and of course there's some hearty cabbage at the market. I know Her Ladyship is partial to a nice bit of cabbage."

"She certainly is, Mr. Dobbs." Cook took the rough piece of paper from Frankie, and ran a finger down the list of vegetables. "I think we'll need something of everything this week. Full house, you know."

"Right you are." Standing uneasily in the kitchen, Frankie fingered his cap. "I was wondering, Mr. Carter, if there was something I might discuss. With both yourself and Mrs. Crawford here."

"Of course, Mr. Dobbs, sit down at the table. Cook, a cup of tea for Mr. Dobbs. What can we do for you?"

Carter faced Frankie across the heavy pine table.

"Well, it's about my girl. She's a bright lass, very bright . . ." Frankie faltered, looked at his shining boots and twisted his cap. "Since 'er mother died, well, we was going to send 'er on to the big school . . . and she got a scholarship and all . . . but there's the money for the special clothes and books, and what with the doctor's bills . . ."

Cook placed a cup of tea in front of Frankie, leaned toward him, and covered his hand with hers. "You're a good man, Mr. Dobbs. You'll do right by young Maisie."

Frankie shrank at his daughter's name, afraid of what he was about to ask. "I was wonderin' if you had a place for my Maisie 'ere, like. In service. She's a good girl. 'ard worker. Very bright. You won't need to tell 'er anythin' twice. She's well mannered and speaks nicely—'er mother, God rest her soul, saw to that. I thought that after a while, she could go back to night school, you see. Take up where she left off. Loves learnin', does Maisie."

Carter and Cook glanced at each other once again, and Carter spoke quickly. "Mr. Dobbs, it seems you have come at the right time, and in answer to a prayer, hasn't he, Mrs. Crawford?"

Cook looked at Carter and nodded her head in agreement. She had absolutely no idea what he was talking about.

"One of our more junior maids recently left service. Help is needed. Have your girl come to the house at five o'clock today—she can pick up the order for tomorrow's delivery. I think you have to check quantities, don't you, Mrs. Crawford?"

Cook nodded agreement, and looked at the list of vegetables again. They both knew that Frankie Dobbs never had to be told quantities, and always delivered exactly what was needed. Carter continued, "I'll interview her, just to make sure that she is right for the position."

Frankie breathed a sigh of relief.

"Thank you, Mr. Carter, Mrs. Crawford. I'll be getting on now. Maisie will be here at five sharp."

The grieving man left quickly, and before leading his horse away, put his head against the Persephone's soft nose and wept. "It's for the best," he whispered. "It's for the best."

It was the nearest he had come to having "words" with his daughter. As Frankie broke the news to Maisie—that times were difficult, that he was only thinking of her, that he wanted her to be safe, and that the Compton household was a fine place to work—he watched the tears well up in her eyes, her jaw tighten with the effort of not giving in to the pressure to cry, and her fine, long-fingered hands clench into fists held firmly by her sides.

"But Dad, you know you need me here. I can help. I helped when Mum was ill. I can get another job, I can even do this job and come home at night, Dad."

"Maisie, love, we'll still see each other, you know that. Sunday afternoons we can go to the park, take a turn, have a cup of tea. We can go to see yer Nan and Granddad. But at least you'll have a place, a good job. And later on, we can get you into night school, to catch up. I'm all out, love. There's no money, and there's bills to pay. I don't even know if I can keep renting this house. Your mother going . . . ."

Maisie drew away as he reached out to her, turned her back to him, and looked out the window. They hadn't been well off, not by any means, but there used to be enough for a few extras. Now there was nothing, and there was ground to be made up. Then they would be all right. She sighed deeply in resignation.

"Dad, if I work at Lady Rowan's, and if I send you my money, and we make up the bills, then can I come back?"

"Oh, love. Then what would you do? I was thinking you might go on from there. Maybe get out of the Smoke. She's got a place in the country, you know. Down in Kent. She's got contacts, woman like that. You do yer classes at night, you might get yerself a private teaching job at one of them big 'ouses. You don't want to be back 'ere. Yer mother and me wanted so much for you, love."

Her father was tired beyond reckoning. They were both tired beyond reckoning. Too tired for this talk. But she would go to Lady Rowan's to see this Mr. Carter. And so help me, I'll work my way out of that place, thought Maisie. And on my own. I'll work so hard I'll take care of Dad. He won't have to get up at three in the morning by the time I've finished. Maisie bit her lip and looked up at nothing in particular on the wall. You'll see, I'll show him who can take care of herself. Maisie sighed, then reached out and put her arms around her father's waist.

"Dad, I'll go. You're right. Annie Clark down the road is in service now. So's Doreen Watts. Lot of girls are. It'll be all right. I'll see Mr. Carter. I won't let you down, Dad."

"Oh, love. You could never let me down."

Frankie Dobbs hugged his daughter close for a moment longer, then pushed her back. "Now then, this is where you go."

Maisie Dobbs watched her father as he took a short pencil from his waistcoat pocket, licked the lead, and began to scribble directions on the back of a scrap of paper.

CHAPTER NINE

*D*ays after securing the position of in-between maid, Maisie returned to the white four-story mansion in London's Belgravia, at the southern end of Ebury Place. Before reporting for work, Maisie stood in front of the building and looked up, wondering what it might be like to enter such a house through the front door. Transferring the canvas bag containing her clothes, hairbrushes, and several books from her right hand to her left, Maisie took a handkerchief from her coat pocket and wiped her eyes, hoping that no tell-tale marks were left from the tears shed on the bus from Lambeth. She sighed and, making her way to the left of the house, braced her shoulders and held on to the wrought iron banister to steady herself as she walked down the stone steps that led to the kitchen.

Once welcomed by Carter and Mrs. Crawford, Maisie took her belongings to the top floor of the house. The very top floor, the attic reached by "back stairs" from the kitchen. She shared the room with Enid.

Enid was a worldly sixteen-year-old, with pressed rouge on her cheeks and a hint of color on her lips, who had now reached such a high position of authority that she would be called upon to serve in the breakfast room come tomorrow morning. A thin, gangly girl, Enid was friendly enough to Maisie, who felt that circumstances would never give her cause to laugh again.

"That's your bed over there," was Enid's welcome to the shared bedroom. "Make yourself at home. We're up early in the morning. Half past four, five at the latest, so I hope you don't snore and keep me awake."

She grinned at Maisie, her freckled nose crinkling over the teasing remark. Enid was concentrating on her pronunciation, convinced that if she was to get anywhere in the world, she had to work quickly to introduce aitches into her spoken language. Thus every word beginning with the letter *h* was overpronounced, with a breathy start and a rapid completion. *Huh-ome, huh-ouse, huh-ope.* In fact, Enid's rather zealous pursuit of something better resulted in the occasional *h* where *h* had no place.

"H-ave you bin in s-h-ervice before, or is this your first pos-hishun?" asked Enid.

"No, this is my first. My mother passed on and my father thought it better . . . ."

Enid nodded. She never did know what to say when confronted by loss.

"Well, I reckon you'll do all right. You're tall, not as tall as me, mind, but taller than some of them short girls. They reckon the tall ones always do all right, get promoted quickly to serving, being as we look better in the uniform, more, you know, suited to the h-occasion. And you won't find them upstairs doin' any little tests to see if you're an h-onest sort—like puttin' a farthin' under the carpet to see if you take it or leave it on the side. Anyway, come on, Dobbsie, I'll show you where the facilities are. Come along with me."

Enid put her hand on Maisie's shoulder and led her along a dimly lit hallway to the "fac-hilities."

Carter had chosen to introduce her at breakfast. Maisie knew that in some houses the staff weren't introduced until they had reached a higher position, if at all. The practice changed at the Compton residence when Lord Julian had asked a maid to inform Lady Rowan that he would take tea with her in the drawing room, to which the maid had answered, "Yes, Sir. And who shall I say is calling?" Lady Rowan was appalled, and since that time had insisted upon meeting whoever was under her roof, even if the meeting was a short one.

"Your Lordship, Your Ladyship, may I introduce our new downstairs member of staff, Miss Maisie Dobbs." Carter held his hand out toward Maisie, who took one step forward, curtsied, and stepped back to her place alongside Carter.

Lord and Lady Compton were cordial, welcoming Maisie to the household, saying they were absolutely sure that she would be happy there. After a brief encounter, she left the dining room with Carter, to go down to the kitchens and receive her instructions for the day.

"My word, Julian, what a striking girl."

Lord Compton looked over a folded edge of *The Times* toward his wife. "Striking? Yes. Yes, I suppose so. Very young."

"Yes, very young. Very . . . there was something about her, wasn't there?"

"Mmm? About whom?" Lord Julian continued to read the newspaper.

"About Miss Dobbs. Something quite different about her, don't you think? Julian, are you listening?"

"Hmm? Oh, Rowan. Yes. Miss Dobb, Dobbins . . . what was her name? Dobbs?" Lord Julian looked out of the window to recall the conversation. "You know, Rowan, I think you are right. Could be those eyes. Very deep blue. Don't see that very often."

"Julian. I don't think it was the color of her eyes. It was nothing I could put my finger on."

Lady Rowan spread a thin slice of toast with butter and marmalade as Lord Julian turned to the next page of the morning paper. "Yes, Darling, probably nothing."

Within a few days, most people agreed that Maisie Dobbs had indeed settled in well to life at the Compton residence. Her day started at half past four, when she rose and poured cold water from the pitcher on the washstand into a large china bowl. She splashed her face and moistened a cloth to wash her body before hurriedly dressing, then tiptoeing down to the lowest level of the house to fill the coal scuttles.

Her first job was to take heavy coal scuttles to the breakfast room, the drawing room, His Lordship's study, the morning room, and to the hall. Kneeling by each fireplace, she pulled back the black iron grate cover, swept out yesterday's ashes, and placed them in an old empty scuttle. She rolled sheets of yesterday's newspaper, placed them in the grate, then carefully positioned dry kindling on top and lit the newspaper with a match.

As flames licked up and caught on the wood, Maisie leaned forward and balanced bricks of coal, one by one, on the spitting wood. Sitting back, she watched for just a few seconds as the fire crackled and flared into life. Satisfied that the wood and coal had taken the flames, she brushed splinters, coal dust, and ash under the grate, replaced the cover, and put a few more pieces of coal onto the mound before giving the fireplace a quick dust. She was ready to move on to another room.

When she had finished lighting fires in each of the rooms, it was time to fill the scuttles again and feed the fires so that the rooms were ready to warm those who had time to sit by a fire—people who had the time to be warmed by something other than hard work.

Throughout the day Maisie cleaned, ran errands for Cook, and generally served at the bidding of anyone above her in the pecking order, which was almost everyone in the household. But the duties of her waking hours brought a calm to Maisie's life that she had not known since before her mother became ill. She had only to follow the direction of others, and in the rhythm of her daily round, whether blacking the fireplaces, sweeping the stairs, or polishing furniture, there was room for thought—thought of what might be.

Maisie's "day off" was Sunday afternoon. As soon as the heavy clock on the mantelpiece over the kitchen stove struck a single chime at half past eleven, Maisie waited for Cook to look up at her and nod toward the door.

"All right, lass, off you go. And mind you're back by a decent hour!"

It was a feigned warning, because Maisie had nowhere to be at an indecent hour.

Untying her pinafore as she hurried from the kitchen and up the back stairs toward the servants' quarters, Maisie thought that her legs would never carry her as fast as her mind wanted to travel. She quickly changed into a long black skirt that had belonged to her mother, and a clean cotton blouse. She checked her reflection in the mirror just once, pushed her hat onto her head, and reached for her coat and coin purse before rushing through the bedroom door again. She was off to see her father, knowing that at twelve noon he would pull the fob watch from his waistcoat pocket and smile to himself. Frankie Dobbs couldn't wait for his girl to come home so they could spend a few hours together, a precious respite from a work-weary week.

On Sundays, Frankie was always to be found at the stable where he kept his mare, under the dry arches that were part of the Southern construction of Waterloo Bridge. Sunday was the day to clean the horse from head to hoof, to oil the leather traces, polish the brasses, and make sure the cart was ready for another week's work. It was an easy morning, a morning made sweeter by the knowledge that soon Maisie's footsteps would clatter against the cobblestone street leading to the stables.

"Love, you are a sight for sore eyes. How are you, my girl?"

"Well enough, Dad. I'm well enough."

"Let me just finish this, then we'll go home for a cuppa."

Together they worked in the stable, finally leaving the horse to the remainder of her day at rest. After a cup of tea, Frankie would dress in his Sunday best, and father and daughter would catch a bus to Brockwell Park, where they walked together before stopping to eat a packed lunch.

"You should see the library, Dad! I've never seen so many books. Walls of them. About everything."

"You and your books, girl. You keeping up with your reading?"

"Yes, Dad. I go to the public library every week on a Wednesday afternoon. Mrs. Crawford sends me with a list for her and Mr. Carter, and I get books for myself as well. Mind you, Enid says she can't sleep with the light on, so I can't read for long."

"You watch your eyes, my girl, you only get one pair, you know."

"Dad!"

"I know, I'm naggin'. So, what about the other folk downstairs, what're they like, then?"

Father and daughter sat down on a wooden bench overlooking a flowerbed. "Well, you know Mr. Carter and Mrs. Crawford."

"That I do. Good people, both of them."

"Well, anyway, Mrs. Crawford is called 'Cook' and 'Mrs. Crawford' without any—well, without any method to it."

"What do you mean, love?"

"I mean that sometimes she's called 'Cook' or sometimes 'Mrs. Crawford' and there's no rule—sometimes it's both names in one sentence."

Frankie chewed on a sandwich, and nodded his head for Maisie to continue.

"There's two footmen, Arthur and Cedric, and there's Her Ladyship's maid, Nora—she's a bit quiet. Apparently, at the big house, in Kent, there's more staff and a housekeeper, Mrs. Johnson. There's some scullery maids—Dossie, Emily, and Sadie—who help Mrs. Crawford in the kitchen, and of course there's Enid."

"What's she like, then?"

"She's got hair the color of a blazing fire, Dad. Really red, it is. And when she brushes it out at night, it goes right up like this."

Maisie held out her hands to indicate a distance away from the sides of her head, which made Frankie laugh. Something he couldn't understand—how she could look like a child one minute, and like a mature woman the next.

"She nice to you, love?"

"She's all right, Dad. Blows hot and cold, though. One minute she seems full of the joys of spring, and the next, well, I just keep out of her way."

"I might've guessed. Your carrottops are always the same. Remember, love, the more you're yourself, the more it's like you've just put iron shoes on yer feet—they'll 'old you to the ground when that 'ot and cold air comes rushing from 'er direction. That's the key with that sort."

Maisie nodded, as if to take in this important advice, and continued with her story. "The other thing about Enid is that I think she's sweet on Master James."

Frankie laughed again. "Oh! I see it didn't take you long to get wind of the goings-on! What's 'e like, then, this James? Bit old to be called 'Master,' in' 'e?"

"Well, apparently, so I heard Cook saying, His Lordship gave instructions that Master James should be called Master until he proved his worth. Or something like that. He comes into the kitchen sometimes, you know, of an evening, after dinner. I've watched him. He comes in to see Cook, and as he walks by Enid, he always winks at her. She goes all red in the face and looks the other way, but I know she likes him. And Cook pretends to tell him off for coming into her kitchen, as if he was still a little boy, but then she brings out a big plate of ginger biscuits—which he gets stuck into while he's standing there in the kitchen! Drives Mr. Carter mad, it does."

"I should think it does! Likes order, does Mr. Carter. Now then, tell me about the 'ouse itself."

And Maisie smiled, glad to be in the easy company of her father, a man who was given to remark that a person could take him as they found him, there were no airs around Frankie Dobbs. And Frankie was more at peace now. Life itself was easier—easier now that the man knew his daughter to be in good hands. Easier now that the bills were being paid. Yes, thought Frankie Dobbs as he walked with his daughter in the park, it was all getting easier.

*M*aisie was fascinated by the library. It was well used, for both Lord and Lady Compton enjoyed literature, politics, and keeping up with the fancies of intellectual London. But when Maisie opened the door and brought in the coal scuttle at five in the morning, it was a quiet room. The lush velvet curtains kept drafts at bay and allowed warmth to seep into every corner after Maisie had lit the fire ready for whoever would use the room that morning.

Each day she lingered just a little longer before kneeling down to the fireplace, before her hands were blackened by the lighting of fires. Each day she learned a little more about the depth and breadth of knowledge housed in the Comptons' library, and each day her hunger grew. Gradually she became braver, first tentatively touching the leather binding as she read the title on the spine of a book, then taking the text from its place on the shelf and opening the fine onionskin pages at the front of the book.

The library seized Maisie's imagination, rendering the small public library with which she was familiar a very poor runner-up in her estimation. Of all the rooms in the house, she loved this the most. One morning, as she replaced a book to attend to the fireplace, a thought occurred to Maisie.

After her mother's death, she had been used to rising at three in the morning to make her father his tea. It had never hurt her then. In fact, she considered getting up at half past four to be "lying in." So, what if she got up at three in the morning and came down to the library? No one would know. Enid could sleep through the roof falling in over her head, and she had started coming up to bed late over the past week anyway. Lord knows where she had been, but it certainly wasn't out, because Carter locked up the house as if it were the Bank of England every night. She dreaded that Enid might be with Master James. Just two weeks ago, as she was leaving Lady Rowan's sitting room, where she had been sent to collect a tray one evening, Maisie saw Enid and James together on the first-floor land-ing. Without being observed by them, she watched as James ran his fingers through his fair hair and continued speaking with Enid, his gray eyes intent upon her response to his question. Was it a question? Surely it was, because she saw Enid shake her head and look at the carpet, while brushing her right shoe back and forth across the fibers.

And now Enid was never in bed before midnight—which meant that, thankfully, she would be deep in slumber by three o'clock. Maisie resolved to come to the library when the house was asleep. That night, before pulling up the covers and extinguishing the small lamp beside her bed, Maisie pinched the skin on her right arm sharply three times to ensure that she would awake in time to put her plan into action.

The next morning Maisie awakened easily by three o'clock. A chill in the attic room tempted her to forget her plan, but she sat up, deter-mined to go through with it. She washed and dressed with hardly a sound, crept out of the room carrying her shoes and a cardigan, and felt her way downstairs in the dark. In the silent distance, the kitchen clock struck the single chime of a quarter past the hour. She had almost two hours before the coal scuttles had to be filled.

The library was silent and pitch black as Maisie entered. Quickly closing the door behind her, she lit the lamps and made her way to the section that held philosophy books. This was where she would start. She wasn't quite sure which text to start with, but felt that if she just started somewhere, a plan would develop as she went along. The feeling inside that she experienced when she saw the books was akin to the hunger she felt as food was put on the table at the end of the working day. And she knew that she needed this sustenance as surely as her body needed its fuel.

Maisie's fingers tapped along the spines of books until she could bear the electric tingle of excitement no longer. Within minutes, she was seated at the table, opening *The Philosophical Works of David Hume,* and drawing the desk lamp closer to illuminate the pages. Maisie took a small notebook and pencil from her apron pocket, set it down on the desk and wrote the title of the book and the author's name. And she read. For an hour and a half, Maisie read. She read with understanding on a subject she had barely even heard of.

As the library clock chimed a quarter to five, Maisie turned to her notebook and wrote a precis of what she had read, what she understood, and her questions. The clock struck five, Maisie put the notebook and pencil away in her apron pocket, closed the book, replaced it ever so carefully on the shelf, extinguished the desk light, and left the room. She closed the door quietly behind her and went quickly downstairs to fill the coal scuttles. Just a short while later she opened the library door again. Without looking at the shelves, as if eye contact with the spines of the beloved books would give her game away, she set the coal scuttle down and knelt by the grate to build and light the fire.

Each weekday morning Maisie rose at three to visit the library. Sometimes a party at the house would keep the Comptons up until the small hours, and the change in routine made the library expeditions a risk she could not afford. She was liked in the house, though she had been spoken to by Lord and Lady Compton only once, when she had first arrived.

Half past two. Maisie crept out of bed. It was earlier than usual, but she couldn't sleep. She had gone to bed early, so it would be just as well to get up now. Enid slept soundly, which hardly surprised Maisie as the girl hadn't been in bed long. She was becoming a late one, that Enid. As late as Maisie was early. One of these days we'll meet in the doorway, thought Maisie. Then we'll have to do some talking.

The house was silent; only the ticking of clocks accompanied her to the library. Now when she entered the room it was as if she were falling into the arms of an old friend. Even the tentacles of cold receded as she turned on the light, placed her notebook and pencil on the desk, and went to the bookshelves. She took down the book she had been reading for the past three days, sat at the desk, found her place, and commenced.

Frankie Dobbs always said that when she was reading Maisie had "cloth ears." She always seemed instinctively to know the time and when she would need to stop reading to run an errand or complete a chore, but as far as Frankie was concerned, "Those ears don't even work when you've yer nose in a book!" And he loved her all the more for it.

*L*ord and Lady Compton were caught up in the midst of the London season, which Lady Rowan loved for its energy, even if she did have to tolerate some people she considered to be "light." Fortunately late nights usually fell on weekends, but this invitation, in the middle of the week, was not to be missed: an intimate yet sumptuous dinner with one of London's most outspoken hostesses.

"Thank God there's someone with a bigger mouth than mine," Lady Rowan confided to her husband.

Guests were to include some of the leading literary lights of Europe. It was an opportunity for sparkling conversation, definitely not to be missed. Maurice Blanche would accompany them, a rare event, as he was known to shun society gatherings.

After-dinner conversation drifted past midnight. It was only as Maisie Dobbs crept downstairs to the library that Lord and Lady Compton, along with Maurice Blanche, bade their hostess adieu, thanking her profusely for a wonderful evening. They arrived home at three in the morning. Carter had been instructed not to wait up, but an evening supper tray had been left for them in the drawing room. Lady Rowan was still in fine argumentative fettle as Lord Julian led the way.

"I tell you, Maurice, this time you are mistaken. Only last week I was reading—where was I reading—oh yes, that new book. You know, Julian, what was it called? Anyway, I was reading about a new hypothesis that utterly controverts your position."

"Rowan, could we please—" interrupted Lord Julian.

"Julian, no, we couldn't. Pour Maurice a drink. I'll find the book, then you'll see!"

"As you will, Rowan. I am very much looking forward to seeing what you have read. One always welcomes the opportunity to learn," said Maurice Blanche.

While the men settled by the embers of the drawing-room fire, Lady Rowan stormed upstairs to the library. Maisie Dobbs was deep in her book. She heard neither footsteps on the stairs nor the approach of Lady Rowan. She heard nothing until Lady Rowan spoke. And she did not speak until she had watched Maisie for some minutes, watched as the girl sucked on the end of her single braid of thick, black hair, deep in concentration. Occasionally she would turn a page back, reread a sentence, nod her head, then read on.

"Excuse me. Miss Dobbs."

Maisie sat up and closed her eyes tightly, not quite believing that a voice had addressed her.

"Miss Dobbs!"

Maisie shot up from the chair, turned to face Lady Rowan, and quickly bobbed a curtsy. "Sorry, Your Ladyship. Begging your pardon, Ma'am. I've not harmed anything."

"What are you doing, girl?" asked Lady Rowan.

"Reading, Ma'am."

"Well, I can see that. Let me see that book."

Maisie turned, took the book she had been reading, and handed it to Lady Rowan. She stepped back, feet together, hands at her sides. Bloody hell, she was in trouble now.

"Latin? Latin! What on earth are you reading Latin for?"

Lady Rowan's surprise stemmed questions that another employer might have put to the young maid.

"Um . . . well. Um . . . I needed to learn it," replied Maisie.

"You needed to learn it? Why do you need to learn Latin?"

"The other books had Latin in them, so I needed to understand it. To understand the other books, that is."

Maisie shifted her weight from one foot to the other. Now she needed to pee. For her part Lady Rowan was regarding Maisie sternly, yet she felt a strange curiosity to know more about the girl she had already thought unusual.

"Which other books? Show me," demanded Lady Rowan.

One by one Maisie took down the books, her hands shaking, her legs turning to jelly as she moved the library steps from one shelf to another. Whatever happened next, it was sure to be bad. Very bad. And she had let down her dad. How would she tell him she had been sacked? What would she say?

Maisie was so scared that she did not notice that, in her curiosity, Lady Rowan had forgotten the formality with which she would ordinarily address a servant. She asked Maisie about her choice of books, and Maisie, taking up her notebook, recounted what she had learned in her reading, and what questions had led her to each text in turn.

"My, my, young lady. You *have* been busy. All I can remember of Latin is the end of that verse: 'First it killed the Romans, and now it's killing me!' "

Maisie looked at Lady Rowan and smiled. She wasn't sure if it was a joke, but she couldn't stop the grin from forming. It was the first time she had truly smiled since coming to the house. The expression was not lost on Lady Rowan, who felt herself torn between regard for the girl and the appropriate response in such a situation.

"Maisie—Miss Dobbs. There is still time for you to enjoy a short rest before your duties commence. Go back to your room now. I shall need to discuss this incident. In the meantime, do not use the library until you hear from Carter, who will instruct you as to how we will deal with this . . . situation." Lady Rowan felt the requirements of her position pressing upon her, just as it had when she had been taken by Maurice to the East End of London. How could she do what was right, without compromising—how had Maurice described it? Yes, without compromising "the safety of her own pond"?

"Yes, Your Ladyship." Maisie put her notebook into in her pocket, and with tears of fear visibly pricking the inner corners of her eyes, bobbed another curtsy.

Lady Rowan waited until Maisie had left the room before extinguishing the lights. It was only as she walked slowly down the staircase that she remembered that she had gone to the library for a book.

"Bloody fool," she said to herself, and walked toward the drawing room to speak with her husband and Maurice Blanche on a new topic of conversation.

CHAPTER TEN

*M*aisie had hardly been able to concentrate on anything since being discovered. She felt sure that notice to leave the employ of Lord and Lady Compton would soon follow, and was surprised that one week had gone by without any word. Then Carter summoned Maisie to his "office," the term he sometimes used—especially in grave situations where a reprimand was to be meted out—to describe the butler's pantry, a small room adjacent to the kitchen, where he kept meticulous records regarding the running of the house.

Maisie was in a miserable state. The embarrassment of being caught, together with the pain of anticipating her father's dismay at her behavior, was almost too much to bear. And of course, she no longer had access to the Comptons' library. Wringing her already work-reddened hands, Maisie knocked on the door of Mr. Carter's office. Her nails were bitten down to the quick, and she had picked at her cuticles until her fingers were raw. It had been a nerve-wracking week.

"Enter," said Carter, with a tone that was neither soft and welcoming nor overtly displeased. It was a tone that gave nothing away.

"Good morning, Mr. Carter." Maisie bobbed a curtsy as she walked into the small room. "You wanted to see me, Sir?"

"Yes, Maisie. You know why I have summoned you. Lady Compton wishes to meet with you at twelve noon today. Sharp. In the library. I shall myself be in attendance, as will a colleague of both Lord and Lady Compton.

"Yes, Mr. Carter."

Maisie could bear the wait no longer, and although fear was nipping at her throat and chest, she had to know her fate.

"Mr. Carter, Sir?"

"Yes, Maisie?" Carter regarded her over half-moon spectacles.

"Mr. Carter. Can't you just get on with it? Give me the sack now, so that I don't have to—"

"Maisie. No one has said anything about the sack. I am instructed only to accompany you to a meeting with Lady Rowan and Dr. Blanche. I have also been requested to take your notebooks to the library this morning at half past ten. Please bring them to me directly so that I can take them to Lady Rowan."

"But . . ." Maisie did not understand, and although she thought that Carter did not understand either, she suspected he might have an inkling. "Mr. Carter, Sir. What's this all about?"

Carter adjusted his tie and swept an imaginary hair from the cuff of his crisp white shirt. "Maisie, it is most unusual. However, I do not believe your employment here is at an end. In fact, rather the contrary. Now then. The notebooks. Then I believe the sideboard in the dining room is to be waxed and polished this morning, so you had better get on."

Maisie bobbed another curtsy and turned to leave the office.

"And Maisie," said Carter, sweeping back his well-combed gray-at-the-temples hair. "Although respect should always be accorded our employers and their guests, there's no need to keep bobbing up and down like a sewing-machine needle when you are downstairs."

Maisie absentmindedly bobbed again and quickly left the office. She returned fifteen minutes later with her collection of small notebooks for Carter. She was terrified of the meeting that was to take place at twelve noon, and was sure that she would spend half the time until then in the lavatory.

Carter was waiting at the foot of the first-floor stairs at five minutes to twelve when Maisie walked toward him from the landing that led to the lower stairs and the kitchen. He drew his pocket watch from his waistcoat pocket, determined to be not a moment too soon or a second too late.

"Ah, Maisie," he said as she approached, hands clasped together in front of her white pinafore.

Carter looked the girl up and down to check for marks on the pinafore and scuffs on her shoes, for stray tendrils of hair escaping from her white cap.

"Nicely turned out. Good. Let us proceed."

Carter checked his watch once more, turned, and led the way to the library. Maisie had a horrible taste in her mouth. What would her father say when she came home with her small canvas bag and no job? Well, perhaps it was for the best. She missed him something rotten, so perhaps it would be a very good thing. Carter knocked briskly at the door. A voice could be heard within.

"Come in."

Maisie closed her eyes for a second, put her hands behind her back, and crossed her fingers.

"Ah, Carter. Miss Dobbs. Maisie. Do come in."

"Thank you, Ma'am," said Carter. Maisie bobbed her curtsy and looked sideways at Carter. Lady Rowan beckoned Maisie to her.

"Maurice, this is the girl of whom we have been speaking." Then, inclining her head slightly toward Maisie, she said, "I would like to introduce Dr. Maurice Blanche. He knows of our meeting in the library, and I have consulted with him regarding the situation."

Maisie was now utterly confused. What situation? And who was this man? What was going on? Maisie nodded and curtsied to the man standing alongside Lady Rowan.

"Sir," she said in acknowledgment.

She didn't know what to make of this small man. He wasn't as tall as Lady Rowan, and while he looked well fed, there was a wiryness to him. Solid, as her dad would have said. Solid. She couldn't even guess his age, but thought he was older than her dad, but not as old as Grandad. Over fifty, perhaps sixty. He had blue-gray eyes that looked as if they were floating in water, they were that clear. And his hands—they had long fingers with wide nails. Hands that could play the piano, very exact hands that made precise movements. She saw that when he took up her notebooks from a walnut side table and flicked a page or two.

He was a plain dresser, not done up like two penn'orth of hambone like some of them that she'd seen at the house. No, this was a plain man. And he looked right through her. And because she thought that she had nothing to lose and because her dad had told her always to "stand tall," Maisie stiffened her spine, pulled her shoulders back, and looked him straight in the eye as he had looked at her. Then he smiled.

"Miss Dobbs, Maisie. Lady Rowan has spoken with me about your encounter in the library last week."

Here it comes, thought Maisie. She clenched her teeth.

"Now then, come with me."

Maurice Blanche walked to the library table and sat down, then invited Maisie to sit next to him, with her notebooks in front of them.

Lady Rowan nodded at Carter, who remained by the door, as she walked to stand by the window. They watched as Blanche spoke with Maisie.

Gradually he broke down Maisie's shyness and the formalities that separated housemaid and houseguest. Within fifteen minutes the two were in animated conversation. Maurice Blanche asked questions, Maisie answered, often with another question. Clever, thought Carter, very clever. The way that Dr. Blanche drew Maisie out, with his voice, his eyes, a finger tapped upon the page, a question punctuated by a hand placed on the chin to listen. Lady Rowan was equally riveted by the discourse, but her interest was of a more personal nature. Maisie

Dobbs's future was part of her own quest to challenge herself, and what was considered correct in a household such as hers and for a woman of her titled position.

An hour passed. An hour during which Carter was sent to bring tea for Dr. Blanche. Nothing was requested for Maisie. It would never do for a man of Carter's position to be at the service of a maid. Yet Carter sensed that something important was happening, that this was an hour during which the established structure of life in the house was changing. And he foresaw that changes that came as a result of whatever came to pass in this room this morning would affect them all. And these were strange-enough times already, what with old King Edward just dead and King George V's coronation around the corner.

Finally Maurice Blanche asked Maisie to close and collect her books. She did as instructed and drew away from the table to stand next to Carter, while Lady Rowan joined Maurice Blanche at the table.

"Rowan, I am more than satisfied," said Dr. Blanche. "You may reveal our plan to Miss Dobbs and Mr. Carter. Then we shall see if Mr. Carter agrees and how we may begin."

Lady Rowan spoke, first looking at Carter, then at Maisie. "Last week when I came upon Miss Dobbs in the library, I was struck by the breadth of her reading. We know that anyone can take down a book and read, but when I briefly looked at her notebooks I realized that there was also a depth of understanding. You are a very bright girl, Miss Dobbs."

Lady Rowan glanced at Maurice Blanche, who nodded to her to continue.

"I know that this is most unusual. Carter has already been given an indication of my thoughts, and has concurred with my decision. Now I can be more specific. Lord Compton and I are believers in education and opportunity. However, opportunities to contribute directly are rare. Miss Dobbs, we have a proposal for you."

Maisie blushed and looked at her shoes as Lady Rowan continued.

"Under the direction of Dr. Blanche you will continue your

studies here. Dr. Blanche is a busy man, but he will meet with you once every fortnight in the library. Your studies, and the tutorials with Dr. Blanche, must, however, be on your own time and must not interfere in any way with your work in the house. What do you say to that, Maisie?"

Maisie was shocked, but after taking a moment to consider, she flashed the smile that seemed to be working its way back into her life. "Thank you, Ma'am. Sir—Dr. Blanche—thank you."

"Miss Dobbs," said Maurice Blanche, "hold your thanks for the time being. You may not take kindly to me when you have seen my plans for your education."

That night, when Maisie was in bed, she was hardly able to sleep for wondering about the events of the day. Carter had been accommodating, but then he was kind. And the other staff, when they had learned about it later—because that Mrs. Crawford was a right old chatterbox—seemed to be all right with it all, as long as she pulled her weight in the house. There hadn't been any snide comments, or jealousy. But when Enid finally came to bed in the early hours, she wasted no time in voicing a thought that had been at the back of Maisie's mind.

"You'd've thought they would've just sent you to one of those fancy schools, on the QT, like. Or even paid for your uniform and all that, for the school where you won the scholarship. They're not short of a few bob, are they?"

Maisie nodded.

"But you know what I reckon, Mais? To be perf-hectly honest with you. I reckon they knew you would 'ave a rotten time there. What with all them toffs. It would get you down, it would. Reckon that's what it is."

Without waiting for a response, and using her hairbrush as a pointer for emphasis, Enid continued. "And what you've got to remember,

Dobbsie, is that there's them upstairs, and there's us downstairs. There's no middle, never was. So the likes of you and me can't just move up a bit, if that's what you think. We've got to jump, Dobbsie, and bloody 'igh to boot!"

Maisie knew that there was more than a grain of truth in her words. But if Her Ladyship wanted a cause, someone with whom to play 'Lady Bountiful,' she didn't mind being on the receiving end if it meant getting on with her education.

Maisie changed the subject. "So, where were you tonight, Enid?" she asked.

"Never you mind. You can keep that there clever mind of yours on your own business now, and don't you be thinking about mine."

Maisie closed her eyes, then quickly fell asleep. She dreamt of long corridors of books, of Dr. Blanche at the library table, and of Enid. And even with the excitement of her lessons with Dr. Blanche, it was the dream about Enid that remained with her throughout the next day, and for some days to come. And she tried not to think about the dream and Enid, because every time she did, she shivered along the full length of her spine.

CHAPTER ELEVEN

*L*ord Julian Compton knew of his wife's "project" and gave the education of Maisie Dobbs his blessing, although secretly he believed that the exercise would soon falter and any ambitions shown by young Miss Dobbs would be extinguished under the strain of trying to be two very different people, to say nothing of being a girl on the cusp of womanhood. He was intrigued by Maurice Blanche and his interest in Maisie's education, and it was this involvement, rather than his wife's philanthropic gestures, that led him to allow that the project might, in fact, have some merit. He held Maurice Blanche in high esteem, and was even in some awe of the man.

Maisie, for her part, felt no fatigue at the end of a long day. She began her chores in the household at her usual early hour, starting with the lighting of fires, the cleaning of rooms, and the polishing of heavy mahogany furniture. The job of cleaning cutlery fell to the junior footman, though when she handled the solid silver knives and forks, perhaps when cleaning the dining room after dinner guests had departed to the drawing room, she looked with care at the inscription. Each piece of fine cutlery bore the Compton crest, a great hunting dog and a stag together with the words "Let There Be No Ill Will." Maisie pondered the crest as she collected the soiled silverware. The hunter and the hunted, the suggestion of forgiveness between the victor and the victim, and the fact that both stood tall and proud. In fact, Maisie had taken to pondering just about everything that happened in the course of a day, seeing coincidences and patterns in the life around her.

Mrs. Crawford put Maisie's behavior down to her work with Maurice Blanche, an assumption that was, of course, correct.

"I dunno, when I was a girl learning meant your reading, your writing, and your 'rithmetic. None of this lark, this philosophy nonsense."

Mrs. Crawford pointed a floury finger at Maisie, who had just returned from the weekly visit to the library. She was placing books, those for Mrs. Crawford and Mr. Carter, as well as her own, carefully in a kitchen cupboard, so they would not become soiled by the business of the kitchen. Later she would take her selection to her room for more late-night reading. Cook had immediately noted the girth of Maisie's books, and could not resist comment—to which Carter felt bound to respond.

"I am sure that Mr. Blanche knows more about the education of a young person for today's world than either you or I, Cook. But I must say, Maisie, that is rather a large tome, is it not?"

Carter, decanting a fine port, did not stop his task to wait for an answer, but cast his eyes over his spectacles in Maisie's direction.

"Maisie—are you listening to Mr. Carter?"

Carter exchanged glances with Mrs. Crawford, and both rolled their eyes in a compact that hid their true feelings. They were very proud of Maisie Dobbs, and laid some claim in their hearts to the discovery of her intellectual gifts.

"Sorry, Mr. Carter. Were you speaking to me?" She had to remove her little finger from her mouth to speak. Maisie had hurried back from the library to allow an extra few moments to dip into one of her books.

"Yes, Mr. Carter was speaking to you, Maisie—and if I see that finger in your mouth again, I swear I'll paint your nails with carbolic. It's a wonder you've got hands left, they way you chew on those fingers."

"Sorry, Mrs. Crawford. Begging your pardon, Mr. Carter? I'll get going again now. I just thought I'd take a quick peek."

Carter studied the kitchen clock. "You can have five minutes. Cook and I were commenting on the width of that book. It's a fair size. Is Dr. Blanche working you too hard, Maisie?"

"It's Kierkegaard. Mr. Blanche says I should read this because he—Kierkegaard—has had a considerable influence on modern thought. And no, don't worry, I can keep up with everything."

Cook and Carter exchanged glances once again, neither wanting to show ignorance about some newfangled thing that sounded to both of them like "kick the guard."

In the meantime Maisie took a notebook from her apron pocket and began to write down her questions and observations for Maurice Blanche. As Carter had suspected, she had already started reading the book on her way back from the library, and was sufficiently into it to be completely absorbed. Once finished, she replaced the notebook in her pocket, glanced at the heavy oak clock with the pearl white face and bold black numbers that was visible from any angle in the kitchen, and stood up from the table.

"I just need to put my book away, then I'll get on with making up the stove before I do the polishing."

Maisie moved quickly from the room, remembering the house rule that those from "below stairs" never ever ran, but when speed was of the essence, a brisk walk was permissible.

"I don't know how she still manages to see her poor father, what with her work down here, and all that book learning. I will say this for her, she's got some spirit, has that girl." Mrs. Crawford swept her forearm across her brow and continued with the pastry making. Carter had completed the task of decanting the port and was now uncorking brandy, to be carefully poured into a fine cut-crystal decanter. He made no reply to Mrs. Crawford's comments, which rather annoyed the woman, as she was given to strong opinions and the need to defend and discuss them.

"I wonder, Mr. Carter, what will happen when Maisie has a young man. I wonder, you know, what will happen to her. Fish can't survive long out of water, you know."

Mrs. Crawford stopped rolling the pastry and looked at Carter, who remained silent. "I said, Mr. Carter—"

"Cook—Mrs. Crawford—I know what you said. I would suggest that the education of Miss Dobbs is in good hands. I would also suggest that Miss Dobbs is a very determined young woman who will be more successful than most when it comes to surviving outside her established boundaries. Now then, it is not for us to question the decisions of our employers. We can do only what is required of us in the circumstances, don't you think?"

Mrs. Crawford, who had been filling a pastry-lined dish with fresh-sliced apple, added cinnamon and clove with rather more than her usual flourish, replied with a certain asperity, "Right you are, Mr. Carter," before turning her back on him to check the oven.

Maisie's education was indeed going well. Maurice Blanche had encouraged an easy camaraderie while maintaining the certain distance required by his position, and by Maisie's. Within eighteen months of embarking upon the demanding timetable set by Blanche, Maisie was studying at a level of which a master at one of the prestigious private schools of the day would have been proud.

For her part Maisie knew only that the work challenged and excited her. When Maurice handed her a new text, she felt a thrill of anticipation. Would the book be brand new, unread, with pages untouched by another? If so, then Maurice would request a précis of the content, and her assessment of the text.

"Four pages of quarto, if you please. And a word of advice. This man has opinions. Opinions, as we have discussed, are not fact. But of course, as we know, Maisie, they may be the source of truth. I will be speaking with you about the truth demonstrated in this thesis, Maisie, so be prepared!"

Of course, the text may have already been read and in that case, each page would bear penciled notation in Maurice Blanche's small, fine handwriting with its slight slant to the right. A single page of questions would be tucked inside, between the back page and the cover. Maisie knew that each question must be answered.

"I never want to learn that you 'don't know,' Maisie, I want to know what you *think* the answer is to the question. And once more, a word of advice: Stay with the question. The more it troubles you, the more it has to teach you. In time, Maisie, you will find that the larger questions in life share such behavior."

It had been almost two years since Maisie's mother passed away, and still Frankie Dobbs grieved. He swore that it was Maisie who kept him going, for Frankie Dobbs lived for Sundays, and always the ritual was the same.

Although it was not a market day, Frankie would be at the stable with Persephone from an early hour, not as early as on a weekday, but early all the same. He talked softly to his mare, brushing her coat until she shone, caring for mane and tail, and checking hooves that had to pull a heavy load over a considerable distance each day. There was a warm, oaty sweetness to the stable, and here Frankie, often so ungainly when walking down the street or in company, was completely at ease. It was usually as Frankie was halfway through the Sunday morning round of chores that Maisie could be heard walking up the cobblestones toward the stable.

"Dad, I'm here," Maisie called out to him before looking over the half-door and waving. Always she brought something for Frankie from Mrs. Crawford, perhaps a pork pie wrapped in fine white muslin and brown paper, freshly baked bread still warm to the touch, or a steamed apple pudding that needed only "A bit o' warming up over the stove," according to the cook.

Maisie quickly pulled off her coat and rolled up her sleeves. Father and daughter worked together to finish the morning's labor, their talk made easier by their movement. They shared confidences easily as their hands were busy with job of work.

"So, your learning's coming along, is it, Girl?"

"Yes, Dad. Dr. Blanche is looking ahead, he says. Reckons I could be ready for scholarship and entrance exams next year."

"Entrance for what?" asked Frankie, as he moved toward the pump to refill his bucket with water to rinse Persephone's leather reins and traces, which he had just lathered with saddle soap.

"Well, um, university. Dr. Blanche says I can do it. Her ladyship is very keen for me to apply to Cambridge, to Girton College. Says it's the place for an individualist."

"Did she now? Cambridge. Well, there's posh for you, my girl!" Frankie laughed but then looked seriously at Maisie. "As long as you don't push yourself, Love. And Cambridge is a long way off, isn't it? Where would you live? And what about mixing with the type of folk at a place like that"

"I dunno, Dad. I have to live at the college, I think. There are all sorts of rules about that, you know. And I will meet people. I'll be just fine, Dad. Girton is a women's college away in a village, after all."

"Yes, but those other young women have more money than you do, and they've got more, you know, connections, like."

Maisie looked up from brushing Persephone. Even though Frankie had already brushed the horse from head to tail, Maisie loved to feel the warm animal close to her, and knew the horse appreciated her efforts.

"Dad, I'm not a child any more. I'm fifteen now. And I've seen more than a lot of girls my age. Dr. Blanche knows what he is doing."

"Yes, love, I'm sure he does. Clever man, that one. I just worry about you."

Frankie rubbed the cleaned leather with a dry cloth, and hung reins and traces from a hook on the low ceiling. Later, after Maisie's return to Belgravia, Frankie would come back to the stable to feed Persephone, then take down the dry reins, bridle, and traces, and rub warmed neatsfoot oil into the leather.

"Don't worry about me, Dad. I'm doing very well, you know. Now then, where shall we go for our walk? I've got some nice sandwiches and a couple of bottles of ginger beer for us."

$\mathcal{T}$hree days after her visit with Frankie, Maisie walked briskly toward the library for her early-evening lesson. She saw Maurice Blanche on alternate Wednesday evenings, meeting promptly at half past five in the library, for three hours, until Dr. Blanche left to join the Comptons for an informal supper in the dining room. She studied alone until he had finished supper, when both he and Lady Rowan joined Maisie in the library to review her work. Lady Rowan was well pleased with the education of Maisie Dobbs, asking questions and suggesting new areas of study. But this evening a new possibility was discussed.

"Maisie, I think it is time for us to embark on some fieldwork."

Maisie looked first at Blanche, then at Lady Rowan. Botany. It had to be botany.

"Lady Rowan has spoken with Mr. Carter, and next week, on Wednesday, we will be taking an excursion. In fact, I have several such outings planned, and on those afternoons we must meet a little earlier than usual."

"What sort of outings? Where are we going?"

"Various places," said Blanche, "Of historical, social, or economic interest."

Little more was said, but in the following weeks Maisie was taken by Blanche to meet people with whom she would spend time alone in conversation. At first Maurice would remain with her, but as time went on, he would quietly leave the room to allow for conversation between Maisie and his friend, for each person who met with Maisie was considered a "friend" by Maurice Blanche. As far as Maisie was concerned, some of them were a strange lot altogether, and she wasn't sure what Frankie Dobbs would have to say about it all.

"Today we will be meeting with my dear friend Dr. Basil Khan," Maurice Blanche informed Maisie as they journeyed to Hampstead by taxi-cab. "An extraordinary scholar, born in Ceylon, into a very-high-caste family. His first name was given as a mark of respect to one of his father's former colleagues, an Englishman. Khan, as he prefers to be known, is completely blind. He lost his sight in an unfortunate accident, but as these things do, it became the foundation for his life's work."

"What's his life's work?"

"Khan, as you will see, is a man of great wisdom, of insight. His work uses that insight. He grants audiences to politicians, people of commerce, men of the cloth. He came to England as a young man, sent by his parents to see ophthalmic specialists, to no avail. While in England he gained his doctorate in philosophy at Oxford. Then he returned to Ceylon, and later traveled throughout the Indian sub-continent, himself seeking the counsel of wise men. To do this he had to give up the life he had once enjoyed in London and Oxford, which he had ceased to enjoy. Now he resides in Hampstead."

"So why am I to see him?"

"Maisie, we are visiting for him to see *you*. And for you to learn that seeing is not necessarily something one does with the eyes."

The visit to Khan was illuminating for Maisie. His apartments in a grand house were furnished in a simple manner: plain wooden furniture, curtains without pattern or texture, candlelight, and a strange smell that made her cough at first.

"You will get used to it, Maisie. Khan uses incense to bring a fragrant atmosphere to the house."

At first Maisie was timid when led into a large room with only cushions on the floor and an old man sitting with legs crossed. He was positioned by the long French window as if contemplating the view, so that as Maisie and Maurice Blanche walked toward him, Khan was framed by shafts of light, and appeared to have been borne into the room by some mystical means of transportation. Without turning, Khan gestured toward Maisie with his hand.

"Come, child, come sit with me. We have much to speak of."

To her surprise Maurice Blanche motioned Maisie to step forward, and moved toward Khan himself. He leaned down toward Khan, took the old man's bony brown hands in his own, and kissed his lined and furrowed forehead. Khan smiled and nodded, then turned to Maisie.

"Tell me what it is you know, child."

"Um . . ."

Both Khan and Maurice laughed, and the old man with long gray hair and almost colorless eyes smiled kindly at Maisie.

"Yes, a good start. A very good start. Let us talk of knowing."

So Maisie Dobbs—daughter of a costermonger from Lambeth, just south of the water that divided London's rich and poor—began to learn in the way that Maurice had intended, from the centuries of wisdom accumulated by Khan.

With Khan she learned to sit in deliberate silence, and learned too that the stilled mind would give insight beyond the teaching of books and hours of instruction, and that such counsel would support all other learning. When she first sat with Khan, she asked what it was she was to do as she sat with legs crossed on the cushion in front of him. The old man lifted his face to the window, then turned his clear white eyes toward her and said simply, "Pay attention."

Maisie took the practice of sitting with Khan seriously and to heart, with an instinctive knowledge that this work would serve her well. In just a few short years, the lessons learned in the hours with Khan would bring her calm amid the shellfire, the terrible injuries, and the cries of wounded men. But for now, Maurice Blanche told Maisie, it was no small coincidence that she often knew what a person was going to say before he or she spoke, or that she seemed to intuit an event before it had occurred.

CHAPTER TWELVE

"Maisie, you'll ruin your eyes if you read by that good-for-nothing light in the corner—and look at that time, you've to be up in three hours!"

"So have you, Enid, and you aren't anywhere near asleep yet."

"Don't you be worrying about me. I've told you that."

Maisie slipped a page of notes into the book to mark the place, closed the book, and placed it to one side on her small table. She looked directly at Enid.

"And don't you look at me with those eyes either, young Maisie Dobbs. Gives me the willies, it does."

"You are being careful, aren't you, Enid?"

"'Course I am. I told you not to worry."

Khan might be teaching her many things about the human mind, but as far as Maisie was concerned, it didn't take much in the way of foresight to see that Enid was going to get into some trouble before long. In truth it was a surprise that the older girl was not only still as slim as a whip but was still employed at the house in Belgravia at all. But Enid, who was now almost eighteen, was loved by everyone downstairs. Her efforts at correct enunciation still fell short, and sometimes Maisie thought she sounded more like a music hall act than a maid in service. But she, too, had come to love Enid, for her laughter, for the unsought advice she gave so freely, and most of all for her unselfish support of Maisie.

Enid slipped a thick cotton nightdress over her head, pulled on woolen socks, and proceeded carefully to fold her clothes into the chest of drawers by the wall. Shadows cast by the oil lamp flickered on the sloping ceiling of the top-floor bedroom as Enid brushed out her thick hair with a hardy bristle brush.

"One hundred strokes for a good thick head of hair—have I told you that, Mais?"

"Yes, many a time."

Maisie ensured that her books and papers were carefully put away, and clambered into bed.

"Brrrr. It's cold in here."

Enid took an old silk scarf that had been hanging over the cast-iron bedpost, wrapped it around the head of her brush, and began brushing the silk over her hair to bring it to a lustrous shine.

"No, and it ain't getting any warmer. I tell you, Maisie, a chill wind blows through 'ere sometimes, a chill wind."

Maisie turned to face Enid.

"Enid, why don't you like it here?"

Enid stopped brushing, held the brush in her lap, and fingered the scarf. Her shoulders drooped, and when she looked up at Maisie, it was with tears in her eyes.

"Enid, what is it? Is it James? Or that Arthur?"

Maisie had guessed that the reason for Enid's absences over the past year resided in rooms on the third floor. Though it might have been Arthur, the young footman who had come to work at the house a month before Maisie. His position had been elevated since then. He had been given the task of ensuring the good health of the Comptons' Lanchester motorcar, keeping it polished, oiled, and spick and span. She thought that he had taken a shine to Enid, too.

"No, it's not 'im. That one's full of the old bluster, all mouth and trousers, that's Arthur. No, it's not 'im." Enid picked at the hairbrush, taking out long hairs and rolling them between her fingers.

"Come on, Enid. Something makes you sad."

The older girl sighed, the familiar defiance ebbing as Maisie's eyes sought her confidence.

"You know, Maisie, they're all very nice here until you overstep the line. Now you, you'll land on your feet; after all, 'avin' brains is like 'avin' money, even I know that. But me, all I've got is 'oo I am, and 'oo I am i'n't good enough."

"What do you mean?"

"Oh, come on, Maisie, you must've heard talk—they love to talk in the kitchen of this place, 'specially that old Mrs. Crawford." Enid put down the brush, pulled back her bedsheets, and climbed into bed. She turned to face Maisie. "I don't know what it is about them eyes of yours, Mais, but I tell you, the way you look at me makes me want to spill my insides out to you."

Maisie inclined her head for Enid to continue.

"It's James. Master James. That's why His Lordship is talking about sending him away. To Canada. As far away from the likes of me as they can get 'im. It's a wonder they don't send me off too, to look for another job, but 'er Ladyship isn't a bad old bird, really. At least she can keep an eye on me if I'm 'ere—otherwise, who knows? I might just go to Canada meself!"

"Do you love James, Enid?"

Enid rolled to face the ceiling, and in the half-light, Maisie saw a single tear run from the corner of her eye onto the pillow.

"Love 'im? Gawd, Maisie, what business 'ave I got, going in for all that nonsense?"

Enid paused, dabbing at her eyes with a corner of the sheet. "Love don't put food on the table, does it?" She looked at her crumpled handkerchief, dabbed her eyes, and nodded. "I suppose I do, love him, that is. I do love James, but—"

"But what? If you love him, Enid, you can—"

"Can what, Maisie? Can what? No, theres no 'buts' in the matter.

He's going, and when he's gone, I've got my life to get on with. And in some way or another, I've got to get out of this 'ere job. I've got to get on, like you're getting on. But I've not got your cleverness."

"Dr. Blanche says that having a mental picture works. He said once that it's good to have a vision of what the future may hold. He says it's important to keep that in mind."

"Oh, he does, does he? Well, then, I'll start seeing myself all dolled up like a lady, with a nice husband, and a nice house. How about that for a picture?"

"I'll picture that for you too, Enid!"

Enid laughed and rolled over. "I tell you, Maisie Dobbs, you're one of a kind! Now then, you just turn off that thinking and imagining mind of yours, and let's get some kip."

Maisie did as she was told, but as she settled into the quiet of the night, she was sorry that the conversation had ended. It was always like that with Enid, as soon as you got a little closer to her, she moved away. Yet Maisie knew that at this very moment Enid was thinking of James Compton, hoping that if she held on to a picture of them together, it would come to pass. And Maisie thought of them together, too. Of seeing them on the landing, not long after she had come to work at 15 Ebury Place. She had seen them since, once in Brockwell Park when she was walking with her father. They must have thought that no one would recognize James on the south side of the river—his sort rarely ventured across the water. Enid was in her Sunday best: her long deep-lavender coat, which she kept hanging in the wardrobe covered in a white sheet and protected by mothballs. Her black woolen skirt poked out underneath, and you could just about see her laced-up boots, polished to a shine. She wore a white blouse with a high neck and a little sprig of lavender pinned to the front of the collar, right where a brooch might have been, if Enid had owned one. She wore black gloves and an old black hat that Maisie had seen her hold over a steaming pot of water in the kitchen, then work with her hands to mold it into shape, before making it look just like new with a band of purple velvet ribbon. Oh, she did look lovely, with her red hair tied in a loose knot so that you could see it beneath her hat. And James, she remembered him laughing when he was with Enid, and just before she managed to steer her father in another direction, so that Enid and James wouldn't see her, she watched as he took the glove off Enid's right hand and lean over to press his lips to her thin knuckles, then turn it over to the palm and kiss it again. And as he stood up, Enid reached up and flicked back his fair hair, which had flopped into his eyes.

And though she was now snuggled down into the bedclothes and blankets, a hot-water bottle at her feet, Maisie shivered and was frightened. Perhaps she should speak to Dr. Blanche about it, this strange feeling she had at times, as if the future had flashed a picture into her mind, like being at the picture house and seeing only a few seconds' worth of the show.

*J*ust one week after Enid had taken Maisie into her confidence, James Compton departed on a ship bound for Canada. As a result Enid had become less than affable.

"I do wish you would turn out that bloomin' light so that I can get some shut-eye. I'm sick of it, I am. 'Alfway through the night and all I can hear is you turnin' those bloomin' pages over and over."

Maisie looked up from her book, over to the lump that was Enid in the adjoining bed. She could not see Enid's face, for she was curled sideways with her back to Maisie, and the blankets over her head.

"I'm sorry, Enid, I didn't realize—"

Suddenly one arm came over the blankets as Enid pulled herself up into a sitting position, her face furiously red. "Well, you *wouldn't* bloomin' realize, *would* you, Miss Brainy? Always got yer 'ead in a book round 'ere when everyone else is workin'."

"But Enid, I pull my weight. No one else has to do my work for me. I can manage my jobs."

"Oh yes? You can manage your jobs, can you? Well, next time you go over to that mirror to do 'yer 'air, take a look at the sacks of coal under yer eyes. Your idea of pullin' weight is just a bit different from mine. And what with all that other stuff you 'ave to think about, it's a wonder you can get up in the morning. Now then. I'm off t'sleep, and it'd be a good idea if you did the same thing."

Maisie quickly marked her place in the book Maurice had given her earlier in the week, and extinguished the lamp at her bedside. Pulling the covers up to her shoulders and pressing her hands to her sore, watering eyes, she sought refuge from Enid's words. It seemed to Maisie that since Enid confided in her, she had become standoffish and unpleasant, as if her frustrated aspirations to become a lady had caused an unbearable resentment to grow. Maisie had begun to avoid her when Enid lost her temper at being asked to replenish coal in one of the upstairs rooms, and was reprimanded by Carter. But something must have sparked in Carter, for he called Maisie into the butler's pantry next to the kitchen.

"Maisie, I am worried about your ability to manage both your routine in the house and the schedule set by Dr. Blanche."

"Oh, Mr. Carter, I am managing."

"I want you to know that I will be watching, Maisie. I must obviously support Her Ladyship's wishes, but I must also bring it to her attention if changes should be made."

"No, you don't have to do that. I'll manage, sir. I promise."

"Right you are, Maisie. You may continue with your duties. But do make sure, doubly sure, that your work is complete at the end of the day."

"Yes, Mr. Carter."

*I*t was with a heavy heart that Maisie visited Frankie Dobbs on the following Sunday. More than at any other time since she had started lessons with Dr. Blanche, Maisie couldn't wait to leave the house and immerse herself in the warmth of the stable and her father's love.

"There you are. Bit late today, young Maisie, aren't you?"

"Yes, Dad. I was late getting up, then had to stay to finish some jobs, and missed the bus. I had to wait for the next one."

"Oh, so you couldn't get up in time on the one day you come to see your poor old dad?"

"That's not it, honestly, Dad," responded Maisie defensively.

She took off her hat and coat, folded them and put them on top of her basket, which she left just outside the stable door. She walked over to Persephone and rubbed the soft spot behind her ears.

"I was just a bit late, that's all, Dad."

"You doin' too much of that readin'?"

"No, Dad. No, I'm not."

"So how about your week then, Love? What've you been doing?"

"Oh, we had a to-do in the kitchen this week. Mrs. Crawford was experimenting with pouring brandy over the cooked meat and then adding a flame to it. Some new French idea that Lady Compton had asked Carter about. The whole kitchen nearly caught alight. You should have seen it, Dad. It was hilarious!"

Frankie Dobbs stopped work and looked at Maisie.

"What is it, Dad?" The smile seemed to evaporate from her face.

"'Ilarious, was it? I like that. 'ilarious. Can't use ordinary words anymore. Got to use big ones now, 'aven't you?"

"But Dad . . . I thought . . . ."

"That's the trouble with you. Too much of that thinking. I dunno . . . ."

Frankie turned his back on Maisie, the set of his shoulders revealing a seldom-seen anger. "I dunno. I thought this was all very well and all, you gettin' an education. Now I dunno. Next thing you know, you won't want to talk to the likes of me."

"Now that's silly, Dad."

"Silly, am I?" Frankie looked up again, his eyes blazing.

"I didn't mean it like that. What I meant was . . ." Maisie was exhausted. She let her arm drop to her side. Persephone nuzzled her to continue the ear rubbing, but there was no response. Father and daughter stood in stony silence.

How had this happened? How was it that one minute it seemed that everyone was on her side, and the next everyone was against her? What had she done wrong? Maisie went over to an upended box in the corner and slumped down. Her furrowed brow belied her youth as she tried to come to terms with the discord between her beloved father and herself.

"I'm sorry, Dad."

"I'm sorry, too. Sorry that I ever talked to that Mr. Carter in the first place."

"You did right, Dad. I would never have had this opportunity. . . ."

Frankie was also tired. Tired of worrying about Maisie, tired of fearing that she would move into circles above her station and never come back. Tired of feeling not good enough for his daughter. "I know, love. I know. Let's 'ave an end to the words. Just make sure you come back and see your old dad of a Sunday."

Maisie leaned over to Frankie, who had upended another wooden box to sit next to her, put her arms around his neck, and sobbed.

"Come on, love. Let's put the words behind us."

"I miss you, Dad."

"And I miss you, Love."

Father and daughter held on to each other a moment longer, before Frankie announced that they should be getting along to the park if they were to enjoy the best of the day. They worked together to finish jobs in the stable and, leaving Persephone to her day of rest, went to the park for a walk and to eat the sandwiches that Mrs. Crawford had made for Maisie.

As she traveled back to Belgravia that evening, Maisie couldn't help but remember Frankie's outburst, and wondered how she would ever balance her responsibilities. As if that were not enough, Enid's tongue was as sharp as a knife again when Maisie entered the room they shared on the top floor of the house.

"It's a wonder you can bring yourself to see that costermonger father of yours. Isn't he a bit lower class for you now, Maisie?"

Maisie was stunned and hurt by Enid's words. Slights against herself she could handle, but those against her father she would not tolerate. "My father, Enid, is one of the best."

"Hmmph. Thought he wouldn't be good enough, what with you bein' 'er Ladyship's pet."

"Enid, I'm not anyone's pet or favorite. I'm still here, and working hard."

Enid was lying on her back on the bed, pillows plumped up behind her head. She was reading an old copy of *The Lady* magazine while speaking to Maisie.

"Hmmph. Maisie Dobbs, all you've done is give 'er Ladyship a cause. They like causes, do these 'ere toffs. Makes 'er feel like she's doin' something for the lower classes. Right old do-gooder she is, too. And as for that funny old geezer, Blanche, I'd worry about 'im if I was you. D'you really think you can become a lady with all this book lark?"

"I've told you before, Enid—I don't want to be a lady."

Maisie folded her day clothes and put them away in the heavy chest of drawers, then took up her hairbrush and began to unbraid her glossy black hair.

"Then you're as stupid as you are silly lookin'."

Maisie swung around to look directly at Enid.

"What is *wrong* with you? I can't do a thing right!"

"Let me tell you what's wrong with me, young Maisie. What's wrong with me is that I might not be able to do the learning from books that you can, but mark my words, I'll be out of here before you, 'er Ladyship or not."

"But I'm not stopping you—"

In frustration Enid flounced to her feet, pulled back the bed-clothes, and threw herself into bed. Without saying goodnight, she turned her back on Maisie, as had become her habit.

Maisie said nothing more, but climbed into her heavy brass bed to lie upon the hard horsehair mattress between cold white muslin sheets. Without attempting to read her book or work on the assignment Maurice Blanche had given her, she turned out the light.

Jealousy. Now she was beginning to understand jealousy. Together with the exchanges of the past few weeks, and the heated conversation with her father, Maisie was also beginning to feel fully the challenge of following her dream. And she was disturbed, not for the first time, by Enid's words about Lady Rowan. Was she just a temporary diversion for Lady Rowan, a sop to her conscience so she could feel as if she was doing something for society? Maisie couldn't believe this, for time and time again she had seen genuine interest and concern on her employer's face.

"So, Maisie. Let me see your work. How are you progressing with Jung?"

Maisie walked into the library for her meeting with Maurice Blanche and stood before him.

"Sit down, sit down. Let us begin. We have much work to do."

Maisie silently placed her books in front of him.

"What is it, Maisie?"

"I don't think, Dr. Blanche, that I can have lessons with you anymore."

Maurice Blanche said nothing but nodded his head and studied Maisie's countenance. Silence seeped into the space between them, and Maurice immediately noticed the single tear that emerged from Maisie's right eye and drizzled down her face.

"Ah, yes, the challenge of position and place, I think."

Maisie sniffed and met Blanche's look. She nodded.

"Yes. It has been long overdue. We have been fortunate thus far, have we not, Maisie?"

Once again Maisie nodded She expected to be dismissed, as she would in turn dismiss her ambitions and the dream she had nurtured since first planning to visit the Comptons' library at three o'clock in the morning so long ago.

Instead Maurice took up the book he had assigned at their last meeting, along with her notes, and the lessons she had completed in the subjects of English, mathematics, and geography.

Looking through her work, Maurice inclined his head here, and raised his eyebrows there. Maisie said nothing, but inspected her hands and pulled at a loose thread in her white pinafore.

"Maisie. Please complete these two final chapters while I speak with Lady Rowan."

Once again Maisie was left, if only for a short time, to wonder at her fate, and whether all would be well. As Maurice Blanche left the room, Maisie took up the book and turned to the chapters he had indicated. But try as she might, she could not read past the first paragraph of her assignment and retain what she had read. Instead she put her right hand to her mouth and with her teeth worried a hangnail on her little finger. By the time Maurice Blanche returned with Lady Rowan and Carter, Maisie had to plunge her right hand into her pinafore pocket so that the blood now oozing from the cuticle would not be seen.

Clearly much discussion had taken place in the interim. It fell to Carter, as head of the domestic staff, to stand at Lady Rowan's side as she told Maisie of a plan that had been incubating and had just hatched, inspired by her genuine need. It was a plan that would in turn help Maisie. And not a moment too soon.

"Maisie, the Dowager Lady Compton lives in the dower house at Chelstone Manor, in Kent. My mother-in-law is in command of her faculties but has some difficulty in movement, and she does sleep long hours now that she is of advanced age. Her personal maid gave notice some weeks ago, due to impending marriage."

Lady Rowan glanced at Maurice Blanche and at Carter before continuing. "Maisie, I would like to offer you the position."

Maisie said nothing, but looked intently at Lady Rowan, then at

Carter, who simply nodded, then raised an eyebrow, and focused his gaze quickly on her hand in the pinafore pocket.

Maisie stood up straighter, twisted a handkerchief around the sore finger, and brought her hand to her side.

"The Dowager Lady Compton has only a small staff," said Lady Rowan, "as befits her needs. Aside from her personal maid and a nurse, household staff do not live at the dower house but at the manor. When we are in residence, as you know, Carter and Mrs. Crawford travel to Chelstone to join the staff. However, Mrs. Johnson, the housekeeper, is in sole charge of the household at Chelstone while we are in London."

Lady Rowan paused for a moment, walked to the window, and crossed her arms. She took a moment to look out at the garden before turning back into the room to continue.

"Employment with my mother-in-law will allow you some—let us say 'leeway'—to continue your work with Dr. Blanche. In addition you will not be subject to some of the scrutiny that you have experienced in recent weeks, although you *will* report to Mrs. Johnson."

Maisie looked at her feet, then at Carter, Lady Rowan, and Dr. Blanche, all of whom seemed to have grown several inches while Lady Rowan was speaking.

Maisie felt very small. And she was worried about her father.

As she remained silent, Carter raised an eyebrow, indicating that she should speak.

"Is there a bus so I can get back to London to see my father on Sundays?"

"There is a train service from the village, on the branch line via Tonbridge. But you may wish to make the visits to Mr. Dobbs farther apart, since the distance requires several hours of travel," replied Maurice Blanche.

Then he suggested that Maisie be given a day to consider the offer.

"You will see Mr. Carter with your decision tomorrow at five o'clock in the afternoon, Maisie?"

"Yes, sir. Thank you, sir—and thank you, Your Ladyship, Mr. Carter."

"Right you are. I will bid you goodnight."

Carter bowed to Lady Rowan, as did Dr. Blanche, while Maisie bobbed a curtsy, and put her hand back in her pocket, lest the company see her handkerchief bloodied from the bitten hangnail.

"I think, Mr. Carter, that Maisie should continue with her household responsibilities this evening, rather than her assignments from me. Such endeavors will be a useful accompaniment to the process of coming to a decision."

"Right you are, sir. Maisie?"

Maisie curtsied again, then left the room to return to her duties.

Blanche walked over to the window and looked out at the gardens. He had anticipated young Maisie's challenges, which had come later than he might have expected. How he despised wasted talent! He knew that the move to Kent would be a good one for her, but the decision to pursue her opportunity was one Maisie alone would have to make. He left the house, wending his way to familiar streets south of the Thames.

*I*t surprised the staff when Frankie Dobbs came unsummoned to the back door of the kitchen the next morning, to report that some very nice lettuces and tomatoes had just been brought in from Jersey, and would Mrs. Crawford be needing some for the dinner party on Friday night?

Usually Frankie would not see Maisie when he came to the house to deliver fruit and vegetables each week, but on this occasion Mrs. Crawford took no time at all to summon Maisie to see her father, for she knew that the motive for Frankie Dobbs's appearance extended beyond urgent notification of what was best at Covent Garden market.

"Dad, . . . Dad!" cried Maisie as she went to her father, put her arms around his waist, and held him to her.

"Now then, now then. What's all this? What will Mr. Carter say?"

"Oh Dad, I'm *so* glad you came to the house. What a coincidence!"

Maisie looked at her father inquisitively, then followed him up the outside stairs to the street, where Persephone waited, contentedly eating from the nosebag of oats attached to her bridle. Maisie told Frankie about the new position she had been offered with the Dowager Lady Compton.

"Just as well I 'appened by, then, innit, Love? Sounds like just what you need. Your mother and me always wanted to live in the country, thought it would be better for you than the Smoke. Go on. You go, love. You'll still see me."

"So you don't mind then, Dad?"

"No, I don't mind at all. I reckon bein' down there in the country will be a real treat for you. Hard work, mind, but a treat all the same."

Maisie gave Carter her answer that evening. It was agreed with Lady Rowan that she should leave at the end of the month. Yet even though he wanted her to see and learn all there was to see and learn, Frankie often felt as if fine sand were slipping through his fingers whenever he thought of his girl, Maisie.

CHAPTER THIRTEEN

aisie first came to Chelstone Manor in the autumn of 1913. She had traveled by train to Tonbridge, where she changed for Chelstone, on a small branch line. She'd brought one bag with her, containing clothes and personal belongings, and a small trunk in which she carried books, paper, and a clutch of assignments written in Maurice Blanche's compact almost indecipherable hand. And in her mind's eye Maisie carried a vision. During their last lesson before she left for Chelstone, he had asked Maisie what she might do with this education, this opportunity.

"Um, I don't really know, Dr. Blanche. I always thought I could teach. My mum wanted me to be a teacher. It's a good job for me, teaching."

"But?"

Maisie looked at Maurice Blanche, at the bright eyes that looked into the soul of a person so that they naturally revealed to him in words what he could silently observe.

"But. But I think I want to do something like what you do, Dr. Blanche."

Maurice Blanche made a church and steeple with his hands, and rested his upper lip on his forefingers. Two minutes passed before he looked up at Maisie.

"And what do I do, Maisie?"

"You heal people. That is, I *think* you heal people. In all sorts of ways. That's what I think."

Blanche nodded, leaned back in his chair, and looked out of the library window to the walled gardens of 15 Ebury Place.

"Yes, I think you could say that, Maisie."

"And I think you find out the truth. I think you look at what is right and wrong. And I think you have had lots of different . . . educations."

"Yes, Maisie, that is all correct. But what about that vision?"

"I want to go to Cambridge. To Girton College. Like you said, it's possible for an ordinary person like me to go, you know, as long as I can work and pass the exams."

"I don't think I ever used the word 'ordinary' to describe you, Maisie."

Maisie blushed, and Maurice continued with his questions. "And what will you study, Maisie?"

"I'm not sure. I am interested in the moral sciences, sir. When you told me about the different subjects—psychology, ethics, philosophy, logic—that's what I most wanted to study. I've already done lots of assignments in those subjects, and I like the work. It's not so—well—definite, is it? Sometimes it's like a maze, with no answers, only more questions. I like that, you know. I like the search. And it's what you want, isn't it, Dr. Blanche?"

Maisie looked at Maurice, and waited for his response.

"It is not what I want that is pertinent here, Maisie, but what you are drawn to. I will, however, concur that you have a certain gift for understanding and appreciating the constituent subjects of the moral sciences curriculum. Now then, you are young yet, Maisie. We have plenty of time for more discussion of this subject. Perhaps we should look at your assignments—but remember to keep those hallowed halls of Girton College uppermost in your mind."

$\mathcal{T}$he old lady was not too demanding, and there was the nurse to take a good deal of the responsibility for her care. Maisie ensured that the dowager's rooms were always warm, that her clothes were freshly laundered and laid out each day. She brushed her fine gray hair and twisted it into a bun which the dowager wore under a lace cap. She read to the dowager, and brought meals to her from the main house. For much of the time, the old lady slept in her rooms, or sat by the window with her eyes closed. Occasionally, on a fine day, Maisie would take her outside in a wheelchair, or support her as she stood in the garden, insisting that she was quite well enough to attend to a dead rose, or reach up to inhale the scent of fresh apple blossom. Then she tired and leaned on Maisie as she was assisted to her chair once again. But for much of the time Maisie was lonely.

There was little conversation with staff up at the manor, and despite everything, Maisie missed Enid and her wicked sense of humor. The other members of staff at Chelstone would not speak with her readily, or joke with her, or treat her as one of their own. Yet though she missed the people she had come to love, she did enjoy having solitude for her studies. Each Saturday, Maisie walked into the village to post a brown-paper-wrapped package to Dr. Blanche, and each Saturday she picked up a new envelope with her latest assignment, and his comments on her work of the week before. In January 1914 Maurice decided that Maisie was ready to take the Girton College entrance examinations.

$\mathcal{I}$n March, Maurice accompanied Maisie to Cambridge for the examinations, meeting her early at Liverpool Street Station for the journey to Cambridge, then on to the small village of Girton, home of the famous ladies' college of Cambridge University. She remembered watching from the train window as the streets of London gave way to farmland that was soft in the way that Kent was soft, but instead of the green undulating hills of the Weald of Kent, with hedges dividing a patchwork quilt of farms, woodland, and small villages, the Cambridgeshire fens were flat, so that a person could see for miles and miles into the distance.

The grand buildings of Cambridge, the wonderful gardens of Girton College two miles north of the town, the large lecture hall, being taken to a desk, the papers put in front of her, the hours and hours of questions and answers, the nib of her pen cutting into the joint at the top of the second finger of her right hand as she quickly filled page after page with her fine, bold script, were unforgettable. Thirst had suddenly gripped at her throat until she felt faint for lack of breath as she left the hall, whose ceiling now seemed to be moving down toward her. Her head was spinning as she leaned on Maurice, who had been waiting for her. He steadied her, instructing her to breathe deeply, as they walked slowly to the village teashop.

While hot tea was poured and fresh scones placed in front of them, Maurice allowed Maisie to rest before asking for her account of each question on the examination papers, and her responses to them. He nodded as she described her answers, occasionally sipping tea or wiping a crumb from the corner of his mouth.

"I believe, Maisie, that you have done very well."

"I don't know, Dr. Blanche, sir. But I did my best."

"Of course. Of course."

"Dr. Blanche. You went to Oxford, didn't you?"

"Yes, indeed, Maisie—and I was only a little younger than you at the time. Of course, as I am male, a degree could be conferred upon me. But there will be a time, I hope before too long, when women will also earn degrees for their advanced academic studies."

Maisie flicked the long braid of jet black hair from her shoulder and felt its weight along her spine as she sat back in her chair to listen to Maurice.

"And I was also fortunate to study in Paris at the Sorbonne, and in Edinburgh."

"Scotland."

"I'm glad to see that you have a grasp of geography, Maisie." Maurice looked over his spectacles at Maisie and smiled at her. "Yes, the Department of Legal Medicine."

"What did you do there, Dr. Blanche?"

"Learned to read the story told by a dead body. Especially when the person did not die of natural causes."

"Oh . . ." said Maisie, temporarily bereft of speech. She pushed away the crumbly scone and took a long sip of the soothing tea. Maisie slowly regained energy after the ordeal of the past few hours, which she had endured along with several dozen other hopeful students. "Dr. Blanche. May I ask you a question?"

"Of course."

"Why did you want to learn about the dead?"

"Ah. A good question, Maisie. Suffice it to say that sometimes one's calling finds one first. When I first came to Oxford it was to study economics and politics; then I went to the Sorbonne to study philosophy—so you see we have similar interests there—but it was as I traveled, seeing so much suffering, that medicine found me."

"And legal medicine? The dead bodies?"

Maurice looked at his watch. "That is a story for another time. Let us now walk over to the college again, where no doubt you will be studying later this very year. The gardens really are quite lovely."

*T*he Comptons had gathered a coterie of important and influential guests, not only to sample the delights of a July weekend in the country but for animated discussion and conjecture upon the discord that had been festering in Europe since June, when the Austrian archduke was assassinated in Serbia. It was predicted that the conflict, which had started two years earlier, in 1912, in the Balkans, would become general war, and as the Kaiser's armies reportedly moved into position along the Belgian border, fear of its escalation grew. Dread stalked Europe, snaking its way from the corridors of government to the households of ordinary people.

Carter was in full battle mode for the onslaught of visitors, while Mrs. Crawford held her territory in the kitchen, blasting out orders to any maid or footman who came within range of her verbal fire. Lady Rowan swore she could hear Cook's voice reverberating through every wooden beam in the medieval manor house, though even she declined to intervene at such a time.

"Rowan, we have the very best cook in London and Kent, but I fear we also have the one with the loudest voice."

"Don't worry, Julian, you know she'll pipe down when everything's in its place and the guests start to arrive."

"Indeed, indeed. In the meantime, I wonder if I should tell the War Office about her, in advance. She could put a seasoned general to shame—have you seen how she marshals her troops? I should have every new subaltern serve in Cook Crawford's battalion for a month. We could overcome the Hun by launching meat pies clear across France and into the Kaiser's palace!"

"Julian, don't be absurd—and don't be so full of certainty that Britain will be at war," said Lady Rowan. "By the way, I understand that our Miss Dobbs received a letter from Girton this morning."

"Did she, by Jove? Well, not before time, my dear. I don't think I could bear to look at those nail-bitten fingers holding onto the tea tray any longer."

"She's had a hard life, Julian." Lady Rowan looked out of the windows and over the land surrounding Chelstone Manor. "We can't presume to imagine how difficult it has been for her. She's such a bright girl."

"And for each Maisie Dobbs, there are probably ten more that you can't save. Remember, we may not have done her any favors, Rowan. Life can be very difficult for someone of her class at Cambridge."

"Yes, I know, Julian. But times are changing. I am glad that we were able to contribute in some way."

She turned from the window to look at her husband. "Now then, shall we go downstairs to see what news the letter from Girton has brought? I don't know if you've noticed, but it has gone awfully quiet in the house."

Lord and Lady Compton went together to the large drawing room, where Lord Julian rang the bell for Carter. The impeccably turned-out and always punctual butler answered the call within a minute.

"Your Lordship, Your Ladyship."

"Carter, what news does Miss Dobbs have from Cambridge?"

"Very, very good news, M'Lord. Miss Dobbs has been accepted. We are all terribly proud of her."

"Oh, that's wonderful, wonderful!" Lady Rowan clapped her hands. "We must get word to Maurice, Julian. Carter, send Miss Dobbs to see us immediately."

CHAPTER FOURTEEN

*M*aisie could not wait to tell Frankie Dobbs her news in person, and as soon as she could, traveled by train to Charing Cross Station, and from there to the small soot-blackened terraced house that had once been her home.

"Well, what do you know? Our little Maisie all grown up and going away to the university. Blow me down, your mum would have been chuffed."

Frankie Dobbs held his daughter by the shoulders and looked into her eyes, his own smarting with tears of pride—and of concern.

"Do you think you're ready for this, love?"

Frankie pulled out a chair and beckoned Maisie to sit with him by the coal stove in the small kitchen. "It's a big step, isn't it?"

"I'll do all right, Dad. I've won a place, and next year if I do well, I might get a college scholarship. That's what I'm aiming for. Lord and Lady Compton will be my sponsors, for the first year, anyway, and I've been putting a bit by as well. Lady Rowan is going to give me some of her day clothes that she doesn't want, and Mrs.

Crawford said she'll help me with tailoring them to fit me, although there are strict rules about what I can wear. Not much different from a maid's uniform, but without the pinny, from what I can make out."

Maisie rubbed her father's hands, which seemed strangely cold.

"I told you, I'll be all right, Dad. And at Christmas, Easter, and summer, I can come back to the house to earn some more money."

Frankie Dobbs could barely meet his daughter's eyes, knowing only too well that it would be nigh on impossible for Maisie to return to the Comptons' employ once she had left. He knew how it was in those houses, and once she had moved beyond her station, she could never go back. She'd been lucky so far, but after she left, she wouldn't be so easily accepted. The gap between Maisie and the other staff would become a chasm. And what worried Frankie more than anything was that Maisie might not ever fit in to *any* station, that she would forever be betwixt and between.

"So when will you be leaving?"

"I'll start in the autumn. They call it the Michaelmas term, you know, like those mauve Michaelmas daisies that bloom in September, the ones Mum used to love. I had to get special permission because I'm not quite eighteen."

Frankie got up from his seat and rubbed at his back. He wanted to get the conversation back to a point at which he could voice his offer.

"Well, talking about 'avin' a bit more, like we were before we started talking about the daisies, I've got something for you, love." Frankie reached up and took down a large earthenware flour jar from the shelf above the stove.

"Here you are, Love. After I paid off the debts, you know, after your mother . . . I started putting a bit by each week meself. For you. Knowing that you'd be doing something important one day, where a bit extra might come in 'andy."

Maisie took the jar, her hands shaking. She lifted the lid and looked into the earthenware depths. There were pound notes, some brand new ten-shilling notes, florins, half-crowns, and shillings. The jar was full of Frankie Dobbs's savings for Maisie.

"Oh, Dad . . ." Maisie stood up and, clutching the jar of money with one hand and her father with the other, held him to her.

In August 1914 people still went about their business, and war seemed to be something that had nothing to do with ordinary life. But then a boy she knew in the village was in uniform, and certain foods were just a little more difficult to find. A footman at the Belgravia house enlisted, and so did the grooms and young gardeners at Chelstone. Then one weekend Maisie was called to Lady Rowan's sitting room at Chelstone.

"Maisie, I am beside myself. The grooms have all enlisted, and I am fearfully worried about my hunters. I have spoken to all sorts of people, but the young men are going into the services. Look, I know this is unusual, but I wonder, do you think your father might consider the position?"

"Well, M'Lady, I don't really know. There's Persephone, and his business."

"There is a cottage in the grounds for him if he wants it. You'll be able to see him when you are not at Girton, of course, and his mare can be stabled here. They will both be well looked after."

The next day Maisie traveled by train to London to see her father. To her complete surprise, Frankie Dobbs said he would "think about it" when she told him of the offer from Lady Rowan. "After all, I'm not getting any younger, and neither is Persephone. She could do with a bit o' the old fresh country air. And 'er Ladyship's been very good to you, so come to think of it, if I 'elped 'er out, it'd be only right. It's not as if I'm a stranger to Kent, 'aving been down there picking the old 'ops every year when I was a bit of a nipper meself."

Frankie Dobbs and Persephone moved from Lambeth on a misty, unseasonably cold morning in late August 1914, to take up residence in the groom's cottage and stables, respectively, at Chelstone Manor. Instead of rising at three o'clock to take Persephone to Covent Garden market and then setting out on his rounds, Frankie now enjoyed a lie-in before rising at five o'clock to feed Lady Rowan's hunters and Persephone, who seemed to be relishing her own retirement. In a short time Frankie Dobbs was being feted by Lady Rowan as the man who knew everything there was to know about the grooming, feeding, and well-being of horses. But it was a deeper knowledge that would endear him to her for the rest of her life.

Only days remained before Maisie was to leave for Cambridge, so time spent in each other's company was of prime importance to Maisie and her father. They had resumed the ritual of working together in making a fuss of Persephone as often as possible. It was on such an occasion, while they were working and talking about the latest war news, that Lady Rowan paid a surprise visit.

"I say, anybody there?"

Maisie snapped to attention, but Frankie Dobbs, while respectful, simply replied, "In 'ere with Persephone, Your Ladyship."

"Mr. Dobbs. Thank goodness. I am beside myself."

Maisie immediately went to Lady Rowan, who always claimed to be "beside herself" in a crisis, despite a demeanor that suggested otherwise.

"Mr. Dobbs, they are coming to take my hunters—and possibly even your mare. Lord Compton has received word from the War Office that our horses are to be inspected for service this week. They are coming on Tuesday to take them. I *cannot* let them go. I don't want to be unpatriotic, but they are my hunters."

"And they ain't taking my Persephone either, Your Ladyship."

Frankie Dobbs walked toward his faithful old horse, who nuzzled at his jacket for the treat she knew would be forthcoming. He took sweet apple pieces from his pocket and held them out to Persephone, feeling the comforting warmth of her velvety nose in his hand, before turning back to Lady Rowan.

"Tuesday, eh? You leave it to me."

"Oh, Mr. Dobbs—everything depends upon you. What will you do? Take them somewhere and hide them?"

Frankie laughed. "Oh no. I think I might be seen running away with this little lot, Your Ladyship. No, I won't have to run anywhere. But here's one thing—" Frankie Dobbs looked at Maisie and at Lady Rowan. "I don't want anyone coming in these stables until I say so. And, Your Ladyship, I'll come to the 'ouse on Tuesday mornin' and tell you what to say. But the main thing is, whatever you see or 'ear, you're not to mind or to say anything else, other than what I tell you. You've got to trust me."

Lady Rowan stood taller, regained her composure, and looked directly at Frankie Dobbs. "I trust you implicitly."

Maisie's father nodded, tipped his cap toward Lady Rowan, and then smiled at Maisie. The stately woman walked toward the stable door, then turned around. "Mr. Dobbs. One thing we spoke about only briefly when you first came to Chelstone. I seem to remember that you were at a racing yard as a boy."

"Newmarket, Your Ladyship. From the time I was twelve to the time I came back to 'elp my father with the business at nineteen. Bit big for a jockey, I was."

"I expect you learned quite a thing or two about horses, didn't you?"

"Oh yes, Your Ladyship. Quite a thing or two. Saw a lot, good and bad."

The men from the War Office came to Chelstone at lunchtime on Tuesday. Lady Rowan led them to the stables apologizing profusely and explaining, as she had been instructed by Frankie Dobbs, that she feared her horses might not be suitable for service as they had contracted a sickness that even her groom could not cure. They were met by Frankie Dobbs, who stood in tears by Sultan, her jet black hunter.

The once-noble horse hung his head low as foam dropped from his open mouth. His eyes rolled back in his head as he struggled for breath. Lady Rowan gasped and looked at Frankie, who would not meet her alarmed eyes with his own.

"By God, what is wrong with the beast?" asked the tall man in uniform, who held a baton under his arm. He stepped carefully toward Sultan, avoiding any soiled straw that might compromise the shine on his highly polished boots.

"Not anything I've seen for years. Caused by worm. Bacteria," Frankie Dobbs replied, and spoke to Lady Rowan directly. "I'm sorry, Your Ladyship. We'll probably lose them all by tomorrow. That old cart 'orse will be first. On account of 'er age."

The men stopped briefly to glance into Persephone's stall, where Frankie Dobbs's faithful horse lay on the ground.

"Lady Compton. Our sympathies. The country needs one hundred and sixty-five thousand horses, but we need them to be fit, strong, and able to be of service on the battlefield."

Lady Rowan's tears were genuine. She had been primed by Frankie as to what she should say, but had not been prepared for what she would see. "Yes . . . yes . . . indeed. I wish you luck, gentlemen."

The two men were soon gone. After seeing them off, Lady Rowan ran immediately to the stables once again, where Frankie Dobbs was working furiously to pour a chalky liquid down Sultan's throat. Maisie was in another stall, feeding the liquid to Ralph. Persephone and Hamlet were on their feet.

Lady Rowan said nothing, but walked over to Hamlet, and touched the pale, drawn skin around his eyes. As she brought her hand away she noticed the white powder on her gloves and smiled.

"Mr. Dobbs, I shall never ask what you did today. But I will remember this forever. I know what I asked of you was wrong, but I just couldn't bear to lose them."

"And I couldn't bear to lose Persephone, Your Ladyship. But I 'ave to warn you. This war is far from over. You keep these 'ere horses on your land. Don't let anyone outside see them, just them as works 'ere. Times like these changes folk. Keep the animals close to 'ome."

Lady Rowan nodded and gave a carrot to each horse in turn.

"Oh, and by the way, Your Ladyship. I wonder if Mrs. Crawford could use two and a half dozen egg yolks? Terrible waste if she can't."

*T*en household staff sat down to dinner at the big table in the kitchen at Chelstone Manor on Maisie's last night before leaving for Cambridge. She was on the cusp of her new life. The Comptons were in residence, so the servants whom Maisie loved from the Belgravia house were there to see her off.

Carter sat at the head of the table in the carver's chair, and Mrs. Crawford sat at the opposite end within easy striking distance of the big cast-iron coal-fired stove. Maisie sat next to her father and opposite Enid. Even Enid, who had been summoned from the London house to assist with late-summer entertaining at Chelstone, joined in the fun and looked happy: She had brightened up considerably since Mr. James had returned from Canada.

"Gaw lummy, I think the world's spinnin' even faster these days. What with the war, Master James coming home, Maisie goin' to Cambridge—Cambridge, our Maisie Dobbs! Then there's all the important people coming tomorrow to meet with Lord Compton," said Cook, as she took her seat after a final check on the apple pie.

"All arrangements are in order, Mrs. Crawford. We will make a final round of inspection after our little celebration here. Now then . . ."

Standing up, Carter cleared his throat and smiled. "I'll ask you to join me in a toast."

Chairs scraped backward, people coughed as they stood up and nudged one another. The entire complement of household staff turned to face Maisie, who blushed as all eyes were upon her.

"To our own Maisie Dobbs! Congratulations, Maisie. We've all seen you work hard, and we know you will be a credit to Lord and Lady Compton, to your father—and to us all. So we've got a small token of our affection. For you to use at the university."

Mrs. Crawford reached under the table and took out a large flat box, which she passed down the table to Carter with one hand, while the other rubbed at her now tearful eyes with a large white hand-kerchief.

"From all the staff at Chelstone Manor and the Compton residence in London—Maisie, we're proud of you."

Maisie blushed, and reached for the plain brown cardboard box. "Oh, my goodness. Oh, dear. Oh—"

"Just open it, Mais, for Gawd's sake!" said Enid, inspiring a scowl from Mrs. Crawford.

Maisie pulled at the string, took off the lid, and drew back the fine tissue paper to reveal a butter-soft yet sturdy black leather document case with a silver clasp.

"Oh . . . oh . . . it's . . . it's . . . beautiful! Thank you, thank you. All of you."

Carter wasted no time in taking his glass and continuing with the toast. "To our own Maisie Dobbs . . ."

Voices echoed around the table.

"To Maisie Dobbs."

"Well done, Mais."

"You show 'em for us, Maisie!"

"Maisie Dobbs!"

Maisie nodded, whispering, "Thank you . . . thank you . . . thank you."

"And before we sit down," said Carter, as the assembled group were bending halfway down to their seats again. "To our country, to our boys who are going over to France. Godspeed and God save the King!"

"God save the King."

The following day Maisie stood on the station platform, this time with an even larger trunk of books that far outweighed her case of personal belongings. She clutched her black document case tightly, afraid that she would lose this most wonderful gift. Carter and Mrs. Crawford had chosen it, maintaining that Maisie Dobbs should not have to go to university without a smart case for her papers.

On her journey up to Cambridge, when Maisie changed trains at Tonbridge for the main service to London, she was taken aback by the multitude of uniformed men lining up on the platform. Freshly posted handbills gave a hint of things to come:

LONDON, BRIGHTON & SOUTH COAST RAILWAYS
MOBILIZATION OF TROOPS
PASSENGERS ARE HEREBY NOTIFIED THAT IT MAY BE NECESSARY
TO SUSPEND OR ALTER TRAINS WITHOUT PREVIOUS NOTICE

It was clear that the journey to Cambridge would be a long one. Sweethearts and the newly married held tightly to each other amid the crush of bodies on the platform. Mothers cried into sodden handkerchiefs; sons assured them, "I'll be back before you know it," and fathers stood stoically silent.

Maisie passed a father and son standing uncomfortably together in the grip of unspoken emotion. As she brushed by, she saw the older man clap his son on the shoulder. He pursed his lips together, firmly clamping his grief in place, while the son looked down at his feet. A small Border collie sat still between them, secure on a leash held by the son. The panting dog looked between father and son as they began to speak quietly.

"You mind and do your best, son. Your mother would have been proud of you."

"I know, Dad," said the son, moving his gaze to his father's lapels.

"And you mind you keep your head out of the way of the Kaiser's boys, lad. We don't want you messing up that uniform, do we?"

The boy laughed, for he was a boy and not yet a man.

"All right, Dad, I'll keep my boots shined, and you look after Patch."

"Safe as houses, me and Patch. We'll be waiting for you when you come home, son."

Maisie watched as the man pressed his hand down even harder on the young man's shoulder. "Listen to that. Your train is coming in. This is it, time to be off. You mind and do your best."

The son nodded, bent down to stroke the dog, who playfully wagged her tail and jumped up to lick the boy's face. He met his father's eyes only briefly, and after passing the leash to the older man, was suddenly swallowed up in a sea of moving khaki. A guard with a megaphone ordered, "Civilians to keep back from the train" as the older man stood on tiptoe, trying to catch one last glimpse of his departing son.

Maisie moved away to allow the soldiers to board their train, and watched the man bend down, pick up the dog, and bury his face in the animal's thick coat. And as his shoulders shook with the grief he dared not show, the dog twisted her head to lick comfort into his neck.

CHAPTER FIFTEEN

*U*pon arrival at Girton College, Maisie registered with the Porter's Lodge and was directed to the room that had been assigned to her for the academic year. Assured that the trunk of books would be brought up to her room in due course, clutching her bag, she began to leave the lodge, following the directions given by the porter, who suddenly called her back. "Oh, Miss! A parcel arrived today for you. Urgent delivery, to be given to you immediately."

Maisie took the brown paper parcel and immediately recognized the small slanted writing. It was from Maurice Blanche.

Few women were already in residence when Maisie arrived, and the hallways were quiet as she made her way to her room. She was anxious to unwrap the parcel, and paid hardly any attention to her new surroundings after opening the door to her room. Instead she quickly put her belongings down by the wardrobe and, taking a seat in the small armchair, began to open the package. Under the brown paper, a layer of tissue covered a letter from Maurice, and a leather-bound book with blank pages. Inside the cover of the book, Maurice had copied the words of Søren Kierkegaard, words that he had quoted to her from memory in their last meeting before her journey to Cambridge. It was as if Maurice were in the room with her, so strong was his voice in her mind as she read the words: "There is nothing of which every man is so afraid, as getting to know how enormously much he is capable of doing and becoming." She closed the book, continuing to hold it as she read the letter in which Maurice spoke of the gift:

> In seeking to fill your mind, I omitted to instruct you in the opposite exercise. This small book is for your daily writings, when the day is newborn and before you embark upon the richness of study and intellectual encounter. My instruction, Maisie, is to simply write a page each day. There is no set subject, save that which the waking mind has held close in sleep.

Suddenly the loud crash of a door swinging back on its hinges, followed by the double thump of two large leather suitcases landing one after the other on the floor of the room next door, heralded the arrival of her neighbor. Amplified by the empty corridor, she heard a deep sigh followed by the sound of a foot kicking one of the cases.

"What I wouldn't give for a gin and tonic!"

A second later, with wrapping paper still between her fingers and her head raised to follow the audible wake of her neighbor, Maisie heard footsteps coming toward her room. In her hurry to open the parcel from Maurice, she had left her door ajar, allowing the young woman immediate access.

A fashionably dressed girl with dark chestnut hair stood in front of her, and held out her finely manicured hand. "Priscilla Evernden. Delighted to meet you—Maisie Dobbs, isn't it? Wouldn't happen to have a cigarette, would you?"

*I*t seemed to Maisie that she lived two lives at Cambridge. There were her days of study and learning, which began in her room before dawn, and ended after her lectures and tutorials with more study in the evening. She spent Saturday afternoons and Sunday mornings in the college chapel, rolling bandages and knitting socks, gloves, and scarves for men at the front. It was a cold winter in the trenches, and no sooner had word gone out that men needed warm clothes than every woman suddenly seemed to be knitting.

At least Maisie felt that she was doing something for the war, but it was her studies that were always at the forefront of her mind. If anything, the endless talk of war seemed to her a distraction, something that she just wanted to be over, so that she could get on with her life at Cambridge—and whatever might come after.

There were times when Maisie was thankful that a very bright spark was resident in the next room. Priscilla seemed to gravitate toward Maisie and, surprising Maisie herself, appeared to enjoy her company.

"My dear girl, how many pairs of these infernal socks must one knit? I am sure I have kitted out an entire battalion."

Another sharp observation from Priscilla Evernden. In truth Maisie loved Priscilla's theatrical tone as much as she had loved Enid's down-to-earth wit, and she was only too aware that, though miles apart in their upbringing, the two girls shared a ready exuberance that Maisie envied. Despite her early fumblings with the language of the aristocracy, Enid was sure of who she was and sure of what she wanted to be. Priscilla was equally sure of herself, and Maisie loved the sweep and flourish of her language, punctuated as it was by exaggerated movements of her hands and arms.

"You seem to be doing quite well, really," said Maisie.

"Oh, sod it!" said Priscilla as she fumbled with her knitting needles, "I fear, dear Maisie, that you are clearly made of knitting stock, one only has to look at that plait hanging down your back. Good Lord, girl, that plait could be a loaf at Harvest Festival! Obviously you have been bred for knitting."

Maisie blushed. Over the years the edges had been knocked away from her London accent. She might not pass for the aristocracy, but she could certainly be taken for a clergyman's daughter. And not one bred for knitting.

"I hardly think so, Pris."

"Well, I suppose not. One only has to look at your academic work, and those books that you read. Anyone who can read those turgid tomes can make short work of a sock. Dear God, give me a drink that bites back and good tale of love and lust any day of the week."

Maisie dropped a stitch, and looked up at Priscilla. "Now, don't tell me that, Pris. Why did you come up to Cambridge?"

Priscilla was tall, giving the impression of strength, though she carried no extra weight. Her chestnut hair hung loose around her shoulders, and she wore a man's shirt with a pair of man's trousers, "borrowed" from her brother before he left for France. She claimed that they wouldn't be in fashion by the time he returned anyway, and swore that she would only wear them indoors.

"Dear girl, I came to Cambridge because I could, and because my dear mother and father were ready to fling themselves burning into the lake rather than have me roll in through the window at two in the morning again. Out of sight, out of mind, darling. . . . Oh my dear Lord, look at this sock! I don't know what I am doing wrong here, but it's like knitting into a funnel."

Maisie looked up from her work.

"Let me see."

"Whoopee! M. Dobbs to the rescue."

Priscilla got up from her place on the old armchair, where she had been sitting sideways with her legs dangling over the arm, while Maisie sat on the floor on a cushion.

"I'm going out now, and to hell with Miss What's-Her-Name downstairs' curfew."

"Priscilla, what if you get caught? You're not supposed to be out late. You could be sent down for this."

"Dear Maisie, I will not get caught, because I will not be coming in late. If anyone asks, I know you will say that I've taken to my bed. And of course, when I come in at the crack of dawn tomorrow—

well—I needed the early morning fresh air to clear the mind after my indisposition."

Minutes later Priscilla reappeared, dressed from head to toe in evening wear, and carrying a small bag.

"One thing you have to admit about war, darling—there's nothing quite like a man in uniform. See you at breakfast—and for heaven's sake do stop fretting!"

"*G*ood Lord, Maisie Dobbs, where do you think you are going with those books?"

Priscilla Evernden was leaning out of the window of Maisie's room, and turned back to draw upon the cigarette she gamely smoked through a long ivory holder. It was the end of her second term at Girton, and Maisie was packing to go back to Chelstone for Easter.

"Well, Pris, I don't want to fall behind in my work, so I thought it wouldn't hurt—"

"Tell me, Maisie, when do you ever have fun, girl?"

Maisie reddened and began to fold a cotton blouse. The intensity of her movements as she ran the side of her hand along the creases and patted down the collar revealed her discomfort.

"I enjoy reading, Priscilla. I enjoy my studies here."

"Hmmm. You'd probably enjoy it a lot more if you went out a bit. You were only away for a few days at Christmas."

Maisie smarted, remembering her return to a depressed household at the end of her first term. The war had not ended by Christmas—as predicted—and, though nothing was said, Maisie felt that others found her studies frivolous at a time when so many women were volunteering for jobs previously held by men who had enlisted to serve their country.

Holding a woolen cardigan by the shoulders, Maisie folded it and placed it in her case before looking up at Priscilla. "You know,

Priscilla, life is different for some people. I don't go back to my horses, cars, and parties. You know that."

Priscilla walked toward the armchair and sat down, folding her legs to one side. Once again she drew heavily on the cigarette, leaned her head back, and blew smoke rings toward the ceiling. Then, holding her cigarette to one side, she looked at Maisie directly. "For all my strange, peculiar privileged ways, Maisie, I am quite acute. You wear your sackcloth and ashes a little too proudly at times. We both know that you will do terribly well here. Academically. But I tell you this, Maisie—we are all a long time dead when we go, if you know what I mean. This is our only ride on the merry-go-round."

She drew again on the cigarette and continued. "I have three brothers in France now. Do you think I'm going to sit here and mourn? Hell, no! I'm going to have fun enough for all of us. Enough fun for this time on earth. And just because it took a tremendous leap for you to be here doesn't mean that you can't enjoy life along with all this—this—studying." She waved a hand toward the books.

Maisie looked up from her packing. "You don't understand."

"Well, perhaps I don't. But here's what I do know. You don't have to rush back to wherever it is you are rushing back to. Not this evening, anyway. Why not go tomorrow? Come out with me tonight. We may not have a chance again."

"What do you mean?"

"Oh, look at me, Maisie. I really am not cut out for all this. I received a severe reprimand when I arrived back here after my last evening out, and was reminded that when I took up my place, I had denied another, more deserving young woman the opportunity to study. Which is true, no getting away from it. So, I'm leaving—and quite frankly, I'm sick of sitting on the sidelines either listening to crusty old dons or knitting socks when I can do something far more useful. And who knows, I might even have an adventure!"

"What are you going to do?"

Maisie walked over to the chair and sat on the arm, next to Priscilla.

"Got to find yourself a new person to share rooms with, Maisie. I'm off to France."

Maisie drew breath sharply. Priscilla was the last person she thought would enlist for service. "Will you nurse?"

"Good Lord, no! Did you see my church hall bandages? If there's one thing I cannot do, it's walk around playing Florence Nightingale in a long frock—although I will have to get a First Aid Nursing Certificate. No, I have other arrows to my bow."

Maisie laughed. The thought of the dilettante Priscilla having skills that could be used in France was worthy of mirth.

"You may laugh, Maisie. But you've never seen me drive. I'm off to be a Fannie!"

"A what?"

"Fannie. F-A-N-Y. First Aid Nursing Yeomanry. An all-women ambulance corps. Actually they are not in France yet—although from what I understand, it might not be long, as Mrs. McDougal—she's the head of FANY—is planning to ask the War Office to consider using women drivers for motor ambulances. Apparently you have to be twenty-three to go to France, so I am extending the truth a little—and don't ask me how, Maisie, please."

"When did you learn to drive?"

"Three brothers, Maisie." Priscilla leaned forward to take the cigarette stub from the holder, and to press in a fresh cigarette, which she took from an engraved silver case drawn from her pocket. "When you grow up with three brothers you forget your cuts, scrapes, and bruises, and concentrate on your bowling arm, on coming back in one piece from the hunting field, and on not being run over by the lugworms when they come to the table. And unless you show that you are as good at everything as they are, you find that you spend virtually all your time running behind them screaming like a banshee, 'Me too, me too!'"

Priscilla looked over her shoulder to the gardens beyond the window and bit her bottom lip. She turned and continued telling her story.

"The chauffeur taught us all to drive. At first it was only going to be the boys, but I threatened to tell all if I was not included. And now the fact is, my dear, I simply cannot have them in France without me. It's 'Me too, me too!'"

Priscilla wiped the hint of a tear from the inner corner of her left eye and smiled.

"So, what do you say to a party this evening? Despite my dismal record, I have permission to go out—probably because they will soon see the back of me, and also the hostess this evening is a benefactor. How about it, Maisie? You can go back to wherever it is you go to wash the ashes from your sackcloth tomorrow."

Maisie smiled and looked at Priscilla, sparkling in defiance of what was considered good behavior for young women at Girton. There was something about her friend that reminded her of Lady Rowan.

"Whose party?"

Priscilla blew another smoke ring.

"Given by family friends, the Lynches, for their son, Simon. Royal Army Medical Corps. Brilliant doctor. Always the one who remained at the bottom of the tree just in case anyone fell from the top branches, when we were children. He leaves for France in a day or two."

"Will they mind?"

"Maisie, I could turn up with a tribe and no one would turn a hair. The Lynch family are like that. Oh, do come. Simon will adore it. The more the merrier for his send-off."

Maisie smiled at Priscilla. Perhaps it *would* do her good. And Priscilla was leaving.

"What about permission?"

"Don't worry, I'll take care of that—and I promise, all above board. I'll telephone Margaret Lynch to make the necessary arrangements."

Maisie bit her lip for just a second longer.

"Yes. I'll come. Though I've nothing to wear, Pris."

"No excuse, Maisie darling, absolutely no excuse. Come with me!"

Priscilla took Maisie by the arm and led her to her own adjacent room. Pointing to the chair for Maisie to take a seat, she pulled at least a dozen gowns of various colors, fabrics, and styles from her wardrobe and threw them on the bed, determined to find the perfect dress for Maisie.

"I think this midnight blue is really you, Maisie. Here, let's just pull the belt—oh gosh, you are a skinny thing aren't you? Now let me just pin this here . . ."

"Pris, I look like two penn'orth of hambone trussed up for the butcher's window."

"There. That's just perfect," replied Priscilla, "Now step back, step back. Lovely. Very nice. You shall have that dress. Have your Mrs. Whatever-Her-Name-Is at Chelstone hem it properly for you."

"But, Priscilla—"

"Nonsense. It's yours. And make the most of it—I saw a bill posted yesterday that I memorized just to remind myself to have some fun while I can."

Priscilla stood to attention, mimicked a salute, and affected an authoritarian mode of speech: TO DRESS EXTRAVAGANTLY IN WARTIME IS WORSE THAN BAD FORM. IT IS UNPATRIOTIC!

She began to laugh as she continued adjusting the blue silk dress on Maisie's slender frame.

"I'll have no need of evening dresses in France, and besides, there will be new styles to choose from when I get back."

Maisie nodded and looked down at the dress. "There's another thing, Pris."

Priscilla took up her cigarette, placed her hand on her hip, and raised an eyebrow. "Now what's your excuse, Maisie?"

"Priscilla, I can't dance."

"Oh, good Lord, girl!"

Priscilla stubbed out the cigarette in the overflowing ashtray, walked over to her gramophone near the window, selected a record from the cabinet below, placed it on the turntable, wound it up using the small handle at the side of the machine, and set the arm across the record. As the needle caught the first spiral ridge in the thick black disc, Priscilla danced toward Maisie.

"Keep the dress on. You'll need to practice in what you'll be wearing tonight. Right. Now then, start by watching me."

Priscilla positioned her hands on imaginary shoulders in front of her, as if held in the arms of a young man, and as the music began she continued.

"Feet like so, and forward, side, together; back, side, together; watch me, Maisie. And forward, side, together . . ."

A car had been sent to collect Priscilla and Maisie, and as they climbed aboard for the journey to the Lynches' large house in Grantchester, Maisie felt butterflies in her stomach. It was the first time she had ever been to a party that had not been held in a kitchen. There were special Christmas and Easter dinners downstairs at the Belgravia house and at Chelstone, and of course she had been given a wonderful sendoff by the staff. But this was a real party.

Margaret Lynch came to greet Priscilla as soon as her arrival was announced. "Priscilla, darling. So good of you to come. Simon is dying for news of the boys. He can't wait to get over there, you know."

"I have much to tell, Margaret. But let me introduce my friend, Maisie Dobbs."

"How lovely to meet you, my dear. Any friend of Priscilla's is welcome here."

"Thank you, Mrs. Lynch." Maisie started to bob, only to feel a sharp kick from Priscilla.

"Now then, you girls, let's see if we can get a couple of these young gentlemen to escort you in to the dining room. Oh, there's Simon now. Simon!"

Simon. Captain Simon Lynch, RAMC. He had greeted Priscilla as one would greet a tomboy sister, asking for news of her brothers, his childhood friends. And as he turned to Maisie, she felt a shiver that began in her ankles and seemed to end in the pit of her stomach.

"A pleasure to meet you, Miss Dobbs. And will the British Army be at your mercy as you sit behind the wheel of a baker's lorry, converted and pressed into service as an ambulance?"

Priscilla gave Simon a playful thump on the arm as Maisie met his green eyes. She blushed and quickly looked at the ground. "No. I think I would be a terrible driver, Captain Lynch."

"Simon. Oh, do call me Simon. Now then, I think I'd like a Girton lass on each arm. After all, this is my last evening before I leave."

As a string quartet began to play, Simon Lynch crooked an elbow toward each girl and led them into the dining room.

Simon had completely drawn Maisie from her shell of shyness and embarrassment, and had made her laugh until her sides ached. And she had danced. Oh, how Maisie Dobbs had danced that evening, so that when it was time to leave, to return to Girton, Captain Simon Lynch made a gracious sweeping bow before her and kissed her hand.

"Miss Dobbs, you have put my feet to shame this evening. No wonder Priscilla kept you locked up at Girton."

"Don't take my name in vain, Lynchie—you brute! And it's a book of rules that keeps us all locked up, remember."

"Until we meet again, fair maiden."

Simon stepped back and turned toward Priscilla. "And I'll bet my boots that any wounded in your ambulance will go running back to the trenches rather than put up with your driving!"

Simon, Priscilla, and Maisie laughed together. The evening had sparkled.

CHAPTER SIXTEEN

he young women arrived back at the college in the nick
of time before their extended curfew—arranged at the
request of The Honorable Mrs. Margaret Lynch—
expired. Just six hours later, standing on the station platform waiting
for the early train that would take her to London for her connection
to Chelstone, Maisie replayed, yet again, the events of the evening. In
her excitement she had not slept a wink, and now that same excitement rendered her almost oblivious to the chilly air around her.
Maisie held her coat closer to her body and up to her neck, feeling
only the memory of sheer silk next to her skin.

As Maisie reflected upon the three of them laughing just before
they left the party, she realized that it was laughter that held within it
the sadness of a bigger departure. The gaiety of Simon's party had an
undercurrent of fear. She had twice looked at Margaret Lynch, only
to see the woman watching her son, hand to her mouth, as if any
minute she would rush to him and encircle his body in her protec-
tive arms.

Her fear was not without cause, for the people of Britain were only
just receiving news of the tens of thousands of casualties from the

spring offensive of 1915. From a land of quiet farms in the French countryside, the Somme Valley was now a place writ large in newspaper headlines, inspiring angry and opinionated debate. The Somme was indelibly enscribed on the hearts of those who had lost a son, a father, brother, or friend. And for those bidding farewell, there was only fearful anticipation until the son, father, brother, or friend was home once again.

From Liverpool Street, Maisie traveled to Charing Cross for the journey to Kent. The station was a melee of khaki, ambulances, red crosses, and pain. Trains brought wounded to be taken to the London hospitals, nurses scurried back and forth, orderlies led walking wounded to waiting ambulances, and young, new spit-and-polished soldiers looked white-faced at those disembarking.

As she glanced at her ticket and began to walk toward her platform, Maisie was suddenly distracted by a splash of vibrant red hair in the distance. She knew only one person with hair so striking, and that was Enid. Maisie stopped and looked again.

Enid. It was definitely Enid. Enid with her hand on the arm of an officer of the Royal Flying Corps. And the officer in question was the young man who loved ginger biscuits: James Compton. Maisie watched as they stopped in the crowd and stood closer together, whispering. James would be on his way down to Kent, most probably on the same train as Maisie, except that she would not be traveling first class. From there Maisie knew that James would be joining his squadron. He was saying good-bye to Enid, who no longer worked for the Comptons. Mrs. Crawford had informed Maisie in a letter that Enid had left their employ. She was now working in a munitions factory, earning more money than she could ever have dreamed of earning in service.

Though she knew it was intrusive, Maisie felt compelled to stare as the two said good-bye. As she watched, she knew in her heart that Enid and James were truly in love, that this was not infatuation or social climbing on Enid's part. She lowered her head and walked away so that she would not be seen by either of them. Yet even as she walked, Maisie could not help turning to watch the couple once again, magnetized by two young people clearly speaking of love amid the teeming emotion around them. And while she looked, as if bidden by the strength of her gaze, Enid turned her head and met Maisie's eyes.

Enid held her head up defiantly, the vibrant red hair even brighter against her skin tone, which was slightly yellow, a result of exposure to cordite in the munitions factory. Maisie inclined her head and was acknowledged by Enid, who then turned back to James and pressed her lips to his.

Maisie was sitting at a cramped table in the station tea shop when Enid found her.

"You've missed the train to Chelstone, Mais."

"Hello, Enid. Yes, I know, I'll just wait until the next one."

Enid sat down in front of Maisie.

"So you know."

"Yes. But it doesn't make any difference."

"I should bloody 'ope not! I'm away from them all now, and what James does is 'is business."

"Yes. Yes, it is."

"And I'm earning real money now." Enid brushed her hair back from her shoulders. "So, how are you my very clever little friend? Cambridge University treating you well?"

"Enid, please. Let me be." Maisie lifted the cup to her lips. The strong tea was bitter, but its heat was soothing. The sweet joy of meeting Simon Lynch seemed half a world away as she looked once again at Enid.

Suddenly Enid's eyes smarted as if stung, and she began to weep. "I'm sorry. I'm sorry, Mais. I've been so rotten to you. To everyone. I'm just so worried. I lost him once. When 'e went to Canada. When they sent him away because of me. And now 'e's going to France. Up in one of them things—I've 'eard they only last three weeks over there before they cop it, them flyin' boys—and if God 'ad wanted us to leave the ground, I reckon we'd 'ave wings growin' out of our backs by now, don't you?"

"Now then, now then." Maisie moved around to sit next to Enid and put her arms around her. Enid pulled out a handkerchief, wiped her eyes, and blew her nose.

"Least I feel as if I'm doing something. Making shells, like. Least I'm not just sitting on my bum while them boys get shot to bits over there. Oh, James . . . ."

"Come on, Enid. He'll be all right. Remember what Mrs. Crawford says about James—he's got nine lives."

Enid sniffed again. "I'm sorry, Maisie. Really I am. But it just gets me 'ere sometimes." Enid punched at her middle. "They look down their noses at me, think I'm not good enough. And 'ere I am working like a trooper."

Maisie sat with Enid until she became calm, as the ache of farewell gave way to anger, tears, and eventually calm and fatigue.

"Maisie, I never meant anything. Really, I didn't. James will come back, I know he will. And this war is changing everything. 'ave you noticed that? When the likes of me can earn a good living even in wartime, the likes of the better-offs will have to change, won't they?"

"You could be right there, Enid."

"Gaw, lummy . . . look at that time. I've got to get back to the arsenal. I'm not even s'posed to leave the 'ostel without permission. I'm working in a special section now, handling the more volatile—that's what they call it—the more volatile explosives, and we earn more money, specially as we're 'avin' to do double shifts. All the girls get tired, so it gets a bit tricky, tapping the ends of the shells to check 'em, and all that. But I'm careful, like, so they promoted me. Must'a bin workin' for that Carter for all them years. I learned to be careful."

"Good for you, Enid."

The two women left the tea shop and walked together toward the bus stop just outside the station, where Enid would catch a bus to work. As they were bidding farewell, a man shouted behind them. "Make way, move along, make way, please."

A train carrying wounded soldiers had arrived, and the orderlies were hurriedly trying to bring stretchers through to the waiting ambulances. Maisie and Enid stood aside and looked on as the wounded passed by, still in mud-caked and bloody uniforms, often crying out as scurrying stretcher-bearers accidentally jarred shell-blasted arms and legs. Maisie gasped and leaned against Enid when she looked into the eyes of a man who had lost most of the dressings from his face.

After the wounded had passed Enid turned to Maisie to say good-bye. The young women embraced, and as they did so, Maisie felt a shiver of fear that made her tighten her hold on Enid.

"Come on, come on, let's not get maudlin, Mais." Enid loosened her grasp.

"You mind how you go, Enid," said Maisie.

"Like I always said, Maisie Dobbs, don't you worry about me."

"But I do."

"You want to worry about something, Maisie? Let me give you a bit of advice. You worry about what you can do for these boys." She pointed toward the ambulances waiting outside the station entrance. "You worry about whatever it is you can *do*. Must be off now. Give my love to Lady Bountiful for me!"

It seemed to Maisie that one second she was with Enid, and then she was alone. She walked toward the platform for the penultimate part of her journey home to her father's cottage next to the stables at Chelstone. With trains delayed and canceled due to troop movements, it would once again be many hours before she reached her destination.

The journey to Kent was long and arduous. Blackout blinds were pulled down, in compliance with government orders issued in anticipation of Zeppelin raids, and the train moved slowly in the darkness. Several times the train pulled into a siding to allow a troop train go by, and each time Maisie closed her eyes and remembered the injured men rushed into waiting ambulances at Charing Cross.

Time and again she fell into a deep yet brief slumber, and in her half waking saw Enid at work in the munitions factory, at the toil that caused her skin to turn yellow and her hair to spark when she brushed it back. Maisie remembered Enid's face in the distance, reflecting the love she felt as she looked at James Compton.

She wondered about love, and how it must feel, and thought back to last night, which seemed so many nights ago, and touched the place on her right hand where Simon Lynch had placed his lips in a farewell kiss.

As the train drew in to Chelstone station late at night, Maisie saw Frankie standing by his horse and cart. Persephone stood proudly, her coat's gloss equaled only by the shine of the leather traces that Maisie could see even in the half-light. Maisie ran to Frankie and was swept up into his arms.

"My Maisie, home from the university. My word, you're a sight for your dad."

"It's grand to be back with you, Dad."

"Come on, let me have that case and let's get going."

As they drove back to the house in darkness, dim lanterns set at the front of the cart swinging to and fro with each of Persephone's heavy footfalls, Maisie told Frankie her news and answered his many questions. Of course she mentioned the meeting with Enid, although Maisie left out all mention of James Compton.

"The arsenal, eh? Blimey, let's 'ope she wasn't there this afternoon."

"What do you mean, Dad?"

"Well, you know 'is Lordship is with the War Office and all that. Well, 'e gets news before even the papers, you know, special messenger, like. He's very well—"

"Dad, what's happened?"

"'is Lordship received a telegram late this afternoon. The special part of the factory went up this afternoon, the place where they 'andle the 'eavy explosives. Just as the new shift came on. Twenty-two of them munitions girls killed outright."

Maisie knew that Enid was dead. She did not need the confirmation that came the next morning, as Lord Compton told Carter that Enid had been among the young women killed and that he should take care of informing the staff in a manner that he saw fit. Not for the first time, Maisie considered how so much in life could change in such a short time. Priscilla enlisting for service, the wonderful evening, meeting Simon Lynch—and Enid. But of the events that had passed in just three days, the picture that remained with Maisie Dobbs was of Enid, swishing back her long red hair and looking straight at Maisie with a challenge. A haunting challenge.

"You worry what you can do for these boys, Maisie. You worry about whatever it is you can *do*."

CHAPTER SEVENTEEN

aisie caught sight of the London Hospital in the distance and did not take her eyes off its austere eighteenth-century buildings until the bus had shuddered to a halt, allowing her to clamber down the steps from the upper deck to the street below. She looked up at the buildings, then at the visitors filing in, people leaving, many in tears, and the ambulances drawing alongside to allow their wounded and bloody cargo to be taken to the safety of the wards.

Maisie closed her eyes and took a deep breath, as if about to jump from a precipice into the unknown.

"'scuse me, Miss, comin' through. You'll get run over if you stand there, young lady."

Maisie opened her eyes and moved quickly to allow a hospital porter through carrying two large boxes.

"Can I 'elp you, Miss? Look a bit lost to me."

"Yes. Where do I enlist for nursing service?"

"You bloomin' angel, you. You'll be just the medicine some of these poor lads need, and that's a fact!"

Positioning his left foot awkwardly against the inside of his opposite shin, the porter held the boxes steady on his knee with one hand, pushed back his flat cap, and used his free hand to direct Maisie.

"You go through that door there, turn left down the long green-tiled corridor, turn right at the end to the stairs. Up the stairs, to the right, and you'll see the enlisting office. And don't mind them in there, love—they pay them extra to wear a face as long as a week, as if a smile would crack 'em open!"

Maisie thanked the man, who doffed his cap quickly before grabbing the boxes, which were about to fall to the ground, and then went on his way.

The long corridor was busy with people lost in the huge building, and others pointing fingers and waving arms to show them the way to reach a certain ward. Taking her identification papers and letters of recommendation out of her bag, Maisie walked quickly up the disinfectant-cleaned tile staircase and across the landing to the enlisting office for nurses. The woman who took Maisie's papers glanced at her over her wire-rimmed spectacles.

"Age?"

"Twenty-two."

She looked up at Maisie again, and peered over the top of her spectacles.

"Young-looking twenty-two, aren't you?"

"Yes, that's what they said when I went to university."

"Well, if you're old enough for university, you're old enough for this. And doing more good while you're about it."

The woman leafed through the papers again, looking quickly at the letter with the Compton crest that attested to Maisie's competence and age. There would be no questions regarding the authenticity of documents that bore not only an impressive livery but the name of a well-known figure at the War Office, a man quoted in newspapers from the *Daily Sketch* to *The Times*, commenting on dispatches from France.

Maisie had taken the sheets of fine linen paper from the bureau in the library at Chelstone, and written what was needed. Emboldened by Enid's challenge, she had felt only the shallowest wave of guilt. She was going to do her part for the boys, for those who had given of themselves on the fields of France.

"*Y*ou've done *what?* Are you mad, Maisie? What about your university learning? After all that work, all that . . . ."

Frankie turned his back on Maisie and shook his head. He was silent, staring out of the scullery window of the groom's cottage, out toward the paddocks where three very healthy horses were grazing. Maisie knew better than to interrupt until he had finished.

"After all that fuss and bother . . . ."

"It's only a postponement, Dad. I can go back. I will go back. As soon as the war is over."

Frankie swung around, tears of fear and frustration welling in his eyes.

"That's all very well, but what if you get sent over there? To France. Blimey, if you wanted to do something useful, my girl, I'm sure 'is Lordship could've got a job for a bright one like you. I've a mind to go up to that hospital and shop you for your tales—you must've said you were older than you are. I tell you, I never thought I'd see the day when my daughter told a lie."

"Dad, please understand—"

"Oh, I understand all right. Just like your mother, and I've lost her. I can't lose you, Maisie."

Maisie walked over to her father and put her hand on his shoulder. "You won't lose me Dad. You watch. You'll be proud of me."

Frankie Dobbs dropped his head and leaned into his daughter's embrace. "I've always been proud of you, Maisie. That's not the point."

As a member of the Voluntary Aid Detachment, Maisie's duties seemed to consist of daily round of mopping floors, lining up beds so that not one was out of place, and being at the beck and call of the senior nurses. She had obtained a deferment from Girton, and no sooner had the letter been posted, along with another to Priscilla, than Maisie put her dream behind her and with the same resolve that had taken her to university, she vowed to bring comfort to the men coming home from France.

Maisie became a VAD nurse at the London Hospital in May, amid the never-ending influx of casualties from the spring offensive of 1915. It was a hot summer, and one in which Maisie saw little rest and spent only a few hours at her lodgings in Whitechapel.

Sweeping a stray tendril of hair under her white cap, Maisie immersed her hands into a sinkful of scalding hot water, and scrubbed at an assortment of glass bottles, bowls, and measuring jugs with a bristle brush. It was not the first time in her life that her hands were raw or her legs and back ached. But it could be worse, she thought, as she drained the suds and began to rinse the glassware. For a moment she allowed her hands to remain in the water as it began to cool, and looked straight ahead through the window to the dusk-dusted rooftops beyond.

"Dobbs, I don't think you've got all day to rinse a few bottles, not when there are a dozen other jobs for you to do before you go off duty."

Maisie jumped as her name was spoken, quickly rushing to apologize for her tardiness.

"Don't waste time, Dobbs. Finish this job quickly. Sister wants to see you now."

The nurse who spoke to her was one of the regulars, not a volunteer, and Maisie immediately reverted to the bobbed curtsy of her days in service. The seniority of the regular nurses demanded respect, immediate attention, and complete deference.

Maisie finished her task, made sure that not a bottle or cloth was out of place, then went quickly to see Sister, checking her hair, cap, and apron as she trotted along the green-and-cream-tiled corridor.

"Nurses never run, Dobbs. They walk briskly."

Maisie stopped, bit her bottom lip, and turned around, hands by her sides and balled into fists. Sister, the most senior nurse on the ward. And the most feared, even by the men who joked that she should be sent out to France—that would send the Hun running.

"I'm sorry, Sister."

"My office, Dobbs."

"Yes, Sister."

Sister led the way into her office, with its green-tiled walls, dark wood floor, and equally dark wooden furniture, and walked around to the opposite side of her desk, sweeping her long blue dress and bright white apron aside to avoid their catching on the corner. A silver buckle shone at the front of her apron, and her scarflike cap was starched. Not a hair was out of place.

"I'll get quickly to the point. As you know we are losing many of our staff to join detachments in France. We therefore need to move our nurses and volunteers up through the ranks—and of course we need to keep many of our regular nurses here to keep up standards and direct care of the wounded. Your promotion today to Special Military Probationer means more responsibility in the ward, Dobbs. Along with Rigson, Dornhill, and White, you must be prepared to serve in military hospitals overseas if needed. That will be in one year, at the end of your training. Let me see . . ."

The austere woman shuffled papers in a file on the desk in front of her.

"Yes, you'll be twenty-three at the end of the year, according to your records. Eligible for duty abroad. Good."

Sister looked up at Maisie again, then checked the time on the small watch pinned to her apron. "I have already spoken to the other VADs in question during their duty earlier today. Now then, from tomorrow you will join doctors' rounds each day to observe and assist, in addition to your other duties. Is that understood?"

"Yes, Sister."

"Then you are dismissed, Dobbs."

Maisie left the office and walked slowly toward the kitchen.

Yes, sooner than she had thought, she would be in France. Possibly this time next year. How she longed to see Maurice, how she ached to speak with him. For here was time again, the trickster, changing the circumstances of her life in an instant. Yet she knew that Maurice would ask her if she was not herself the trickster. She had lied about her age unashamedly to do this work, and now she was burdened by doubt. Could she do what was required of her? Could she live up to Enid's memory?

CHAPTER EIGHTEEN

*M*aisie pulled herself away from the side rail of the ship. She had never dreamed that seasickness could be this bad. A salty wind blew around her head and nipped at her ears as she struggled to keep the heavy woolen cape drawn across her aching body. Nothing in the world could top this. Nothing could be this unbearable.

"Here, miss, old merchant navy trick for the indisposition . . ."

She looked sideways from the place she had claimed, holding on to a handrail that led to a cabin door, then rushed to the side of the boat again. She felt a strong hand between her shoulder blades and pushed against the guard rail bring herself to a standing position. A member of the crew, sensibly wearing foul-weather clothing, with his cap miraculously still on his head, held out a tin mug of hot cocoa and a lump of Madeira cake. Maisie put her hand to her mouth in terror.

"What you do is, when you think you're going to lose your insides again, you take a bite o' this and a quick swig of cocoa. And you do it every time you feel queasy. Then it'll go away; you'll see."

Maisie looked at the man, shook her head, and leaned over the side rail. Exhausted to the core, she stood up again and held out her hands for the cake and cocoa. It had to be worth a go.

Iris Rigson, Dottie Dornhill, Bess White, and Maisie Dobbs had set sail with a small contingent of nurses on July 20, 1916, bound for service in France. Iris, Dottie, and Bess had not suffered unduly on the requisitioned freighter, now in the service of king and country, ferrying supplies—and in this case nurses, too—between England and France. But Maisie Dobbs, granddaughter of a lighterman on the Thames, was embarrassingly seasick. Whatever the battlefield had to offer, it could not possibly make her feel worse than this, though she had in her pocket a letter from Priscilla, who had been sent to France in January with the first FANY convoy. The censors might be able to take out words, but they could not delete the emotion poured from inkwell to paper. Priscilla was exhausted, if not in body then in mind. Her words seemed to bite through the edges of Maisie's thoughts and expectations. For just a moment, as she fingered the letter in her pocket, she felt as if she were a ghostly presence watching over Priscilla as she worked. Priscilla had written:

My back is killing me, Maisie. Florrie the Lorry did not want to go to work this morning, so I did double duty with the starting handle. I had only two hours rest last night, after a twenty-hour shift. Maisie, I can only barely remember the last time I slept for more than just a few hours. My clothes are becoming one with my body, and I dread to imagine how I must reek! Mind you, one simply cannot go on about one's aching back and stinging eyes when faced with the good humor of these boys, even as they are suffering the pain of torn limbs and the terror of seeing comrades die. Despite rain that seems to come down in buckets here, there are some days that suddenly get very hot and humid indeed, especially if you are lugging around the added weight of a heavy uniform glued to your body. Many of the boys have taken a knife to their woolen trousers to get some relief from the chafing of army issue cloth. I suppose it's less for the doctors to cut away, but loaded on to Florrie they look like schoolboys who've taken a wrong turning into hell. I had a boy die on me yesterday. Maisie, his eyes were as deep a blue as that dress you wore to Simon's party, and he could not have been more than seventeen. Poor lad hadn't even begun to shave, just a bit of fluff on his chin. I wanted to just sit there and weep. But you know, you just have to go on. If I stood around in mourning for them, another poor boy would die for want of an ambulance. I don't know what the papers are saying, but here's

Priscilla's letter was abruptly halted by heavy black ink of the censor's pen.

"Here she is. Maisie o' the high seas!" Iris announced as Maisie returned to the cabin.

"Blimey, Maisie, how're you now, then?" Dottie came over to Maisie and put an arm around her shoulder. "Come and sit down. We'll soon be there. Le Havre can't be much longer—can it?" She looked at the other nurses, their heavy capes drawn around them, and settled Maisie into a seat. "You poor little mite, Dobbs. There's nothing of you to start with. Never you mind, we'll soon be in Le Havre. Get us a nice cuppa. That's if the French can make tea."

Iris felt Maisie's forehead and looked at her watch. "You do seem a bit better, though."

Maisie looked at the other girls and leaned against Iris. "Cocoa and cake," she muttered, and promptly fell into a deep sleep.

From Le Havre the train journey to Rouen passed uneventfully. The young women were tired from the journey but managed to keep

awake long enough to watch their first few minutes of foreign soil speed past. Arriving at the port of Rouen, the nurses were met by a medical officer, and taken to the Hotel St. Georges, where they expected to stay for two nights while they waited for orders.

"Let's get ourselves a nice wash and have a cup of tea downstairs," suggested Iris as they settled into the room all four women were to share.

Iris was a tall, big-boned girl, whose uniform always looked rather too small for her. She considered this a blessing. The unfashionably long and impractical woolen dress of the uniform was shorter on her than on the other nurses. Not only could she move with greater ease, but soon she would avoid having her hemline drag in the never-ending mud, the bane of a nurse's life in France.

"How are you feeling, Dobbs?" asked the soft-spoken Bess, maintaining the discipline of hospital address.

"Much better, thank you. And a cup of tea would be just lovely."

The women each unpacked their few belongings, washed faces and hands at the large white enameled stone sink, and brushed hair back into place. As usual Maisie struggled to fasten the stray tendrils of jet black hair that crept out from under her hat. When they left the room, the women looked almost as fresh as they had in the early hours of the morning, when they had joined their train at Charing Cross for the journey to Folkestone, their port of departure for France.

"Look at those cakes. My word, never seen a pastry like that before; it's a wonder they can do that in wartime," said Dottie.

"No, and you've never tasted a cup of tea like this before either."

Iris winced at the weak tea and reached out to take one of the delicate pastries from the china plate placed in the center of the table.

Maisie was quiet, looking around her at the rather aged grandeur of the dining room at the Hotel St. Georges. Large mirrors were positioned on each wall, and ornate archways led into the lounge on one side and the marble-floored lobby on the other. Waiters ran back and forth, elegant in black trousers that shone with too much pressing, white shirts, black ties, and long white aprons. They were all older men, for the younger men had gone to war.

The clientele was mainly military personnel, and the hotel was packed with officers going on leave or passing through on their way back to join their regiments. Some were with sweethearts or wives, still others with parents, the fortunate ones whose people could make a journey across the Channel to bid them farewell in France.

Maisie sipped her tea, feeling the warmth, if not the flavor, reach the core of her tired body. She was aware of the conversation at their table, a familiar to-ing and fro-ing of observations and opinions, a giggle here, a raised voice there. But for the most part, as the journey to France ebbed away behind her, Maisie was lost in her own thoughts.

"Excuse me, it's Miss Dobbs, isn't it?"

Maisie was jolted from her daydream back into the dining room. She jumped up and turned to face the person who had spoken to her.

"Oh my goodness!" said Maisie, spilling tea onto the white cloth.

Captain Simon Lynch quickly took her elbow to steady Maisie, and greeted her with a broad smile, which he then extended to her table companions, who had immediately stopped all conversation, indeed all movement, to look at the man who had come to the table to see Maisie.

"Captain Lynch. Well, what a surprise this is!"

Maisie regained her composure and took Simon's offered hand. A waiter quickly and efficiently replaced the tablecloth and offered to bring a chair for Simon, who declined, commenting to her companions that he had just been leaving when he had seen his friend, Miss Dobbs.

Simon turned again to Maisie, and as he did so she noticed that he seemed older. Not just in years, for it was just over a year since they had first met. No, he was older in his soul. His eyes were ringed with gray skin, lines had formed on his fresh young man's face, and already gray hair was showing at his temples. Yet he could be no more than twenty-six.

"Just here for two days' leave. Not enough time for Blighty, I'm afraid. I'd heard from Pris that you'd joined up."

"How is she? Have you seen her?"

"Our paths crossed only once. She brought wounded men to my hospital, but, well, we didn't have time to stand and chat." Simon looked at his hands, then back at Maisie. "So, do you know where you are going yet?"

"No, we get our orders tomorrow morning, perhaps even this evening. Seems a bit chaotic, really."

Simon laughed.

"Chaotic? You haven't seen chaotic until you've been out there."

"I'm sorry." Maisie rubbed her hands together. "What I meant was—"

"No, *I'm* sorry. That was horrible of me. And, yes, it *is* chaotic. The right arm of the British army hardly seems to know what the left arm's doing. Look, I have to dash off now, but, I wonder, is there any chance that you could have dinner with me tomorrow evening? Or do you have to be chaperoned?"

Simon grinned and looked into Maisie's eyes.

"Well, um, well . . ."

Maisie looked sideways at her companions, who were continuing with their tea quietly in order to listen to the conversation. She caught Iris's eye and saw the other woman smile, nod her head and mouth the word "Go." Maisie turned back to Simon.

"Yes, Captain Lynch. Dinner would be lovely. And, yes, actually I do have to be chaperoned, so my friends will be dining nearby."

"Right you are. Let's make it an early one then, I'll meet you in the lobby at six o'clock. In fact, I'll meet you all in the lobby at six o'clock!"

Simon bowed, bade good-bye to the nurses, smiled at Maisie, and moved to go.

"Oh, and by the way—that uniform—it's almost as stunning as the blue silk dress."

And then he was gone.

Maisie took her place once again, amid the giggles of Iris, Dottie, and Bess.

"And what silk dress might that be, Dobbs?"

"You kept that one quiet, didn't you?"

"Sure you want a chaperone?"

Maisie blushed at the teasing, which she knew would continue for some time. She was about to explain that Simon was only a friend of a friend when an RAMC officer approached their table.

"Dobbs, White, Dornhill, and Rigson? Good. Orders are here, and travel warrants. Sorry. You won't be going to the same place. White and Dornhill together at the base hospital. Dobbs and Rigson, you're going to the Fourteenth Casualty Clearing Station— enjoy it here while you can."

And with that he was gone, clutching several large manila envelopes under his arm while negotiating his way through the busy dining room, in search of other nurses on his list.

The four women sat in silence for a few minutes, looking at the brown manila envelopes.

"Well, he's a bundle of joy, isn't he?" said Iris, taking a knife from the table and slicing open the envelope.

"Dobbsie, my girl, we are indeed off to the Fourteenth Casualty Clearing Station, near Bailleul, like Cheerful Charlie over there said. A CCS, that's as near to the battlefield as nurses are allowed, isn't it?"

"And we're at the base hospital here in Rouen, so we won't be going far, will we, Bess?"

"Well, there we are, then. Let's make the most of it, that's what I say. And let's get some sleep."

Iris dabbed at her mouth with her table napkin, and a waiter scurried over to pull out her chair.

"Yes, good idea. At least one of us needs her sleep if she's to be walking out with an officer!"

"Oh, Dottie, he's just—"

Maisie rushed to defend herself as the women left the table, but her protestations were lost amid the teasing and banter.

*R*emembering the events of her dinner with Simon Lynch took Maisie's mind off the journey. First by train, then by field ambulance along mud-filled and rutted roads, Maisie and Iris traveled to the casualty clearing station where they would be based until due for leave in four months' time.

As the train moved slowly along, though it was still light, Maisie had a sense of darkness descending. Gunmetal gray clouds loomed overhead, splashes of rain streaked across the windows, and when the train stopped at a station, the sound of heavy artillery in the distance seemed to echo and reverberate along the tracks. Even the birds had been silenced by the mighty orchestra of battle. With the sights and sounds of war around them, people in the landscape loomed with a stark intensity.

Maisie watched from the train window as lines of people trudged along, and more lines of battered humanity appeared to be strung out into the distance. Whole families were leaving communities close to the battlefields, seeking a place of safety with relatives in other towns and villages. Yet the river of civilian evacuation was a stream compared to the long column of marching soldiers, battle weary in weathered uniforms. Young men with faces prematurely aged, showing fatigue and fear as well as a determined levity.

> What's the use of worrying?
> It never was worthwhile, so
> Pack all your troubles in your old kit-bag,
> And smile, smile, smile.

The marching songs rang out, and as their train passed by, Iris and

Maisie leaned out of the slow-moving carriages, waved to the soldiers, and joined in their songs.

It's a long way to Tipperary, it's a long way to go;
It's a long way to Tipperary, to the sweetest girl I know;
Good-bye Piccadilly, farewell Leicester Square,
It's a long, long way to Tipperary, but my heart's right there.

With a final wave, Iris and Maisie pulled up the window, and tried to make themselves comfortable again on the prickly wool train seating.

"Funny that your young man's not that many miles from us, isn't it, Dobbs?" Iris looked inquiringly at Maisie when they were settled.

"Oh, for goodness sake, he's not my young man. He's just an old friend of a very good friend of mine. It really is a coincidence that I saw him at all."

"That's as may be, Dobbsie, but I saw the way you two were looking at each other, and I'd say that you were a-courting. Right pair of turtle doves, if you ask me."

"Nonsense. And don't you go repeating this silliness either, Iris. Please. I hardly know him—and I could get into trouble!"

"Blue silk dress eh?"

Iris continued to tease Maisie.

Iris, Dottie, and Bess had taken a table next to Maisie and Simon at dinner, lest it be thought that she was dining completely without a chaperone. But surprising even herself, Maisie hardly noticed other people in the hotel dining room. From the time he had greeted her in the lobby, at six o'clock as arranged, and held out his arm to her, Maisie and Simon Lynch had eyes only for each other.

Now Maisie lowered her eyelids and feigned sleep, which effectively silenced Iris. Left in peace, she was able to envision the dining room again, the waiters running to and fro, and the busyness of people enjoying last farewells or a few days respite from the business of war. And there, at the table with her, was Simon.

Simon who made her laugh with his jokes, putting her at ease.

Simon who asked her why she had become a nurse, and when she told the story of Enid, leaned across and took her hand. "She must have meant a lot to you, your friend."

"Yes, yes, she did . . . she made me think about all sorts of things. While I was busy with my head in a book, she would bring me down to earth with a thud. Yes . . . she made me reconsider my opinions on more than one occasion."

Simon did not release Maisie's hand, and for a moment their eyes met again and they were silent. Abashed, Maisie pulled her hand away and took up her fork. She poked at her food.

"I hope I didn't embarrass you. I, I didn't think—"

"Oh no. That's all right." Maisie blushed.

"It's a strange thing, war. Maisie, you must prepare yourself for what you are going to see. This past year . . . the Somme . . . I cannot tell you what injuries the men suffer. As a doctor I was trained to deal with one surgical case at a time: I operated on a leg, or a chest, or an arm. But these men are brought in with multiple gaping wounds, I—"

Simon stopped speaking and reached for his glass of claret, which he gripped but did not pick up. He stared into the wine, at the deep red liquid, and then closed his eyes. As he did so, Maisie saw again the lines that crept from the edges of his eyelids to his temples, the creases on his forehead, and the dark circles above his cheekbones.

"I came here thinking I could save every one of them, but half the time—" Simon hesitated, swallowed deeply, and looked directly at Maisie.

"It's so very good to see you, Maisie. It reminds me of how it was before I left England. How I felt about being a doctor. And how very much I hoped that I would see you again."

Maisie blushed again but smiled at Simon.

"Yes, Simon. I am glad too."

Without thinking she reached for his hand, which he took and gripped tightly. Suddenly aware of the proximity of other diners, Maisie released her hold, and they took up their knives and forks.

"Now then, tell me all about Lady Rowan. I've heard of her, of course. She has quite a reputation as a staunch supporter of the suffragettes. And I've heard that Lord Julian is an absolute saint— although I doubt he has much time to worry about what she's up to, now that he's at the War Office."

Conversation slipped into the exchanging of stories, of opinions and observations, and by the time dinner was over, Maisie noticed that they had spoken of their dreams, of what they would do "when the war's over."

In that moment she remembered Maurice, walking with her in the orchard one day while at Chelstone, as she broke the news that she had requested a deferment of her place at Cambridge, that she had enlisted at the London Hospital.

She remembered him looking into the distance and speaking, very quietly, almost to himself. "Such is the legacy of war . . . the discarded dreams of children . . . the waste. The tragedy."

Simon looked at his watch. "Well, sadly, Maisie, I must go. I have meetings while I'm here, I'm afraid. So much for leave, eh?"

"Yes, I have to go, too. We set off early tomorrow morning."

As Maisie placed her white linen table napkin alongside her plate, Simon watched her intently. "Would you mind very much if I wrote to you? It may take a while, but letters can be sent up the line. I'll work out something."

"Yes, that would be lovely. Please write."

Simon rose to pull out Maisie's chair, and as he did so Maisie noticed her three friends at an adjoining table, all holding coffee cups to their lips and looking at her over the rims of the cups. She had forgotten they were there.

In the lobby Simon once again made a sweeping bow. "You may be clad in that wonderfully practical nursing attire, Miss Dobbs, but in my eyes you will forever be wearing a stunning blue silk dress."

Maisie shook hands with Simon, and bade him good-bye before joining the three nurses standing directly behind her, and doubtless waiting to begin teasing her once again.

*M*aisie and Iris saw the tents in the distance, a musty afternoon cordite-laden fog lingered overhead, and a heavy ground mist was moving up and around them.

"I'm freezing just looking at that lot, and it's nowhere near winter yet," said Iris.

"I know what you mean. Looks bleak, doesn't it?"

Maisie pulled her cape around her body, though the day was not that cold.

The main tents had giant red crosses painted on top, and beyond were bell tents that were home to the nursing contingent of the casualty clearing station. The ambulance moved slowly along the rutted road, and as they came closer to the encampment, it was clear that they were in the midst of receiving wounded.

The ambulance pulled alongside the officers' tent, where records were kept and orders given. All around them people moved quickly, some shouting, others carrying fresh supplies. Iris and Maisie stepped down and had barely taken up their bags when a sister rushed up to them.

"No time to dawdle. We need you now—time for the paperwork and receiving line later! Get your capes off, your aprons on, and report immediately to the main tent. It's the deep end for you two."

Two hours later, as Maisie stood over a young man, cutting heavy uniform cloth away from an arm partially severed by shellfire, Maisie remembered Simon's words: "You must prepare yourself for what you are going to see."

Quickly pushing the still-fresh words to the back of her mind, and brushing the sweat from her forehead with the back of her bloodied hand, Maisie felt as if she were in the eye of the storm. The young soldier lying in front of her was conscious, watching her face all the time, searching for the glimmer of expression that would give away her assessment of his wounds. But the sisters of the London Hospital had taught their nurses well: Never, never ever change your expression at the sight of a wound—they'll be looking into your eyes to see their future. Look straight back at them.

As Maisie worked quickly, taking up disinfectant and swabs, a surgeon accompanied by nurses and medical orderlies moved from one soldier to the next, cutting away skin, bone and muscle, pulling shrapnel from the bodies of boys who had taken on the toil of men.

The soldier continued to stare into Maisie's eyes as she prepared his wounds for the surgeon's knife. Following the trail of blood and flesh, Maisie cut away more uniform, taking her scissors to his trousers, pulling at the bindings around his lower leg. And as she felt her hand sink into the terrible injuries to his thigh, the soldier cleared his throat to speak.

"Rugby player's legs, those."

"I thought so," said Maisie as she continued to work on his leg, "You can always tell the rugby players."

"Nurse, nurse," the soldier reached out toward her with his uninjured hand, "Nurse, could you hold my hand?"

And as Maisie took his hand in hers, the young man smiled.

"Thank you, nurse."

Suddenly Maisie was aware that someone was bending back the soldier's fingers and moving his arm to his side, and she looked up at the nursing sister in charge. An army chaplain placed his hand on her shoulder for barely a second before lifting it to perform last rites over the young soldier's not-yet-cold body, while two stretcher-bearers waited to remove him to allow room for more wounded.

"Oh, I'm sorry—"

"No time for sorry," said the sister. "He's been gone less than a minute anyway. You did all you could. Now then, there's work to do here. No time to stop and think about it. Just got to get on with it. There's plenty more waiting outside that need your helping hand."

Brushing back a stray hair with the back of her hand once again, Maisie prepared the table as best she could for the next soldier.

"'Allo, Nurse. Going to make me all better, are you?" said the man as the stretcher bearers quickly but carefully placed him on the table.

Maisie looked straight into the man's eyes and saw intense pain masked by the attempt at humor. Taking up scissors and swabs, along with the pungent garlic juice used to disinfect wounds, she breathed deeply and smiled.

"Yes. I'm going to make you all better, young man. Now then, hold still."

CHAPTER NINETEEN

*M*aisie awoke in the tent she shared with Iris. Snuggling under her blankets, she looked over at her friend and, in the half sleep of early morning, thought for a moment that it was Enid, but realized that it was the bump of Iris's behind forming a mound in the bed as she, too, curled herself against the early morning chill.

She took a deep breath. The chill air notwithstanding, Maisie suddenly sat up, pulling the blanket around her shoulders as she did so. She must do everything in her power to keep a calm head, to brace herself for the day, and to prepare herself for the elements. Rain had started to fall again. Rain that soaked into the ground to form a stew of mud and filthy water that seeped up into the cloth of her long woolen dress, making it hang heavily against her ankles as she worked again and again to clean and bandage wounds. By the end of each day the mud had worked its way up to her knees, and time and time again she told herself that she was warm, really, that her feet felt dry, really. Then at night, she and Iris would hang up their dresses to allow the moisture to evaporate, and check each other's bodies for the battlefield lice that seemed to know no defeat.

"You first, Maisie," said Iris, still clutching the bedcovers around her body.

"You just don't want to be the one to crack the ice."

"What ice?"

"I told you, Iris, there was a layer of ice on the top of that water yesterday."

"No!"

Iris turned over in her cot to look at Maisie, who sat cross-legged on her bed.

"I don't know how you can sit like that, Dobbs. Now then, are you telling me there was ice on the water? It's not even proper winter yet."

"Yes. Even though it's not proper winter."

Maisie took another deep breath, which, when exhaled, turned to steamy fog in front of her face. She cast the blanket aside and nimbly ran over to the water pitcher and bowl that stood on top of a wooden chest.

"And the sitting in the morning—it's what helps to keep me from freezing solid all day, Iris. It clears my head. You should try it!"

"Hmmmph!"

Iris turned over in bed and tried to ignore her cold feet.

Maisie poked her finger into the water pitcher. She cracked the thin layer of ice as if tentatively testing a piecrust, then gripped the handle of the pitcher with both hands and poured freezing cold water into the bowl. Reaching over to the side of the chest, Maisie unhooked a flannel cloth, which she steeped in the water. After wringing it out, Maisie unbuttoned the front of her nightgown and washed first her face, then under her arms and up to her neck. Oh, what she would give for a bath! To sit in a deep bathtub filled with piping hot water and soap bubbles coming up to her ears.

Again she plunged the cloth into the cold water, squeezed the excess water back into the bowl, and this time lifted her nightgown and washed between her legs and down to her knees. A nice hot bath. For hours. She wouldn't come out for hours. She'd keep twiddling that hot tap with her big toe, and she wouldn't come out until every last molecule of mud, blood, sweat, and tears had been washed away.

Taking down her still-damp dress, which had been hanging from a wire she and Iris had rigged up inside the tent, Maisie checked every seam and in the hem for lice. It was the morning drill: Check for lice everywhere, and when you've finished checking, check some more, because lice are crafty little beggars. She dressed quickly, finally slipping a white armband with a red cross just above the elbow of her right sleeve, and taking out a fresh apron and attaching a silver watch pin to the left side of the bib. Along with the black leather document case, which now held her writing paper and letters received, the nurse's watch was her talisman from home, a gift from Lady Rowan.

Finally Maisie placed a towel on her cot and leaned over it to brush her hair, looking carefully for lice falling out. She and Iris checked each other's hair every night or, if they were on duty at night, whenever they were both in the tent and awake at the same time. But Maisie always checked again in the morning, brushing her hair over a towel until her head spun. Then she quickly pinned her hair up into a bun, and placed her cap on her head.

"I'm all finished, Iris."

"Right you are, Dobbsie." Iris shivered under her bedclothes. "Lord knows what this will be like in the real winter."

"At least we're not up to our waists in mud in the trenches, Iris. Least we're not piling up bodies to make a wall to protect us. Not like the boys."

"You're right there, as always," said Iris as she leaped from bed and began the morning ritual that Maisie had just finished. "Brrrr . . . I 'spect you're going over to see if there's a letter from your young man."

Maisie rolled her eyes. "I've told you, Iris. He's not—"

"Yes, I know, I know. He's not your young man. Well then, go and get your letter from your special friend of a friend then, and leave me to my delousing, if you don't mind!"

The young women laughed, as Maisie pulled back the tent flap, leaving Iris to her morning ablutions. Picking her way across wooden boards covering mud and puddles, Maisie made her way to the cooks' tent to get tea and bread for breakfast.

"There you are, Sister, get this down you." The orderly on duty held out a large enamel mug along with a slice of bread and dripping for Maisie, addressing her as "sister" in the way that soldiers called all nurses, regardless of rank, "sister."

"And a little something else for you, passed on to me this morning." He reached into his pocket and brought out a simple brown envelope that clearly contained a long letter, such was the thickness of the packet. The envelope was crumpled and bore stains of the four sets of dirty hands it had passed through before reaching its destination.

The letters from Simon Lynch to Maisie Dobbs would never travel through the censor's office, passed as they were from orderly to ambulance driver to stretcher bearer to cook. Her letters in return were passed in the same way, from person to person. And each time a letter changed hands, there would be a comment exchanged, a remark about young love, or that it was all very well for him, Captain Romantic over there.

The writers said nothing of love when the first letter, from Simon to Maisie, was sent and received. But in the way that two people who are of one mind on any subject move closer, as if their heads were drawn together by thoughts that ran parallel toward a future destination, so the letters of Simon and Maisie became more frequent, one hardly waiting for the other to reply before setting pen to paper again. Bearing up under exhaustion that weighed on their backs and pushed like a fist between their shoulder blades, Simon and Maisie, each in a tent several miles apart, and each by the strained light of an oil lamp, would write quickly and urgently of days amid the detritus of war. And though both knew that war, and the ever-present breath of despair might have added urgency to their need to be together again, they began unashamedly to declare their feelings in the letters that were passed from hand to hand. Feelings that, with each shared experience and story, grew deeper. Then Simon wrote:

> My Dearest Maisie of the Blue Silk Dress,
>   I have been on duty for 30 hours without so much as sitting down for five minutes. Wounded started coming in again at eleven yesterday morning. I have bent over so many bodies, so many wounds that I fear I have lost count. I seem to remember only the eyes, and I remember the eyes because in them I see the same shock, the same disbelief, and the same resignation. Today I saw, in quick succession, a man and his son. They had joined up together, I suspect one or both lying about their age. And they had the same eyes. The very same. Perhaps what I see in each man is that no matter what their age (and by golly, some of them shouldn't be out of school), they seem so very old.
>   I am due for a short leave in three weeks. I will receive orders soon. I plan to go back to Rouen for two days. I remember you said that you would be due for leave soon, too. Would it be too presumptuous for me to ask if we might possibly meet in Rouen? I so long to see you, Maisie, and to be taken from this misery by your wonderful smile and inspiring good sense. Do write to let me know.

Iris had leave at the same time as Maisie, providing Maisie with a female companion. The journey to Rouen seemed long and drawn out, until finally they reached the Hotel St. Georges.

"I swear I cannot wait to get into that bath, Maisie Dobbs."

"Me too, Iris. I wonder if we can get our dresses cleaned. I've another day dress with me that I haven't worn. How about you?"

"Yes, me too. Not supposed to be out of uniform, but for goodness sake, this dress will walk to the laundry if I don't take it."

Maisie and Iris hurried immediately to their assigned room. The ceilings seemed extraordinarily high and there was chipped paint on the walls and doorframe. The room itself was small and simple, containing two single beds and a washstand, but after several months of living with the roof of a leaking tent barely six inches above their heads, they saw only grandeur. Two bathrooms were situated along the red-carpeted corridor, and the ever vigilant Iris immediately checked to see whether either was already occupied.

"One already gone, I'm afraid, and he's singing at the top of his voice."

"Golly, I am just aching for a nice hot bath," said Maisie.

"Tell you what. I'll put on my day dress and see if I can get our laundry done, while you draw a bath. We can top and tail it—check for the dreaded lice at the same time. It'll save waiting. Did you see the officers coming in after us? Bet they'll be bagging the bathrooms a bit sharpish."

"Don't some officers get rooms with bathrooms?"

"Oh, yes. Forgot that. Privilege and all that."

Iris and Maisie had discarded their uniform dresses quickly, and Iris gathered the laundry and walked toward the door.

"Never know, Maisie, p'raps your Captain Lynch will let you use *his* bathroom."

"Iris!"

"Only joking, Dobbsie. Now then, go bag us a bathroom."

The bathtub easily accommodated the two women, who lay back in the steaming water and audibly allowed the tension of the past few months to drain away.

"Bit more hot water, Maisie. Another five minutes and we'll swap ends."

"And about time!"

Maisie turned on the hot tap and pulled the plug to allow some of the cooler water out at the same time. After wallowing for another five minutes, they swapped ends, giggling as they moved, and continued to linger in the soothing steamy heat.

"Maisie," said Iris, as she leaned back, trying to comfortably position her head between the heavy taps, "Maisie, do you think your Captain Lynch will ask you to marry him, then?"

"Iris—"

"No, I'm not kidding you on now. I'm serious. What with the war and all. Makes you a bit more serious, doesn't it? Look at Bess White—gets a letter from her sweetheart, says he's going home on leave, she goes on leave, and boom! There they are—married, and him back at the front."

Maisie leaned forward, dipped her head in the water and sat up, sweeping back the long dark tresses.

"Here's what I do know, Iris. I know that when this is over, when the war is done with, I'm going back to university. That's what I know. Besides, when the war's over, I don't know if I'll be . . . well, Simon comes from a good family."

Iris looked at Maisie, then sat up and took hold of her hand.

"I know exactly what you are just about to say, Maisie, and let me tell you this, in case you haven't noticed. We are living in different times now. This war has made everything different. I've seen the letters from your dad, and from that Carter and Mrs. Whatsername with the pies. Those people, Maisie, are your family, and they are every bit as good as Simon's. And you are every bit as good as anyone Captain Simon Lynch will ever meet."

Maisie held on to Iris's hand, bit her bottom lip, and nodded. "It's just that—I can't explain it, but I have a feeling here," she held her hand to her chest, "that things will change. I know, I know, Iris, what you're going to say, 'It's the war. . . .' But I know this feeling. I know it to be true. And I know that everything will change."

"Come on. This water's going to your head, Maisie Dobbs. You are a grand nurse, Dobbsie, but I tell you, sometimes I wonder about all your wondering."

Iris put her hands on either side of the bath and levered herself up. She stepped out onto the tiled floor, grabbed one of the sturdy white towels, and began to dry herself. Maisie continued to sit in the rapidly cooling water while Iris dressed.

"Come on, dreamer. We'd better get a move on. That's if you want to see young Captain Lynch for dinner this evening. What time did he say to meet him?"

"The note said seven o'clock. By the desk in the main corridor as you come into the hotel."

Wearing a plain gray day dress, her hair up in a bun, and accompanied by Iris, Maisie walked down the wide sweeping staircase of the hotel. She had tried not to anticipate meeting with Simon again, in case she imagined too much, in case the expectation of excited conversation, of hands held, of feelings expressed, was to clash with reality.

Iris was accompanying Maisie, but had already made up her mind to retire early. Not that she should, really. Fraternizing between men and women in uniform was frowned upon. But with a bit of luck, Maisie's young man would have a nice friend for company. Chaperone, my eye! thought Iris. Nothing like being the piggy in the middle.

Maisie and Simon Lynch saw each other at exactly the same time, and moved quickly through the throng of visitors. The thumping of Maisie's heart seemed to radiate to her throat, and stopped the words of greeting she had so carefully planned. Simon simply stood in front of her, took both her hands in his and looked into her eyes.

"I thought I would never see you again, Maisie."

Maisie nodded and looked down at their hands held together.

A deep, throaty "Ahem!" brought Simon and Maisie's attention back into the room. Iris was looking at her feet, inspecting the soles of her shoes, when the man accompanying Simon spoke.

"Think you could introduce us, Lynch? Don't know how you folks do things, but where I'm from, we try to get acquainted."

"Oh, I'm sorry. Please forgive me. Maisie, Iris, may I introduce Captain Charles Hayden. Currently sporting a British uniform, but as you can hear, he's an American. Good man came over here with the Massachusetts General Hospital contingent to do his bit. God bless them all. We've been exchanging notes about dealing with gas poisoning. Charles—Miss Maisie Dobbs and Miss Iris Rigson."

"And delighted to meet you. It was worth coming all this way. And Lynch was becoming a bit of a bore, as you might say. Well, are we going to eat, or stand here all evening? Personally I'm for eating."

"Me too," said Iris.

Charles Hayden provided the group with a much-needed dose of humor at dinner, and as time passed the waves of conversation shifted, so that the voices of Hayden and Iris could be heard above all others, laughing loudly, teasing, and generally exchanging good cheer. Instinctively they had assumed the task of allowing their friends the intimacy that can be had, even in a crowded room, when two people want only to be with each other.

"I have longed to see you, Maisie, and yet now that you are here, I hardly know what to say."

"Yes, I know."

Simon turned his body toward Maisie and reached for her hand.

"Talk to me about anything, Maisie. I want to know everything about you. Even if you've already told me in a letter. I want to hear your voice. Start anywhere, but not with the war. Tell me about London, Kent, about your father, your mother—and what about that funny little man Maurice Blanche? Tell me about it all, Maisie."

Maisie smiled, looked briefly across the table at Iris laughing with her head back.

"I'll tell you about my father. Francis. Known to just about everyone as Frankie. He has three loves in his life. My mother, who died when I was a child, me, and Persephone, his horse."

Maisie and Simon each unfolded tales of their lives that transported them from the memory of more recent experiences. Even after dinner had ended, the two walked close together along a cobblestone street that led to nowhere in particular and back again. For two days Simon and Maisie were almost exclusively with each other, apart only when Simon kissed her hand at the end of each day and watched as she climbed the stairs to the room she shared with Iris.

"Well, we're off tomorrow, Maisie. Back to the delightful Maison Tent."

"Have you enjoyed yourself, Iris?"

"Thank God for Chuck—that's what he calls himself—Hayden. Nice man, good company. We swapped sweetheart stories while you collected stars in your eyes."

"Iris, I'm sorry. I can't thank you enough."

"Oh, Maisie, don't get me wrong. It was a very nice time I had. Seriously, like I said, he was good company. Left his wife and young son behind to come over here with other American doctors and nurses. Misses his family something rotten. I told him all about my Sid. Blimey, I dunno if I would've come over here if I didn't have to."

"You didn't have to come here, Iris."

"I know. But there again I did, because it's my country that's here in this war. They're our boys and I'm a nurse. But they didn't; the Americans didn't have to come here. Though Charles seems to think it won't be long before they're in."

Iris began packing her small bag ready for the journey back to the casualty clearing station. "Made a nice job of the uniforms they did, here in the hotel laundry. And in double-quick time. Enjoy the clean dress, my girl; we'll be in mud up to our knees before long. And fighting off the lice again."

"Oh don't, Iris. . . ."

$\mathscr{S}$imon accompanied Maisie and Iris to the station, and while Iris walked along to the platform for their train, Simon and Maisie stood together. Maisie shivered.

"I'll write as usual."

"That would be lovely, Simon. Gosh, it's cold."

Simon looked at her and without thinking put his arms around her.

"Please," Maisie protested weakly.

"Don't worry. No nasty sisters around to report you for dawdling with an unscrupulous RAMC captain."

Maisie laughed and shivered at the same time, moving her body closer to Simon. He held her to him and kissed her first on her forehead, then, as she looked up at him, Simon leaned down and kissed Maisie again on her cheek, then her lips.

"Simon, I—"

"Oh dear, will I get you into terrible trouble?"

She looked up at him, then around at the other travelers, none of whom seemed to notice the pair, and giggled nervously.

"Well, you might if someone sees us, Simon."

The guard signaled a loud whistle to alert passengers that the train would soon be leaving. Steam from the heavy engine was pushed up and out onto the platform. It was time for Simon and Maisie to part.

"Maisie. Look, I have a leave coming up again in a few months. Back to England. When's your leave? Perhaps it will be at the same time."

"I'll let you know, Simon. I'll let you know. I must run. I'll miss the train."

Simon held Maisie to him, and as the train signaled the "all aboard," she pulled herself away and ran along the platform. Iris was leaning out of the window of their carriage waving to her. She clambered aboard and sat down heavily on the seat just as the train began to move.

"I thought I'd be leaving without you, Dobbs."

"Not to worry, Iris. I'm here."

"Yes. You're here, Dobbsie. But I think you've left your heart behind with a certain young man."

Catching her breath as the train pulled out of the station, Maisie closed her eyes and thought of Simon. And as she saw his face in her mind's eye, the pressure returned to her chest. Rain slanted down across the windows as the fields of France seemed to rumble past with the movement of the train. Maisie looked out at this country she had willingly come to, so close to home, yet so far away from all that she loved. Almost. Simon was near.

CHAPTER TWENTY

*O*n a cold, wintry morning in February 1917, with the sun barely visible through the morning fog, Maisie pulled the wool cape around her shoulders and walked back to the tent she shared with Iris. Burning a hole in her pocket were two letters. One was from Simon. The other contained her leave papers. Her fingers were crossed.

"So, did you get it?" asked Iris, as Maisie tore at the small buff-colored envelope.

"Wait a minute, wait a minute. Yes! Yes! Yes!"

Maisie jumped up and down. She was going on leave. A real leave. Allowing two days for travel, she would have three days at home. Three days! One whole day more than her last leave, which was— she couldn't even remember. She immediately opened Simon's letter, scanned the lines of fine, right-slanted handwriting and jumped up and down again.

"Yes, Yes! He's got it, he's got leave!"

And the dates, April 15 to 20, were almost the same as hers. They would have two days together. Two whole days.

Iris smiled and shook her head. Oh, how that girl had changed.

Not in her work. No, the skill and compassion she brought to her work were as unquestionable as ever. But this joy, this excitement, was something new.

"Dobbsie, I do believe you are becoming a normal young woman!"

"Nonsense. I've always been normal," said Maisie, continuing to read Simon's letter.

"No, you haven't. I can tell. Taken life far too seriously, you have."

Iris reached for her cape and shivered. "And you can't do that in these times, Maisie. Take your work seriously, yes. But the rest of it, it'll drive you mad."

Iris carefully positioned her cap so that the red cross was in the center of her crown, and the point of the linen square was centered at the back of her head, just grazing the area between her shoulder blades.

"Ready, then?"

"Yes, I'm ready."

"Good. Let's get to work."

The weeks seemed to drag on, yet when Maisie looked back at the time between the arrival of her leave papers and the moment when which she walked onto the boat for the crossing back to Folkestone, it seemed that time had flown. As she stowed her bags, sought out hot cocoa and cake, Maisie almost dreaded the start of her leave, for by this time next week, she would be back in France. It would be over.

The crossing was calmer than last time, and though the sea was not quite like a millpond, the boat did not seem to pitch and toss as violently as before, and the tops of waves did not suddenly rear up and cover the deck. The nausea of her previous journey was not repeated to the same extent, yet a band of pressure around her forehead caused her to lean against the rail, counting off the quarter hours until land came in sight. She breathed in, waiting for sea saltiness to give way to the clear air of the county of Kent.

Oh, how she ached to see her father, to be drawn into the warm, steamy atmosphere of Mrs. Crawford's kitchen. In France she had dreamed of Kent, of apple orchards in full blossom, primroses and bluebells carpeting the woodland, and the soft countryside stretching out before her.

She longed to be home. She could hardly wait to see Simon.

Maisie disembarked, walking down the gangway and toward the port buildings. As she came through into the main waiting area, she saw her father, cap in hand, anxiously searching the sea of faces for her. Pushing her way through people jostling for extra height to see over the heads of others to the line of weary passengers, Maisie pulled at her father's arm.

"Dad! What are you doing here?"

"Darlin' girl. Couldn't wait for you to get to Chelstone, could I? So, I took the day off, like, and came down to meet you off the boat. Gawd, this ain't 'alf a busy old place! Come on, let me get that bag of yours, and let's get out of this lot. Never could stand a crowd, even at the market."

Maisie laughed and, still holding tightly to his arm, followed as he pushed his way through the surging throng making their way to the station.

The journey to Chelstone took another two hours, first by train to Tonbridge, then by the small branch line down to Chelstone. In a field across from the station, Persephone was grazing, her cart resting just inside the gate.

"Just a minute, love. Won't take me long to get old Persephone ready for you. Stationmaster let me leave the old girl here. I know it's not a fancy motorcar, but I thought you'd appreciate a ride home on the old cart with Persephone."

"That I do, Dad."

They rode in silence for a while, Frankie Dobbs with his arm around his daughter's shoulder.

"'Ard to know what to say to you, love. Bet you don't really want to talk about it, do you?"

"No. Not now, Dad. I'm not home for long. I'll be back there soon enough."

"And how long will I see you for?"

Frankie looked sideways at Maisie.

"Well, I'll be seeing a friend while I'm on leave. But we've got all day tomorrow."

"Is that all I get? Blimey, this Captain Lynch must be an interestin' fella."

Maisie swung round to her father.

"How do you know—?"

"Now then, now then. Just you 'old your 'orses, young lady. You're still my girl, and that's a fact."

Frankie grinned at Maisie. "There's a letter waiting indoors for you. Just sent to Miss Dobbs at Chelstone Manor. Got 'is name printed on the back of the envelope. Very posh. Knows your old Dad's the groom, does 'e?"

"Yes. He does, Dad. He knows who you are and who I am."

"Good. That's all right then. Look forward to meeting the man."

"Well, I don't know . . . ."

Frankie put his arm around Maisie again, and in the security of her father's embrace and his love for her, she slept as she had not been able to sleep since she left for France.

"*W*ell, I never. Look at you. All skin and bone, Maisie, all skin and bone."

Mrs. Crawford drew Maisie to her, then pushed away to inspect her from head to toe.

"A good dinner, that's what you need, my girl. Thank heavens we are all down here now, have been ever since her ladyship said it was too dangerous in London, what with the Zeppelin raids. Anyway, at least I can get a good dinner down you. That's what you need—a good dinner."

Maisie had hardly stepped from Frankie Dobbs's cart before the "welcome homes" began. And it seemed that one welcome was followed by another. She had been immediately summoned to the drawing room to meet with Lady Rowan. Already the short leave was turning into a whirlwind, but the next day Maisie spent time only with her father, alone.

Frankie Dobbs and Maisie groomed the horses together, walked across farmland, and speculated on the apple crop that would surely be the result of such fine hearty white blossom. And sitting alone in the gardens at Chelstone, Maisie wondered about the war, and how it was that such blooms could give joy to the soul, when one only had to stand on cliffs overlooking the Channel to hear the boom of cannons on the battlefields of France.

On the second day of her leave, Maisie was to see Simon in London, a meeting arranged in letters passed between their respective medical stations in France. She would meet his parents at the family's London home during their first day together. They both knew better than to have Simon suggest she stay at the house, as an overnight invitation would come only after a more formal luncheon meeting, the invitation for which had arrived from Mrs. Lynch, and along with Simon's letter, had awaited Maisie's return to Chelstone. Simon wrote that he couldn't wait to see her.

Frankie Dobbs took Maisie to the station, and they stood awkwardly on the platform to wait for the local train, which would connect with the London train at Tonbridge.

"Now, you make sure you don't overdo it. That Crawford woman was right. Skin and bone you are. You're like your mother, a tall drink of water in a dress."

"I'll eat them out of house and home, Dad."

"And you mind yourself, Maisie. I've not met this young man, but seeing as you've been invited by his people, I'm sure he's a fine person. And a doctor. But you mind yourself, Maisie."

"Dad, I'll be back on the train this evening—"

"Maisie. It's in 'ere that I'm talking about."

Frankie Dobbs pressed his hand to the place that still held grief for his departed wife.

"I'm talking about your 'eart, Maisie. Mind out for your 'eart."

*T*he sun was shining by the time the engine met the end-of-the-line buffers at Charing Cross station. Maisie checked her face in the shell-shaped mirror on the bulkhead between the carriages. She had never been one to fuss over her appearance, but this was different. This was important.

Once again butterflies were holding court in her stomach, and once again she was filled with the joyous anticipation of seeing Simon Lynch. She opened the heavy wooden door and stepped down onto the platform.

"Maisie!"

"Simon!"

The young officer swept Maisie up into his arms and unashamedly kissed her, much to the delight of people rushing to catch trains, or anxiously waiting for loved ones on the platform. There was usually little cause for humor or delight at a wartime railway station, filled as they often were with war wounded, anxious farewells, and the bittersweet greetings of those who would have such a short time together.

"I have missed you so much. I can hardly believe we are here."

Maisie laughed, laughed until the tears fell down her cheeks. How she would hate to say good-bye.

The time spent at the Lynches' London house could not have been more perfect. Simon's parents welcomed Maisie into their home with great affection, as if she were part of the family. Mrs. Lynch personally showed Maisie to a guest room to "repair after the long journey."

Maisie's fears that she might have to field questions about her father's line of business proved to be unfounded, and she was asked only about her time at Cambridge and whether she might return when the war was over. Simon's parents understood that talk of "intentions" was almost futile at such a time, and the joy of having a dear son home was not to be sullied by questions that might give rise to discord. Time was too short.

Simon and Maisie had one more day together, then Maisie would leave early on Sunday morning for France. After lunch Simon escorted Maisie to Charing Cross Station again, and spoke of what they would do the next day.

"So, I've managed to get the car, lucky, eh? I'll leave early for Chelstone, then we can have a nice day out together—perhaps go on to the Downs."

"That would be lovely."

"What is it, Maisie?"

Maisie looked at her watch, and at the many men and women in uniform at the station.

"Remember to come to the groom's cottage, Simon. Not to the main house."

"Oh, I see. You're worried about me coming to Chelstone, aren't you?"

Maisie looked at her hands, and at Simon. "A little."

"It doesn't matter to me, Maisie. We both know that there are bigger things to worry about. Besides, it's me that has to worry about Chelstone, what with the formidable Mrs. Crawford waiting to render judgment!"

Maisie laughed. "Yes, Simon, you may have a good point there!"

Simon held her hand and escorted her to the platform. The arrival of her train had just been announced.

"Tomorrow will be our last day together." said Simon. "I wish I understood time, Maisie. It vanishes through one's fingers."

He held her hands together in front of his chest, and touched each of her fingertips in turn.

"Maurice says that only when we have a respect for time will we have learned something of the art of living."

"Ah, yes, the wise man Maurice. Perhaps I'll meet him one day."

Maisie looked into Simon's eyes and shivered. "Yes, perhaps. One day."

Simon arrived at Chelstone at half past nine the next morning. Maisie had been up since half past five, first helping Frankie with the horses, then going for a walk, mentally preparing for Simon's arrival. She strolled through the apple orchards, heavy with blossom, then to the paddock beyond.

Half of what was, before the war, grazing for horses, was now a large vegetable garden providing fresh produce not only for Chelstone Manor but also for a wider community. In a time of war, flowers and shrubs were seen to be an extravagance, so every cottage garden in the village was almost bereft of blooms. Even the smallest postage stamp of land was needed for growing vegetables.

Maisie made her way back to the cottage and waited for Simon. Eventually the crackle of tires on gravel heralded his arrival. Frankie drew the curtains aside to look out the window in the small parlor.

"Looks like your young man is here."

Maisie rushed from the room, while Frankie stood in front of the mirror, adjusted his neckerchief and pulled down the hem of his best waistcoat. He rubbed his chin, just to make sure, and took off the flat cap that almost never left his head. Before going to the door to meet Captain Simon Lynch, Frankie took up the cherished sepia photograph of a woman who looked so much like the girl who had run joyously to the door. She was tall and slender, dressed in a dark skirt and a cotton blouse with wide leg-o'-mutton sleeves. Though she had fussed with her hair in anticipation of having the photograph taken with her two-year-old daughter, there were still stray curls creeping onto her forehead.

Frankie ran his finger across the glass, tracing the line of the woman's face. He spoke to the image tenderly, as if she were in the room with him, for Frankie Dobbs had prayed for her spirit to be at his side today.

"I know, I know . . . go easy on 'im. I wish you was 'ere now, Love. I could do with a bit of 'elp with this."

Frankie replaced the photograph, and with one last look in the mirror, just to make sure that he wouldn't let Maisie down, he walked from the cottage to greet the man to whom his daughter had run so eagerly.

For hours Simon and Maisie talked, first on the journey by motor car across to Sussex, then throughout lunch at a small inn. It was only after they had parked the car by a clump of trees and walked high up on the South Downs, seagulls whooping overhead, that they spent time in silence. Their pace aligned as they walked along the rough path on the crest of the hills overlooking the Channel. They moved closer together, hands brushing but not quite touching.

The day was warm, but Maisie still felt cold. It was a cold that had seeped into her bones in France and now seemed never to leave her. Simon sat down on the grass under a tree, and beckoned her to sit next to him. As she sat down he took her hand and grimaced, then playfully reached for one of her walking shoes, untied the laces, and held her foot in his hand.

"Goodness, woman, how can anyone be that cold and not be dead!"

Maisie laughed along with Simon.

"It's that French mud that does it, gets right into your bones."

The laughter subsided, and seconds later they were both silent.

"Will you definitely return to Cambridge after the war?"

"Yes. And you, Simon?"

"Oh, I think I'll be for the quiet life, you know. Country doctor. Delivering babies, dealing with measles, mumps, hunters' accidents, farmworkers' ailments, that sort of thing. I'll grow old in corduroy and tweed, smoke a pipe, and swat my grandchildren on their little behinds when they wake me from my afternoon snooze."

Simon leaned forward, plucked a blade of grass, and twisted it between his long fingers. "What about after Cambridge, Maisie?"

"I'm not sure."

Conversation ebbed as Simon and Maisie looked out over the sea, both daring their imagination to wander tentatively into the future. Maisie sighed deeply, and Simon held her to him. As if reading her thoughts, he spoke.

"It's hard to think about the future when you've seen so many passing through who don't have tomorrow, let alone next year. No future at all."

"Yes."

It was all she could say.

"Maisie. Maisie, I know this is rather soon, possibly even presumptuous, but, Maisie, when this is all over, this war, when we are back here in England . . . would you marry me?"

Maisie inhaled sharply, her skin prickly with emotion. What was that emotion? She wanted to say "Yes" but something stopped her.

"I know, I know, you don't have to say anything. It's the thought of corduroy trousers and tweeds isn't it?"

"No, Simon. No. It was just a surprise."

"Maisie, I love you."

He took her hand and looked deeply into her eyes.

"Yes. And I love you too, Simon. I love you too."

Simon drove Maisie back to Chelstone, and brought the car to a halt on the road at the end of the driveway that led to the manor. He leaned over and took Maisie's left hand.

"You never gave me an answer, Maisie."

"I know. It's just me, Simon. And doing what we have to do. In France. I want to wait until it's over. Until there's no more . . . no more . . . death. I can't say yes to something so important until we're home again. Until we're safe."

Simon nodded, his compassion for her feelings at war with his disappointment.

"But Simon. I do love you. Very much."

Simon did not speak, but cupped Maisie's face in his hands, and kissed her deeply. At first, Maisie began to pull away, afraid that someone from the manor might see, but as Simon's arms enfolded her, she returned his kiss, reaching for his neck to pull him closer. Suddenly Maisie was aware of moisture on her face and, pulling away, she looked into Simon's eyes and touched her cheek where their tears had met.

"God, I wish this war would end," Simon wiped the back of his hand across his eyes, before facing her once again. He kissed her gently on the lips. "I love you, Maisie, and I want you to be my wife. I promise that as soon as this war is over, I will walk across miles of trenches to find you, and I will stand there in my muddy clothes until you say 'Yes!'"

They kissed once more. Then, taking up her bag, Maisie asked Simon to let her walk back to the house alone. She did not want to suffer a difficult farewell, possibly in front of her father and whoever else might be in the gardens to witness their parting. Simon objected, on the grounds that no gentleman would allow a lady to walk unaccompanied to her home, but Maisie was adamant, reminding Simon that she had walked along that lane many a time, and often with a heavy basket.

Simon did not argue her decision. Instead of more words, they held each other close and kissed. She went swiftly from the motorcar and along the driveway, eventually hearing Simon start the engine in the distance and pull away onto the road.

*M*aisie insisted that she travel alone back to Folkestone, and Frankie, seeing a new maturity and independence in his daughter, agreed to allow Lady Rowan's new chauffeur, an older man passed over for military service, to take her to the station. Maisie said good-bye to her father at home. She had no stomach for more platform farewells.

It was on her journey to Folkestone, and then to France, that she thought back over the events of the days she had spent on leave. She remembered Simon's easy camaraderie with her father, his smile upon introduction, and how he immediately began asking about the horses and allowed himself to be led to the stables so that Frankie Dobbs was relaxed in the domain over which he was the obvious master.

Time and again Maisie replayed Simon's proposal in her head, and, though she would no doubt receive a letter from him soon, considered how she avoided making a commitment. She knew only too well the source of such reticence.

As the train moved through the early morning mist of a Kentish springtime, Maisie breathed deeply, as if to remember the aroma of freedom. Though there had yet to be a victor in this great war that had begun almost three years ago, Maurice had written to her that they had, all of them, on all sides, lost their freedom. The freedom to think hopefully of the future.

It was later, much later, more than ten years after the war, that Maisie remembered every thought that had entered her mind on the journey back to the battlefield hospital.

She remembered praying to see Simon just one more time.

SUMMER 1929

aisie took the underground from Warren Street to Charing Cross, then changed to the District Line for Victoria. As the train rocked from side to side, Maisie wondered what the evening's conversation with Lady Rowan might reveal. She suspected that the farm where James intended to take up residence was the same place that Celia had described over tea.

Leaving the train at Victoria, Maisie made her way out of the underground station, and walked along Lower Belgrave Street toward Ebury Place. And as she walked, she thought of Maurice, who had told her so many times that coincidence could simply be what it appeared to be: two events connected to each other by the thoughts and experience of a person. But he also told Maisie to pay attention to coincidence.

Coincidence was a messenger sent by truth.

Carter took Maisie's cloche and jacket, and welcomed her into the entrance hall. "So lovely to see you, Maisie. How are you? Her ladyship is waiting for you in the drawing room—and very anxious to see you she is, too."

"I'm well, thank you, Mr. Carter. I'll just nip down to see Mrs. Crawford first. I don't want her giving me an earful for not coming straight down to see her."

"A very wise decision, Maisie. You know the way."

Carter left to hang Maisie's outer garments in the cloakroom as Maisie made her way through the door to the right of the entrance hall and downstairs into the kitchen. The stone stairwell was as chilly as she remembered, but as soon as she walked through the door to the kitchen, she was enveloped in the welcoming warmth and mingling aromas that sent her back to her girlhood.

Mrs. Crawford had become hard of hearing, and continued to work as Maisie stood at the threshold of her domain. Maisie wondered if she had ever seen the old cook's hands clear of either flour or water. They were rough and work-worn hands, but Maisie knew that before touching any food, Mrs. Crawford would have stood at the big square earthenware sink and scrubbed her hands with a coarse bristle brush and a bar of coal tar soap. And by the time she plunged her hands into pastry dough, her red, sausage-like fingers would be in stark relief to the white flour. Maisie loved Mrs. Crawford's apple pie, and if she was visiting, there would be a pie for the sweet course *and* a pie for her to take home.

"Mrs. Crawford," said Maisie in a raised voice, "I'm here!"

Mrs. Crawford turned quickly, her purposeful frown transformed into a beaming smile.

"Well, look at you now! Don't you go getting those nice clothes all covered with flour."

Mrs. Crawford rubbed her hands on her pinafore and came toward Maisie with her arms open wide. Maisie was only too pleased to relinquish her body to a hug that was warm and close, even though the old woman was careful to keep her hands away from Maisie's clothes, instead embracing Maisie with pressure from her elbows.

"Are you eating, Maisie? There's nothing of you! I always said that a puff of wind would blow you away clear to Clacton!"

"I promise I'm eating, Mrs. Crawford. In fact, what's for dinner?"

"A nice vegetable soup, followed by roast beef with all the trimmings—and it's not even Sunday. Then there's apple pie and the cheese board."

"Oh my goodness. I'll pop!"

"Not all for you, but mind you eat a good bit of it. His Lordship will be home late again this evening and will have dinner in his study. And if that James comes in with his face as long as a week, they'll probably eat together. Otherwise Master James will eat in his rooms, with his misery for company."

"I thought he had his own flat—I didn't know he was back at home."

"When he likes. I know, I know, you feel sorry for the boy and all that, and you know we all love him—have done since he was but a streak of lightning running around. But the fact is, he's not a boy anymore, is he? And there's plenty of men out there what saw everything over there in France that he did, and they did what we all have to do—they just got on with it instead of moping around like a lost, wet gun dog, all soppy eyes and sodden coat."

Maisie knew that it was no good reasoning with Mrs. Crawford, who had firm ideas when it came to coping with life's ups and downs.

"That's the trouble with these boys of privilege. Not that I'm criticizing, far from it, I've been treated very well by them upstairs, very well. But that James has had too much time to think about it all. Too much going on up there." Mrs. Crawford had gone back to her pastry but tapped the side of her head to emphasize the point. Realizing that she had touched her hair, she went over to the sink to scrub her hands again but lost no time in continuing to make her point.

"Look at the boys who came back and had to get straight out in the farms and the factories—they had wives and families to look out for. You don't see them dragging their heels along, do you? No, that James should be at his lordship's side, taking some of the weight so that His Lordship isn't in the City at all hours. Not right for a man of his age. After all, look at James, he's thirty-eight this year."

Mrs. Crawford came back to her pastry, rolling out the dough with more than a little thumping of the rolling pin on the table. "Have you heard from your father lately?" Mrs. Crawford looked up at Maisie, yet continued flouring the pastry and sizing it to the pie dish.

"Yes. Mind you it's difficult, Mrs. Crawford. It's not as if he ever liked to put pen to paper. But he's still busy at the house. Master James goes down quite a lot to ride, so there's always work with the horses. And Her Ladyship likes to know that her own horses are cared for, even though she can't ride anymore."

"And that's another thing. All that time to go down there to 'think,' if you please. It's like I said, too much money and too much time on his hands."

Suddenly one of the bells over the door rang.

"That'll be Her Ladyship now. She probably reckons I've had long enough with you. Now then, don't forget to come down for your pie to take home when you leave in the morning."

Maisie kissed Mrs. Crawford on the cheek and went upstairs to the drawing room.

"Maisie, how lovely to see you. I had to ring or Mrs. Crawford would have hogged you for the whole evening! Come here to sit by the fire. I expect you know what's for dinner already. I told Julian that you would be dining with me, and he said 'Oh, good, we'll get some apple pie.' Come on, over here."

Lady Rowan tapped the place next to her on the sofa. The two women spoke of Maisie's business and her new clients. For Rowan Compton, Maisie was a breath of fresh air, and she lived vicariously through Maisie's stories.

"And Maurice is keen to see you again soon, you know."

"I thought he would be glad to have a break from me, to tell you the truth."

"Now, then, Maisie. You are like a daughter to him. You are his protégée. You are carrying his torch and shining your own light too. But I know he made a promise to himself to give you a little room for you to make your own way. He said to me, 'Rowan, it is past time to let our Maisie Dobbs fly free.'"

"I'll bet he said a bit more than that. I know Maurice too, Lady Rowan."

"Well, yes. He said that you would always look down as you were flying overhead, and if the ground was good for a landing, in you would come—or something like that. You know, that man talks in parables. I swear that sometimes I think he is the most profound person I know, and at others he infuriates me with his obscurity." Lady Rowan shook her head. "Will you visit him soon, Maisie?"

"Yes, I mean to. In fact, I need to consult with him."

"Anything interesting?"

Maisie smiled at Lady Rowan, without speaking.

"I know, you can't divulge a secret."

"Tell me about James," asked Maisie.

Lady Rowan rolled her eyes, took up her glass from the side table, and sipped her sherry. "James. Oh, that James. I am at a loss, Maisie. I knew it when that boy was a child, too sensitive by half. Have you noticed how we always call him a boy? Even now. It wouldn't be so bad if he were gadding about town wining and dining and getting into mischief. But this malaise . . . I wish he would speak to Maurice. But he won't go to see Maurice, and you know that Maurice won't go to him. One of his riddles, that James must open the door and walk along the path to him."

"Maurice is right, Lady Rowan."

"Well, you would say that, wouldn't you? You're a chip off the old block. By the way, he and your father are like two old peas in a pod down there, ever since Maurice bought the dower house."

"Tell me about James," Maisie prodded her.

Lady Rowan took another sip of her sherry. "Frankly, I'm worried. Julian is also worried, but he expresses it in a different way. He seems to think that if we are all patient, then James will come round, and that he won't be so incredibly depressed anymore."

Maisie did not speak, allowing Lady Rowan to gather her thoughts. Sitting still and allowing the silence to grow, Maisie felt the frustration, misunderstanding, and anger that had built up in the house, permeating every room—along with an expectation that James would one day bound in as the happy-go-lucky young man he had once been.

Carter came in to announce that dinner would be served in the dining room, and led the way. Maisie held out her arm to steady Lady Rowan, who now walked with the aid of a silver-capped cane, as they moved into the dining room.

"Wonderful, Carter, wonderful. Compliments to Mrs. Crawford, as always."

The conversation continued lightly as each dish was served, moving once again to the subject of James only after Carter had left the room.

"Some weeks ago, James met with a wartime colleague who had heard of a farm, coincidentally in Kent, where old soldiers could go to live with others who 'understood.' That was the term they used, 'understood.' As if no one else is able to understand. It seems that this farm is quite a revolutionary idea. It was originally set up for those suffering facial wounds, but now it is open—obviously when a room becomes available—to those with other wounds."

Lady Rowan set her knife and fork down on the plate, reached for her wine, and took a sip before continuing. "Of course, James still suffers pain in his leg and arm from the shrapnel, but Maurice has said that his discomfort is a result of melancholy. Yet James has become most interested in this community of wounded. He has visited, met with the founder, and has decided to go to live at this . . . this farm for the foreseeable future!"

"You seem distressed by his decision, Lady Rowan. Is there anything else?"

"Yes. A lot more. The founder, a man called Adam Jenkins, maintains that because everyone on the battlefield should have been equal, officers and enlisted men, because they all faced the same enemy, then there should be no advantage while in residence at this farm. Which is fair enough, but James said something about giving up his surname and title. Whatever next?" Lady Rowan shook her head.

At once Maisie thought of Vincent Weathershaw. Vincent.

Lady Rowan went on, "I wish to heaven James would go back to Canada. He seemed happy there, before the war, and at least he would be working and useful. Certainly his father would be delighted; it would be a weight off his mind. I know Julian wants to slow up a bit and wishes James would begin to take up the reins. And now he's signing over his money. . . ."

Lady Rowan had hardly touched her food. Instead she ran the fingers of her right hand up and down the stem of her wine glass.

"What do you mean?" Maisie asked.

"Apparently it's one of the stipulations for entering this Retreat or whatever it's called. You come with nothing, to be part of the group. So James has transferred his personal funds to this Jenkins fellow—and it's not just him, others have done the same thing. Thank God his father is still alive and there are limits to what James can actually relinquish financially. Julian is taking steps to protect the estate—and James's future—until he gets over this horrible idea. Of course Julian had already done a lot to shore up the estate when he saw the General Strike coming a few years ago. I married a sensible man, Maisie."

"What does Jenkins do with the money?"

"Well, it's a sizable property to run, and I'm sure the upkeep isn't insignificant. Of course, when one leaves one is refunded any monies remaining and given a statement of account. James said that he saw samples of the statements and refund documents, and he was happy with the arrangements. Mind you, he seemed eager to isolate himself on this farm. He said that people would understand him there. Oh, mind you, he seemed eager to isolate himself on this farm. He said that people would understand him there. As if I don't!"

Lady Rowan reached over and clasped Maisie's hand. Maisie had never seen the usually stoic Lady Rowan so vulnerable.

"Where is James now?"

"Out. Possibly at his club, but he doesn't go there much now. Quite honestly, I don't know where he is. He could be wandering the streets for all I know. Most probably he's spending time with some old comrades. He visits them you know, those that are still institutionalized. He'll probably be back later. Much later. I told him he could remain at Chelstone; after all, it's in the country, there's peace and quiet, and he could do what he likes and come back when he's ready for the City. Lord knows Julian needs his help. But he's determined to go to this farm. I have never felt so . . . so . . . cut off from my son."

Maisie pushed the food around on her plate. There was a time when mother and son had been almost inseparable, sharing a dry wit and a mischievous sense of humor. She remembered being at the London house soon after she received news that she had been accepted by Girton College. James had just returned from Canada, hoping to join the Royal Flying Corps. There was much joy in the household, and as she walked down the outside stairs toward the kitchen, Maisie saw the tall, fair young man through the window, creeping up behind Mrs. Crawford and putting his arms around her ample waist. And as Maisie watched through the condensation that had built up inside the pane of glass, Mrs. Crawford swung around, clipped the young man around the ear, and, laughing, pretended to admonish him. "You, young James, why no sooner are you back than you'll be the death of me. Look at you, you young lout—and if you are after fresh ginger biscuits, I've baked up a batch 'specially for you, though I'm not sure you deserve them now!"

Maisie had walked in through the back door of the kitchen just as James was taking his first bite of a fresh ginger biscuit.

"And look who else is here," said Mrs. Crawford. "Maisie Dobbs, I do believe you are even thinner! My back only has to be turned for one minute, and you're not eating properly."

With crumbs around his mouth, James swallowed the biscuit, and struggled to greet Maisie politely. "Ah, the clever Miss Maisie Dobbs, passing exams that the rest of us mere mortals have nightmares about!"

Then as Mrs. Crawford turned to the stove, James whispered to Maisie, "Tell Enid I'm home."

Later, as she walked past the drawing room on her way to Lord Julian's study to serve afternoon tea, which he had elected to take alone, she saw James and Lady Rowan through the open door. Lady Rowan was laughing heartily, having been whisked by her son into an impromptu dance, accompanied only by the sound of his own booming voice:

> Oh, he floats through the air with the greatest of ease
> The daring young man on the flying trapeze
> His actions are graceful, all girls he does please
> And my love he has stolen away.

"I won't ask you to see James, Maisie," continued Lady Rowan, bringing Maisie back into the present, "I know your opinion will mirror Maurice's, so I know better than to ask. But I wonder. Would you find out something about this farm, or whatever it is? I have to say that I do feel he would be better in the world rather than trying to escape from it."

"I will certainly look into it, Lady Rowan. I'll go down to Kent next week. I have to go anyway, as I need to speak with Maurice, and I must see my father. I'll find out about James's retreat as well."

"Maisie. Take the MG. I know very well that you can drive, so do please take the car. It's not as if I've used it much since Julian bought it for me to run around in—and George drives Julian to the City in the Lanchester."

"Yes, all right, Lady Rowan. It's very kind of you to offer, and I may need to be flexible, so the car will be handy."

"It's almost new, so the young thing should get you there and back with no trouble at all. And Maisie—don't forget to send me your bill!"

Maisie directed conversation to other matters, and soon Lady Rowan was laughing in her old infectious manner. Carter watched as two maids cleared the table and brought in the delicious apple pie, to be served with a generous helping of fresh clotted cream. After dinner Maisie and Lady Rowan returned to the drawing room, to sit beside the fire until Lady Rowan announced that it was past time for her to be in bed.

Maisie made her way to the guest room that had been prepared for her visit. Nora had already unpacked Maisie's small bag and laid out her nightclothes on the bed. Later, as she snuggled closer to the hot water bottle that warmed the sheets, Maisie remembered, as she always did when she slept at the Compton residence, the nights she'd spent in the servants' quarters at the top of the house.

She left before breakfast the next morning, stopping quickly to drink tea with Carter and Mrs. Crawford, and to collect the apple pie. Billy Beale would love that apple pie, thought Maisie. She might need it when she asked him if he would take on a very delicate task for her. In fact, as the plans began to take shape in her mind, she might need more than apple pie for Billy Beale.

CHAPTER TWENTY-TWO

"*R*ight then. Watch carefully, miss. 'Ere's how you start 'er up."

The young chauffeur walked around to the front of the 1927 MG 14/40 two-seater roadster, and put his hand on the engine cover.

"You've basically got your five steps to starting this little motor, very straightforward when you know what you're about, so watch carefully."

George enjoyed the attention that came as a result of his expertise in the maintenance and operation of the Compton's stable of very fine motor cars.

"First you lift your bonnet, like so."

George waited for Maisie to nod her head in understanding before continuing with his instructions, and as he turned his attention once again to the MG, she grinned with amusement at his preening tutorial.

"Right. See this—you turn on your fuel. Got it?"

"Yes, George."

George closed the engine cover, and indicated for Maisie to move away from the side of the car so that he could sit in the driver's seat.

"You set your ignition, you set your throttle, set your choke—three moves, got it?"

"Got it, George."

"You push the starter button—on the floor, Miss—with your foot and—"

The engine roared into life, perhaps somewhat more aggressively than usual, given the enthusiasm of George's lesson.

"There she goes."

George clambered from the seat, held open the door, and, with a sweep of his hand, invited Maisie to take his place.

"Think you've got all that, Miss?"

"Oh yes, George. You explained everything very clearly. As you say, it's very straightforward. A lovely motor."

"Oh, nice little runner, to be sure. 'Cording to them at Morris Garages, this one can do sixty-five miles an hour—up to fifty in the first twenty-five seconds! 'Er ladyship goes out of 'ere like a shot out of a gun, doesn't know where she's going, but goes like a shot anyway. Comes back all red in the face. Worries me with them gears though. Talk about crunch! Makes me cringe when I 'ear it. Thank 'eavens for us all that she don't get out in it much anymore. Now, then, sure of your way?"

"I'm sure, George. Down the Old Kent Road, and just keep on from there, more or less. I've done that journey many a time when I was younger."

"'Course, you was at Chelstone, wasn't you? Mind you, if I were you, I'd go out onto Grosvenor Place, then along Victoria Street, over Westminster Bridge, St. George's Road, and just the other side of the Elephant and Castle. . . ."

"I think I can remember the way, George, and thank you for the advice."

George walked around to the back of the MG and dropped Maisie's bag into the car's rear luggage compartment, while she made herself comfortable in the rich claret leather seat. He checked once again that her door was closed securely before standing back and giving her a mock salute.

Maisie returned the wave as she eased the smart crimson motor car out into the mews. It wasn't until she was across the Thames and past the Elephant and Castle that Maisie felt she could breathe again. At every turn she sat up straight and peered over the steering wheel, making sure that each part of the vehicle was clear of any possible obstruction. She had learned to drive before returning to Cambridge in 1919, but took extra care as it had been quite some time since she'd had an opportunity—although she did not want to admit as much to George. In fact, she did not change from first gear until she was well out of George's hearing, fearing a dreadful roaring as she reacquainted herself with the intricacies of the double-de-clutch maneuver to change gear.

It was a fine day in early June, a day that seemed to predict a long hot summer for 1929. Maisie drove conservatively, partly to minimize chances of damage to the MG and partly to savor the journey. She felt that she only had to smell the air and, blindfolded, she would know she had arrived in Kent. And no matter how many times she came back to Chelstone, every journey reminded her of her early days and months at the house. As Maisie drove, she relaxed and allowed her mind to wander. Memories of that first journey from the house in Belgravia came flooding back. So much had happened so quickly. So much that was unexpected yet, looking back, seemed so very predictable. Ah, as Maurice would say, the wisdom of hindsight!

Drawing to a halt at the side of the road to pull back the roadster's heavy cloth roof, Maisie stood for a moment to look at the medley of wildflowers that lined the grass verge. Arrowheads of sunny yellow charlock were growing alongside clumps of white field mouse-ear, which in turn were busily taking up space and becoming tangled in honeysuckle growing over the hedge. She leaned down to touch the delicate blue flower of the common speedwell, and remembered how she had loved this county from the moment she first came to work for the dowager. It was a soft patchwork-quilt land in which she found solace from missing her father and the Belgravia house.

Maisie had decided already that the day in Kent should become a two or three day excursion. Lady Rowan had given her permission to keep the car for as long as it was needed, and Maisie had packed a small bag in case she chose to stay. The hedgerows, small villages and apple orchards still full of blossom, were working their magic upon her. She stopped briefly at the post office in Sevenoaks.

"I'm looking for a farm, I think it's called The Retreat. I wonder if you might be able to direct me?"

"Certainly, Miss."

The postmaster took a sheet of paper and began to write down an address with some directions.

"You might want to be careful, Miss."

Maisie put her head to one side to indicate that she was listening to any forthcoming advice. "Yes, Miss. Our postman who does the route says it's run like a cross between a monastery and a barracks. You'd've thought that the blokes in there had seen enough of barracks, wouldn't you? There's a gate and a man on duty—you'll have to tell him your business before he'll let you in. They're nice enough, by all accounts, but I've heard that they don't want just anyone wandering about because of the residents."

"Yes, yes indeed," said Maisie, taking the sheet of paper. "Thank you for your advice."

The sun was high in the sky by the time Maisie came out of the post office, and as she touched the door handle of the MG it was warm enough to cause her to flinch. Pay attention, Maurice had always cautioned her. Pay attention to the reactions of your body. It is the wisdom of the self speaking to you. Be aware of concern, of anticipation, of all the feelings that come from the self. They manifest in the body. What is their counsel?

If those from the outside were questioned, albeit in a nonthreatening manner, when they entered, how might it be for the residents, the men who had been ravaged by war, in their coming and going? Maisie decided to drive on toward Chelstone. The Retreat could wait until she had seen Maurice.

Frankie Dobbs put the MG away in the garage and helped Maisie with her bags. She would stay in the small box room at the groom's cottage, which had once been her bedroom and was now always made up ready for her to visit, even though such visits were few and far between.

"We don't see enough of you, Love."

"I know, Dad. But I've been occupied with the business. It's been hard work since Maurice retired."

"It was 'ard work before 'e retired, wasn't it? Mind you, the old boy looks as if 'e's enjoyin' 'avin' a bit of time to 'imself. He comes in 'ere to 'ave a cup of tea with me now'n again, or I'll go over to see 'is roses. It surprised me, what 'e knows about roses. Clever man, that Maurice."

Maisie laughed.

"I have to go over to see him, Dad. It's important."

"Now then, I'm not stupid. I know that I'm not the only reason for you comin' all this way. Mind you, I 'ope I'm the main reason."

"'Course you are, Dad."

Frankie Dobbs finished brewing tea and placed an old enamel mug in front of Maisie, then winked and went to the cupboard for his own large china cup and saucer. As he brought some apple pie out of the larder, Maisie poured tea for them both.

"Maisie. You are lookin' after yourself, aren't you?"

"Yes, Dad. I can take care of myself."

"Well, I know that this work you do is sometimes, well, tricky like. And you're on your own now. Just as long as you're careful."

"Yes, Dad."

Frankie Dobbs sat down at the table with Maisie, reached into his pocket and pulled out a small package wrapped in brown paper and secured with string. "Anyway, I was in the 'ardware shop last week, talking to old Joe Cooke—you know 'ow that man can jaw—and, well, I saw this little thing. Thought it might come in 'andy, like, for you. Natty, innit?"

Maisie raised an eyebrow at her father, wondering if he was teasing her. With nimble fingers, she pulled away the string and opened the paper to reveal a shining new stainless-steel Victorinox pocket knife.

"Old Joe said it was a bit odd, buying a thing like this for me daughter, like, but I said, 'Joe, let me tell you, a daughter on 'er own can make more use of a thing like this, with them little tools, than any of them lads of yours.' In any case, y'never know when it might be just the thing you need, 'specially if you're runnin' all over in that motor."

"Oh, Dad, you shouldn't go spending money on me." Maisie pulled out each tool in turn, then looked at the closed knife in the palm of her hand. "I'll keep it with me all the time, just in case." Maisie slipped the knife into her bag, leaned across the table to kiss her father on the cheek, then reached for her tea.

Father and daughter laughed together, then sat in companionable silence drinking tea and eating apple pie, comfortable with only the heavy tick-tock of the grandfather clock for company. Maisie was thinking about The Retreat, and how she would present the story to Maurice.

Years of working with Maurice had helped Maisie prepare her answers to some of his questions, like a chess player anticipating the moves in a game. But she knew that the ones likely to be most difficult were those that pertained to her own past.

Frankie Dobbs interrupted Maisie's thoughts.

"So, that MG. Nice little motor, is it? What's she like on the corners?"

After tea Maisie walked though the gardens and down to the dower house. Maurice had been invited to use the house after the dowager's death, in 1916, and he had purchased the black-and-white beamed home in 1919. After the war, like many landowners of the day, the Comptons decided to sell parts of the estate, and were delighted when the much-loved house became the property of a friend. The gardens had suffered during the war as groundsmen left to enlist in the army, and land that had lain fallow was requisitioned to grow more produce. At one time it was feared that Chelstone Manor itself would be requisitioned to house army officers, but thankfully, given Lord Julian's work with the War Office, together with the fact that the fifteenth-century ceilings and winding staircases rendered the building unsuitable for such use, the manor itself was spared.

Though Maurice officially became resident at the dower house in 1916, he was hardly seen throughout the war years, and came to Chelstone for short periods, usually only to rest. The staff speculated that he had been overseas, which led to even more gossip about what, exactly, he was doing "over there." Maurice Blanche had become something of an enigma. Yet anyone watching him tend his roses during the scorching summer of 1929, as Maisie did before opening the latched gate leading to the dower house garden, would think that this old man wielding a pair of secateurs and wearing a white shirt, light khaki trousers, brown sandals, and a Panama hat, was not one for whom the word "enigma" was appropriate.

Maisie hardly made a sound, yet Maurice looked up and stared directly at her immediately she walked through the gate. For a minute his expression was unchanged, then his face softened. He smiled broadly, dropped the secateurs into a trug, and held both hands out to Maisie as he walked toward her.

"Ah, Maisie. It has taken you a long time to come to me, yes?"

"Yes, Maurice. I need to talk to you."

"I know, my dear. I know. Shall we walk? I'll not offer you tea, as your dear father will have had you swimming in the liquid by now."

"Yes. Yes, let's walk."

Together they passed through the second latched gate at the far end of the garden, and then walked toward the apple orchards. Maisie unfolded the story of Christopher Davenham, of his wife, Celia, the poor departed Vincent, and how she had first heard about The Retreat.

"So, you have followed your nose, Maisie. And the only 'client' in the case is this Christopher Davenham?"

"Yes. Well, Lady Rowan is a sort of client now, because of James. But we always took on other cases, didn't we? Where we felt truth was asking for our help."

"Indeed. Yes, indeed. But remember, Maisie, remember, truth also came to us as individuals so that we might have a more intimate encounter with the self. Remember the Frenchwoman, Mireille—we both know that my interest in the case came from the fact that she reminded me of my grandmother. There was something there for me to discover about myself, not simply the task of solving a case that the authorities could not begin to comprehend. Now, you, Maisie, what is there here for you?" Maurice pointed a finger and touched the place where Maisie's heart began to beat quickly. "What is there in your heart that needs to be given light and understanding?"

"I've come to terms with the war, Maurice. I'm a different person now," Maisie protested.

The two walked on through the apple trees. Maisie was dressed for the heat and wore a cream linen skirt, with a long, sailor-collared linen blouse and a cream hat to shield her sensitive skin from the beating sun, yet she was still far too warm.

When they had walked for more than an hour, Maurice led them back to the dower house and into the cool drawing room. The room was furnished tastefully, with chairs covered in soft green floral fabrics of summer weight. Matching curtains seemed to reflect the abundant garden, with foxgloves, hollyhocks, and delphiniums framing the exterior of the dower house windows. As the winter months drew in, the light materials would be changed, with heavy green velvet drapes and chair covers bringing a welcome warmth to the room. For now the room was light and airy, and bore the faint aroma of potpourri.

Some indication of Maurice's travels was present, in the form of artworks and ornaments. And if one went into Maurice's study, adjacent to the drawing room, there were two framed letters on the wall, from the governments of France and Britain, thanking Dr. Maurice Blanche for his special services during the Great War of 1914–18.

"I am expecting a visitor this evening, for sherry and some reminiscences. The Chief Constable of Kent, an old friend. I will ask him about this Retreat, Maisie. I believe and trust your instincts. Go there tomorrow, proceed with the plan you have outlined to me, and let us speak again tomorrow evening after dinner—no doubt you will dine with your dear father—and let us also look again at your notes, to see what else speaks to us from the pages."

Maisie nodded agreement. A feeling of anticipation and joy welled up inside her as she realized how very lonely it had been working without Maurice. Before she left the house, Maurice insisted that Maisie wait for one minute.

"A new book. I thought you might be interested. *All Quiet on the Western Front*. It has just been published. You have no doubt read reviews and commentary about it."

Maisie raised an eyebrow, though she would never ignore a recommendation from Maurice Blanche.

"Remember, Maisie, while there is always a victor and a vanquished, on both sides there are innocents. Few are truly evil, and they do not need a war to be at work among us, although war provides them with a timely mask."

"Yes, I suppose you are right there, Maurice. I'll read it. Thank you. And I'll see you tomorrow when I get back from The Retreat."

As Maisie turned to walk down the path and across the garden to the stables and groom's cottage, Maurice stopped her.

"And Maisie, when you visit The Retreat, consider the nature of a mask. We all have our masks, Maisie."

Maisie Dobbs held the book tightly in her hand, nodded, and waved to Maurice Blanche.

CHAPTER TWENTY-THREE

*O*n a bright sunny day The Retreat seemed truly to live up to its name, a place that would afford one sweet respite from the cares of the world. As she drew up to the Gothic cast-iron gate with a pillar of rough stone at either side, Maisie could see through the railings to the sun-drenched farm beyond. The road leading from the entrance to the front of the house was dusty, causing a rippled haze of heat to work its way up toward a blue sky dotted with only a few lintlike clouds.

In the distance she could see a large medieval country farmhouse fronted by apple orchards. A high brick wall restricted further inspection of The Retreat, but as she regarded the subject of her investigation and imagination, she noticed in front of her the pink and red blooms of roses that had grown furiously upward on the other side of the wall, and now seemed to be clambering toward her, to freedom. Each bloom nodded up and down in the breeze, and in that moment the wave of roses reminded Maisie of the men who scrambled from a mud-soaked hell of trenches over the top and into battle. Bleeding from their wounds, millions of young men had died on the sodden ground and barbed wire of no-man's land.

Maisie closed and opened her eyes again quickly, to extinguish the images that presented themselves so readily in her mind's eye and had been haunting her since she had torn at the weeds on Don's grave at Nether Green Cemetery. She reminded herself that she could not afford to be distracted or influenced by her memories.

Maisie was leaning back against the MG's door, looking up at the gates, when a man walked through a smaller pedestrian entrance built into the wall. "Can I help you, Ma'am?"

"Oh yes indeed. Is this The Retreat?"

"Yes it is. And what might your business be here today?"

Maisie smiled at the man and approached him. He was tall and thin, with hair that seemed to be gray before its time. She was about to reply when she saw the long, livid scar running from his forehead across his nose and down to his jaw. There was no left eye where the left eye should have been, not even a glass one. The socket was laid bare, defiantly. And as Maisie looked into the right eye of the disfigured man, she saw that he dared her to turn away. She met the man's gaze directly.

"I have written but have received no reply, so I decided to visit without an appointment. It's about my brother. I understand that he might stay here, at The Retreat, until he is healed."

And remembering how Celia Davenham so delicately touched her own face when speaking of Vincent's wounds, Maisie brought her fingers to her left cheek, mirroring the unseen pain of the wounded man before her. He visibly took a deep breath, and waited a second before replying. "You've come to the right place, Ma'am. Wait here and I'll be back in ten minutes. Mr. . . . . er . . . Major Jenkins is who you need to see, and I'll have to get permission."

Maisie nodded, smiled, and said she would be glad to wait. He hurried back through the pedestrian entrance and, taking a bicycle that had been leaning on the other side of the wall, raced along the driveway toward the house. Maisie squinted to watch as the man, now a speck in the distance, stood the bicycle by a door at the side of the house, then ran inside. Five minutes later the speck came running out of the door, took up the bicycle, and grew larger in her vision as he neared the front gate once more.

"You can come in to meet with Major Jenkins, Ma'am. I'll open the gate for you. Drive slowly to the front of the house, and park your motor by the big fallen tree on the gravel there. Major Jenkins is waiting for you."

"Thank you, Mr. . . . ."

Maisie held her head to one side, seeking a name.

"Archie, Ma'am."

"Thank you, Mr. Archie. Thank you."

"Actually, it's just Archie, Ma'am. We don't use surnames here."

"Oh, I see. Thank you, Archie. Is 'Jenkins' the major's Christian name?"

The man's face reddened, except for the scar, which became pale as the surrounding skin heated.

"No. 'Jenkins' is the major's surname."

"Ah," said Maisie, "I see."

Maisie started the MG and drove to the gravel by the fallen tree as instructed. As she applied the handbrake, the door of the car was opened by a man who wore beige jodhpurs, a white shirt, and tall leather riding boots, and carried a baton.

"Miss Dobbs, I understand. I'm Major Jenkins."

Maisie took the hand offered to balance her as she got out of the car. Jenkins was of average height and build, with dark brown hair, brown eyes, and pale skin that did not seem to match his hair and eye coloring. His hair was so neatly swept back that ridges left by his comb reminded Maisie of a freshly ploughed field. She quickly regarded his face, looking for the scars of war, but there were none. None that were visible.

"Thank you, Major Jenkins. No doubt Archie told you why I am here. Perhaps you could tell me more about The Retreat."

"Indeed. Do come to my office, and we'll have tea and a talk about what we are trying to do here."

Jenkins sat in the Queen Anne chair opposite Maisie, who was seated in an identical chair. Tea had been brought earlier by Richard, another man who seemed not yet to be thirty, who had worked hard to mouth words of greeting to Maisie, his shell-blasted jawbone moving awkwardly as he made an enormous effort to physically frame the voice that came forth from his throat.

For her part Maisie did not draw back from the men at The Retreat, although she was sure she was not seeing those with the more devastating wounds. She had seen such wounds when freshly shattered bone and skin still clung to the men's faces, and scars were the best outcome to be hoped for.

"I read about it, in fact," said Jenkins, "then went over to France to have a look for myself. It seemed that these French chappies had a cracking good idea—provide a place of refuge for the men whose faces were altered, or taken, by war. It was certainly not the easiest thing to get going especially as, just after the war, many of the men here had such terrible injuries."

"What happened to them?"

"Frankly, for some it was just too much—bad enough having the wounds in the first place, but being young and having the girls turn away, not being able to go out without people staring, that sort of thing. To tell you the truth, we lost some—but of course we were their last chance of a bearable life anyway."

Jenkins leaned forward to offer Maisie a biscuit, which she declined with a wave of her hand. He nodded and set the plate down on the tray again.

"Of course, for most of our guests, being here helps. The men have no fear of sitting out in the sun, enjoying life outside. The physical work is good for them. Makes them feel better about themselves. No sitting around in bath chairs and blankets here. We go into Sevenoaks to the pictures occasionally—it's dark in the picture house, no one can see."

"And how long does a patient stay here?"

"Not 'patient,' Miss Dobbs. 'Guest.' We call them guests."

"What about the first names only, Major Jenkins?"

"Ah yes. Reminds them of better times, before they became pawns in the game of war. Millions of khaki ants clambering over the hill and into oblivion. The familiarity of using Christian names only is in stark contrast to the discipline of the battlefield, of this terrible experience. Relinquishing the surname reminds them of what's really important. Which is who they are inside, here." He held his hand to the place just below his rib cage to indicate the center of his body. "Inside. Who they are inside. The war took so much away."

Maisie nodded accord and sipped her tea. Maurice had always encouraged judicious use of both words and silence.

"Now then. Your brother?"

"Yes, Billy. He wasn't injured facially, Major Jenkins. But he walks with some difficulty, and has been so very . . . very . . . unwell. Yes, unwell, since the war."

"Commission?"

"Commission, Major Jenkins?"

"Yes, is he a captain, a second lieutenant?"

"Oh. Actually, Billy was a soldier, a corporal when he was injured."

"Where?"

"The Battle of Messines."

"Oh God. Poor man."

"Yes. Billy saw more than enough. But then they all saw more than enough, didn't they, Major Jenkins? Major Jenkins, why is Billy's rank important?"

"Oh, it's not important, really. Just enables me get a sense of what he might have experienced."

"And how might that have been different for Billy than for, let's say yourself, Major?"

"It's just that we have found that men have different experiences of recovery."

"Are you a doctor?"

"No, Miss Dobbs. Simply a man who wanted to do some good for the men who gave their identity for the good of the country and returned to a people who would rather see their heroes walking tall or at best limping, than reflecting the scars caused by our leaders' ill-conceived decisions."

Maisie took another sip of tea and nodded. It was a fair comment.

She left The Retreat thirty minutes later after a tour of the premises. She had been escorted to her car by Jenkins, who watched as she made her way to the gate at a very sedate five miles per hour, the gravel crackling under the tires like sporadic gunfire.

Archie waited for her, touched his forehead in a partial salute as she approached, and leaned down toward her open window as she drew alongside him.

"So, what do you think? Will your brother be joining us, Ma'am?"

"Yes. Yes I think so, Archie. I believe it would do him a power of good."

"Righty-o. We'll look forward to seeing him, then. Hold on while I open the gate."

Maisie waved as she pulled out onto the road, the roses once again nodding in the breeze as Archie waved her on her way.

While she hadn't flinched or drawn back from his wounds, Maisie felt the discomfort of Archie's injury. The sun shone through the windshield of the MG, its heat and brightness causing her eyes to smart and a sharp pain to move from the socket of her left eye to a place on her forehead. The body empathizing with another's pain, thought Maisie. The subconscious mind alerting her to Archie's agony, though she had been successful in appearing to ignore the scar and empty eye socket.

Maisie didn't go far. Stopping once again in Westerham, she sat on a bench in the old churchyard, took the notebook out of her handbag, and began to write an account of her visit.

A walk through the grounds of The Retreat accompanied by Major Jenkins had revealed very little to her that she did not already know, only now she was familiar with the extent of the house, where the "guest" rooms were, and how the farm worked.

There were twenty-five guests living in the main house and an old oasthouse, no longer used for drying hops—Kent's most famous harvest. Though converted to living quarters years before, the oast-house still bore the strong peppery aroma of warm hops.

The youngest man she met must have been thirty, which meant that he had been shipped to France at about age seventeen. The eldest was no more than forty years of age. Questioning Jenkins, Maisie had learned that although the guests were free to come and go at will, most remained, comfortable in the freedom from stares The Retreat afforded them.

Though the farm was to a large extent self-sufficient, each guest entrusted his personal savings to The Retreat, to draw upon for expenses beyond those of day-to-day living, and to contribute to the cost of helpers. If the farm's produce was bringing in a tidy sum, and providing much of the food, the pooled savings must have earned interest and amounted to a pretty penny in someone's bank account. The thought troubled Maisie.

The needs of the guests seemed to be few. There was no doctor on staff to provide for the physical care of those living with such terrible wounds, and no seasoned professional used to dealing with the emotional needs of those traumatized by war. Some of the men still wore the tin masks that had been provided for them when first recovering from their wounds. But the fine glaze used on tin molded to fit a face ten years younger now provided little respite from the mirror's reflection.

Maisie questioned Jenkins's approach. True, it seemed a benevolent idea, and she knew how successful the "holiday camps" had been in France, providing a resting place for wounded men struggling to return to peacetime life. But if The Retreat had been inspired initially by the success of an idea born of compassion, what fuel drove the engine now? The war was almost eleven years past. Then again, those who lived with its memory were still very much alive.

What about Jenkins? How and where had he served? Clearly the men at The Retreat were troubled as a result of their wounds and their memories. But Jenkins's soul was a troubled in a way that was different. Maisie suspected that his wounds lay deep within.

James would soon be going to The Retreat, so she had to act quickly. It was time to go back to London. Archie thought that The Retreat would do her "brother" a world of good. She wondered how Billy Beale would feel about his newfound siblinghood, and if, in a month, he would feel as if time in the country had done him a power of good.

CHAPTER TWENTY-FOUR

"So what you think is that this Jenkins fella is getting up to no good down there at this Retreat 'e's set up?"

Billy Beale sat in the chair in front of Maisie Dobbs, his hands working around and around the fabric on the perimeter of his cap, which he had taken off when he came to answer Maisie's call. Maisie had lost no time in telling Billy Beale why he had been summoned, and how she needed him to help her.

"Yes, I do, Billy. I would only need you to be there for a week, no, let's say two weeks. To let me know what is happening, what you see."

"Well, you've come to the right person if you want someone what's willing. But I'm not sure I'm your man. Not as if I'm a toff, to mix with the likes of them."

"Billy. You don't need to be a toff. You just need to have some money—"

"And that's even bloomin' funnier. Money—the likes of me!"

"It's taken care of, Billy. As soon as you are accepted as a guest at The Retreat, a sum will be moved from your bank account to Major Adam Jenkins's account."

Billy Beale looked at Maisie and winked. "And I bet I know who's got me a bank account I never 'ad before in me life."

"Yes. It was arranged today."

Suddenly Billy was quiet. He looked again at his cloth cap, and sat with obvious discomfort in the too-small chair opposite Maisie's desk. It was the end of another humid day in London: The summer of 1929 was breaking records for lack of rain, and for heat.

"I'd do anything for you, Miss. I said that when you moved in 'ere to run yer business. I've seen you work all hours 'ere. And I've seen 'ow you 'elp people."

Billy tapped the side of his nose in his usual conspiratorial fashion.

"What you do isn't what you'd call regular. I can see that. And if this 'elps someone, then I'm your man. Like I said before. You 'elped me Miss, when you weren't more than a girl. I remember."

"It could be risky, Billy. I believe this Jenkins is a troubled man, and possibly a dangerous one."

"No. Don't you worry about me. You've explained it all very well. I understand what's involved, Miss. And it won't take me long to set up a line for us, soon as I get the lay of the land. Now then. Let's look at that map again. Mind you—"

Billy rose to look down at the map that Maisie had spread out on the table.

"Just as well the missus is taking the nippers down to 'er sister's in 'astings. You reckon we leave tomorrow?"

"The sooner the better, Billy. Let's go over the plan again, and the story. We'll leave for Chelstone tomorrow. We'll be meeting with Maurice Blanche in the afternoon. He has been seeking some additional information for us from one of his contacts."

"And who might that be, if I may ask?"

"The Chief Constable of Kent."

"Bloody 'ell . . ."

"Quite, Billy. Now then, William Dobbs, we expect a letter from The Retreat to arrive at Chelstone by Friday, so we can drive over on

Saturday. The other gentleman I told you about, who must not see me or know that I am involved in anything to do with The Retreat, will be taking up residence in just a few weeks. I hope to have this . . . this . . . investigation concluded by that time."

"Right you are, Miss. I'd better be getting 'ome then. Got to pack me ol' kit bag again, for the good of me country."

"Dr. Blanche has arranged for your clothes, Billy."

"It wasn't clothes I was going to pack, Sis," said Billy, with an impish smile, "You don't mind if I call you Sis, get used to it, like? I need to pack the other bits and pieces of kit that I'll be needing for this job."

Maisie looked up at Billy Beale and smiled.

"This is good of you, Billy. You were the only person I could ask. I can't tell you how much I appreciate it. Your help will not go unrewarded."

"It already 'as been rewarded. Been getting a bit bored around 'ere anyway. I need a change."

Maisie lingered for a while in the office before leaving, closing the door behind her, and making her way along the hallway to another unmarked door. Here she took a key from her pocket and entered the room. Home. She had moved a few weeks before, when it was clear that she needed to be closer to her work. The bed–sitting room was small, but all that she required was within the walls of this room. And when she needed some respite from the dour familiarity of such spartan accommodations, there was usually an invitation to stay at Ebury Place, or she would go down to Chelstone, to spend time in the calm and comforting company of her father.

"There. Reckon I've got everything."

Billy Beale placed one more bag in the luggage compartment of Lady Rowan's car, and stood to watch Maisie, who was securing her navy blue beret with a long pearl-tipped pin. Her corduroy jacket had been thrown around the shoulders of the driver's seat, giving the impression of a rather stout old man who had just sat down. An observer might have considered the young woman "fast," for today Maisie was wearing a pair of long beige cuffed trousers, with a linen blouse and brown walking shoes.

Maisie looked at her watch and took her place in the driver's seat of the MG.

"Good. Not too late. We'd better get a move on. We need to be at Chelstone by noon."

Billy Beale hesitated.

"What is it, Billy?"

"Nothing really, Miss . . . it's just that . . ." He took the cap from his head and looked up at the sky. "It's just that this is the first time I've left London since I got back from the war. Couldn't face it. O' course the missus 'as been away with the nippers. Been down to Kent with 'er people 'op-picking, and o' course to 'er sister's in 'astings. But not me, Miss."

Maisie said nothing, made no response. She understood the power of reflection well, and as she had done with Celia Davenham just a few short weeks before, she made no move to soothe Billy Beale, allowing him the time he needed to step into the car.

"But you never know, at least I might get a good night's sleep down there in the country." Still he hesitated.

"What do you mean, Billy?"

Maisie shielded her eyes from the morning sun as she looked up at him.

Billy sighed deeply, took a breath, opened the car door, and sat down on the passenger seat. The claret leather of the hardly used seat creaked as Billy moved to make himself comfortable.

"Just can't sleep, Miss. Not for long anyway. 's'bin like that since I got 'ome from France. That many years ago. Soon as I close my eyes, it all comes back."

He looked into the distance as if into the past.

"Blimey, I can almost smell the gas, can 'ardly breathe at times. If I fall asleep straight away, I only wake up fighting for breath. And the pounding in my 'ead. You never forget that pounding, the shells. Mind you, you know that, don't you, Miss?"

And as he spoke, Maisie remembered her homecoming, remembered Maurice taking her again to see Khan, who seemed never to age. In her mind's eye she saw herself sitting with Khan and telling her story, and Maurice sitting with her.

Khan spoke of bearing witness to the pain of another's memories, a ritual as old as time itself, then asked her to tell her story again. And again. And again. She told her story until, exhausted, she had no more story to tell. And Maisie remembered Khan's words, that this nightmare was a dragon that would remain alive, but dormant, waiting insidiously to wake and breathe its fire, until she squarely faced the truth of what had happened to Simon.

"You all right, Miss?"

Billy Beale placed a hand on Maisie's shoulder for just a second.

"Yes, yes, I was just thinking about what you said, Billy. So what do you do when you cannot sleep?"

Billy looked down at his hands and began pulling at the lining of his cap, running the seam between the forefinger and thumb of each hand.

"I get up, so's not to wake the missus. Then I go out. Walking the streets. For hours sometimes. And you know what, Miss? It's not only me, Miss. There's a lot of men I see, 'bout my age, walking the streets. And we all know, Miss, we all know who we are. Old soldiers what keep seeing the battle. That's what we are, Miss. I tell you, sometimes I think we're like the waking dead. Livin' our lives during the day, normal like, then trying to forget something what 'appened years ago. It's like going to the picture 'ouse, only the picture's all in me 'ead."

Maisie inclined her head to show understanding, her silence respectful of Billy's terrible memories, and of this confidence shared. And once again she was drawn back, to that year in the wards after her return from France, working to comfort the men whose minds were ravaged by war. Small comfort indeed. Yet for every one who could not bring his mind back from the last vision of a smoke-filled hell, there were probably dozens like Billy, living now as good father, good husband, good son, good man, but who feared the curtains drawn against darkness, and the light extinguished at the end of the day.

"Ready, Billy?" Maisie asked when Billy put the cap firmly back on his head.

"Reckon I am, Miss. Yes, I reckon I am. Do me the world of good will this, Miss. Bein' useful like."

They spoke little on the journey to Kent. Occasionally Maisie asked Billy questions as they drove along the winding country roads. She wanted to make doubly sure that he understood everything that was required of him. Information. She needed more information. A feel for the place. How did it work when you were on the inside? Was anything amiss?

She spoke to him of intuition, abbreviating the teaching she had received from Maurice and Khan many years before.

"You must listen to the voice inside, Billy," said Maisie, placing her hand to her middle. "Remember even the smallest sensation of unease, for it could well be significant."

Billy had been quick to learn, quick to understand that his impressions were important, just as relevant as facts on a page. As Maisie knew from their first meeting, Billy Beale was sharp, an acute observer of circumstances and people. He was just what she needed. And he was willing.

But was it fair to draw Billy into her work? If she thought that Vincent's death was questionable, was it right to involve Billy? Then again, he would not be at The Retreat for long. And they would be in daily contact. She had promised Maurice that as soon as she had gathered enough information, she would refer her findings to the authorities—if what she found required it.

Maisie knew that her curiosity was drawing both Billy and herself deeper into the mystery of Vincent. And even as she drove she closed her eyes briefly and prayed for the confidence and courage to face whatever was hidden in the darkness.

CHAPTER TWENTY-FIVE

*M*aisie parked the motorcar outside the dower house and led Billy into Maurice Blanche's home, to introduce her old teacher to her new assistant, and to have lunch together before she and Billy proceeded to The Retreat.

They talked about The Retreat, and Billy added weight to Maisie's earlier deliberations about the naming of this place where the wounded of a war over ten years past still sought refuge.

"O' course, it might not be just The Retreat, you know, as in gettin' away from it all into shelter. There's 'The Retreat,' in't there? You know, the bugle call at sunset. S'pose you'd 'ave to be an army man to know that, eh? Like 'retreating from a position' as well. That's what we should've done many a time—would've saved a few lives, and that's a fact."

Maisie set down her knife and fork and nodded thoughtfully.

The Retreat, the ultimate play on words to describe a place for the wounded. But what happened if someone wanted to retreat, as it were, from The Retreat?

"Maisie, while you are visiting your father, before you and

Mr. Beale—or perhaps I should say 'Dobbs' to get him used to the name—anyway, before you depart for The Retreat, I will walk with Mr. Beale in the meadow, just beyond the orchard."

Maisie knew that this was not a chance suggestion, and watched the two men walk toward the meadow, heads together in conversation, the younger man ever so slightly ready to steady the older man lest he falter. If only he knew, she thought, how much the old man feared the faltering of the younger.

As soon as they returned, Maisie took Billy to The Retreat, but before entering, she drove around the perimeter of the estate and parked under the shade of a beech tree.

"It's a retreat all right, innit, Miss? Pity they don't allow visitors for the first month. Wonder what they'll say when I tell them I'm out after two weeks? Prob'ly be a bit upset with me, eh, Miss?"

Billy surveyed the landscape, the fencing, the road, and the distances between landmarks.

"Look, 'ere's what I think. No point trying to get all fancy here, rigging up lines to, y'know, communicate. Why don't I just meet you at the same time every evening, by that bit of fence there, and tell you what I know."

"Well, Billy, it seemed as if we had a good plan, for your safety, that is."

"Don't you worry about me. From what you've said, I don't think I'm that important to the likes of them. I'm just your average bread and butter, aren't I? No big legacies being signed over or anything."

Billy smiled at Maisie and pointed toward the fields between the large house in the distance, and the road.

"Tell you the truth, looking at this landscape now, it's best if we don't mess around with telephone lines coming too near the 'ouse. Draw more attention. No one's goin' to question an old soldier what wants to go off by 'imself for a jaunt of an evenin'. But they might question an old sapper fiddling around with a telephone line in the dark. And you know, Miss, I might be good at that sort of thing, but I never did say I was invisible. And I can't run like I used to, not with the leg 'ere." Billy slapped the side of his leg for emphasis. "But 'ere's what I can do now. I can rig up a line to that telephone box we just passed back there, on the corner as you leave the 'amlet back there. I 'ad a quick look as we drove by—not that I 'ad much time, what with the speed and all—"

Maisie grimaced at Billy, who continued. "It's one of them new ones, a Kiosk Number Four, I think. They 'ave em in places where there ain't no post office—did y'see? It's got a stamp machine on the back, and a pillar-box for letters. Sort of all purpose—mind you, me mate what works on the things says that the stamps get soggy when it rains, and then they all stick together and make a right old mess. So, anyway, getting' back to me and the old lines 'ere, if I need to get 'old of you urgent, like, or if I'm in an 'urry to get out of 'ere, I can always jump through this fence—well, sort of jump, what wiv the leg and all—and use the box and line what I rig up to connect with the outside line at that box up the road. D'you see what I mean, Miss? Then I'll run like a nutter, bad leg an' all!"

Maisie laughed nervously. "Right you are, Billy, I think I follow you. It sounds like a good idea."

Billy opened the car door, pulled himself out of the low seat, and walked around to the luggage compartment. He carefully took out two large old canvas kit bags and placed them on the ground. Taking out spools of cable, "small, so's I can work with them on me own," Billy walked over to the ditch at the base of the perimeter fence.

Moving aside grasses and wildflowers growing innocently at the side of the road, Billy began to unwind the cable into the ditch, moving away from Maisie, who remained in the car. It was a quiet thoroughfare, so they had little to fear from passing traffic, but nevertheless, country folk were apt to be inquisitive about two strangers lingering on the road. Especially if one were seen unraveling cable.

Maisie got out of the car and walked over to the fence, looking out over the land belonging to The Retreat. The perimeter fence, six feet tall and topped with barbed wire, would merge into a stone wall just half a mile along in the opposite direction to the line being laid out by Billy.

The main gate was situated another half mile away from the beginning of the wall. Eventually Billy returned.

"Nicely done, and quick too. Managed to save meself some work by using the bottom wire of this 'ere fence." Billy pulled back the grass to point to the wire in question. "I hear that's what they've done over there in America, y'know—used the fences on farms to make connections between places, like." Billy pushed back his cap, and wiped the back of his hand across his forehead. "Stroke of luck it bein' there—the telephone—see more of them in the towns, don't you? S'pose it's used by them what live in the terraced cottages in the 'amlet. I tell you, no one will see that line, mark my words."

Billy caught his breath, and for the first time Maisie heard the wheezing that revealed gas-damaged lungs. "You shouldn't be running like that, Billy."

"I'm awright, Miss. Now to this end." Billy held up a telephone receiver. "The old 'dog and bone,' Miss. We used to say in the trenches that them as is on the end of the line only bloomin' 'ear 'alf of what's said—and then only what they want to 'ear anyway. Personally, meself, I reckon it's a poor old situation when you 'ave to make out a person's intentions from their voice in a tin cup."

Billy worked on as he spoke, wiring the receiver to a metal box he placed in the ditch before leaning in and connecting lines. He picked up the receiver, turned the dial, and listened. The operator responded at his request for a connection, charges to go to the recipient of the call, and put him through to Maurice's telephone number. They spoke briefly before Billy replaced the receiver on its cradle.

"I know it's not perfect, and it takes a bit o' time, but it might come in 'andy, you never know."

After ensuring that their makeshift telephone was hidden and secure, Billy then cut into the wire of the perimeter fence, forming a "door" through which he could escape, should escape become necessary. He secured the door with spare wire to camouflage the fact that the fence had been tampered with.

The first part of their task finished, Maisie and Billy loaded up the motor car again and drove slowly toward the main entrance to The Retreat. They said little, only speaking to confirm the time at which they would meet each evening.

Billy would take a solitary stroll at seven o'clock, which would bring him to the fence by the large beech tree at half past seven. Maisie would be waiting to meet with him for just a few moments, then he would make his way back to the main house. In all other dealings with the residents of The Retreat, there was to be nothing about him that could be remarked upon. He was to be invisible but for the bed he slept in and the food he consumed. But he was to watch, and listen and report back to Maisie.

"Welcome back to The Retreat, Miss Dobbs," said Archie as he opened the gate.

He walked toward the car, leaned down so that his face was alongside the passenger window, and addressed Billy.

"William, isn't it? The major is waiting to welcome you personally to The Retreat."

Billy Beale took the proffered hand and seemed not to see the terrible scars that had changed Archie's countenance forever. Maisie nodded to Archie, and moved the car slowly along the driveway.

"Poor bleedin' bugger—oh, I am sorry, Miss—I forget meself at times. Least I can get about and no one worries about a bit of a limp. Blimey, that poor fella, with that face. Not that I 'aven't seen worse. Just not seen it for a long time, not close up. That's all."

Maisie slowed the car even more. "Billy, if you have any doubts—"

"Not likely," said Billy, straightening his shoulders. "If there's any funny business going on here that can cause any more damage to these blighters, then I want to do my bit to stop it." He paused to look at Maisie. "Can't blame them for wanting to get away, can you?"

"No, you can't. But there's a lot that can be done for them now."

"Not when you've been through what they've been through. Just want to be left alone 'alf the time, I should think, never mind being messed around with by newfangled ideas of skin medicine and what 'ave you."

The car drew alongside the main building as Adam Jenkins, the major, came through the front door and down the steps toward them.

"Ah, William. Welcome to The Retreat. I am sure you will be comfortable here. Come into my study for tea, then we can get you settled later."

Adam Jenkins led the way, his white shirt once again crisply laundered, leather riding boots polished to a blinding shine, and not a hair out of place. He invited Maisie and Billy to take a seat, standing behind Maisie's chair to hold it for her, then indicating, with a nonchalant sweep of his hand, the seat by the window for Billy.

How strange, thought Maisie, that he should direct Billy to a seat that took the full strength of the late-afternoon sun, rays that would cause Billy to become hot and uncomfortable, and to have to shield his eyes with the hand that he would need to reach out for the teacup as it was offered to him. Strange to unsettle a person so.

Billy met Maisie's look and raised an eyebrow. He knows, thought Maisie. He knows that Jenkins has placed him by the window on purpose.

Ten minutes of seemingly purposeless conversation had been exchanged between Jenkins and Maisie. As befitting his character—the tired veteran of a war over ten years past—Billy was silent. And hot. Maisie looked at Billy again. She saw the perspiration on his brow, his discomfort as he ran the forefinger of his right hand along the edge of his shirt collar.

Jenkins suddenly directed his attention away from Maisie, toward Billy. "My dear man. How remiss of me. How utterly stupid. Move over to this other chair and into the cool of the room immediately."

Jenkins put down his cup and used one hand to beckon Billy away from the window seat, and the other to indicate another seat.

Interesting, thought Maisie. A small gesture, but a subtle and significant one. Was it a ploy to begin to inspire Billy's trust? Placing himself immediately in the role of savior, and of one prepared to acknowledge a mistake. Or was Adam Jenkins genuinely admitting an error of judgment? Was this opening of his outstretched arms a move to render Billy more comfortable in another seat, an act of genuine concern? Or was it perhaps a deliberate action to draw Billy into his circle of admirers? Arms spread wide to bring him within the force of his influence.

Maisie watched Jenkins carefully, while attending to the business of afternoon tea. In her work with Maurice, Maisie had learned much about the charm and charisma of the natural leader, which, taken to an extreme, can become dictatorial and vindictive. Was Adam Jenkins such a man? Or an enlightened and concerned soul?

"Well, it's time to get some pawprints on the page, don't you think?" said Jenkins. He glanced at his watch, stood up, and walked over to a large heavily carved desk. The top was covered in rich brown leather, and only one plain manila file sat waiting for attention on top of a wooden board. He opened the file, checked the papers within, took a fountain pen from the inside pocket of his light linen jacket, and returned to the chair next to Maisie.

"We have received the necessary documents—thank you, Miss Dobbs—pertaining to the financial arrangements." He turned to Billy. "And I know you completely understand the commitment we request upon taking up residency at The Retreat, William. Now, perhaps you would be so kind as to sign here."

He placed the papers on the wooden board to provide a stable writing surface, and passed them to Billy, tapping the place for signature with his forefinger.

After Billy carefully wrote "William Dobbs" in the space indicated, Jenkins rang the bell for an assistant to escort Billy to his quarters, and as he did so, Billy winked at Maisie. Yet when Jenkins turned back to the two supposed siblings, he saw only the blank resignation of the man, and the worry etched in the face of his sister. But Maisie's concern was no act. She *was* worried for Billy. She had to ensure that he was at The Retreat not a moment longer than necessary.

CHAPTER TWENTY-SIX

*M*aisie waited anxiously at Maurice Blanche's cottage. Billy had been at The Retreat for three days, and each evening at seven o'clock, Maisie set off in Lady Rowan's MG, along country lanes filled with the lingering aroma of Queen Anne's Lace and privet, to meet Billy Beale by the perimeter fence, across the road from the ancient beech tree.

Each evening, with summer midges buzzing around her head, she watched as Billy approached. First she would see his head, bobbing up and down in the distance, as he walked across the fallow fields of tall grass. Then as he came closer, his wheaten hair reflected the setting sun, and Maisie wondered why no one noticed Billy Beale taking a walk each evening.

"Evenin', Miss," said Billy as he curled back the fence wire and clambered through.

"Billy, how are you?" As always, Maisie was both relieved and delighted to see Billy. "You've caught the sun, Billy," she remarked.

"Reckon I 'ave at that, Miss." Billy rubbed at his cheeks. "All this working on the land, that's what's done it."

"And how is it, the working on the land?"

"'Not bad at all, Miss. And it seems to do these lads good. You should see some of them. Seems that they were right down in the dumps when they came 'ere. Then slowly, like, the work and the fact that no one looks twice at them starts to give them the, you know, the sort of confidence they need."

"Nothing unusual, Billy?"

"Can't say as there is, Miss. O' course, not that I can go around asking questions, but I keep my eyes open, and it seems like it's all on the up and up. The major is a funny bloke, but 'e's doing 'is bit, i'n'e? And now that there's space 'ere, what with some fellas gone, they're taking other blokes, with other injuries, not just to the face and 'ead, like. But you know that, don't you, otherwise I wouldn't be 'ere, not with this fine lookin' physog."

Billy grinned at Maisie and rubbed his chin.

"Quite, Billy. So is everyone happy there?"

"I should say so, Miss. Not much to dislike, is there? Mind you, there is one bloke, has some terrible scars on his face, just 'ere."

Billy turned his head to the right, and with the forefinger of his left hand indicated a line going from his ear, to his jaw, then to his chest. He grimaced, then continued.

"I think 'e's 'ad enough of being out 'ere—says that he feels good and well enough to get back to the real world."

"And what does the major say to that?"

"I don't know that 'e's said anything, Miss. I think they like 'em to give it some thought, you know, them as wants to leave."

"What makes you say that? What would stop someone from just leaving? It's in the contract that you can leave when you want."

"Well, what I've 'eard is that some blokes get back their confidence and next thing you know, they want to go back out, face the world. Then when they get back out, they find that it ain't all that rosy, that they get the stares an' all. Apparently that's 'appened a few times, and the blokes topped themselves."

"Is that what you've heard, Billy?"

"'ere and there. You 'ear talk. They think that this fella, who's wanting to get back to what 'e calls the 'real world,' is worrying the major. Seems the major has said 'e's . . . what was it 'e was supposed to 'ave said?"

Billy closed his eyes and scratched the back of his head. As he did so, Maisie saw the red sunburn at his neck, the farm laborer's "collar."

"That's it. The major 'as said 'e's suspectible."

"Do you mean susceptible, Billy?"

Billy smiled again. "Yes, reckon that's it, Miss."

"Anything else, Billy?"

"Not really, Miss. The major seems a really good bloke, Miss. I don't know what 'appened to those fellas you found out about. P'raps they left and then was the type what couldn't stand up to bein' on the out-side. But I will say this. There's blokes 'ere what love the major, you know. Think 'e's a lifesaver. And I s'pose 'e is really, when you think about it. Given some boys a way of life since the war, boys who thought they 'ad none."

Maisie noted Billy's comments on index cards and nodded her head. Slipping the cards and the pencil into her work-worn black document case with the silver clasp, she looked directly at Billy.

"Same time tomorrow evening, Billy?"

"Yes, Miss. Although, Miss . . . can we make it a bit earlier? 'bout 'alf past six? Some of the boys are 'aving a snooker tournament. Like to give it a go if I can. Join in with a bit of fun, like."

Maisie was silent for some seconds before replying. "Right you are, Billy. But keep your eyes open, won't you?"

"Don't worry, Miss. If there's anything funny goin' on 'ere I'll find out all about it."

Maisie watched as Billy turned and walked through the field again. She walked back across the road, opened the car door, and sat down in the driver's seat, leaving the door ajar to watch Billy become but a speck in the distance.

Had she made a mistake? Had her gift, her intuition, played tricks on her? Were the deaths of Vincent—and the other boys who used only one name—suicide? Or simply coincidence? She sighed as she started up the MG again.

Maisie spent her days at Chelstone close to the telephone. She would pass a precious hour or two with her father each day, but quickly returned to the dower house in case she was needed. Together she and Maurice went over old cases for clues and inspiration, and speculated over the details of life at The Retreat.

"I would very much have liked to see the postmortem findings on our friend Vincent, and his colleagues."

"I located the inquest proceedings, and it seems that they were all attributed to 'accidental death' in some form or another."

"Indeed, Maisie. But I would like to inspect the details, to observe through the eyes of the examiner, so that hopefully I might see what he did not. Let's go back over the notes. Who conducted Vincent's postmortem?"

Maisie passed Maurice the report.

"Hmmm. Signed by the coroner, and not the attending examiner."

Maurice stood up and walked around the room.

"To solve a problem, walk around," he said, noticing her smile.

How often in the past had they worked together in this way, Maisie sitting on the floor, legs crossed in front of her, Maurice in his leather chair. He would get up, pace the floor with his hands together as if in prayer, while Maisie closed her eyes in meditation and breathed deeply, as she had been instructed years ago by Khan.

Suddenly Maurice stopped walking, and at almost the same moment, so close that neither would have been able to say who was first, Maisie came to her feet.

"What is it that you find so interesting about the reports, Maisie?"

She looked at Maurice. "It is not the actual contents of the report, Maurice. It is the lack of detail. There's nothing to go on, no loose threads. There's not the slightest particle of information for us to work with."

"Correct. It is too clean. Far too clean. Let me see . . ." Maurice flipped the pages back. "Ah, yes. Let me telephone my friend the chief inspector. He should be able to help me." He looked at the time, it was half past nine in the evening. "Indeed, he should be delighted to help me—his interior will have been warmed by his second single malt of the evening."

Maisie took her place on the cushion again and waited for Maurice. She heard his muffled voice coming from the room next door, the rhythm of his speech not quite English yet not quite Continental. The telephone receiver was replaced on the cradle with an audible thump, and Maurice returned.

"Interesting. Extremely interesting. It seems that the attending examiner in the case of Vincent, and likely also in the other cases, was on call in the early hours of the morning, with his duty ending at half past eight—and so was able to go to The Retreat immediately after he was summoned. He returned home after completing his cursory examination and writing a brief report. His name, Maisie, is Jenkins. Armstrong Jenkins. Something of a coincidence, I think. And the examination lists time of death at . . . let me see . . . yes, it was at five o'clock in the morning."

"Dawn," said Maisie.

Maisie leafed through the papers that she had spread across Maurice's desk. Her mentor came to her side.

"Maurice. They died at dawn. The time of death for each of the men buried at Nether Green is dawn."

"An almost mystical hour, don't you think, Maisie?"

Maurice clasped his hands behind his back and walked to the window.

"A time when the light is most likely to deceive the eye, a time between sleep and waking. A time when a man is likely to be at his weakest. Dawn is a time when soft veils are draped across reality, creating illusion and cheating truth. It is said, Maisie, it is darkest just before dawn."

"So there's still nothing much to tell you, Miss."

Billy Beale stood with his hands in the pockets of his light sailcloth summer trousers, and kicked at the dry ground between his feet. He had been at The Retreat for only a week.

"Don't worry, Billy. It wasn't definite that you would find something. You're only going to be here a short time anyway. I just thought that some inside observations might be helpful."

Maisie moved to stand next to Billy, and without his noticing, adopted the same stance. She was wearing trousers again, and a light cotton blouse, so it was easy for her to place her hands in her pockets, emulating Billy's pose exactly.

He's embarrassed about something, thought Maisie. There's something he doesn't want to tell me. As Billy moved in discomfort, so did Maisie. She closed her eyes and felt Billy's dilemma.

"And you think this Adam Jenkins is a good man, do you, Billy?"

Billy kicked at the ground again, and though his face was tanned from working on the land, she saw a deep blush move from his chin to his cheeks.

"Well, yes, reckon I do, Miss. And I feel awful, at times. After what 'e's done for them, 'ere I am sniffin' around for something nasty."

"I can see how that might be difficult for you, Billy. You admire Adam Jenkins."

"Yes. Yes, I admire the man."

"That's good, Billy."

Maisie turned to face Billy and with the intensity of her gaze compelled him to look back at her.

"That's good. That you admire the man. It'll make your time here easier, and what I ask you to do easier."

"'ow do you mean?"

"Just go about your business, Billy. Just go about doing what you have to do here. You don't have to do anything other than be yourself. Although I do request two things: That we keep to our evening meetings, that's one. The other is that you take care to maintain your assumed name. Do not give anything away. Is that clear?"

Billy relaxed as Maisie spoke to him, and nodded his head.

"I just want to know about your days. That's all, Billy. Then next week I'll come and collect you. In fact, I'll come tomorrow if you want."

"No. No, miss. I'll stay on as we agreed. Don't expect I'll find anything, though. These 'ere meetings might get a bit boring."

Maisie nodded her head, and continued to mirror Billy's movements with her own.

"Just one more thing, Billy. About the man who wanted to leave. Remember, you told me about him? What's happened to him?"

"Can't say as I've seen 'im for a day or so. Mind you, that's not unusual, if one of the fellas wants to 'ave a bit of time alone. Like they do."

Billy stopped speaking, kicked his feet at the ground, then looked up at Maisie.

"What is it, Billy?"

"Just a thought, though. So keen to leave, 'e was. End of the month, 'e said. Wouldn't think 'e wanted any time to 'imself, now I come to think about it."

Maisie made no move to agree or disagree. "Like I said, Billy. You don't need to go snooping around. Just meet me here every day."

"Right you are, Miss. Now then. Best be going, before I'm missed."

Maisie waited a second before responding to Billy's movement toward the fence.

"Billy . . ."

"Yes, Miss?"

With his good knee bent, ready to go through the hole in the fence, Billy turned to meet Maisie's direct stare.

"Billy. Don't you think that someone would understand that you just needed some time to yourself—if you're back a bit late, that is?"

"Oh, they might do, Miss," Billy replied thoughtfully. Then with a wink added, "But not when I'm due to defend my snooker title in 'alf an hour."

Maisie smiled as Billy climbed through on to the other side of the fence, and secured the wire. But instead of going back to the car, she remained in the same place to watch Billy Beale once again walk across the fields, back to his temporary life at The Retreat.

"*O*h, please don't worry about the car, my dear. Heavens above, I can't even drive the thing, not with my hip at the moment. Besides, I think your need is greater than mine, and you are working in my interests."

Maisie had been holding the telephone receiver away from her ear while Lady Rowan spoke, but brought the receiver closer to reply.

"Thank you. I was worried. But I should have it back to you by the middle of next week."

"Right you are. Now, tell me. What's happening? James is due to leave for The Retreat in ten days. And heaven knows he won't be spoken to about anything. Not even to his father. I swear he hasn't been the same since that girl—"

"Yes, Lady Rowan. I know."

"And if it weren't for you, I would be absolutely frantic."

"Lady Rowan, may I speak to Lord Julian please?"

"Yes, yes . . . I know, I am just about to become tedious. He's in his study. I'll just nip next door to get him. Won't wait for Carter, it would take all day."

Maisie smiled. It would probably take a while for Lady Rowan to walk next door to the study to get Lord Julian. She hadn't been able to "nip" anywhere for some time.

Eventually, she heard Lord Julian Compton's voice. "Maisie, what can I do for you?"

"Lord Julian. In confidence."

"Of course."

"I wonder if you could help me with some information that I believe you may be able to obtain for me from your former contacts at the War Office."

"I'll do what I can—what do you need, Maisie?"

"Jenkins. Major Adam Jenkins. I need to see his service record, if at all possible."

"I've already obtained it, m'dear. Didn't like the sound of this Retreat business when I heard about it from James. Got the service record in my office now. Didn't know he called himself Major, though. I only heard him called Jenkins by James."

"The men at The Retreat call him Major."

"That's interesting. Jenkins was just a lieutenant."

"Is there anything else there, Lord Julian? Any other anomalies?"

"Of course a service record is limited. He was discharged though, medical discharge."

"Where to?"

"Craiglockhart."

"Oh."

"Yes. Right up your alley I'd say, Maisie. Mind you, he was a mild case, apparently. Of course I don't have a record of his treatment. Just the notes of his commanding officer. Says that he went gaga after a couple of chaps in his command deserted. Seems to have been an innocuous fellow, quite frankly. Got a commission based on need rather than any military talent, I would say, from the record. Officers were dropping like flies, if you remember. Well, of course you remember. Mind you, the chap's obviously got a business head on him, setting up this Retreat."

"The men seem to adore him for what he's done there. Providing a place for them to go," said Maisie.

"Yes, I've got to hand it to him. Now he's opened the doors to those who sustained other injuries. Like James. Bit like a monastery though, if you ask me, wanting people to sign over their assets. Mind you, if the idea is a place of refuge forever . . . ."

"Yes."

"Shame, isn't it? That we only like our heroes out in the street when they are looking their best and their uniforms are 'spit and polished,' and not when they're showing us the wounds they suffered on our behalf. Well, anything else, m'dear?"

"No. I think that's all. Is there any chance that I might see—?"

"I'll have it sent down to Chelstone in the morning."

"Thank you, Lord Julian. You've been most helpful."

Maisie had spent most of that day at the dower house with Maurice, taking only a short break to visit Frankie Dobbs. She declined to sleep in the small bedroom that had always been hers at the groom's cottage, instead electing to remain by Maurice's telephone, just in case Billy needed her. Time and again she ran through the details of events and research information she had accumulated.

Adam Jenkins had lied about his status. But was it a lie, or had a man simply called him "major" and it stuck? She remembered her grandfather, working on the Thames boats. People called him The Commander, but he had never been in the navy, never commanded anything. It was just a nickname, the source of which had been lost over the years. But how did Jenkins, "an innocuous little man," assume such power? Billy had become a believer, and the men seemed to adore him. Was fear a factor? Was there a deeper connection between Vincent and Jenkins? And what about Armstrong Jenkins? Family member, or coincidence?

She had missed something. Something very significant. And as she reexamined, in her mind's eye, each piece of collected evidence that had led her to this place, she considered Maurice's words, and felt as if each day, all day, she was living in the moment before dawn broke. Maisie thought back, to that earlier dawn, more than ten years earlier. The beginning of the end, that was what it had been.

CHAPTER TWENTY-SEVEN

*T*he time is drawing closer, is it not my dear?" Maurice asked her now. He looked at the grandfather clock, patiently tick-tocking the seconds away.

"Yes it is. Maurice, I want to take Billy out of The Retreat."

"Indeed. Yes. Away from Jenkins. It is interesting, Maisie, how a time of war can give a human being purpose. Especially when that purpose, that power, so to speak, is derived from something so essentially evil."

Maurice reached forward from his chair towards the wooden pipe stand that hung on the chimney breast. He selected a pipe, took tobacco and matches from the same place, and leaned back, glancing again at the clock. He watched Maisie as he took a finger-and-thumb's worth of tobacco from the pouch, and pressed it into the bowl of the pipe.

"Your thoughts, Maisie?"

Maurice struck a match on the raw brick of the fireplace, and drawing on the pipe, held the flame to the tobacco. Maisie found the sweet aroma pungent, yet this ritual of lighting and smoking a pipe soothed her. She knew Maurice to indulge in a pipe only when the crux of a matter was at hand. And having the truth revealed, no matter how harsh, was always a relief.

"I was thinking of evil. Of war. Of the loss of innocence, really. And innocents."

"Yes. Indeed. Yes. The loss of that which is innocent. One could argue, that if it were not for war, then Jenkins—"

The clock struck the half hour. It was time for Maisie to leave to meet Billy Beale. Maurice stood, reaching out to the mantelpiece to steady himself with his right hand.

"You will be back at what time?"

"By half past eight."

"I will see you then."

Maisie left the cottage quickly, and Maurice moved to the window to watch her leave. They needed to say little to each other. He had been her mentor since she was a young girl, and she had learned well. Yes, he had been right to retire. And right to be ready to support her as she took on the practice in her own name.

"*B*illy. Good timing. How are you?"

"Doin' awright, Miss. Yourself?"

Without responding to his question, Maisie continued with her own.

"Any news?"

"Well, I've been thinking a bit and keeping my eyes open."

"Yes."

"And I've noticed that the fella who wanted to leave ain't around."

"Perhaps he's left, gone home."

"No, no. Not in the book."

"What book?"

"I found out there's a book. By the gatehouse. Records the ins and outs, if you know what I mean. Took a walk over to 'ave a word with old Archie the other day, and it looks like the bread delivery is all that's gone on in a week."

"And Jenkins?"

"Chummy as ever."

"Billy, I think it's time for you to leave."

"No—no, Miss. I'm safe as 'houses. Sort of like it 'ere, really. And no one's looking twice at me."

"You don't know that, Billy."

"One more night, then, anyway. I want to find out where this fella's gone. I tell you, I keep my eyes peeled, like I said, and one minute 'e's there and the next 'e's not. Mind you, there is someone in the sick bay."

"And who tends the sick bay?"

"Well, there's a fella who was a medic in the war, 'e does all your basic stuff, like. Then this other fella came up today. In a car, doctor's bag and all. I was working in the front garden at the time. Dead ringer for Jenkins actually. Bit bigger, mind. But you could see it round 'ere." Billy rubbed his chin and jaw. "'round the chops."

"Yes. I know who that is," Maisie whispered as she wrote notes on an index card.

"What, Miss?"

"No. Nothing. Billy, listen, I know you think that Jenkins is essentially a good man, but I fear that you may now be in some danger. You are an innocent person brought into my work because I needed information. That must change. It's time for you to leave."

Billy Beale turned to Maisie and looked deeply into her eyes. "You know, Miss, when we first met, when I said I'd seen you before, after that shell got me leg. Did you recognize me?"

Maisie closed her eyes briefly, looked at the ground to compose herself and then directly at Billy. "Yes. I recognized you, Billy. Some people you never forget."

"I know. I told you, I would never forget you and that doctor. Could've 'ad my leg off, 'e could. Anyone else would've just chopped the leg and got me out of there. But 'im, that doctor, even in those conditions, like, 'e tried to do more."

Billy gazed out across the land to The Retreat.

"And I know what 'appened. I know what 'appened after I left. 'eard about it. Amazing you weren't killed."

Maisie did not speak but instead slowly began to remove the pins that held her long black hair in a neat chignon. She turned her head to one side and lifted her hair. And as she drew back the tresses, she revealed a purple scar weaving a path from just above her hairline at the nape of her neck, through her hair and into her scalp.

"Long hair, Billy, hides a multitude of sins."

His eyes beginning to smart, Billy looked toward The Retreat again, as if checking to see that everything was still in its place. He said nothing about the scar, but pressed his lips together and shook his head.

"I'll stay 'ere until tomorrow, Miss. I know you need me to be at this place at least another day. I'll meet you 'ere at half past seven tomorrow, and I'll 'ave me kit bag with me. No one will see me, don't you worry."

Billy did not wait for Maisie to respond, but clambered back through the fence. And as she had each evening for more than a week now, Maisie watched Billy limp across the field to The Retreat.

"I'll be here," whispered Maisie. "I'll be here."

Maisie did not go to bed, and was not encouraged to do so by Maurice. She knew that the time of reckoning could come soon. Yes, if Jenkins was to make his move, it would be now. If not, then the investigation would lie dormant; the file would remain open.

She sat on the floor, legs crossed, watching first the night grow darker, then the early hours of the morning edge slowly toward dawn. The clock struck the half hour. Half past four. She breathed in deeply and closed her eyes. Suddenly the telephone rang, its shrill bell piercing the quiet of the night. Maisie opened her eyes and came to her feet quickly. Before it could ring a second time, she answered the call.

"Billy."

"Yes. Miss, something's goin' on down 'ere."

"First, Billy—are you safe?"

"No one's seen me leave. I crept out, kept close to the wall, came straight across the field and through the fence to the old dog 'n' bone 'ere."

"Good. Now—what's happening?"

Billy caught his breath. "I couldn't sleep last night, Miss. Kept thinking about, y'know, what we'd talked about."

"Yes, Billy."

Maisie turned to the door as she spoke and nodded her head to Maurice, who had entered the room dressed as he had been when he had bidden her goodnight. He had not slept either.

"Anyway. 'bout—well, blimey, must 've been over 'alf an hour ago now—I 'eard a bit of a racket outside, sounded like a sack bein' dragged around. So, I goes to the window to see what's what."

"Go on, Billy. And keep looking around you."

"Don't you worry, Miss, I'm keepin' me eyes peeled. Anyway, it was 'im, bein' dragged away down the dirt road."

"Who?"

"The fella that wanted to leave. Could see 'im plain as day, in the light coming from the door."

"Where does the dirt road lead to—the quarry?"

"Yes, Miss. That's right."

Maisie took a deep breath.

"Billy, here's what you are to do. Go into the hamlet. Keep very close to the side of the road. Do not be seen. There may be someone else coming from that direction heading for The Retreat. Do not let him see you. Meet me by the oak tree on the green. Go now."

Maisie replaced the receiver. There was no time to allow Billy Beale another question before ending the call.

Maurice handed Maisie her jacket and hat and took up his own. She opened her mouth to protest, but was silenced by Maurice's raised hand.

"Maisie, I never, ever said that you were too young for the many risks you have taken. Do not now tell me to stay at home because I am too old!"

$\mathscr{B}$illy clambered out of the ditch and stretched his wounded leg. Kneeling had made him sore, and he rubbed at his cramped muscles. The sound of a breaking twig in the silence of the early morning hours, as leaves rustled in a cool breeze, made him snap to attention. He remained perfectly still.

"Now I'm bleedin' 'earin' things," whispered Billy into the dawn chill that caught his chest and forced his heart to beat faster, so fast he could hear it echo in his ears.

"Like waitin' for that bleedin' whistle to go off for the charge, it is."

Billy took his bag by the handle and slung it over his shoulder. Looking both ways, he began to cross the road to take advantage of the overhanging branches that would shield him as he made his way along the lane into the hamlet. But as he moved, his leg cramped again.

"Blimey, come on, come on, leg! Don't bleedin' let me down now."

Billy tried to straighten his body, but as he moved, his war wounds came to life, shooting pain through him as he tried to take a step.

"I'm afraid you've let yourself down, William," a man's voice intoned.

"Who's that? Who's there?" Billy fell backward, his arms flailing as he tried to regain balance.

Adam Jenkins stepped out of the half-light in front of Billy. Archie stood with him, together with two other longtime residents of The Retreat.

"Desertion is what we call it. When you leave before your time."

"I just, well, I just wanted to 'ave a bit of a walk, Sir," said Billy, nervously running his fingers through his hair.

"Well, a fine time to be walking, William. Or perhaps you prefer 'Billy?' A fine time for a stroll."

Jenkins signaled to Archie and the other men, who pinioned Billy's hands behind his back and tightly secured a black cloth across his eyes.

"Desertion, Billy. Terrible thing. Nothing worse in a soldier. Nothing worse."

Maisie drew up alongside the oak tree in the hamlet of Hart's Lea. There was no sign of Billy.

"Maurice, he's not here," said Maisie, as she swung the car in the direction of The Retreat, and accelerated. "We've got to find him."

Maisie drove at high speed along the lane to The Retreat, scanning the side of the road as she maneuvered the car. Beside her Maurice was silent. Abruptly she swung the car onto the verge by the beech tree and got out. Kneeling on the verge, she ran her fingers over the rough ground. In the early light of morning, she could see signs of a scuffle.

Yes, they had Billy.

Maurice climbed out of the car, with some difficulty, and joined Maisie.

"I must find him, Maurice. His life is in danger."

"Yes, go, Maisie. But I would advise that this is the time—"

Maisie sighed, "Of course, you're right, Maurice. Over here I think we might be in luck."

Lowering herself into the ditch on the other side of the road, near the perimeter fence of The Retreat, Maisie reached down, and pulled up Billy's makeshift telephone.

"Thank God! They didn't find it—they must have arrived just after he replaced the receiver. I'm not really sure how you—"

"Go now, Maisie. I will see to it. I may be old, but such things are not beyond the scope of my intelligence."

Maisie rushed over to the MG, opened the door, and took out the black jacket that Maurice had handed her when they left the house. Pulling on the jacket, Maisie was about to close the door of the car, when she stopped and instead reached behind the driver's seat for her bag. She hurriedly took out the new Victorinox knife, slipped it into the pocket of her trousers, and closed the car door. Maisie crossed the road, pausing only to touch Maurice's shoulder with her hand, before pulling back the wire and squeezing through the hole in the fence. She ran quickly across the field, aided by the grainy light of sunrise.

At first Maisie took care to step quietly past the farm buildings, but soon realized that they were deserted, a fact that did not surprise her. "He will probably want to set an example to the residents," Maisie had said to Maurice as they left the dower house. "He'll have an audience. An 'innocuous' little man would love an audience."

Maisie squinted at the silver watch pinned to the left breast pocket of her jacket. The watch that to this day was her talisman. Time had survived with her, but now time was marching on. Billy was in grave danger. She must be quick

Within minutes she reached the quarry, and as she ran, the memories cascaded into her mind. She must get to him. Simon had saved him, and so must she. She must get to Billy.

She slowed to a walk and quietly crept into the mouth of the quarry, keeping close to the rough sandstone entrance so that she would not be seen. Maisie gasped as she scanned the tableau before her. A sea of men were seated on chairs, facing a raised platform with a wooden structure placed upon it. With their damaged faces, once so very dear to a mother, father, or sweetheart, they were now reduced to gargoyles by a war that, for them, had never ended. There were men without noses or jaws, men who searched for light with empty eye sockets, men with only half a face where once a full-formed smile had beamed. She choked back tears, her blue eyes searching for Billy Beale.

As the rising sun struggled against the remains of night, Maisie realized that the wooden structure was a rough gallows. Suddenly, the men's faces moved. Maisie followed their gaze. Jenkins walked toward the platform from another direction. He took center stage, and raised his hand. At his signal Archie and another man came toward the platform, half guiding, half dragging a blindfolded man between them. It was Billy. As she watched, Billy—jovial, willing Billy Beale—who surely would have given his life for her, was placed on his knees in front of the gallows, and held captive in the taut hangman's noose. It would need only one sharp tug from the two men working in unison to do its terrible work.

The audience stood unmoved, yet in fear; their eyes, behind the terrible deformities war had dealt them, showing terror. And in that dreadful moment when she thought that the strong, fast legs that had borne her to this place had become paralyzed, Maisie was haunted by the past and present coming together as one. She knew that she must take action, but what could stop this madness immediately, without the men rising up against her—such was Jenkins's control over them—and without risking Billy's immediate death? "Fight like with like," she whispered, remembering one of Maurice's lessons, and as she uttered the words, a picture flashed into her mind, a memory, of being on the train with Iris, of watching the soldiers as they marched off to battle, singing as they beat a path to death's door. There was no secret route along which she could stealthily make her way to Billy's side. She had only one option. For just a second Maisie closed her eyes, pulled her shoulders back, and stood as tall as she could. She breathed deeply, cleared her throat, and began to walk slowly toward the platform. For Billy she must be a fearless warrior. And as the men became aware of her presence, she looked at their faces, smiled kindly, and began to sing.

> There's a rose that grows
> In No-Mans' Land
> And it's wonderful to see

Though it's sprayed with tears
It will live for years
In my garden of memory . . .

As she gained on the platform, now keeping her eyes focused on Jenkins, Maisie heard a deep resonant voice join her own. Then another voice echoed alongside her, and another, until her lone voice had become one with a choir of men singing in unison, their low voices a dawn chorus that echoed around the quarry.

It's the one red rose
The soldier knows
It's the work of the Master's hand
'Mid the war's great curse,
Stands the Red Cross Nurse
She's the Rose of No-Man's Land . . .

Maisie banished all fear as she stood on the ground below Jenkins. Dressed in the uniform of an officer who had served in the Great War, he stood with eyes blazing. She avoided looking at Billy, instead meeting Jenkins's glare while ascending the steps to the platform. The men continued to sing softly behind her, finding solace in the gentle rhythm of a much-loved song. Standing in front of Jenkins, she maintained eye contact. Her action had silenced him, but in mirroring his posture, she knew of his inner confusion, his torment, and his pain. And in looking into his eyes, she knew that he was mad.

"Major Jenkins . . ." She addressed the officer in front of her, who seemed to regain a sense of place and time.

"You can't stop this, you know. This man is a disgrace to his country," he pointed his baton towards Billy. "A deserter."

"By what authority, Major Jenkins? Where are your orders?"

Jenkins's eyes flashed in confusion. Maisie heard Billy groan as the rope cut into his neck.

"Has this man received a court-martial? A fair trial?"

Voices murmured behind her as Jenkins's audience, the wounded "guests" of The Retreat, began to voice dissent. She had to be in control of each moment, for if one word were out of place, the men could easily become an angry mob—dangerous not only to this mind-injured man in front of her but to Billy and herself.

"A trial? Haven't got time for trials, you know. Got to get on with it! Got a job to do, without having to tolerate time wasters like this one." He pointed his baton at Billy again, then brought it to his side and tapped it against his shining leather boots.

"We *do* have time, Major." Maisie held her breath as she took her chance. Billy had begun to choke. She had to make her bravest move.

Though Maurice had cautioned Maisie in the use of touch, he had also stressed the power inherent in physical connection: "When we reach to place a hand on a sore knee or an aching back, we are really reaching into our primordial healing resources. Judicious use of the energy of touch can transform, as the power of our aura soothes the place that is injured."

"Major Jenkins," said Maisie, in a low voice. "It's over. . . the war is over. You can rest now . . . you can rest. . . ." And as she whispered the words, she raised a hand, stepped closer to him, and instinctively held her palm against the place where she felt his heart to be. For a moment there was no movement as Jenkins closed his eyes. He began to tremble, and with her fingertips Maisie could feel him struggle to regain control of his body—and his mind.

The onlookers gasped as Jenkins began to weep. Falling to his knees, he pulled his Webley Mk IV service revolver from its holster and held the barrel to his head.

"No," said Maisie firmly, but softly, and with a move so gentle that Jenkins barely felt the revolver leave his grasp, she took the weapon from his hand.

At that moment, as the audience watched in a stunned silence that paralyzed all movement, she saw lights beginning to illuminate the entrance to the quarry. Uniformed men ran toward the platform, shouting, "Stop, police!" She abandoned Jenkins, who was rocking back and forth, clasping his arms about his body, and moaning with a rasping, guttural cry.

Maisie pushed the revolver into her pocket and moved quickly toward the lifeless body of Billy Beale. Archie and his assistant were nowhere to be seen. Maisie quickly took out her pocket knife and, holding back the flesh on Billy's neck with the fingers of her left hand, she slipped the blade against the rope, and freed Billy from the hangman's noose. As Billy fell toward her, Maisie tried to take his weight, and stumbled. She was aware that Jenkins was now flanked by two policemen, and that all around her the frozen moment had thawed into frenzied activity.

"Billy, look at me, Billy," said Maisie, regaining balance.

She slapped his face on both sides, and felt his wrist for a pulse.

Billy choked, and his eyes rolled up into their sockets as his hands instinctively clamored to free his neck from the constriction that he could still feel at his throat.

"Steady on, Miss, steady on, for Gawd's sake."

Billy choked, his gas-damaged lungs wheezing with the enormous effort of fighting for breath. As he tried to sit up, Maisie supported him with her arms around his shoulders.

"It's awright, Miss. I'm not a goner. Let me get some air. Some air."

"Can you see me, Billy?"

Billy Beale looked at Maisie, who was now on her knees beside him.

"I'm awright now that you're 'ere, even if you are a bit 'eavy 'anded. Mind you . . ." he coughed, wiping away the blood and spittle that came up from his throat, "I thought you'd never get over chattin' wiv that bleedin' lunatic there." Billy pointed toward Jenkins, then brought his hand back to his mouth as he coughed another deep, rasping cough.

"May I have a word, Miss Dobbs?" The man looking down at her beckoned the police doctor to attend to Billy, then held out a hand to Maisie. Grasping his outstretched hand, she drew herself up to a standing position and brushed back the locks of black hair that were hanging around her face. The man held out his right hand again. "Detective Inspector Stratton. Murder Squad. Your colleague is in good hands. Now, if I may have a word."

Maisie quickly appraised the man, who was standing in front of her. Stratton was more than six feet tall, well-built, and confident, without the posturing that she had seen before in men of high rank. His hair, almost as black as her own, except for wisps of gray at the temples, was swept back. He wore corduroy trousers and a tweed jacket with leather at the elbows. He held a brown felt hat with a black grosgrain band in his left hand. Like a country doctor, observed Maisie. "Yes. Yes, of course, Detective Inspector Stratton. I . . . ."

". . . Should have known better, Miss Dobbs? Yes, probably, you should have known better. However, I have been briefed by Dr. Blanche, and I realize that you were in a situation where not a moment could be lost. Suffice it to say that this is not the time for discussion or reprimand. I must ask you, though, to make yourself available for questioning in connection with this case, perhaps tomorrow?"

"Yes, but—"

"Miss Dobbs, I have to attend to the suspect now, but, in the meantime—"

"Yes?" Maisie was flushed, tired, and indignant.

"Good work, Miss Dobbs. A calm head—very good work." Detective Inspector Stratton shook hands with Maisie once again, and was just about to walk away when she called him back.

"Oh, Inspector, just a moment. . . ." Maisie held out the service revolver she had taken from Jenkins. "I think you'll need this for your evidence bag."

Stratton took the revolver, checked the barrel, and removed the ammunition before placing the weapon safely in his own pocket. He inclined his head toward Maisie and smiled, then turned toward Jenkins, who was now flanked by two members of the Kent Constabulary. Maisie watched as Stratton commenced the official caution: "'You are not obliged to say anything unless you wish to do so, but what you say may be put into writing and given in evidence.'"

Maisie looked around at Billy, to satisfy herself that he was safe—he was now on his feet and speaking with the doctor—then surveyed the scene in front of her. She watched as Maurice Blanche walked among the terrified audience of 'old soldiers' who still seemed so very young, his calming presence infectious as he stood with the men, placing a hand on a shoulder for support, or holding a weeping man to him unashamedly. The men seemed to understand his strength, and clustered around to listen to his soothing words. She saw him motion to Stratton, who sent policemen to lead the residents of The Retreat away one by one. They were men for whom the terror of war had been replayed and whose trust had been shattered. First by their country, and now by a single man. They were men who would have to face the world in which there was no retreat. Maurice was right, they were all innocents. Perhaps even Jenkins.

Jenkins was now in handcuffs and being led to a waiting Invicta police car that had been brought into the mouth of the quarry, his unsoiled polished boots and Sam Browne belt shining against a pressed uniform. Not a hair on his head was out of place. He was still the perfectly turned-out officer.

CHAPTER TWENTY-EIGHT

$\mathcal{S}$o, what I want to know," said Billy, sitting in Maurice Blanche's favorite wing chair, next to the fireplace in the dower house, "Is 'ow did you get on to Adam Jenkins in the end. And I tell you, 'e certainly 'ad me there. I was beginnin' t'think 'e was a crackin' bloke."

Maisie sat on a large cushion on the floor sipping tea, while Maurice was comfortable on the sofa opposite Billy. She set down her cup and saucer on the floor and rubbed at her cold feet.

"I had a feeling, here." Maisie touched the place between her ribs, at the base of her breastbone. "There was something wrong from the beginning. Of course you know about Vincent. And the others. That was a mistake on Jenkins's part, suggesting to Vincent's family that he be interred at Nether Green because it's a big cemetery, with lots of soldiers' graves. It was a mistake because he used it several times."

Maisie took a sip of her tea and continued. "I questioned the coincidence of several men buried with only their Christian names to identify them. Then I found out that they were all from the same place. The Retreat."

"And what else?" asked Billy, waving a hand to disperse the smoke from Maurice's pipe.

"A mistrust—on my part—of someone who wields so much power. The inspiration for The Retreat was admirable. Such places have worked well in France. But, for the most part, those places were set up for soldiers with disfiguring wounds to go to on holiday, not to be there forever. And using only Christian names was Jenkins's innovation. Stripping away a person's name is a very basic manner of control. It's done in all sorts of institutions, such as the army—for example, they called you 'corporal,' not 'Billy,' or possibly—rarely—even 'Beale.'"

Billy nodded.

"The irony is, that it was one of the first men to live at The Retreat, Vincent Weathershaw, who gave him the idea for the Christian-names-only mode of address."

Maisie caught her breath and continued.

"More evidence came to hand after you went to The Retreat. Each cause of death was different—there was even a drowning listed—yet each could be attributed to asphyxiation of some sort. To the untrained eye, an accident. The word of the examiner would not be questioned. No police were involved, they were considered to be deaths from 'accidental' or 'natural' causes—and as the men were all seeking relief from torment by coming to The Retreat, the families had no lingering questions. In fact, there was often relief that the loved one would not have to suffer anymore," said Maisie.

"Indeed." Maurice looked at Maisie, who did not return his gaze. He took up the story. "Then there was Jenkins's own history. How could someone who had given his superiors cause to refer to him as "innocuous" have gained such power? Maisie telephoned the doctor who had supervised his care at Craiglockhart—the hospital in Scotland where shell-shocked officers were sent during the war. The poet Siegfried Sassoon was there."

"Well, sir, I ain't never bin much of a one for poetry." Billy waved smoke away from his face once more.

"The doctor, who is now at the Maudsley psychiatric hospital in

London, informed me that Jenkins's mental state was not as serious as some," said Maisie, "But there was cause for concern."

"I'll bet there was." Billy rubbed at the red weal left by the rope at his neck.

"You know what happened to deserters, Billy?"

Billy looked at his hands and turned them back and forth, inspecting first the palms, then his knuckles. "Yes. Yes I do, Miss."

"They were taken and shot. At dawn. We talked about it. Some of them just young boys of seventeen or eighteen—they were scared out of their wits. It's been rumored that there was even a case of two being shot for accidentally falling asleep while on duty." Tears came to Maisie's eyes and she pursed her lips together. "Jenkins was the commanding officer instructed to deal with a desertion. 'Innocuous' Jenkins. Much against his will—and apparently he did question his orders—he was instructed to preside over such an execution."

"And . . ."

Billy sat forward in the leather chair.

"He carried out orders. Had he not, then he might well have been subject to the same fate. To disobey would have been insubordination."

Maisie got up from the floor and walked to the window. Maurice's eyes followed her, then turned to Billy. "The mind can do strange things, Billy. Just as we can become used to pain, so we can become used to experience, and in some cases a distasteful experience is made more palatable if we embrace it."

"Like putting sugar in the castor oil."

"Something of that order. Jenkins's sugar was the power he claimed. One might argue that it was the only way for him to stomach the situation. He was not a man strong in spirit. So close was he to the act of desertion that it made him detest the actual deserter, and in meting out this terrible, terrible punishment, he maintained control over the part of him that would have run away. He became very good at dealing with battlefield deserters. Indeed, he enjoyed a level of success, we understand, that he did not enjoy in other areas of responsibility."

Maurice looked again at Maisie, who turned to face Billy. "Jenkins's idea of founding The Retreat was formed in good faith. But once again the need for control emerged. The chain of murders began when one of the men wanted to leave. Jenkins felt the man's decision keenly. He was, in effect, deserting The Retreat. For Jenkins, his mind deeply affected by the war, there was only one course of action. And then one death made the others easier."

"Blimey," whispered Billy.

"Had you been at The Retreat longer, you too would have heard it said that it was difficult to depart with one's life. Obviously he could not shoot a man—it would not be easy for the medical examiner to disguise the truth of such a wound—but he could use a more dramatic method. This gallows in the quarry would not break a man's neck, but would deprive the body of oxygen for just about long enough to take a life. A death that it would be easy to attribute to suicide or accident. And he must have been in a hurry with you, Billy, because with the others, a heavy cloth was wrapped around the noose. The rope marks were not as livid as the necklace you're now wearing."

Billy once again rubbed at his neck. "I reckon it's all bleedin' wrong, this 'ere business of shootin' deserters. I tell you, 'alf of us didn't know what the bloody 'ell we were supposed to be doin' over there anyway. I know the officers, specially the young ones, didn't."

Maurice pointed the stem of his pipe at Billy, ready to comment. "Interesting point, Billy. You may be interested to know that Ernest Thurtle, an American by birth, now the MP for Whitechapel, has worked hard in Parliament to have the practice banned—it wouldn't surprise me if a new law were passed in the next year or so."

"About bloody time, too! And talkin' about deserters, what's the connection with Vincent Weathershaw? Remember me finding out that there was something that went on with 'im?"

"Yes," continued Maisie. "From what we know, Weathershaw was disciplined because he complained about the practice of military execution. He was vocal about it too, upsetting higher-ups. He was injured before he could be stripped of his commission and court-martialed for insubordination."

Billy whistled between his teeth. "This gets worse."

"It did for Weathershaw. He came to The Retreat in good faith, a terribly disfigured man. He had known something of Jenkins while in convalescence, but at The Retreat he found out about his reputation as a battlefield executioner. Vincent had put two and two together, so Jenkins decided he had to go. He'd suffered terrible depression, poor man, so accident or suicide was entirely believable."

"Poor sod. What about this other Jenkins?"

"Cousin. We thought Armstrong Jenkins was a brother, but he's not, he's a cousin. Surprisingly, Adam Jenkins was not in it for the money. His reward was the sensation of control. King of all he surveyed, and with a legion of serfs who listened to his every word, and despite what they heard, adored him. And that is the part of the puzzle that is most intriguing."

"Indeed," said Maurice. "Most intriguing."

"That despite the rumors, such as they were, and the demise of those who 'left' The Retreat, Jenkins was held in very high regard by the men."

Billy blushed.

"An interesting phenomenon," said Maurice. "Such control over a group of people. It is, I fear, something that we shall see again, especially in times such as this, when people are seeking answers to unfathomable questions, for leadership in their uncertainty, and for a connection with others of like experience. Indeed, there is a word to describe such a group, gathered under one all-powerful leader, taken from the practice of seeking answers in the occult. What Jenkins founded could be described as a cult."

"This is givin' me the shivers," said Billy, rubbing his arms.

Maisie took up the story again. "Armstrong Jenkins was the one who persuaded his cousin to have the men sign over their assets. And for a man coming into The Retreat, so desperately unhappy that he would willingly cloister himself, it was not such a huge step.

Armstrong held the purse strings. He came to this area to work as medical examiner when The Retreat opened. Like his cousin, his is a case of power laced with evil."

"I'll say. Gaw blimey, that was close."

"I made three telephone calls before our last meeting in the lane, and what I learned alerted me to the level of your danger. One was to the Maudsley, to speak to Adam Jenkins's doctor; one was to the county coroner, to confirm Armstrong Jenkins's history, and finally one to Maurice's friend, the Chief Constable, to inform him of my suspicions. It was his intention to begin an investigation of The Retreat the following day—but of course events overtook him. Billy, I wanted you to relinquish your task as soon as you told me that another man wished to leave The Retreat. But you were adamant."

Billy met Maisie's eyes with his own. "I told you, Miss, I didn't want to let you down. I wanted to do something for you. Like you and that doctor did for me. You never did it 'alf-'earted because you was all tired out. You had men linin' up all over the place, yet you saved my leg. When I got 'ome, the doc said it was the best bit of battlefield leg saving 'e'd ever seen."

Tears smarted in Maisie's eyes. She thought the pain had ceased. She hated this tide of tears that came in, bidden by truth.

"And I know it's a bit off the subject, like, but I wanted to ask you somethin', and I . . . I dunno . . . I just felt you didn't want to talk about it, and who can blame you? But . . . what 'appened to 'im? What 'appened to that doctor?"

A strained silence fell upon the room. The excited explanation of events at The Retreat gave way to embarrassment. Maurice sighed, his brow furrowed, as he watched Maisie, who sat with her head in her hands.

"Look, I 'ope I ain't said anythin' wrong . . . I'm sorry if it was out of turn. It ain't none of my business, is it? I thought you were a bit sweet on each other, that's all. I remember thinking that. So I thought you'd know. The man saved my leg, probably even my life. But I'm sorry. Shouldn't 'ave said anythin'." Billy picked up his jacket as if to leave the room.

"Billy. Wait. Yes. Yes, I should have told you. About Captain Lynch. It's only fair that you should know. After what you've done for me, it's only fair."

Maurice moved to Maisie's side and took her hand in his. She answered Billy's question.

CHAPTER TWENTY-NINE

$\mathcal{J}$t seemed to Maisie that no sooner had she returned to the casualty clearing station, from her leave at home with Simon, than droves of injured were brought in. As day stretched into night, the few hours' sleep that Maisie managed to claim each night offered only a brief respite from the war.

"Did you remember to tie the scarf, Maisie?" asked Iris, referring to the cloth tied to the tent pole, which would indicate to the orderlies that the nurses inside were on the first shift to be called if wounded came in at night.

"Yes. It's there, Iris. 'Night."

"'Night, Maisie."

Often Maisie would fall into a deep sleep immediately upon climbing into her cot. Time and again her dreaming mind took her back to Chelstone, walking toward her father in the orchard. Yet as she came closer to him, he moved away, reaching up to pick rosy red apples before moving on. She would call out to him, and he would turn and wave, but he did not stop, he did not wait for her. This Frankie Dobbs simply picked the deep red apples, placed them in his wicker basket, and moved through the long grass of late summer. Such was the weight he carried, that rich red juice ran from the bottom of the basket, leaving a trail for her to follow. She tried to run faster, yet her long, heavy woolen dress soaked up the red juice, clung to her legs, and caught in the grass, and as the distance between them extended, Maisie cried out to him. "Dad, Dad, Dad!"

"Bloody hell, whatever is the matter with you?"

Iris sat up in bed and looked across at Maisie who, in her sudden wakefulness, lay on her back staring straight toward the top of the main tent pole, her violet eyes following drops of rainwater as they squeezed through the canvas and ran down to the ground.

"Are you all right?"

Iris leaned over and nudged Maisie.

"Yes. Yes, thanks. Bad dream. It was a bad dream."

"Not even time to get up yet. Brrr. Why doesn't it ever seem to get warm here? Here we are in the third week of May, and I'm freezing!"

Maisie did not answer, but drew the blankets closer to her jaw.

"We've got another half an hour. Then let's get up and go and get ourselves a mug of that strong tea," said Iris, making an attempt to reclaim the comfort of deep sleep.

"Looks like we've got some 'elp coming in today, ladies."

One of the medical officers sat down with Iris and Maisie, ready to gossip as he sipped scalding tea and took a bite out of the thick crust of bread.

"Lord, do we need it! There's never enough doctors, let alone nurses," said Iris, taking her mug and sitting down on a bench next to Maisie.

"What's happened?" asked Maisie.

"Think they're coming in from the hospital up the line. We've been getting so many in each day 'ere, and someone pushing a pencil at a desk finally got wind of it. Some docs are being moved. Down 'ere first."

Maisie and Iris looked at each other. She had written to Simon only yesterday. He had said nothing to her about being moved. Was it possible that he was one of the doctors being sent to the casualty clearing station?

"Mind you, they might not like it much, what with them shells coming in a bit closer lately," added the medical officer.

"I thought the red cross meant that we were safe from the shelling," said Iris, cupping her hands around her mug.

"Well, it's supposed to be safe. Red crosses mark neutral territory."

"When will they arrive . . . from the hospital?" asked Maisie, barely disguising her excitement. Excitement laced with trepidation.

"End of the week, by all accounts."

❖

It was late afternoon when new medical personnel began to appear. Maisie was walking through the ward, with men in various stages of recovery waiting for transportation to a military hospital in beds on either side of her, when she saw the silhouette she knew so well on the other side of the canvas flap that formed a wall between the ward and the medicines area. It was the place where nurses prepared dressings, measured powders, made notes, and stood to weep, just for a moment, when another patient was lost.

He was here. In the same place. They were together.

Without rushing, and continuing to check her patients as she made her way toward Simon, Maisie struggled to control her beating heart. Just before she drew back the flap of canvas, she took a deep breath, closed her eyes, then walked through into the medicines area.

He was on his own, looking through the pile of records, and familiarizing himself with the stocks of medicines and dressings. As Maisie entered, Simon looked up. For a moment neither moved.

Simon broke the silence, holding out his hand and taking hers.

"Why didn't you tell me in your letter?" whispered Maisie, looking around, fearful that someone might see her speaking with Simon.

"I didn't know I'd be sent. Not until yesterday." He smiled. "But now we're together. Couldn't believe my luck, Maisie."

She held his hand tighter. "I am so glad. So glad that you are here. And safe."

"Good omen, don't you think? That we're here in the same place."

In the distance Maisie heard a wounded soldier calling for her, "Sister. In 'ere. Quick."

Simon held onto Maisie's hand for a second before she rushed to attend to her patient.

"I love you, Maisie," he said, and brought her hand to his lips.

She nodded, smiled, and ran to her duties.

Working side by side was easier than either had thought it might be. For three days, wounded were brought in to the hospital and, time and time again, Maisie saw another side of the Simon she loved, the Simon who had stolen her heart as she danced in a blue silk dress. He was a brilliant doctor.

Even under the most intense pressure, Simon Lynch worked not just to save a life but to make that soldier's life bearable when the soldiering was done. With Maisie at his side, ready to pass instruments to him even before he asked—to clear the blood from wounds as he brought shattered bones together and stitched vicious lacerations—Simon used every ounce of knowledge garnered in the hospitals of England and in the operating tents of the battlefield.

"Right, on to the next one," said Simon, as one patient was moved and orderlies pushed forward with another soldier on a stretcher.

"What's waiting for us in the line?"

"Sir, we've got about a dozen legs, four very nasty heads, three chests, three arms, and five feet—and that's only as far as the corner. Ambulances coming in all the time, sir."

"Make sure we get the ones who can travel on the road as soon as possible. We need the room, and they need to be at the base hospital."

"Yes sir."

The orderlies hurried away to bring in the next soldier, while Simon looked down at the wounded man now dependent upon his judgment and skill, a young man with hair the color of sun-drenched wheat, and a leg torn apart by shrapnel. A young man who watched his every move so intently.

"Will you be able to save me leg, sir? Don't want to be an ol' peg-leg, do I?"

"Don't worry. I'll do my best. Can't have you not able to chase the ladies, can we, Corporal?" Simon smiled at the man, despite his exhaustion.

Maisie looked up at Simon, then down at the corporal, and as Simon removed the shrapnel, she cleaned the bleeding wounds so that he could see the extent of the injury. To keep the soldier's spirits up—this man so conscious of everything happening around him—Maisie would look up for a second from her work and smile at him. And as Simon cut skin and brought together flesh, muscle, and bone that had been torn apart, the soldier took heart. For though he could not see Maisie's smile through the white linen mask that shielded part of her face, her warm blue eyes told the soldier what he wanted to hear. That all would be well.

"Right. On your way to Blighty you are, my man. Done the best for you here, and God knows you've done your best for Blighty. The sooner you get home, the sooner they'll get you moving again. Rest assured, Corporal, the leg is staying with its owner."

"Thank you, Captain, sir. Thank you, Sister. Never forget you, ever."

The soldier looked intently at Simon and Maisie, fighting the morphine to remember their faces. A "Blighty," a wound sufficiently severe to warrant being sent back to England—and he would keep his leg. He was a lucky man.

"This one's ready for transport. We're ready for the next one."

Simon called out to the orderlies, and Maisie prepared the table as Corporal William Beale was taken to an ambulance for transfer to a base hospital closer to the port. He would be home within two days.

"*I* feel sorry for the ones who are left," said Maisie.

She and Simon were walking by moonlight along a corridor of ground between the tents, quiet and ready to part quickly should they be seen together. Distant sporadic gunfire punctured their conversation.

"Me too. Though the ones I ache for are the ones who are injured so terribly, so visibly to the face or limbs. And the ones whose injuries can't be seen."

"In the London Hospital, there were many times when a woman cried with relief at the passing of her husband or son. They had wounds that the family couldn't cope with—that people on the street couldn't bear to see."

She moved closer to Simon, who took her hand.

"It'll be over soon. It has to be, Maisie. The war just can't go on like this. Sometimes I feel as if I'm doctoring in a slaughterhouse. One body of raw flesh after another."

Simon stopped and drew Maisie to him and kissed her. "My Maisie of the blue silk dress. I'm still waiting for an answer."

Maisie drew back and looked into Simon's eyes. "Simon, I said to ask again when this is over. When I can see a future."

"That's the trouble," said Simon, beginning to tease her, "Sometimes I think you *can* see the future—and it gives me chills!"

He held her to him again. "I tell you what, Maisie. I promise that I won't ask you again until the war is over. We'll walk together on the South Downs and you can give me your answer then. How about it?"

Maisie smiled and looked into his eyes, bright in the moonlight. Simon, Simon, my love, she thought, how I fear this question. "Yes. Yes, Simon. Ask me again on the South Downs. When the war is over."

And Simon threw back his head and laughed, without thought for who might hear him.

"*God* . . . ."

Simon's lips were drawn across his teeth as he looked at the wound to the soldier's chest, and uttered his plea to the heavens. Maisie immediately began cleaning the hole created by shrapnel, while Simon stanched the flow of blood. Nurses, doctors, anesthetists, orderlies, and stretcher-bearers were everywhere, rushing, running, working to save lives.

Maisie wiped the sweat from Simon's brow and continued to work on the wound. Simon inspected the extent of the injury. Lights flickered, and the tent shuddered.

"God, I can hardly even see in here."

Suddenly it seemed as if the battlefield had come to the hospital. As they worked to save the lives of men being brought in by the dozen, the tent shook again with the impact of a shell at close quarters.

"What the bloody hell . . .?"

"Sir, sir, I think we're coming under fire," an orderly shouted across to Simon. The operating tent was becoming part of the battlefield itself. Maisie swallowed the sour liquid that had come up from her stomach and into her mouth. She looked at Simon, and to combat her fear, she smiled at him. For one second he returned her smile broadly, then turned again to his patient. They could not stop.

"Well, then. Let's get on with it!"

Let's get on with it.

Those were the last words she heard Simon speak.

Let's get on with it.

CHAPTER THIRTY

*J*t was on a warm afternoon in late September that Maisie stepped out of the MG and looked up at the front of an imposing Georgian building in Richmond. Two Grecian-style columns stood at either side of the steps, which in turn led to the heavy oak doors of the main entrance. The house had once been a grand home with gardens that extended down toward the Thames, where the great river grew broader on its meandering journey from the village of Thame in Oxfordshire, after it emerged as a small stream. From Richmond it would rush on toward London, through the city, and into the sea, fresh and salt water meeting in a swirling mass. Maisie loved to look at the river. There was calm to be found in viewing water. And Maisie wanted to remain calm. She would walk to the water and back, to get her bearings.

The Retreat affair had been brought to its conclusion. Jenkins was now at Broadmoor, incarcerated with those who were considered mentally ill and dangerous. Archie and others involved in Jenkins's wrongdoing at The Retreat were also in institutions where they would find a measure of compassion and solace. They were not being held "at His Majesty's Pleasure" but would be released in time. Other men had returned to families or to their solitary lives, some finding renewed understanding.

Billy Beale found that he did not really enjoy publicity, that it was enough for him to go about his business each day, though if a person needed help, then he, Billy Beale, was the man.

"Of course, the missus don't mind gettin' a bit extra when she goes into that skinflint butcher for a nice bit of lamb, and the attention's brought a bit of a smile to 'er face. But me, I dunno. I'm not your big one for bein' noticed on the street."

Maisie laughed at Billy, who daily told of the latest encounter that came as a result of being the hero of events at The Retreat. He was supervising the placement of her new office furniture, which had just been moved to a larger room on the first floor of a grand building in Fitzroy Square, just around the corner from the Warren Street premises. Finally giving in to Lady Rowan's insistent nagging, Maisie would now be living in her own rooms at the Belgravia house.

"Look, my dear, Julian and I have decided to spend most of our dotage at Chelstone. Of course we'll come up for the Season, and for the theater and so on. But it is so much calmer in Kent, don't you think?"

"Well, Lady Rowan . . . ."

"Oh, no, I suppose it wasn't that calm for you, was it?" Lady Rowan laughed and continued. "Anyway, with James on his way to Canada to take care of our business interests again—thank heavens—the house will be all but empty. We'll have a skeleton staff here, naturally. Maisie, I must insist you take over the third-floor living rooms. In fact, I need you to."

Eventually Maisie concurred. Despite the fact that business was coming in at a respectable clip, Billy was now working for her, and money saved on her own rent would contribute to his wages.

As was Maurice's habit at the closure of a case, Maisie had visited the places of significance in The Retreat affair. During her apprenticeship, she had learned the importance of such a ritual, not only to ensure the integrity of notes that would be kept for reference, but for what Maurice referred to as a "personal accounting," to allow her to begin to work with new energy on the next case.

Maisie had walked once more in Mecklenburg Square, though she did not seek a meeting with Celia Davenham. She had received a letter from Celia after events at The Retreat became headline news. Celia had not referred to the inconsistency with the surname Maisie had given, but instead thanked her for helping to put Vincent's memory to rest.

She took tea at Fortnum & Mason, and at Nether Green Cemetery she placed fresh daisies on the graves of Vincent and his neighbor Donald, and stopped to speak to the groundsman whose son rested in a place overlooked by passing trains.

Maisie drove down to Kent in early September, when the spicy fragrance of dry hops still hung in the warm air of an Indian summer. She passed lorries and open-top buses carrying families back to the East End of London after their annual pilgrimage to harvest the hops, and smiled when she heard the sound of old songs lingering on the breeze. There was nothing like singing together to make a long journey pass quickly.

She drew the car alongside menacing heavy iron gates, and looked up, not at blooms, but this time at blood red rosehips overgrown on the wall. The Retreat was closed. Heavy chains hung on the gates and a sign with the insignia of the Kent Constabulary instructed trespassers to keep out.

*B*ecause memories had been given new life by her investigation, they too were part of her personal accounting. Maisie wrote letters to Priscilla, now living with her husband and three young sons in the South of France, each boy bearing the middle name of an uncle he would never know; to the famous American surgeon Charles Hayden and his family; and to Iris, who lived in Devon with her mother. Like many young women who came of age in the years 1914–18, Iris had no husband, for her sweetheart had been lost in the war. Maisie's letters did not tell the story of The Retreat, but only reminded the recipients that she thought of them often, and was well.

Now, as Maisie stood in the gardens of the grand house, looking out over the river and reflecting once again upon how much had happened in such a short time, she knew that for her future to spread out in front of her, she must face the past.

She was ready.

The conversation demanded by Billy had untied a knot in her past, one that bound her to the war in France over ten years ago.

Yes, it was time. It was more than time.

"*M*iss Dobbs, isn't it?"

The woman at the reception desk smiled up at Maisie, her red lipstick accentuating a broad smile that eased the way for visitors to the house. She crossed Maisie's name off the register of expected guests and leaned forward, pointing with her pen.

"Go along the corridor to your left, just over there, then down to the nurses' office. On the right. Can't miss it. They're expecting you. Staff Nurse will take you on from there."

"Thank you."

Maisie followed the directions, walking slowly. Massive flower arrangements on each side of the marble corridor gave forth a fragrance that soothed her, just as the sight of water had calmed her before she entered. Yes, she was glad she had made this decision. For some reason it was not so hard now. She was stronger. The final part of her healing was near.

She tapped on the door of the nurses' office, which was slightly ajar, and looked in.

"I'm Maisie Dobbs, visiting . . . ."

The staff nurse came to her.

"Yes. Good morning. Lovely to have a visitor. We don't see many here."

"Oh?"

"No. Difficult for the families. But you'd be surprised what a difference it makes."

"Yes. I was a nurse."

The staff nurse smiled. "Yes. I know. His mother told us you would be coming. Very pleased, she was. Very happy about it. Told us all . . . well, never mind. Come with me. It's a lovely day, isn't it?"

"Where is he?"

"The conservatory. Lovely and warm in there. The sun shines in. They love the conservatory."

The staff nurse led the way down the corridor, turned left again, and opened a door into the large glass extension to the main building, a huge room filled with exotic plants and trees. Staff Nurse had not stopped talking since they left the nurses' office; they do that to put the new visitors at ease, thought Maisie.

"This was originally called the Winter Gardens, built by the owner so the ladies of the house could take a turn in the winter without going outside into the cold. You can have quite the walk in here. It's a bit too big to call it a conservatory, I suppose. But that's what we call it."

She motioned to Maisie once again. "This way, over to the fountain. Loves the water, he does."

The staff nurse pointed to an open window. "And though it's warm, it doesn't get too warm, if you know what I mean. We open the windows to let the breeze blow through in summer, and it still feels like summer, doesn't it? Ah. Here he is."

Maisie looked in the direction of her outstretched hand, at the man in a wheelchair with his back to them. He was facing the fountain, his head inclined to one side. The staff nurse walked over to the man, stood in front of him, and leaned over to speak. As she did so she gently tapped his hand. Maisie remained still.

"Captain Lynch. Got a visitor, you have. Come to see you. A very beautiful lady."

The man did not move. He remained facing the fountain. The staff nurse smiled at him, tucked in the blanket covering his knees, and then gave Maisie a broad smile before joining her.

"Would you like me to stay for a while?"

"No, no. I'll be fine." Maisie bit her lip.

"Right you are. About twenty minutes? I'll come back for you then. Never find your way out of the jungle alone!"

"Thank you, Staff Nurse."

The woman nodded, checked the time on the watch pinned to her apron, and walked away along the brick path overhung with branches. Maisie went to Simon and sat down in front of him, on the low wall surrounding the fountain. She looked up at this man she had loved so deeply, with all the intensity of a first love, a love forged in the desperate heat of wartime. Maisie looked at the face she had not seen since 1917, a face now so changed.

"Hello, my love," said Maisie.

There was no response. The eyes stared at a place in the distance beyond Maisie, a place that only he could see. The face was scarred, the hair growing in a shock of gray along scars that lay livid across the top of his skull.

Maisie put her hand to his face and, running her fingers along the jagged lines, wondered how it could be that the outcome of wounds was so different. That scars so similar on the outside concealed a different, far deeper injury. In comparison, her own wounds from the same exploding shell had been superficial. Yet Simon's impairment freed him from all sensation of the deeper wound: that of a broken heart.

Simon still did not move. She took his hands in hers and began to speak. "Forgive me, my love. Forgive me for not coming to you. I was so afraid. So afraid of not remembering you as we were together, as you were. . . ."

She rubbed his hands. They were warm to the touch, so warm she could feel the cold in her own.

"At first people asked me why I didn't come, and I said I didn't feel well enough to see you. Then as each month, each year passed, it was as if the memory of you—of us . . . the explosion—were encased in fine tissue-paper."

Maisie bit her lip, constantly kneading Simon's still hands as she spoke her confession. "I felt as if I were looking through a window to my own past, and instead of being transparent, my view was becoming more and more opaque, until eventually the time had passed. The time for coming to see you had passed."

Breathing deeply, Maisie closed her eyes and gathered her thoughts, then continued, her voice less strained as the weight of formerly unspoken words was lightened.

"Dad, Lady Rowan, Priscilla—they all stopped asking after a while. I kept them at arm's length. All except Maurice. Maurice sees through everything. He said that even if people couldn't see my tissue-paper armor, they could feel it, and would not ask again. But he knew, Maurice knew, that I would have to come one day. He said that the truth grows even more powerful when it is suppressed, and that often it takes only one small crack to bring down the wall, to release it. And that's what happened, Simon. The wall I built fell down. And I have been so filled with shame for being unable to face the truth of what happened to you."

Simon sat still in his wheelchair, his hands unmoving, though blood colored his skin.

"Simon, my love. I never did tell you my answer. You see, I knew that something dreadful was going to happen. I couldn't promise you marriage, a future, when I could see no future. Forgive me, dear Simon, forgive me."

Maisie looked around, trying to see what Simon's stare focused upon, and was surprised to see that it was the window, where they were reflected together. She, wearing her blue suit and a blue cloche, her hair in a chignon at the base of her neck. A few tendrils of hair, always the same few tendrils of black hair, had flown free and fallen down around her forehead and cheeks. She could barely see his facial wounds in the reflection. The glass was playing tricks, showing her the old Simon, the young doctor she had fallen in love with so long ago.

Maisie turned to face Simon again. A thin line of saliva had emerged from the side of his mouth and had begun to run down his chin. She took a fresh linen handkerchief from her handbag, wiped the moisture away, and held his hand once again, in silence, until the staff nurse returned.

"How are we, then?" She leaned forward to look at Simon, then turned to smile at Maisie. "And how about you?" she asked.

"Fine. Yes, I'm fine," she swallowed and returned the nurse's smile.

"Good. Bet you've done him the world of good." Staff Nurse looked at Simon again and patted his hand. "Hasn't she, Captain Lynch? Done you a power of good!"

Simon remained perfectly still.

"Let me lead you out of the maze here, Miss Dobbs."

As she walked away, Maisie stopped to look back at Simon, then at his reflection in the windowpane. There he was. Forever the young, dashing Simon Lynch who had stolen her heart.

"*W*ill you come again?"

They had reached the main door of the house. A grand house that was now a home for men stranded in time by the Great War, men trapped in the caverns of their own minds, never to return.

"Yes. Yes I will come again. Thank you."

"Right you are then. Just let us know. Loves a visitor, does Captain Lynch."

aisie drove back into London, waving to Jack Barker as the MG screeched around the corner into Warren Street, before stopping at her new office in Fitzroy Square. She parked the car in front of the building and watched as Billy positioned a new brass nameplate with tacks, then stood back to appraise the suitability of his placement before securing the plate with screws. He rubbed his chin and moved the plate twice more. Finally he nodded his head, satisfied that he had found exactly the right place for her name, a place that would let callers know that M. Dobbs, Psychologist and Investigator, was open for business.

Maisie continued to watch as Billy worked, polishing the brass to a glowing shine. Then Billy looked up and saw Maisie in the MG. He waved and, rubbing his hands on a cloth, walked down the steps and opened the car door for her to get out.

"Better get weaving, Miss."

"Why, what's happened?"

"That Detective Inspector Stratton from Scotland Yard, the Murder Squad fella. Been on the 'dog and bone' four times already. Urgent, like. Needs to be 'in conference' with you about a case."

"Golly!" said Maisie, grabbing the old black document case from the passenger seat.

"I know. 'ow about that? We'd better get to work, 'adn't we, Miss?"

Maisie raised an eyebrow and walked with Billy to the door. She ran her fingers along the engraving on the brass plate, and turned to her new assistant.

It was time to go to work.

"Well then, Billy—let's get on with it!"

ACKNOWLEDGMENTS

irst and foremost, I am indebted to Holly Rose, my friend and writing pal who read the initial tentative pages of *Maisie Dobbs* and pressed me to continue. Adair Lara, my writing mentor, was the first to suggest I consider writing fiction, and later, after my "accident horribilis," when *Maisie Dobbs* was barely half written, insisted that convalescence was an ideal time to finish the book—broken arm notwithstanding.

I have been truly blessed in my association with Amy Rennert and Randi Murray of the Amy Rennert Agency, for their wise counsel, wonderful humor, hard work, and most of all, their enthusiastic belief in *Maisie Dobbs*. I am equally blessed in my editor, Laura Hruska, who has the qualities that make her one of the best—including, I believe, psychic powers that enable her to see into my mind.

My godmother, Dorothy Lindqvist, first took me to London's Imperial War Museum when I was a child, an experience that brought a new reality to my grandfather's stories of the Great War of 1914–18. Now, years later, many thanks must go to the museum for its amazing resources, and to the staff who were most helpful during my research visits.

The following people kindly responded to emails and phone calls, providing me with detail that has brought color and texture to the life and experience of Maisie Dobbs: Kate Perry, Senior Archivist at Girton College; Sarah Manser, Director of Press and Public Relations at The Ritz, London; Barbara Griffiths at BT Group Archives, London; John Day, Chairman of the MG Car Club Vintage Register; and Alison Driver of the Press & PR Department of Fortnum & Mason, London. For his dry wit and dogged investigative skills, my utmost gratitude goes to Victor—who knows who he is.

On a personal level thanks must go to my parents, Albert and Joyce Winspear, for their great memories of "old London," and their recollections of my grandfather's postwar experiences; my brother, John, for his encouragement; my friend Kas Salazar, who constantly reminds me of my creative priorities; and last—but certainly not least—my husband and cheerleader, John Morell, for his unfailing support, and for sharing our home with a woman called Maisie Dobbs.